S0-BBA-778

THE CRACKED THRONE

Be sure to read all the novels in
JOSHUA PALMATIER's
acclaimed fantasy trilogy from DAW:

THE SKEWED THRONE (Book One)
THE CRACKED THRONE (Book Two)
THE VACANT THRONE (Book Three, coming in 2007)

JOSHUA PALMATIER

DAW BOOKS, INC.

DONALD A. WOLLHEIM, FOUNDER
375 Hudson Street, New York, NY 10014
ELIZABETH R. WOLLHEIM
SHEILA E. GILBERT
PUBLISHERS
http://www.dawbooks.com

Copyright © 2006 by Joshua Palmatier.

All rights reserved.

Jacket art by Steve Stone.

DAW Books Collectors No. 1382.

DAW Books are distributed by Penguin Group (USA) Inc.

Book designed by Elizabeth Glover.

All characters and events in this book are fictitious.
All resemblance to persons living or dead is strictly coincidental.

The scanning, uploading and distribution of this book via the Internet or via any other means without the permission of the publisher is illegal, and punishable by law. Please purchase only authorized electronic editions, and do not participate in or encourage the electronic piracy of copyrighted materials. Your support of the author's rights is appreciated.

First Printing, November 2006
1   2   3   4   5   6   7   8   9

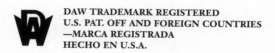
DAW TRADEMARK REGISTERED
U.S. PAT. OFF AND FOREIGN COUNTRIES
—MARCA REGISTRADA
HECHO EN U.S.A.

PRINTED IN THE U.S.A.

*This work is dedicated to
my editor, Sheila Gilbert, and my agent, Amy Stout.
Bold adventurers both.
Without them, this book would not be . . .
and would not be half as good.*

Acknowledgments

The Usual Suspects:

Ariel Guzman, a good friend, who is my first reader and who always manages to keep things real, even in a fantasy.

Patricia Bray and Jennifer Dunne, two fellow writers. We all get together once a week to talk shop . . . and end up drinking, gaming, and being thankful there isn't a fan webcam watching us. That we know of.

Steve Stone, the artist who has brought all of my novels to life with such great covers. The Ochean is perfect!

The Family: My brothers, Jason and Jacob; my sisters-in-law, Janet and Chrissie; and my mother. Without their support, I wouldn't remain sane long enough to get anything written.

And finally, the most important person in my life, George. For all the little things, especially the understanding that I have to write, even if he doesn't understand what I write or why.

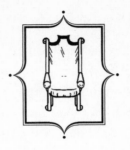

Chapter 1

I CROUCHED DOWN BEHIND a pile of broken stone to catch my breath and gazed down the darkened narrow in the warren of buildings of the Dredge. In the moonlight, the alley was mainly shadow, with edges of dull light. Water gleamed in a thin stream in the alley's center. No doorways, no windows here. At least none that I could see.

A sound came from behind, a rattle of stone against stone.

I spun, breath catching, heard my heart thudding in my ears, poised on the verge of bolting. My feet skidded in the wet dirt on the cobbles—

But there was nothing behind me. The alley was as dark as it was ahead. There were many places to hide, but nowhere to escape to. He could be waiting for me, hidden in any of the shadows, ready to pounce if I turned back.

A sob tightened my chest and I fought it back, closed my eyes against the sensation. I breathed in slowly, tried to calm myself.

Use the river.

The thought slid across the darkness behind my eyes and I frowned. But then there was the unmistakable tread of a foot, moving cautiously, and far, far too close.

My eyes flew open, my heart shuddered, and I lurched out from the shelter of the broken stone into the alley, moving almost blindly, eyes catching glimpses of heaped stone, piles of shattered crates, and rotting refuse. My bare feet pounded against the slick cobbles, splashed in the trickling stream. I heard a curse, and a hail of loose dirt and stone as someone pushed away from a crumbling wall, then heavy footfalls. A cold sliver of fear lanced down my side, sharp with pain. I slapped a hand against it, tried to force it away, and then the alley turned.

I swerved too late, felt my feet skid in the muck, slip, begin to pull out from under me, and then I slammed into the mud-brick wall in the corner. My breath whooshed from my lungs, but I didn't pause. I used the wall to catch my balance, shoved away from it before I'd truly gained purchase, and stumbled down the left turn.

A door. I needed a door, a window, an escape.

Behind, the footfalls burst into a run. Someone shouted, cursed as he stumbled into a stack of garbage, tripped, and fell.

I darted along the new alley. Still nothing. No door, no window. I sobbed, breath hitching in my throat. The dagger of pain in my side dug deeper. I was no longer running smoothly, the pain too harsh, making me stumble. I'd been running too long.

A cloud moved across the moon. The alley plunged itself into total darkness. I stumbled to a halt, leaned heavily against one wall, one hand still clutching my side. My breath came in ragged gasps. Too loud, too filled with desolation. My eyes widened as I tried to catch even the faintest light, but there was nothing. Only the reek of shit and stone, rot and death.

The footsteps behind stopped.

I drew a deep breath, held it to listen.

Breathing. He was still there. But he'd learned caution. I'd hurt him when I'd first escaped, bitten into the fleshy part of his hand hard enough to break the skin, then shook it like a dog with a rat carcass while he screamed. I could still taste the blood in my mouth and smiled with grim satisfaction. He'd let his guard down, but that wouldn't happen again.

Use the river!

I tried to slip into that other world, tried to force everything to blur and gray, tried to suppress all sound into a dull wind—something I'd been able to do without thought since I was six; something I'd relied on to survive on my own since then—but nothing happened.

The river was gone.

Choking down a sob, smile fading, I turned to the wall I could no longer see, pressed my shoulder against it a moment, then, with effort, forced my weight away and began edging down its length. With my shoulder scraping the stone for support, I ran with one hand ahead of me, felt for a corner, an edge, an opening. I'd only get one chance at escape.

Behind, the man heard my movements and edged forward. But he came too fast in the total darkness. His foot splashed in the stream, and then he stumbled over loose stone. I heard a bark of pain, followed by a bitten-off curse. But he got back up. I heard clothing rustling against stone, more cautious this time.

My fingers slid off the stone wall in front of me into open space. I halted, explored with my hand.

Another corner. The alley turned again.

I edged around the side. The sounds of pursuit quieted, but I pushed on. He wasn't going to give up, even in the dark. I'd hurt him too much for that, dared to defy him in front of all the others, dared to run.

A sense of uselessness, of total despair, washed over me. I tasted it, like grit in the back of my throat, and forced it back with a hard swallow. For a moment, I leaned more weight against the wall, heard my tattered clothes scraping harshly against the mud-brick. But I kept moving. Why couldn't he just leave me alone? Why couldn't he just let me go? He had other workers. He didn't need me.

But I knew. It was because I'd bitten him. I could still hear his howl of shock and rage.

"I won't go back," I mumbled, too softly for anyone to hear, voice choked with tears and anger.

My fingers found another opening: a window, its edges ragged and broken with decayed stone.

With a surge of hope, I stepped back from the wall, placed both hands on the crumbling ledge, and pushed my small form upward. Stone ground into my stomach and the sharp pain in my side lanced down into my leg. I began to flail, tilting forward. I couldn't see where the window led, but it didn't matter. Anywhere was better than here.

I began to fall forward into the darkness, gasping with effort and triumph.

A hand latched onto my ankle.

"No!" I screamed, hope flailing desperately in my chest. "I won't go back! I won't!"

"You bloody well will," the man grunted.

Another hand grabbed the waist of my breeches, gripped the cloth tight, and as the man heaved, I felt myself lifted up off the window's ledge by the pants and ankle and thrown backward, out into the alley.

I hit the opposite wall hard. As I collapsed to the ground, no longer able to breathe, the moon reappeared from behind the clouds, startlingly bright. I tried to catch myself with my hands, but I had no strength left. My arms crumpled and the side of my face struck the mud-slicked cobbles. Pain jolted through my jaw, and I tasted fresh blood. My own blood. I moaned.

The man didn't give me time to recuperate. My arms still use-

less, my hands grasping feebly at nothing, the man kicked me hard
in the stomach, the force of the blow throwing me onto my back. I
coughed as blood trickled down into my throat, tried to curl into a
protective ball, but a hand latched onto the front of my shirt and
hauled me upright. The man loomed over me, then jerked me in
close, my feet no longer touching the ground.

"Thought you could run, eh?" Putrid breath blew across my
face. "No one runs from Corum."

My head rolled sideways, no longer under my own control. I
had no more strength left. And for the first time I saw my attacker.

His face was screwed up into a snarl of hatred, eyes sharp and
black in the moonlight, teeth yellowed and crooked. Brown hair lay
in tangles on fatty, bulging skin, a few locks twisted and tied together with thin, colored string.

"No one," he said again when he saw he'd caught my attention.

I spat into his face.

He hesitated a single moment, trembling in shock. Then he
growled and threw me again.

I hit the mud-brick wall, bounced off it into something wooden
resting in another corner, where the alley turned yet again. I caught
myself on its edge, one hand holding, the other slipping off and
splashing into collected water.

A rain barrel. Or what was left of one.

I steadied myself, pulled myself upright so that I was kneeling
over the water.

And then I froze.

Confusion stabbed deep into my gut as I stared down into the
reflection on the rippled surface of the water.

It wasn't me. It was a boy, not yet ten. Round face with smooth
skin encrusted with the Dredge, with dirt and blood and tears.
Light brown eyes wide and desperate. Hair short and crawling with
lice.

Then the reflection of the moon in the water was eclipsed by Corum's shadow.

I jerked back, but Corum was too quick. His hand fell onto the back of my head, fingers curling tight in my hair. I screamed as Corum, nearly three times my height and weight, dropped to one knee beside me and in a rough voice spat, "No one!"

He placed his other hand over the one wrapped in my hair, then thrust my head downward. Stagnant water closed up and over my ears, drowning out my screams, drowning out Corum's harsh breathing as he held me down with his full weight. I struggled, pushed back from the barrel, kicked my legs, writhed and squirmed and fought. Water splashed out of the barrel, soaked into my clothing. But there was no purchase, no strength left in me, and then water filled my mouth and I drew it in, pulled its coldness down into my lungs and I felt it filling me, seeping into every part of my body. And as it touched my arms, I felt my struggling relax, felt my arms go numb and slack. Strength ebbed from my legs. And then I felt myself sinking, down and down into the depths of the barrel, down and down forever.

As I sank, I suddenly realized why I couldn't use the river.

Because this wasn't me dying. It was someone else. Someone who lived in the slums beyond the Dredge.

And then I woke.

†

I lurched out of the dream with a sharp cry, choking on the slick coolness of rainwater even though my mouth was dry. Sick, I crawled to the edge of the immense bed, arms tangled in sweaty sheets, and coughed into the darkness of the room. Harsh, racking coughs, as if I were trying to purge my lungs of nonexistent water.

When the coughing faded, I fell back onto the bed, my entire body trembling with weakness. I swallowed, throat raw, then felt the strangeness of the room around me and sat up slowly.

The Mistress' chambers.

Because I was the new Mistress.

I shuddered, drew my knees up to my chest and hugged them close, the unfamiliar cloth of the shift I wore rustling in the darkness.

As the last of the dream faded, reality returned. Except that the dream felt more real. I knew the Dredge, knew the warren of alleys and niches filled with filth and refuse. From the age of six until I'd fled to the upper city at fifteen, I'd spent my life living in its decaying buildings, surviving off of the streets any way I could, stealing my food, rooting through the garbage for that discarded chunk of moldy cheese, that weevil-ridden crust of bread. I was a thief, gutterscum, spat upon and kicked out of the way. The only reason I'd survived as long as I had was because of the Seeker assassin, Erick . . . and because of the river.

For a moment, I let the darkened room around me shift, let myself sink into the special sight that I called the river. The blackness shifted to a lighter gray, took on edges and forms as I picked up the faint moonlight seeping around the drawn curtains leading to the balcony. It was like sliding beneath the surface of water, and as I pushed myself deeper, the details of the room clarified. Still gray, but now they were visible when before there hadn't been enough light.

But it was more than that now, different than what it had been even on the Dredge. Because now I had the power of the Skewed Throne augmenting the river. I could feel the throne pulsing around me, heightening my awareness, taking it beyond what I was used to. The new power felt raw, almost unwieldy, barely under control.

I shifted my focus, turned back to the bedroom.

It was large, the largest room I'd ever slept in, even after I'd escaped the Dredge and taken up residence in the merchant Borund's manse as his bodyguard. The bed stood against one wall, four posts rising from its corners, the canopy tied high above bowing down toward me. Tables stood at various points about the room, mixed in with potted trees and plants, a settee, chairs. Large wardrobes stood off to my left, and chests with linens and clothes, none of the contents mine. One of the tables held a large pitcher filled with water set in a basin so that I could wash my face in the morning; another held the dagger I'd taken from an ex-guardsman after he'd tried to rape me and I'd killed him. I'd only been eleven then.

Across the room, opposite the bed, were a set of double doors leading to the antechamber and the rest of the palace. In the grayness of the river, I could sense the two guardsmen who waited on the other side of the doors, in the antechamber itself. They were arguing, their voices too low for me to catch. But their emotions coursed through the river like a current. Fear and uncertainty; mostly uncertainty. They must have heard me thrashing around in my sleep, couldn't decide whether to enter the room.

Before I'd taken control of the throne, I wouldn't have been able to sense their emotions in such detail. I wouldn't have been able to sense them at all, since they were behind a closed door. On the Dredge and then later in the upper city as a bodyguard for Borund, I needed to be able to see my targets before I could use the river against them. But now, with the power of the throne behind me . . .

The guardsmen didn't know what to think of their new Mistress, of the seventeen-year-old girl who had somehow entered the palace two nights ago dressed as a page boy, had slipped through all of the patrols, had bypassed every guardsman, and somehow made it to the throne room and taken control of the Skewed Throne.

I pushed the river away, let the darkness of the room return, the emotions of the two guardsmen fade. I'd done more than taken control of the throne, though. Because whoever controlled the throne controlled the entire city of Amenkor.

I pulled my knees in tighter, tried to suppress a sudden flare of anger but failed.

I'd never intended to seize the throne. I'd been sent by the administrator Avrell, the First of the Mistress, and Borund after I'd escaped the Dredge. Sent to kill the previous Mistress so that someone else could take her place. They'd claimed it was the only way to get the insane Mistress off the throne, that they'd tried everything else and failed; that if it wasn't done soon, the city would never survive the winter. In her insanity, the previous Mistress had blockaded the harbor and cut off trade when food was desperately needed, had allowed a quarter of the city and a significant portion of the stored food to burn, had ordered the city and palace guardsmen not to help in putting out the fire. She had to be removed, and I was the only one who could do it. Because I'd been trained by the Seeker Erick to be an assassin . . . and because of the river. I was the only one who could get close enough to kill her.

So I'd agreed. Because I'd believed the Mistress *had* gone insane, and because Erick, my mentor, convinced me that I was the only one who could succeed.

But it had been a trap. The Mistress had been waiting for me, had manipulated the guardsmen and servants of the palace so that I would make it to the throne room unimpeded.

Instead of killing her, I'd been forced to touch the Skewed Throne.

My anger flared higher—at Avrell, at Borund, and especially at Erick's betrayal—but it paled at the sudden surge of horror at the memory of the throne.

I shuddered, stifled a moan, laid my head down on my knees and closed my eyes, felt the exhaustion that had plagued me since that night washing over me.

I let myself sink back into the river, dove deep, heading straight for the edge of the spherical White Fire that burned continuously now at my core. A power separate from the river, the Fire had saved me more than once on the Dredge, flaring up to forewarn me of danger, of threats that I had not yet seen. And now it protected me from the voices within the throne and their immense force. I would never have survived the Skewed Throne without it. The voices would have crushed me, smothered me beneath their weight.

I winced as I grew closer to the boundary, drew a slow steadying breath as I felt the throbbing pulse of the throne's power, and halted just outside the seething barrier of white flame.

On the far side, a maelstrom of voices roared, almost deafening. Hundreds upon hundreds of voices clamoring for my attention, screaming defiance and hatred, pleading for release, for pity, all of them trying to take over at once. They were the voices of all of the previous Mistresses, all who had sat upon the throne and ruled Amenkor since the throne was created, as well as the voices of any who had dared to touch it since then. Hundreds of Mistresses; even more of those who had touched the throne and not had the power to survive. I felt the pressure of their personalities, of their emotions, against my face like heat, white-hot and hissing. Anger and hatred and raw desperation—all trapped by the throne.

And now trapped by the Fire as well. After being thrust onto the throne, forced to face its power, I'd used the White Fire to capture those voices. I'd surrounded them in its protective flame and now held them deep inside myself with the power of the river.

The voices had driven the previous Mistress to the edge of madness. But she'd managed to lure me to the throne room by distracting the guards, had managed to use the throne to overpower me and shove me forcibly onto its seat.

And then she'd given me a choice: die and let the city of Amenkor die with me during the coming winter, or claim the power of the throne myself and release her, giving the city a chance to survive.

My anger returned, hot and fluid and bitter. It hadn't been much of a choice at all.

I let the river go again with a hard thrust, sat up straight in the Mistress' bed—my bed now—legs folded so I could rest my elbows on my knees. If they wanted a new Mistress, then I'd be Mistress. But I was tired of being manipulated, of being given choices that were not choices at all.

One of the guards knocked on the door to the antechamber, followed by a muffled argument, pitched high with concern.

I scowled. When the knocking resumed, more urgent, I slid off the bed and moved to the door, walking carefully through the unfamiliar room in the darkness.

I jerked the door open, the two guards outside stepping back sharply. They regained their composure quickly, standing stiffly at attention, but still a little uncertain. One of them was one of the previous Mistress' palace guardsmen, the other was one of the assassin Seekers.

"What?" I spat.

The regular guardsman, the one who had knocked on the door, licked his lips, glanced toward the Seeker for reassurance, then answered. "We heard a cry—"

"If there'd been an assassin," I said, "I'd have been dead by the time you decided to open the door."

The guardsman stood, mouth open, with no idea what to say.

I moved to close the door, but the Seeker stepped forward.

"Is everything all right, Mistress?"

My stomach clenched, a sudden wave of loneliness, of desolation and instability and doubt washing over me.

Two days ago, I'd been a bodyguard for a somewhat powerful merchant. Today, I ruled the entire city—a city on the verge of winter starvation.

A chill shivered through my skin, tingling, raising the hairs on my arms.

I swallowed, met the Seeker's eyes. Dark eyes, with a dangerous glint that I recognized. I'd seen it in Erick's eyes when I was fourteen and he'd found me in an alley off the Dredge, vomiting over the corpse of the second man I'd killed. Erick, the man who had trained me, had given me the chance to escape the Dredge when I was fifteen and become a bodyguard for Borund.

This man had the same stance as Erick, totally relaxed, fluid, with an edge of death. But unlike Erick, this man had few scars lining his face, had less gray in his dark hair, his nose more pointed and straight because it had never been broken.

Unlike the regular guardsman, the Seeker carried a dagger instead of a sword, wore leathers instead of armor. Of the two, he was the more dangerous, and yet I felt more comfortable speaking to him than to the palace guardsman.

"I'm fine," I said, then hesitated.

I could feel myself trembling, alternately hot with rage and cold with terror at the thought of what I would be expected to do as Mistress.

The room behind me suddenly felt both too large and too confining.

I drew in a ragged breath and let it out slowly. "No," I said. "No, I think I need some air. Take me to the roof of the palace."

The Seeker nodded, then said in a carefully neutral voice, "You should probably change."

I glanced down at my sweat-matted shift, rumpled and wrinkled, then glared at both of the guards before closing the door without a word.

✝

The Seeker guarding the door to my chambers led me to the roof of the palace, halting at the opening to the stairwell with a nod. Dressed in Eryn's white robes, the predawn air felt chill and close, still damp with the autumn rains and with a bite of winter. As I moved to the low wall at the edge of the roof overlooking the port of Amenkor, I repressed a shudder at the robe's unfamiliar weight and movement. I was used to close-fitting clothes, shirts and breeches, nothing loose that would interfere with my dagger, with my movements. But the previous Mistress did not have breeches, did not carry a dagger. And someone had removed the page boy's clothes I'd worn to infiltrate the palace. The white robes, with bands of gold embroidery around the neck and hem, were the only clothes I could find.

I glared out over the city of Amenkor in irritation, trying not to scratch myself. Things would have to change, starting with the clothes.

On the harbor, ships rocked in the waves, silhouetted against the water by the reflected moonlight. All but those guarding the harbor's entrance were at the docks, where they'd been since the previous Mistress had blockaded the harbor. A few were loading cargo, by the light of torches lining the wharf, but I couldn't see which ships in the darkness, could only see vague forms moving in the glow of the lanterns along the docks. Closer in, there was a patch of darkness where the warehouses had burned, the buildings nothing but charred husks.

I felt a weight of guilt settle onto my shoulders, a clench of nausea tug at my stomach. I may not have started the fire that destroyed the warehouse district, but the lantern that *had* started it had been thrown at me by a boy attempting to save himself from my blade.

I turned away from the black scar, toward the barely discernible streets, the River, and the outer walls of the city.

At the same time, I heard footsteps behind me.

I slid beneath the river, felt the world shift to gray, the sounds of the night muting to a soft wind, and targeted the woman who approached.

Eryn, the previous Mistress.

I tensed, back rigid, comforted by the presence of my dagger at my side, tucked into a makeshift belt. I'd seen little of the previous Mistress since I'd released her from the throne and assumed power. There'd been little time. I'd spent a full day seated on the throne, afraid to let my guard down, afraid the voices would overtake me the moment I turned my back. Eventually, I'd isolated them behind the Fire, stabilized it so that it burned without conscious thought. Only then had I stepped away from the throne.

But the effort had drained me. I'd collapsed in exhaustion almost immediately, been taken to the Mistress' chambers to rest. When I'd woken, after only a few hours of sleep, the palace had been in turmoil, the guardsmen seething with anger, the servants confused. Nothing had been accomplished, all of Avrell's time spent calming everyone down.

There'd been nothing I could do at the time, so I'd retired early, still exhausted . . . and dreamed.

Eryn moved up beside me, placed her hands on the stone parapet of the tower, and gazed out over the city. In the moonlight, her hair was blue-black, her skin washed a pale white, as white as the simple dress she wore. She held herself formally, head high, chin lifted. Not arrogant, but assured. The stance of a ruler.

I felt small beside her. And not only because I was two hands shorter and probably less than half her age.

"Couldn't sleep?" she asked a moment later, after a heavy sigh.

I shifted, slipped into a stance the Seeker watching us would have recognized, and answered, "No." It came out harsher than I'd intended. I suddenly wondered where she had slept last night, what she had done while the palace was in chaos.

She turned toward me, eyes narrowed, lips pursed. She looked exhausted as well, dark smudges beneath her eyes, her skin tight, as if she'd been sobbing for hours. It had aged her. Instead of the nearly forty-year-old woman who'd so confidently bested me a few nights before, she appeared fifty . . . and totally defeated.

I found my anger and wariness faltering, forced myself to remember that this was the woman who had almost killed me days before.

"It's hard," she said, tight and controlled. "I've lived so long with the voices of the throne that now that they're gone . . ." She grimaced, shrugged, then laughed bitterly, no humor touching her eyes. "I know I'd be dead by now, if you hadn't come to kill me. I could never have withstood the throne. It was too powerful, and the voices . . . they were wearing me down. They would have driven me insane eventually. But still . . ."

I said nothing. I'd seen the insanity in her eyes in the throne room, seen how much she'd fought to hold herself together at the end.

Eryn straightened. "I think . . ." Her voice had changed, some of the bitterness seeping away. "I think, if you hadn't come, I would have thrown myself from this very wall."

I stilled, startled, then shifted forward so I could see down the height of the wall, down past the gaps of the inset windows, past the banners, to the stairs at the wall's base.

The stone of the steps gleamed white in the moonlight.

Something tightened in my chest, and I pulled back from the edge with a sharp gasp. For a brief moment, the world tilted around me, and I felt off-balance, dizzy with the height. I placed my hands carefully on the stone wall to steady myself and felt the last of my wariness vanish, lost in the thudding of my heart.

"You used to come here often," I said. "Avrell said that on the night the warehouses burned, you came up here to watch the fire. He said that you smiled."

Eryn didn't answer at first. She simply stood, staring down at the stone steps below, her eyes distant. Almost contemplative.

"That wasn't me standing here that night," she said, her eyes haunted and lost. "It was the throne."

For a horrible moment, I thought she was on the verge of jumping as she'd planned earlier. I could see it in her eyes, almost like the madness I'd seen in the throne room before, but somehow more terrifying because she was so calm.

But then the moment passed. Her eyes narrowed and she turned away from the wall, from the steps far below, and looked at me.

"You dreamed," she said. There was no doubt in her voice. The assured woman who'd first stood beside me had returned.

I thought about lying, but saw no point. She'd been the Mistress for longer than I'd been alive. "Yes."

She frowned. "That's unusual. It took at least three months after I assumed the throne before I dreamed. Tell me, what happened in this dream?"

"I drowned," I said curtly. "A man shoved my head into a rain barrel and I drowned. Except it wasn't me, it was a boy I didn't know."

Eryn nodded, turning back toward the city. "And do you know where this happened?"

"The slums beyond the Dredge."

"And did you see the man who killed you—or rather, did this boy you don't know see him?"

"Yes. His name was Corum."

"Then you must send the Seekers after this Corum. He is a mark. He deserves to die."

I felt a warm surge of satisfaction course through my blood at the thought. My hand closed into a fist about the hilt of my dagger. Corum's face rose sharp and clear in my mind and my jaw clenched with hatred. "I can look for him myself. I can kill him."

Eryn turned sharply at the harshness in my voice, her eyes going wide in alarm. "Varis," she said, taking a tentative step forward.

Beneath the river, her movement was slow, almost languid. I'd sunk deeper than I'd intended, had let the world gray almost to black, the city spread out below me—once half lost in the darkness before dawn—now sharp with edges and clearly defined. And there was a tug on the currents, a pull. Nothing focused or clear, but a scent. I doubt I would have sensed it without the added power of the throne behind me. I faced it, reached out for it, and found myself focusing across the buildings of the merchants' quarter, across the wharf and the harbor, across the real River that emptied into the bay, to where the cobbled street called the Dredge ran into the slums of the city. The scent grew clearer, more intense. As sharp and fresh as new-fallen rain—

And suddenly I knew I *could* find him, could find Corum wherever he hid on the Dredge, using the river, using the throne. I could already smell his putrid breath, could feel my dagger sliding up beneath his ribs. I could taste his death.

"Varis, no!"

Eryn's voice was hollow, distant. But then she slapped me, hard, the stinging sensation piercing through the eddies of the river like a blade. I pulled back from the edge of the city with a jerk, snapped back into myself at the edge of the palace wall hard enough I stumbled back. Eryn was already there, holding me up, steadying me. Her face was a steel mask of terrified anger, cold and stark in the moonlight.

"Never do that again!" she spat. "Never reach out like that using the Sight or the throne!"

"But I can find him," I gasped, still disoriented. I felt an urge to vomit, but fought the sensation down, swallowed hard as I caught my balance. "I can scent him—"

"No!" she growled. "It's too dangerous. Reaching like that, extending yourself out so far. . . ." She shook her head. "You could lose yourself, never find your way back. Previous Mistresses have been lost in such attempts before. No. It's better to send the Seekers. That's what they've been trained for." She squeezed my shoulder, locked gazes with me, her voice brittle. "Tell me you will not try that again. Tell me!"

I nodded, still feeling sick. "I won't."

"You'll send the Seekers?"

I nodded again.

The terror began to fade from Eryn's eyes. "Good." She loosened her grip and stepped back, eyeing me carefully. Then she sighed. "Good. Now you should get some rest. Avrell and the others will want to talk to you tomorrow. There are things you must decide on, and decide on quickly, if Amenkor is to survive."

"If it's to survive what?"

Eryn hesitated, her eyes searching. But I was still shaking from the . . . the Reaching into the Dredge.

Eryn's mouth turned in a sudden frown. "Winter," she said. "If we're to survive winter, of course."

Then she turned and walked steadily to the stairs, without looking back.

†

I stayed on the tower to watch the dawn. To the east, over the hazy shadow of mountains, the sky lightened. I'd never seen what lay beyond the city of Amenkor, had always been hidden inside the streets, unable to see what was outside of the walls and buildings. From the tower of the palace, though, as the sun rose, I could see how the city crowded around the enclosed bay and the River. To the north, the Dredge ran up into the decaying buildings of the slums, which clung to the rocky cliffs of the northern portion of the harbor before reaching the top of a ridge and spilling over beyond view. To the south, the land fell away steeply from the edge of the outer wall of the palace toward a coastline dotted with windswept trees. A road cut through the landscape in both directions—north and south—intersecting another road heading from Amenkor to the east, toward the mountains.

I stared at the road and River snaking out into the foothills of the mountains, eyes wide. The entire landscape was covered with trees, more trees than I'd ever seen, could ever have imagined. I followed the dense forest as it faded into the haze at the base of the mountains, noted a cleft in the peaks in the far distance: the pass that led to the lands beyond.

As the sun rose higher, dawn slipping away, I turned back to the city below.

Amenkor. The real Amenkor.

My Amenkor.

I leaned forward, stone gritty beneath my palms, and stared out over the streets, over the water of the river and the harbor, over the two juts of land that reached out to enclose the bay, protecting it. Barely discernible in the distance, at the ends of each jut of land, I could see two towers, like sentinels at the harbor's entrance. And before that entrance I could see the Mistress' ships blocking the watercourse, preventing all ships from entering.

And leaving.

I frowned. But I shrugged aside the sudden uneasiness and turned back to the city. Lights had been doused and people had begun to emerge into the streets. As the cries of the dockworkers and hawkers on the wharf began to filter up to the tower, I turned to where the Seeker waited patiently. With a nod, we descended.

Erick was waiting outside the Mistress' chambers. He was alone, aside from the palace guardsman I'd left outside the door earlier, and he smiled when he saw me, the skin crinkling around his eyes.

I halted, the Seeker who accompanied me stepping to one side behind me. My eyes narrowed in anger, my hands tightening in the folds of my white robes. I hadn't seen him since he, Borund, and Avrell had convinced me to kill the Mistress. Like Eryn, he appeared haggard, older than he was.

"Varis," he began.

"Don't," I said, cutting him off, moving forward and past him to the door. "I don't want to talk to you."

"Varis, wait."

I stormed through the antechamber into the Mistress' rooms, paused when I saw the neatly folded page boy's clothes stacked on the chest at the bed's base, then turned and strode to where the curtains were drawn across the glass doorway that led to the balcony. I halted before them, but did not pull them back.

I heard Erick enter behind me, heard the door close.

"Varis." His voice was hard, commanding. The same voice he'd used to train me to be an assassin in the slums of Amenkor. But things had changed in the last few weeks. He was no longer my mentor, had not been my mentor for two years, since I'd left the Dredge. Neither he, nor Borund, nor Avrell, could command me now.

I spun. "What?"

Erick stood just inside the door, back straight, eyes dark, jaw tight, clearly angry. He crossed his hands over his chest, spaced his feet a shoulder's width apart, and said nothing. The scars that lined his face, that marked him as dangerous even when he was relaxed, stood out in the light.

For a moment, I saw him as he had appeared on the Dredge almost four years before, when he'd found me: cold, arrogant, and unreadable. A guardsman. A Seeker. I was nothing then. A wisp of a girl barely surviving off the dregs of Amenkor. Gutterscum. I'd looked no further than the next rotted apple or scabbed potato.

But he'd changed all that. I'd discovered he wasn't as cold and arrogant and distant as he had seemed.

The anger I felt began to ebb, to drain away as the silence between us deepened. But it didn't vanish completely.

"Did you know?"

His forehead creased in confusion. "Know about what?"

"Did you know it was a trap! That they sent me to kill the Mistress simply to get me into the palace, to get me to the throne room?"

He shook his head. "No." A flat denial. No hesitation.

I looked hard into his eyes, wanting to believe him, and found them completely open, nothing hidden. The tension in my shoulders released and I turned away. "Good," I said, my voice still sharp, even though I felt a wave of relief. I hadn't realized how betrayed I'd felt, how horribly deep it had cut me, until I'd seen him.

Behind, I heard Erick move a few steps farther into the room.

"I don't think Borund knew either," he said. "He and Avrell only wanted me to convince you to kill the Mistress. They thought I'd have a better chance at it than they would by themselves. They thought you trusted me. Neither one of them mentioned anything about you becoming the Mistress."

I grunted without comment.

Erick was quiet for a long moment, then added, "It took them a long time to convince me that killing her was necessary. And in the end they didn't convince me that she was insane. You did."

Startled, I turned to see his face. "What do you mean?"

He moved forward, until he stood only a few paces away. "You knew that something was wrong with the Mistress when she sent me to kill Mari. You knew Mari wasn't a mark just by looking at her. After that I began to question every mark the Mistress sent me after. By the time Avrell and Borund approached me, I already knew that the Mistress was insane and that something needed to be done. But I didn't know what. All they had to do was convince me that killing her was the only option."

"But you don't think Borund intended for me to become the Mistress? Or Avrell?"

"Borund, no. I don't know about Avrell."

I thought back to that meeting only four days before. I'd thought then that Avrell was hiding something, that there was something he wasn't telling me, something he'd kept back. I hadn't gotten the same sense from Borund or Erick. Was it possible Avrell hadn't known the Mistress' plans? Had he been manipulated by her as well?

I shook my head in annoyance and moved to the chest where the page boy's clothes rested. On top of the neatly folded linen shirt lay a key.

I reached down and picked it up. It was the key to the room that held the archer's niche I'd used to bypass Baill's guards during their watch. Avrell had given it to me, along with the page boy's clothes.

"I don't think Borund knew either," I said, distracted. Then I sighed and set the key back onto the clothes, turning away.

"I don't want to be the Mistress, Erick."

Erick snorted. "But you are. Nothing can change that now."

I felt a surge of rebellion. Erick must have seen me tense.

"Where would you go, Varis? You can't go back to the Dredge. You spent too much time as Borund's bodyguard to return to living off the slums. And could you be a bodyguard now? After what's happened here?"

I thought about the Dredge. But Erick was right. There was

nothing for me there. I'd left that long ago, had abandoned it after killing Bloodmark. But I could become a bodyguard again. Not with Borund, no. Not now. But still . . .

I ran my hand over the page boy's clothes and felt for the voices of the throne in the recesses of my mind, still kept at bay by the Fire. If I let the Fire relax just a little, let it dampen . . .

I felt a flush of heat flow through me, tingling in my skin, coursing along my arms, across my shoulders, down my legs. And then the heat flowed outward, suffused and surrounded me completely, extending out through the room, through the palace, and then out farther . . . until it reached the edges of the city itself, pulsing in sync with my blood.

I could feel the city, from the palace to the Dredge, from the River to the two towers that guarded the harbor. Its heartbeat matched mine. Its life flowed through my veins.

I drew in a deep steadying breath, then pushed back the sensation of the city, forced the power behind the protective curtain of Fire again. My hand slid from the page boy's clothing to my side. Erick was right about being a bodyguard as well. How could I return to that now? I was bound to the throne, and through it to the city. Bound by my own choice. Eryn may have lured me into the throne room and forced me to touch the throne, but in the end she hadn't forced me to assume its powers, hadn't forced me to take control. It had been my decision. I could have said no.

"These aren't even my clothes," I said and turned away from the page boy's clothing toward Erick. "I want my own clothes."

Erick grinned. "Let's see what we can find. Then we need to find Avrell. He has a meeting set up with the rest of the people in control of the palace staff. They're all anxious to meet the new Mistress of Amenkor."

I shot him a hard glare but his grin only widened.

†

". . . no idea what she's going to want, Matron Ireen. You'll have to ask her when she arrives."

I heard Avrell's voice the moment Erick opened the door to the meeting room, his tone calm and casual but tinged with irritation. He drew breath to continue, but someone else coughed discreetly and there was a loud rustle of cloth and the scraping of chairs.

A small group of men and women rose from their seats as the door opened fully, Erick stepping into the room in front of me and then to one side. The moment I caught their collective gaze, I reached for my dagger and slid beneath the river, but managed to keep from drawing the blade. Instead, I gripped its hilt, hard enough that my knuckles turned white. Then I scanned the room.

A simple table with seven chairs sat in the middle of the room. A few potted trees rested in two of the corners, the other two taken up by small tables with trays of cheeses and fruit and a pitcher with glasses for drinks. The wall behind the tall chair at the head of the table was covered with a white banner with the gold insignia of the Mistress: the stylized marking of the Skewed Throne—three slashes; one horizontal, the two others angled down and out from that, one shorter than the other. All of the remaining walls were bare.

There were six people waiting at the table. Avrell and Nathem I already knew, both administrators of the Mistress, the First and Second respectively. Next to Nathem stood a woman I had never met before, broad shouldered and older, dressed in the Mistress' whites, her face squinched up into a penetrating frown. With one quick glance, she took in my brown breeches, soft-skin shoes, and the loose linen shirt Erick had borrowed from one of the guardsmen. Then she harrumphed and shook her head in disapproval. The shirt was too large and the breeches itched, but the shoes were well worn and comfortable. I shifted beneath her hostile glare, even though beneath the river she was completely gray and so not a real threat. Both Avrell and Nathem, dressed in the blue-and-gold robes of the Mistress' order, appeared gray as well.

But the three men on the other side of the table were not gray. Baill, captain of the palace guard, stood rigid, face set, hands folded comfortably over his sword belt. His eyes held mine with a reserved look, but they noticed everything: my clothes, my dagger, my hair hanging loose and uncombed about my face. His reaction was impossible to read. Beside him, also dressed in the burgundy silk shirts and brown breeches of guardsmen, were two men I did not know. The first was tall and thin, with the same cold, casual, dangerous look that surrounded Erick. A Seeker. He wore no visible weapons and nodded to Erick before turning his attention to me. When he saw my clothes, a small smile lit in his eyes and his lips twitched. The second man was shorter than the Seeker and wore a sword. He barely glanced in my direction. All three appeared red.

After a long, uncomfortable moment, Avrell cleared his throat and said to the room in general, "May I present Varis, the Mistress of Amenkor."

Another awkward pause, and then everyone gave a short bow, Avrell and Nathem first, with Baill giving a belated brief nod at the end.

Erick moved to the far side of the room and stood behind a high-backed chair, resting his hand on one corner of its back.

"If the Mistress would care to sit," Avrell said, motioning to the chair.

I shot him a glare, but he was too much the diplomat to react. Nothing touched his dark brown eyes as he gave me a casual smile. He was too practiced, had spent too much time around Mistresses and the throne. To all appearances, my seizing of the throne had come as a pleasant surprise.

But I didn't trust him. If he'd helped Eryn to lure me to the throne room, then he'd manipulated me without remorse. And if not, then he'd hired me to kill her, betraying the woman he was supposed to protect. I couldn't afford to trust him.

Captain Baill was no better. Numerous merchants within the city had been murdered during the last year by a consortium of men led by the merchant Alendor in an attempt to take over all of the city's trade. Baill had been suspected of helping the consortium, although he'd done nothing but what the previous Mistress had commanded, so nothing could be proved.

Uneasy, I glanced around the room once more, then stepped around Avrell's side of the room to the chair. As I moved, the guards posted outside the room closed the door behind me and all but Avrell and Erick took seats.

"Let's begin by introducing everyone," Avrell said. "Avrell Tremain, the First of the Mistress." He bowed his head again, then motioned to his left. "This is Nathem Ordaven, the Second of the Mistress—"

"I know."

Nathem seemed startled and somewhat nervous, his brow creasing in thought as he tried to figure out how I knew him. But we'd never met officially. I only knew him because I'd overheard Avrell speaking with him about the Mistress while I was inside the palace, on my way to the throne room.

"I see," Avrell said smoothly. But he shared a troubled glance with Erick that made me smile with satisfaction. He moved on, motioning to the woman. "Matron Ireen is the head of the Mistress' servants. She'll handle all of your needs—clothing, food, whatever you want. She'll want to speak with you at length *after* the meeting."

Ireen had shifted forward, ready to speak, but under Avrell's glare she sank back in her seat and crossed her arms on her ample chest with a grunt.

Avrell turned toward Baill. "And this is Captain Baill Gorret of the palace guard. I'll leave it to you to introduce the others, Captain Baill."

Baill gave Avrell a dark look, then stood and motioned to his right. "Karl Westen, Captain of the Seekers, and Arthur Catrell, Captain of the city guard."

He sat as the other two guardsmen nodded.

An unsettled silence followed, as if everyone were waiting for something. Captain Catrell sighed and shifted with nervous agitation, his gaze darting around the spare room as if distracted. Nathem still seemed deep in thought. Baill simply stared at me, his expression unreadable, neither curious like most of the others, nor contemptuous.

For a long moment, I stared back, but then I shifted my gaze to Avrell. "What have you done with the previous Mistress, Eryn?"

Caught off guard, Avrell sat forward and in an uncertain voice said, "I didn't know what to do with her. We've never had an . . . ex-Mistress, so to speak. So I assigned her rooms in the palace and allowed her to keep her usual servants." He recovered his poise as he spoke. "She's been part of the palace since she was eight, and she doesn't really have any other place to go. Were there . . . other arrangements you wished to make?"

I frowned. With a simple inflection, he'd made it sound as if any other arrangements would be unreasonable.

"No," I said grudgingly. I didn't know if keeping her in the palace was a mistake or not, but for now I was willing to wait.

But I felt as if I'd been manipulated again, the decision taken away from me.

With irritation I didn't bother to suppress, I asked, "What did you want to talk about?"

"There are many things to discuss," Avrell said, nodding as if the meeting were back on track. "The blockade of the harbor, the work to be done in the warehouse district after the recent fire, the food shortage and the advent of winter, the sudden cessation of communication with the Boreaite Isles, but I think the first thing that needs to be discussed is the—"

"I think," Baill interrupted, voice loud to override Avrell. Avrell's gaze narrowed as he looked across the table at Baill; Baill's gaze never shifted away from me. "I think the first thing that needs to be discussed is how Varis managed to get into the throne room of the palace without being discovered by the guard."

Nathem drew in a sharp breath, and Captain Catrell's attention suddenly focused as he shifted forward in his chair.

With a casual movement, Baill turned to Avrell. "She couldn't have done it without help," Baill continued. His voice was as calm and collected as Avrell's, but there was a deadlier undercurrent to it, a threat of violent death.

Avrell did not flinch. "I helped her. I let her in through the tunnels beneath the outer walls, gave her maps of the palace, and told her the movements of the guards."

The captain of the city guard grunted as if punched. "You compromised the Mistress' security? What for?"

Avrell glanced toward Captain Catrell, but only briefly, his eyes dropping to the table before turning back to Baill with a challenge. "I wanted Varis to kill the Mistress."

There was a brief moment of silence. Then Captain Catrell stood and in a surprisingly smooth movement brought his sword to bear, the blade reaching across the table toward Avrell's throat without wavering.

"Then you are a traitor," he said simply.

No one in the room moved. Avrell held the gaze of the captain of the city guard, not even glancing down at the sword.

"I made a vow to protect the throne and the city of Amenkor," Avrell said with a tinge of disdain. "Not the Mistress herself."

To one side, I saw Baill frown and shift in his seat as if uncomfortable. He no longer seemed as certain as he had a moment before.

"Besides," Avrell continued, turning his attention to me, still refusing to acknowledge the presence of the sword, "I could only get Varis into the palace. There was nothing I could do about the guardsmen after that. It was the Mistress' own luck that Varis made it to the throne room without being seen."

Avrell's gaze locked onto mine, but it was completely unreadable. I thought about the key he'd given me to get into the inner sanctum of the palace, the key to the archer's niche. But then I realized that Avrell was right. The key could only get me so far. It was the Mistress herself who had distracted the guards beyond that point.

Grudgingly, feeling as if I'd been cornered again, forced into speaking against my will, I said, "It wasn't luck."

With a glare at Avrell, I turned to Baill. "The Mistress—the previous Mistress—lured me to the throne room herself. She wanted me to ascend to the throne. She's the one that diverted the guardsmen from the outer corridor so that I could enter the inner sanctum."

Baill considered for a long moment, his gaze never wavering from mine. Something flickered behind his eyes, there and then gone, too quickly for me to read. Then he nodded. "Lower your sword, Arthur. I believe her."

Captain Catrell hesitated, then resheathed his sword and sat down.

"Now," Avrell said. "About the food shortage—"

"No."

A look of annoyance passed over Avrell's face and he turned toward me with a frown. "No?"

I drew in a deep breath and leaned forward, letting my anger touch my voice. I was tired of being manipulated. "If we're going to discuss the food shortage, I want all the remaining merchants here. Borund in particular."

"But if we're going to be able to find more resources to replace those lost in the fire in the warehouse district, we need to act quickly. Winter is approaching fast. We have only a few more days left to send out ships. After that, there won't be enough time for the ships to travel to the other cities, trade and load cargo, and return before the seas become too rough for safe passage. We can't wait for the merchants. We need to act now!"

I glared at Avrell, and then felt something shift. A strange warmth enfolded me, and suddenly the room grew distant, as if somehow I'd taken a step back from the table, even though I was still seated.

In a cold voice, I said, "The ships belong to the merchants, or are owned outright by their captains. I will not order them to sea without the merchant's or the captain's consent."

Without waiting for a response, I shifted my attention to Captain Catrell. "Can you send guardsmen to Merchant Borund's manse?"

"Of course."

"Then send them. Tell him the blockade on the harbor is lifted, that he may send ships out at once if he wishes, and that they are to find and buy whatever food they can and return. They will be compensated by the palace. Also tell him to gather together the resources he has left in the city, those that weren't destroyed by the fire in the warehouse district. He is to bring a report to the palace tomorrow morning, early. Get from him the names of all of the remaining merchants in Amenkor and give the same message to them. I want the entire merchants' guild to be represented at this meeting."

Captain Catrell stared, stunned, then nodded and said, "Very well." He sat a little straighter in his seat and no longer seemed as distracted as before.

Baill leaned forward. "So the blockade is to be lifted?"

"Yes."

Baill nodded with approval and leaned back in his seat. Avrell had told Borund and me that Baill refused to lift the blockade, had made it seem as if Baill was at fault, that Baill's claim that the Mistress had ordered the blockade kept even after the merchants protested was a lie. Now I began to wonder.

What if Captain Baill *had* simply been following the Mistress' orders? We had no evidence he'd been working for the consortium at all.

"Was there anything else?" I asked, in a tone that suggested there shouldn't be.

Everyone in the room stilled, as if they'd all drawn a sharp breath and were holding it. No one said anything.

I suddenly wanted to leave, the urge like a prickling sensation across my back. The room felt too hot, too closed in and dense. And still distant.

I stood. "Good."

"But what of the guard patrols in the city?" Avrell said abruptly, standing as well. "And the arrangements for your servants?" He motioned toward Ireen.

The prickling sensation across my back increased. "Keep the patrols. As for the servants. . . ." My gaze fell on Ireen, who sat forward expectantly, face set into a stern frown. "Do whatever you want."

The frown vanished, replaced by confused shock, followed by stern elation.

I suddenly pitied the servants of the palace. Ireen seemed a harsh mistress.

I stalked from the room, Erick following with a slight frown. I ignored Avrell's attempt to catch my attention, but he raised his voice to shout after me, "We need to discuss the political situation with the rest of the coast! We'll have to discuss it at some point!" The others stood awkwardly, nodding as I passed.

Once out into the hall, I turned toward the Mistress' chambers, four palace guardsmen falling into step behind Erick. As we moved through the corridors, passing servants in the hallways and rooms who paused in their work to gaze after the new Mistress with blatant curiosity, the sense of distance dissipated and the tension in my shoulders loosened. But I still felt agitated. The river roiled around me, but I didn't want to let it go. All I could think about was Avrell. And Baill.

Back in the Mistress' chambers, I began pacing the room, Erick closing the doors behind us, the four guardsmen remaining outside, two in the corridor and two in the antechamber.

"You *will* have to speak to Avrell at length," Erick said. "He can tell you everything you need to know about being the Mistress. At least regarding the everyday workings of the palace."

I frowned but didn't answer, circled the room, to the bed, the low table with the basin and pitcher of water, the doors looking out onto the balcony. Someone had entered while I was gone, had drawn back the curtains and opened the doors so that the breeze could enter the room. I could see the entrance to the harbor, the view slightly different from what I'd seen from the rooftop. This looked out along the southern jut of land, rather than the main part of the city and the river. But the view didn't hold me, and I returned to the bed.

My hands itched.

I halted, staring at them a moment before sinking down into a seat on the bed.

Then I looked up at Erick.

"What is it?" he asked.

"I don't know."

Except I did.

Erick nodded as if he understood, then moved to a second table I hadn't noticed before. A platter of fruit had been set out, and a pitcher of some type of dark red drink.

He picked up a few grapes.

I glowered at his back, then said, "It's not simple anymore."

"What do you mean?"

I sighed, looked back down at my hands. "On the Dredge, it was only about survival. I hunted—for food, for the easiest target, and then later for marks you sent me after. Whatever it took to survive. Then, for Borund, I hunted again—for those targeting Borund."

Erick turned. "And now you don't know what to hunt for?"

"Yes. No." I shook my head in annoyance. "It's more than that."

Erick hesitated, then came forward. "No, it's not. You're still hunting, just as you hunted for Borund. Except this time you're hunting those that are targeting the city."

My hand still itched and with a casual move I drew my dagger, held it before me. The blade was worn, the handle nicked. A guardsman's dagger. I could still feel the blade slashing across the ex-guardsman's throat, the motion awkward and fumbling, inexperienced, but it had been enough. He'd been the first man I'd killed. My first mark. After that, the process had been easy: identify the mark and kill.

Identify and kill.

Simple.

"Except now the marks are winter and starvation," I said, and looked at Erick. "I can't hunt starvation. I can't kill winter."

A troubled look crossed his face, but at the same time the sound of bells came through the window to the balcony, followed by the low bellow of a horn, sounding close, as if originating from the palace itself.

Erick moved to the balcony. I trailed behind, putting away my dagger.

The balcony was long and narrow, with a few flowering vines on trellises in the corners and a black wrought-iron railing encircling all three sides. As I moved up to its edge, I let the Fire relax and felt the pulse of the city course through me.

In the harbor, the Mistress' ships were pulling back from the entrance, moving swiftly and silently. On the docks, there was a sudden frenzy of activity as men began to load cargo that had rested idle on the wharf for days. A few of the merchant ships that had remained loaded even after the blockade were already tossing their lines and pushing away from the docks.

Erick grunted. "The tide is good. They should be able to leave quickly." Then he turned to me, motioning to the ships below. "You are hunting, Varis," he said. "But you're using ships instead of a dagger."

I glanced toward him, uncertain what to say. But the tension in my shoulders had completely faded. And there was no prickling sensation along my shoulders, no itching in my hands.

I leaned my weight forward onto the railing and watched the ships, *felt* them as they glided through the water. Fixing my attention on the lead merchant ship, I followed it, feeling a sense of elation as it surged forward under the wind. Sails whuffled, snapping taut as they belled out, men scrambling on the deck and through the rigging. I felt the tension of the men's muscles, felt their sweat. Then I noticed the flag flying on its highest mast: gold on a red field. Borund's flag.

Of course. He would have known the blockade would be lifted soon after he'd learned I'd seized the throne. He'd been waiting for it. It must have been his ships loading up at the docks before dawn.

Borund's ship neared the entrance to the harbor, then slid through the ends of the two juts of land and the watchtowers, passing out into the darker blue ocean. As it passed the towers, my connection to the ship began to fade. I felt a painful sense of loss as the sensation of wood and rope and water, of the men's sweat and blood, slipped away, then ended.

Apparently, the power of the throne and its connection to the city ended at the entrance to the harbor.

I sighed, watched the remaining ships for a long moment, then felt a familiar tug on the currents of the city.

I turned, straightened where I stood.

The Dredge.

My eyes narrowed.

"I have a mark for you," I said, then turned toward Erick.

He stood, back rigid, eyes dark and serious, as deadly as he'd appeared to me at first on the Dredge. "I live to serve, my Mistress."

I shivered, uneasy at the words, but nodded in response. "His name is Corum."

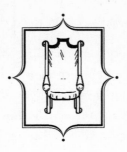

Chapter 2

I WOKE TO BRIGHT SUNLIGHT, the sound of midmorning bells from the city below, and a hollow sense of fear.

I couldn't do this. I was a hunter, an assassin, a thief. I didn't know the first thing about ruling a city.

Something clattered and I turned my head sharply, the fear quashed, my hand sliding up under my pillow to the hilt of my dagger. Three servants dressed in white, all young girls around fifteen years old, moved about the room, setting down trays of cheese, opening the curtains and balcony doors, and laying out clothes for the day. I watched them cautiously, but none of them approached and finally the tension bled away.

I dragged myself into a seated position on the edge of the bed, moving slowly, one hand raised to my head. I'd slept later than I'd wanted, but the lack of sleep over the last few nights had finally caught up to me. I moaned, yawned, then scrubbed at my gritty eyes. I felt as if someone had beat me senseless and left me for dead in a back alley.

Someone coughed and I glanced up to see one of the servants—a girl close to my age, with blonde hair, a roundish face, and soft gray eyes—standing before me holding out a cup of something brown and steaming. It smelled of dead, dried leaves.

The girl ducked her head and muttered, "Mistress." She watched me closely behind lowered lashes. A quick touch on the river revealed she was gray. All three servants were gray.

I frowned but took the warm cup. Bringing it close, I breathed in the steam, wrinkled my nose at the smell. This close it smelled more like muddy water. But I could actually see small pieces of crumbled leaves floating in it.

"What is it?"

The girl seemed surprised. "It's tea, Mistress. From Marland."

I took a tentative sip, expecting it to taste as if I'd licked a mud-brick on the Dredge. Instead, its warmth seeped into my chest, the bitterness making my tongue tingle. It did taste like dirt, but not like the stagnant rot on the Dredge. More like the gardens surrounding Borund's manse. Earthy, like loam.

I unconsciously straightened as I took another sip, no longer feeling so exhausted.

After I'd drunk half the cup, the gray-eyed girl nodded to one of the other servants, who brought forward a stack of clothes. "Some of the merchants have already arrived and are waiting to see you, Mistress."

Borund.

I stood, setting the cup aside on the bed. "Where are my clothes?"

The gray-eyed girl frowned and picked up the cup before it could spill. "Right here," she said, motioning to the second servant, who unfolded a white-and-gold dress.

I grimaced. "No, where are *my* clothes? The breeches and shirt I wore yesterday?"

"Oh! The Matron said we should remove them."

My eyes narrowed, and the gray-eyed girl took a tentative step back. "The Matron?"

"I–Ireen," she stammered.

I recalled Ireen's elation yesterday and suddenly regretted telling her she could do whatever she wanted.

"Find them."

The gray-eyed girl cast a terrified glance toward the girl holding the clothing. "We—we can't."

My eyes narrowed further. "Why not?"

The girl swallowed and seemed on the verge of bolting from the room. "Matron Ireen—" she began, voice tight, eyes wide, then finished in a low rush, head bowed, "Matron Ireen had them burned."

I drew in a breath to respond, then halted, too stunned to know what to say. "Burned?"

The girl nodded.

Anger flooded me. My hands itched for my dagger, but I managed to keep myself in check.

"Find me some breeches and a shirt," I said with suppressed rage. "And get rid of all these . . . dresses. Breeches and tunics, that's all I want to wear. Go to Master Borund's manse and get all my clothes from there if you have to."

"Yes, Mistress. Right away."

The girl backed off, dragging the servant holding the offending dress with her. They held a hissed conversation, punctuated by hand gestures, and then both girls nodded formally in my direction and fled the room.

I wondered how many of them were true Servants—girls who could sense and use the river like me, girls that could one day be the Mistress if they could learn to control the throne well enough. They were here because someone had noticed they had the talent and had brought them here to learn to use it. But because of that, they were as dangerous to me as Avrell and Baill.

A soft footfall sounded and I spun, eyes catching the last girl on the far side of the room. She stilled, tried a tentative smile and a small bow, then began a frantic and unnecessary rearrangement of the curtains.

I sighed and thought of Erick, suddenly wishing I hadn't sent him after Corum after all, that I'd sent one of the other Seekers instead. I was surrounded by people I couldn't trust; having him here would have given me someone I could rely on.

I scanned the room, the hollow feeling in my gut returning. With a small push, I let the Fire relax and felt the sensation of the city flow through me, let the voices of the throne rush forward. Not far enough to overwhelm me, but enough so I could hear distinct voices clamoring for attention.

I ignored them, focusing instead on the city. Closing my eyes, I reached out, wary of Eryn's warning about pushing myself too far. I thought of Erick, of how he felt when I saw him beneath the river, about his scent—sweat mixed with a tang of oranges.

After a moment, I sensed him in the city, somewhere on the Dredge, lost in the darker turmoil of the emotions of the people that lived there, that *survived* there. I smiled, the tension in my shoulders relaxing as I felt him moving, as I drew in the tang of orange that surrounded me.

Erick was hunting.

I felt a momentary urge to take my dagger and join him, escape from this palace with all its meetings and servants and guardsmen. For a moment, I gave in, let myself drift forward, heading toward the Dredge on the flows of the river, following Erick's scent, Eryn's warning forgotten.

But when the sensation began to stretch, when I could no longer feel a tenuous connection to my body, before the last threads broke, I pulled back.

The feeling had been glorious . . . and frightening at the same time.

I breathed in one last calming breath, then shifted my attention to the Dredge itself, to the seething roil of desperation. I couldn't pick out individuals, couldn't even narrow my focus down to a street, but I sensed that it was possible. It wasn't the same as stretching toward Erick, or even Reaching to find Corum as I'd done on the tower. I'd had a known scent to follow then, something concrete to focus on. Without that scent, the eddies and currents were a jumbled mess, too complex to separate. For now.

But I could sense the fear. The people of the Dredge were terrified. The tension on the river was palpable, a tension I recognized because I'd survived on the Dredge for so long on my own. Winter was approaching, and the Dredge would be the hardest hit. The people in the slums were worried about where their next chunk of bread or gobbet of meat would come from.

There had to be a way to help them, to feed them this winter and beyond.

I pushed the voices and the city back, let the river slide away with a sigh, and turned my attention to Borund and the merchants.

✝

An hour later Marielle, the gray-eyed servant, led me through the palace to one of the sitting rooms, where Avrell, Borund, and two other merchants were waiting, talking animatedly. I heard their voices from two corridors away.

"—but look at what happened in the warehouse fires!" Borund spat, his voice easy to recognize.

"I realize that," Avrell countered, voice as slick and fluid as it had been during the meeting the day before. "But in the interest of organization and control—"

"It won't matter how well organized or controlled it is if some other disaster wipes out the remaining supplies. We cannot take the risk!"

All voices ceased as Marielle and I entered, all four men turning toward me with dissatisfied, angry frowns. With a faint twinge of surprise, I realized I'd already been in this room. Low tables and pillows were scattered among plants and a few latticework screens designed to provide small alcoves for private conversations. I'd hidden in one of those screened-off alcoves when I'd infiltrated the palace, had overheard Avrell and Nathem discussing the decision to kill the Mistress.

Once the merchants realized who had interrupted, their anger faded, replaced by cautious but curious frowns from the two merchants I didn't know, and a genuine smile from Borund. Warmth flooded through me at the smile, and I grinned in return. Borund was dressed in his formal red and gold merchant's coat and ruffled white shirt, the wire rims of his glasses catching the light. He was mostly bald, skin shiny on the top of his head, but with gray-brown, wispy hair above his ears and circling around to the back.

"Varis," he said, rising to give a low bow at the waist. The others rose as well. "I mean . . . Mistress. May I introduce Merchants Regin and Yvan."

Both merchants gave stiff bows. They were dressed much like Borund, but with different colors: Regin wore a dark blue-and-gold coat, while Yvan's was cream-colored, with black embroidery. Yvan was fat, with cold, hard, intelligent eyes and a shiny, completely bald head. Regin was thin, poised, and had long, wavy, dark hair.

"Forgive me," Regin said, surveying my clothes. Marielle had found boots, breeches, and a white shirt that actually fit. My dagger was tucked into one of the soft-sided boots. "I did not recognize you, Mistress."

My eyes narrowed, but I couldn't decide whether he'd meant it as an insult or not. "What were you arguing about? And where are the rest of the merchants?"

"This is all that's left," Borund answered, then glanced angrily at Avrell. "And we've been arguing over where the supplies we have should be kept. I think they should be moved to various locations throughout the city, to protect them and to make it easier to distribute them once winter sets in. Avrell wants to store them in a central location."

"We can keep better control over the supplies and their distribution if they are in one location," Avrell countered. "The palace, for instance. It would be easier for the city and palace guards to protect them if they were not scattered throughout the city."

Borund snorted. "But look at the fire in the warehouse district. With one mishap, we lost close to half of our winter storage. Granted, most of it was Alendor's, but . . ."

"Alendor," I interrupted, moving forward to take a seat on one of the pillows, legs crossed so I could rest my elbows on my knees. "What happened to him?"

The merchants shifted uncomfortably where they stood, then slowly took their seats around me, along with Avrell. Marielle was nowhere to be seen.

"No one has seen him since the night of the warehouse fires," Avrell said. He cast me a warning glance to keep quiet, motioning slightly toward Regin and Yvan. Neither of them knew I'd followed Alendor into the warehouse district that night in order to kill him, to break the consortium of merchants he'd built up. The consortium had been buying up and hoarding the resources of the city to form a monopoly, killing off any competing merchants. Instead of killing Alendor, I'd ended up killing his son, Cristoph, and in the process the warehouse district had caught fire.

"Tarrence—and the merchants in the city that we know were part of Alendor's consortium—all scrambled to leave the day after the fire," Avrell continued.

"How do you know?" Borund asked.

"Once I knew who was part of the consortium, I had them watched by the city guard. I also have sources scattered both inside and outside the city. Tarrence, for example, was sighted yesterday south of here, in the port city of Kent."

Borund grunted with grudging respect.

"Is that all?" I asked.

Everyone stilled.

"What do you mean?" Regin asked, his voice tinged with condescension.

I bristled where I sat, turning my full attention on Regin. I noted his merchant's jacket had more gold embroidery than Borund's. Borund had told me once that the color of the jackets indicated what commodity the merchants had dealt in when they applied for membership in the guild—red for wine, blue for fish, cream for dairy—and that symbols in the embroidery indicated what they currently dealt in. More embroidery indicated a more powerful merchant.

Judging by his embroidery, Regin outranked Borund in the guild.

"Alendor tried to seize control of *all* trade within the city," I said, "tried to seize control of the merchants' guild, of all resources within Amenkor, including your own. He ordered the deaths of members of the guild itself, as well as merchants from other cities along the coast. Are you saying the guild isn't even searching for him?"

Yvan snorted, but it was Regin who answered, his voice laced with anger.

"Of course we're searching for him. The guild itself has condemned him and all of those that were part of the consortium. Their licenses to the guild hall have been revoked and all of their rights rescinded. In effect, they can no longer legally act as merchants, either within the city of Amenkor or any of the ports that recognize the merchants' guild as a power. Alendor's name means nothing. All connections to any trading houses along the Frigean coast are gone. He has been destroyed as a merchant. He's not in the city, and he has nowhere else to run to, nowhere he can expect safe haven, at least from the merchants' guild. What more do you expect us to do?"

Regin halted, his jaw clenched. Raw hatred blazed in his eyes, but it was not directed at me. Alendor's betrayal had cut Regin deeply. He wanted more than just Alendor's downfall. He wanted Alendor dead.

I drew back from Regin's gaze, glanced quickly at Borund and Yvan, saw the same rage in their eyes, then turned to Avrell.

"Is there anything else that can be done?"

"Outside of the city?" He thought for a moment, then nodded. "You, as Mistress of Amenkor, can contact the rulers of the surrounding cities and warn them of Alendor and his cohorts, ask them to use their own guard to watch for him and—if he is found—send him back to Amenkor for punishment. Those that we have good relations with at the moment—Venitte, Merrell, some others—will agree, and if they find him, return him to us." He hesitated a moment, then added, "You can also send the Seekers."

I straightened where I sat, but before I could say anything, he halted me with a frown.

"There is a risk in sending the Seekers after targets beyond the city of Amenkor. The rulers of the surrounding cities do not take kindly to having Amenkor assassins roaming their streets in search of citizens."

"Even for known criminals?"

"Even for known criminals. Sending the Seekers beyond Amenkor should only be done in an extreme situation. Since we don't even know in which direction Alendor may have run . . ."

He let the thought trail off and I grimaced.

"I want him found," I said, and heard more emotion in my own voice than I had intended. I could still hear Alendor's voice ordering Borund's death, could hear the cold, businesslike finality in it.

"He will be found," Avrell answered. "My contacts in all of the ports will keep their eyes open. He cannot hide forever."

Not completely satisfied, I turned to Regin. "What about the other ports? Have you sent word to them, warned them?"

Borund cleared his throat. "Our main form of communication with the guilds in other cities is through our ships. Since the harbor has been closed to trade . . ." He shrugged.

Regin picked up the thread. "We sent word overland, but that takes time. Now that the harbor is open again, the word will spread more quickly. The merchants' guild will keep its eyes open for Alendor as well."

I nodded. "And what of Alendor's—and the other merchants'—resources?"

"They couldn't have loaded everything up and left, at least not by ship," Avrell said. "The harbor had been blockaded by then. And taking everything by wagon or cart would have attracted too much notice. They must have left something behind. But I have no idea where they may have stored goods besides the warehouse district. That's a guild matter."

Regin stirred. "I believe we can search the guild records to see what property each of the members of the consortium owned. Then, perhaps, with the city guard's help, any stores left behind could be seized by the guild and allocated to the remaining guild members—"

"How?" Yvan interrupted. His voice was like stone grating against stone, rumbling from his chest as if from the bottom of an empty barrel.

"I don't understand—" Regin began, but Yvan cut him off.

"How are you going to allocate it to the remaining guild members? Evenly? By percentage of the share in the guild? By status?

Does Borund gain more from the seizure simply because he owns more property than I do?"

"I'm certain that the guild can come up with a fair method of distributing what we seize." Regin's voice was laced with heat and an undertone of warning.

Unconsciously I slid beneath the river and almost recoiled at the blatant hostility I found seething on the currents. Hostility toward each other that had not shown in the merchants' faces a few moments before.

Yvan shifted forward, the motion requiring some effort. His voice was laced with suspicion. "Perhaps we should discuss that among the guild members before we attempt to seize any abandoned property."

"That," Regin declared, going rigid, "would be a waste of time."

The two locked gazes, both bristling, like two mongrel dogs on the Dredge preparing to fight over a rotting fish head. Yvan leaned farther forward, ready to respond. . . .

And another voice intervened, sliding smoothly along the currents of the river.

Take it. Take it all.

I tensed, my forehead creasing as I frowned. The soft, sibilant voice was barely more than a whisper, and with it came the heady scent of oak and wine. I breathed in the scent deeply, then halted.

The voice had come from the river, had come from the throne.

Pushing the argument between Regin and Yvan into the background rush of the wind, I dove deep, caught the scent again and followed it, down and down, until I came up to the edge of the spherical Fire at my core that kept the voices of the Skewed Throne in check. Through the white blaze I could sense a woman, the smell of oak and wine strong, constant. An older woman, her essence solid and consistent, removed from the rest of the maelstrom of the other voices. I could feel her holding herself together, resisting the pull of the rest of the throne.

Who are you? I demanded, but she ignored me.

Look at them. Her voice shook with contempt, with the effort to hold herself together against the chaos. *Look at them bickering. How petty.*

I turned back, saw Regin and Yvan arguing, Borund breaking in now and then, trying to calm them down. Both men seethed with aggression, both trying to gain the upper hand.

I felt a bubble of contempt well up inside me, acid with anger.

They're fighting over food, Varis. Over food that belongs to the city. Food that the city needs to survive. We won't last through the winter if they control everything. They'll hoard it, ration it, give themselves more and give the people of the Dredge less. They don't care about the gutterscum. They'd rather the gutterscum die.

The bubble of contempt rose higher. I could taste it now, the anger like ash in the back of my throat.

Behind the Fire, I felt the presence of the woman ease forward, closer to the white flames. They reacted, the wall of the sphere thickening, pulsing, but the woman didn't waver, didn't back off.

You're the Mistress, Varis, she whispered softly. *The city and everything in it is yours.*

The Fire thickened even more. Regin and Yvan were close together now, faces barely inches apart, eyes locked, both hard and unrelenting. Avrell sat back silently, watching, his eyes intent, calculating. Borund sat nervously, uncertain whether he should interfere more than he already had.

You can simply take everything, the woman said, voice low and reasonable, and so close now I could almost feel it, like a breath against my neck, cold and vibrant. *Let me help you, Varis. Let me out . . . so I can help.*

I snapped around.

"No!"

I forced the Fire toward her, eyes blazing, and the woman jerked back with a cry of fear and hatred. I'd startled her out of her carefully held control, and with a shriek of triumph the maelstrom of the throne took her, dragging her down as she cursed and screamed.

Within moments she was lost, trapped again by the throne, her scent mingling with all the others.

I turned back, a sheen of sweat touching my forehead, the palms of my hands. Avrell, Borund, and the two merchants were watching me, startled, and I suddenly realized I'd shouted out loud. And that the bubble of contempt and anger remained.

I glared at both Regin and Yvan. Regin drew breath to speak, but he never got the chance.

"Enough," I spat. The raw edge in my voice silenced everyone, forced Yvan to lean back in shock. I was breathing hard, almost shaking. But the woman, whoever she had been, was right. I *was* the Mistress.

"The guild will get none of the resources left behind by the consortium." Regin and Yvan instantly shifted forward to protest, but I cut them off. "Everything will be seized by the Skewed Throne, stored by the palace wherever I see fit, and protected by the city guard. That can be done?"

I glanced at Avrell for confirmation, suddenly uncertain, and he nodded once, abruptly, as shocked as the merchants. But Avrell was recovering already. I could see it in his eyes, along with approval.

"You," I said, turning back to Regin, "will provide the guard with a list of all of the properties owned by Alendor and the consortium, as well as lists of all the food you and the remaining merchants have stored in the city."

"But," Regin interposed, "the trade of the city has always been carried out by the merchants' guild."

"Not this winter."

"Mistress," Yvan began, voice as slick and reasonable as the woman from the Fire's had been, and just as false.

"No," I growled. "This winter the merchants will work with me so that everyone gets fed and survives to the spring harvest. Everyone." I switched my attention back to Regin. "Don't force me to seize more than just the consortium's property, Master Regin."

Regin halted, his eyes hooded with anger at the threat, but he backed off. Yvan did the same, reluctantly, with a low, dangerous grumble.

There was a moment of tense silence, then everyone turned at a clink of glass, movements sharp. Marielle stood uncertainly in the entryway, holding a large platter of food and drink. She bowed slightly, balancing the weight of the platter.

"I thought some food and wine would be appreciated," she said, glancing in my direction, eyes questioning.

I nodded.

As she went about setting up the food at the various tables, the tension in the room eased. No one spoke, Regin and Yvan watching me carefully, Borund glancing back and forth between them and Avrell. Avrell was subdued, hands folded neatly in his lap, his eyes hooded, deep in thought.

When Marielle came forward offering drinks, Borund coughed. "Mistress, I've brought the lists of my own resources within the city, as well as those I have stored in other cities that there is still time to reach before winter. As you requested."

He passed the papers to me, script neat and orderly on every page. But it was completely meaningless because I couldn't read.

I hesitated, staring down at the pages in my hand blankly. All of the confidence I'd felt a moment before fled, replaced by a sudden sense of inadequacy. A shudder ran through me, and I became aware of how Regin and Yvan must see me: a fraud. Gutterscum risen above her station. A street player, mimicking the Mistress.

The awkward silence in the room shifted. Both Regin and Yvan sat back uncomfortably. Borund suddenly realized his mistake and began to color.

Before the full horror could set in, I felt a hand against my arm. I jumped.

Avrell had leaned forward to take the papers. "Allow me, Mistress?"

I nodded and he took the papers, sat back, and glanced through each page, lips thinning.

After a long moment, he looked toward Regin and Yvan. "And your own reports?"

Both Regin and Yvan straightened where they sat, but said nothing.

"The Mistress did request that you bring a report with you today, did she not?"

"Yes, but—"

"I see."

Regin bristled. "It was not possible to get a full accounting in such a short amount of time."

Avrell blinked. "Are you telling me that one of the most powerful merchants—no, now that Alendor is gone, you are *the* most powerful merchant in Amenkor, are you not?"

Regin nodded.

"Are you telling me, then, that the most powerful merchant in Amenkor does not know what his own assets are on a day's notice? I find that impossible to believe, Master Regin. Most impossible." Avrell's eyes darkened, his voice tinged with anger.

Regin fidgeted where he sat, then exhaled. "A report will be sent immediately."

Avrell turned his stare on Yvan, who grumbled, "From my house as well."

"Good." Avrell shot a questioning glance toward me, but I had not quite recovered and motioned for him to continue. "Then we can turn to the real question: do we have enough to survive the winter? Taking into account all of the combined merchant houses and their resources, sparing nothing."

"And the fact that we must feed the entire city," I interjected, shooting a hard look at Regin. "*All* of it. Those on the Dredge included."

Regin frowned, glancing toward Borund and Yvan before turning back to me.

I read the answer in his eyes before he spoke.

"No."

There was a collective, drawn-out silence. No one reached for their drinks, or the small plates of food Marielle had set beside each one of us as we spoke. Marielle herself stood silently beside the tray of food, her fingers drumming lightly against the side of the bottle of wine. Her eyes caught mine, wide and fearful. She bit her lip before turning away.

"How bad is it?" Avrell finally asked.

Borund stirred. "Right now, there's enough that the entire city won't starve, but not enough to feed everyone. I'd say we can feed half the population for the winter with what we have already stored in the city, making certain assumptions about what portion of Alendor's supplies remain. Some of what was lost can be replaced if we bring in whatever the fishing boats can catch over the next month, before the water becomes too hazardous to fish."

"What about the ships that have already left?" I asked.

Regin shook his head. "They're trading mainly for land goods—fruits, vegetables, salted meats, and grains. If all of them find trade goods it's possible that they will return with enough food to supplement what we have and last through to the early spring harvest, but we aren't the only city facing starvation this season. The autumn harvest was not good anywhere on the Frigean coast—too much rain in some parts, not enough in others—and the trade routes to Kandish across the mountains and to the other eastern countries were cut off."

"Why?"

"Heavy snowfall in the passes would account for some of it, but not all," Avrell said. He seemed as troubled as the merchants. "Something more serious has happened to the east, but we have had no word yet on what that might have been. None of our envoys have returned, and I've received no messages from any of my diplomatic sources. There was a certain amount of political unrest in the area in the last few years, especially regarding the aging emperor and his succession. It's possible that he has died and there is a succession war going on that has closed down the communication lines. But this is purely speculation."

Avrell's report was followed by silence. I knew nothing of the eastern cities.

Regin cleared his throat. "The ships we sent should return with some food, since each of us had some stored in other cities—"

"If the rulers of those cities haven't seized it yet," Yvan rumbled.

Regin frowned but continued as if he hadn't been interrupted. "However, I'm not certain how many new resources they will be able to find and purchase."

"Hopefully, it will be enough," Borund said, his voice low.

"When will we know?" I asked.

"I don't know," Regin answered. "The earliest the ships will return is sometime next week. We can expect them to arrive any time after that for about two weeks, but a month from now we can't expect any more to return. The seas will be too rough for safe passage. That's why it was imperative that the harbor be reopened now. It will take a month for some of the ships to reach their intended ports and then return."

Another moment of silence.

"Then send out the fishing fleets," I said abruptly. "Bring in as much fish and crab as you can. We'll determine how to distribute what we have later, once we have a full accounting from everyone, and once the ships have returned. In the meantime, I suggest we start rationing now."

Regin and Yvan took this as a dismissal, downing their glasses of wine quickly before exiting with perfunctory bows. Borund followed more slowly.

As he stepped to the outer corridor, he paused to give a respectful bow. "It is good to see you well, Va—" He caught himself with a self-deprecating smile. "Mistress."

Then he left. I watched his departing back and realized that things had changed irrevocably between us. I was no longer his bodyguard, no longer took his orders. But there was still an intangible connection between us. We'd always been uncertain of how to treat each other.

But his absence didn't hurt as much as Erick's.

Avrell sipped at his wine, set it aside slowly before turning to me. "You cannot read, can you?"

I felt myself harden defensively. "There's no need to read on the Dredge, and Borund never found the time to teach me."

"I see." Avrell reached down to collect the loose pages of Borund's report, not reacting to my anger. "We shall have to find someone to teach you. Perhaps Marielle?"

Marielle stilled at the mention of her name, a thread of fear coursing through the river. A fear associated with Avrell. But it was fleeting. Without a word, she turned back to picking up the plates and glasses the merchants had left behind.

"In the meantime," Avrell continued, "I can keep track of all of the reports and papers that you need."

I frowned. I didn't know how much I trusted Avrell—didn't

know how much I trusted *anyone* yet, besides Erick and Borund. But there was no one else.

Avrell stood when I said nothing, gave a short bow, and then left, moving slowly. I watched his retreating back, then said softly to myself, "One month."

†

Westen, captain of the Seekers, was waiting for me outside the meeting room where I'd met with Avrell and the merchants. He stood leaning casually against one wall, body relaxed, arms crossed in front of his chest. The stance sent a shiver of recognition through me, rewoke the ache I'd felt since rising that morning.

Erick had stood that way while waiting outside my niche to give me a new mark.

When I hesitated, Westen pushed himself away from the wall and smiled. "I'd like to speak to you, if you have the time."

I was suddenly aware of the four guardsmen who'd fallen in around me. Without looking, I sensed that they were all Seekers, their presence too still, the tension on the river sharp and ready.

The hairs on the nape of my neck stirred. The palace guardsmen who had accompanied me to the meeting had been replaced.

"Do I have a choice?"

The corner of his mouth twitched, and he motioned me forward, falling into step beside me. "You are the Mistress. You always have a choice."

I snorted, felt the other four Seekers reposition themselves behind us. We moved deeper into the palace, passing open windows looking out onto gardens and through wide rooms decorated with trees and tables. We passed a few servants, all of whom paused and nodded or bowed their heads as I passed. Westen said nothing for a long while, content to simply walk beside me. But he never relaxed, the tension that all Seekers radiated never faltering.

When he finally did speak, his soft voice startled me. He'd said nothing at all during the meeting the day before, but for some reason, I'd expected his voice to be harsh, like the Dredge.

"Erick's told me much about you," he said.

Wary, I glanced at his face, at the dark brown hair, the dark eyes, the nose that had been broken at least twice. There was none of the deadly danger I associated with the Seekers in those eyes now. I felt myself relaxing. "Such as?"

He grinned. "He told me how you killed that man the first time he saw you, how you used the dagger to slice the cord wrapped around your neck, how you punched the dagger into his chest."

I snorted. "I didn't punch the dagger into his chest. The man fell on top of me. I was lucky the dagger was pointing up. And I puked after the man died."

Westen chuckled. "Everyone reacts differently after their first kill. Puking is not uncommon."

I frowned. That man hadn't been my first kill—and Erick knew that. He hadn't told Westen everything, then.

"He also told me how you helped him hunt for his marks in the slums beyond the Dredge," Westen continued. "How you eventually helped him kill them as well."

"Yes."

"And he told me of Bloodmark."

I halted at the tone in his voice and he turned to face me.

"What about Bloodmark?"

Westen was no longer smiling. "Bloodmark wasn't one of your marks, was he? He wasn't someone the Mistress had sent Erick to find, to judge?"

"No."

"And yet you hunted him down and killed him."

I felt a flush of shame course through me, old shame that I thought had faded. But this tasted fresh and bitter against my tongue. "He killed the baker and his wife—people who helped me survive the slums, who cared for me—for no other reason than to hurt me. He deserved to die."

Westen watched me closely, his eyes searching my face, then he grunted. "Perhaps. But back then it wasn't your decision to make, was it?"

He turned away, continued walking down the length of the corridor. We'd descended to the level of the courtyard and the main gates, but were on the opposite side of the palace. I didn't recognize any of the rooms. None of this had been on the maps Avrell had given me when I infiltrated the palace and was making my way to the throne room.

Reluctantly, I followed Westen as he emerged into an open room with darkened alcoves on either side, a door on the far side, and nothing else. The floor and walls were bare stone—no tapestries or banners, no furniture or potted plants. Tall metal sconces with bowls of burning oil at the top lined the walls, three on each side of the room.

Westen halted halfway to the far side, turning to face me. "But none of that matters now. You are the Mistress, and I agree that Bloodmark needed to die." Belatedly, I realized that the four Seekers that had accompanied us were gone. We were the only two in the room. "What's more interesting is that Erick told me he trained you. I'd like to see how much you've learned."

And with that, he drew his dagger.

I stopped, ten paces from the door, only five paces away from Westen. His voice had grown even softer, and the dark dangerous glint that I recognized in all the Seekers had returned to his eyes. I kicked myself for having followed him, for allowing myself to be drawn into an unknown part of the palace, into a room I didn't know how to escape. On the Dredge, such a mistake would have meant rape at the very least. More likely death.

Or both.

"Go ahead," Westen said. "Draw your dagger. You are the Mistress, and unlike Avrell or Baill or any of the other guardsmen, the Seekers are sworn to the Mistress, sworn to *protect* the Mistress, not the city and the throne."

Angry at myself, I reached for my dagger, slid into a stance that made Westen nod in approval, still uncertain what the Seeker intended. At the same time I slid beneath the river, wrapped the currents around me, and reached toward the Seeker captain. He held no malice, no hatred; he didn't intend to hurt me.

"You don't report to Baill?" I asked, and even before Westen answered, I felt myself slipping into old rhythms, into old patterns that I'd learned while sparring with Erick in the back alleys and decaying courtyards of the slums of Amenkor. I hadn't trained with Erick in over two years, hadn't faced a true Seeker since then.

"No. The Seekers report only to the Mistress." He grinned slightly. "To you. We consult with Baill as a courtesy. And even then . . ." He shrugged.

And then he attacked.

He cleared the five paces between us with a speed I never expected, faster than Erick, faster than anyone I'd ever seen before, his blade flashing out and to the side. I barked in surprise, lunged hard to the left, his dagger slashing through the space where I'd just stood, and in the same movement I twisted, dropping my weight down onto one hand and sweeping out with my foot in an attempt to trip him, momentum and a push with my supporting arm thrusting me back up into a crouch when my foot connected with empty air. Heart pounding in my throat, breath coming harder, I pushed myself deeper into the river, felt the textures of the room darken, tasted the burning oil on the air, the smoke and the sweat and the blood. New sweat, but also old. The blood old as well.

"This is a training room," I murmured, my attention shifting back to Westen, who crouched as I did a few paces away.

"Yes," he said, but he spoke in a distracted voice, his attention on me, his eyes hard, measuring, judging. "For the Seekers."

Then he spun forward, his motions fluid, graceful, his weight perfectly balanced. As I parried, raising a hand to block his forearm, thrusting him away even as I sliced in tight with my own dagger, I found myself sinking deeper, found the room itself fading, until there was only Westen, only the subtle shift in stance, the liquid and deadly flick of his dagger, the movements of his arms, his feet, his body. He *flowed*, a slow and dangerous dance, closing in for a wicked cut, a sharp block, a vicious slash, and then away to circle, to watch, and then back again, smoother than Erick had ever been.

There was no sound except the rustle of cloth, a grunt, a gasp as a hand connected with chest or an elbow with a thigh. Sweat broke out in my armpits, slicked my arms and chest beneath my breasts, the white shirt Marielle had found for me stuck to my skin. My hair grew matted and clung to my neck in wet tendrils. And still Westen attacked, sweat sheening his own face, his eyes narrowing as he moved faster, his tactics changing, his thrusts aimed toward my chest at first, then shifting to my legs, then my back, testing me and withdrawing before striking again.

Then Westen closed in hard and quick, changing tactics yet again, one hand clamping around my free wrist and twisting me around, catching me across my chest with my own arm, pulling me in tight to his body, so that I couldn't move, my dagger arm caught in the strange embrace.

I spat a curse, breath heaving in and out through clenched teeth.

I felt Westen shift, but not enough for me to break free. His breath cooled the sweat of my neck as he leaned in close. He wasn't even breathing hard.

"You're only defending yourself," he whispered. "I want you to attack."

Before I could respond, his dagger snicked across my arm, slicing through cloth and scoring along flesh as he released me and he thrust me away. I hissed, in both shock and pain, stumbled to a halt and stared down dumbfounded at the beads of blood welling in the rent of cloth, staining the fabric in bright little circles.

A scratch, nothing more, the blood already congealing. But during all of the sparring with Erick, he had never intentionally drawn blood.

"But . . . I'm the Mistress," I hissed, shooting Westen an angry glare.

He shook his head, face deadly serious. "Not here. Here you're only a Seeker. Now attack!"

Anger flaring, I slid into a new crouch. Westen responded, circling. Vaguely, I sensed others in the room now, hidden in the darkness behind the alcoves, watching. But I ignored them, focused exclusively on Westen, watched his muscles as they tensed and relaxed, watched his eyes as they watched me.

I lunged forward, not as graceful as Westen, not as smooth, but I had the river and I used it. Pushing along its flows, I saw where Westen intended to shift, saw his movements before he made them, before his muscles even flexed, tasted his blade as it arced through the air, every motion distinct and brittle under the gray glare of the river. My blade flicked in hard and sharp, caught nothing but air as Westen twisted, but I brought it back in tight again, shifting my grip, and felt it catch cloth. Westen barked out in surprise, even though I knew I hadn't touched skin with the blade, couldn't taste the blood on the river, and in the moment of his distraction the palm of my empty hand slammed into the joint of his shoulder.

He staggered back, his arm hanging momentarily limp, his dagger falling from his hand and clattering to the floor. Even as he recovered, slipping into a new stance, his empty dagger hand flexed, fingers clenching. The numbness was already wearing off, so I pressed my attack, hoping to take him down now and end this while he was defenseless.

But even as I closed in, he grinned, as if he knew what I was going to do, and the next thing I knew his other hand punched forward and struck me in the gut. All strength fled from my legs, and I dropped to my knees with a sharp cry, my dagger forgotten as pain flashed upward from my stomach, hot and visceral. One arm still twitching back to life, he twisted my dagger hand up behind my back with the other, my own hand going numb, and I heard my dagger clatter to the stone floor.

Both of us gasping, Westen once again behind me, my hand throbbing with pain in his grip, he chuckled.

"Erick taught you many things, but you still have much to learn."

He waited, the heat and intensity of the fight bleeding out of the room, out of our bodies. Then he let my hand go.

I sagged forward, coughed as I relaxed enough to taste the acrid smoke in the air, my throat dry.

Then Westen stood before me, one hand extended to help me up. His eyes were bright.

"I look forward to training you in the ways of the Seeker, my Mistress," he said, and then he grasped my hand and pulled me to my feet.

†

I followed Borund as we approached the throng of angry people outside the closed doors of the gates to the inner ward, eyes scanning the crowd as he pressed ahead, shoulders tensed as I tried to stay close, my hand on my dagger, the river pulsing around me. But no one seemed interested in Borund, and no one seemed interested in me. I was just his bodyguard. Everyone was focused on the guardsmen at the gates, demanding answers, demanding to know why the harbor had been shut, why their ships and cargo were being kept in the city.

Someone shoved me into Borund's back and I hissed, apprehension rising as the angry crowd pushed closer. I barely had enough room to wield my dagger to protect Borund if necessary and felt sweat break out between my shoulders.

I was about to grab Borund's shoulder and pull him back when he turned and swore, eyes blazing.

"We'll never get into the palace. They've closed the gates, and this crowd isn't likely to disperse any time soon. Damn! I need to know what's going on!"

I drew breath to suggest retreating to the guild hall, feeling as if I'd done this all before, the sensation prickling along the nape of my neck, but a boy with a round face and dressed as a dockworker stepped from the crowd. When I saw him, my uneasiness grew, my hand falling to my dagger. But the boy was gray. Harmless.

Yet I felt I knew him, even though I'd never seen him before.

"Master Borund?" the boy asked.

Borund frowned. "Yes?"

"Avrell, the First of the Mistress, would like to see you," the boy said. "He said to give you this."

The boy held out a chunk of stone, the outline of a snail embedded in one side.

Borund drew in a breath sharply.

We followed the dock boy through the edge of the mob, at first heading toward the gates, then angling away, passing into a side street running parallel to the palace wall. We passed no one, the buildings mostly vacant.

A cloud drifted overhead, the bright sunlight fading to a dull gray. I shivered.

The boy ducked into a small building that had once been a stable. The reek of manure still clung to the musty air inside, but there were no horses. Instead, the building was packed tight with marked crates, straw poking out through the cracks between the wood.

Borund gasped as the dock boy led us into a narrow space between the stacked crates. "Capthian red! Crates of it! I haven't been able to get this since last winter, not a single crate!"

Irritated the boy motioned for us to hurry, and I felt tension crawl across my shoulder blades again. As if I were missing something. Something important. I shrugged it aside as the narrow path between the crates turned, branched once, then opened up into a small niche that barely fit the three of us hunched over. The dock boy shoved us out of the way, then pulled at a chunk of the plank flooring. A section lifted upward, cut with a ragged edge so that it couldn't be seen when set in place. I stared down into the rounded opening below. I could see that it dropped down into a thin tunnel, even though there was no light.

Borund hesitated, glancing toward me for confirmation.

"It's safe," I said. "It drops down to a tunnel. There's no one down there, and I can see a lantern ready to be lit."

Borund nodded and managed to lower himself down into the hole.

The dock boy stared at me the entire time.

"How did you know there was a lantern?" he finally asked. "It's too dark to see it."

I didn't answer, simply dropped down smoothly after Borund as he moved to light the waiting lantern. Then I turned, expecting to see the dock boy staring down at me through the circular opening.

But it wasn't the dock boy anymore. It was Eryn.

JOSHUA PALMATIER

I shouted, lunged in front of Borund to protect him, drew my
dagger without thought, the weight of the blade heavier than
usual.

At the edge of the tunnel's entrance, Eryn's face darkened into
stern concern, eyes tight, lips thin. She knelt at the edge of the
hole, hands gripping the edge of the entrance tightly, the motion
sharp and urgent.

"Do you see, Varis? Do you see?"

Then the lantern flared to life behind me, yellow light pulsing
outward in a blinding flash, and I jerked awake.

✝

I gasped and flailed in the bedsheets, heart pounding. But then I
recognized the room, realized I'd been dreaming, and collapsed
back onto the tangled sheets, breathing shallow and fast.

Slowly, my heart rate slackened, and my breathing eased. When
I felt calm, I slid out of bed and padded to the dressing table to
pour myself some water, moving through the now familiar room
without pausing, wincing only slightly from the bruises I'd received
the last few weeks while training with Westen. Washing the sour
taste of sleep from my mouth, I drifted to the balcony, letting the
doors swing shut behind me.

Staring out over the darkness, I frowned. This was the third
time in the last three weeks that I'd had the same dream. Except
that it wasn't truly a dream. It was a memory, from when I'd been
a bodyguard for Borund. I remembered it clearly, heard the bells
tolling in the harbor as word was spread that no ships were to leave
the city, felt Borund's rage that the Mistress would dare do such a
thing. We'd tried to go to the palace to find out why, but the gates
had been sealed. Then the dock boy had shown up and taken us to
Avrell.

The first two times I'd relived the memory as I slept, nothing had changed. We'd entered the tunnel, crawled through the passages to the palace. And then the dream had ended.

But this time, Eryn had appeared.

I hadn't thought much about the dreams before. But now . . .

I shivered and stood straighter, rubbing my upper arms for warmth. The night air was sharp. In the three weeks since the meeting with Avrell and the merchants, the signs of winter had become more obvious. The air had gotten colder, the daylight thinner. The vines of the plants on the balcony had begun to turn brown, some of the leaves dropping to the floor.

And the day before, Marielle had pointed out across the harbor to the barely discernible waves of the ocean. "See?" she'd said. "There are more whitecaps now, no matter how the wind blows. And the spray of the waves pounding against the rocks is higher."

I glanced down at the wharf in the moonlight, counted the masts of the ships at dock, and frowned in thought.

Since becoming Mistress, I'd settled into the steady pattern of the palace, become familiar with the eddies and flows of the guardsmen, of the servants and the supplicants from the city, with an occasional break—never announced, always at random—when Westen would appear and escort me down to the training room. Avrell had guided me through the first few rough days, when I'd been forced to see and hear grievances from the people of the city and the guilds and then asked to make a decision. At first, such grievances had occurred every day, but as the days edged toward winter, they slowed to a trickle.

At one point, Avrell had muttered that we were fortunate I'd taken control of the throne at the beginning of winter. When I'd asked him why, he'd said that there were few envoys and delegations from the surrounding cities during winter. Everything of major political importance had already been settled, and he'd have time to familiarize me with the coast and all of its cities during the winter months.

I'd scowled at him in annoyance. I already disliked dealing with the squabbles of those in the city. I didn't want to think about dealing with the entire coast. He'd already started tutoring me, though, a few hours a day spent discussing the other city-states along the coast—Venitte, Marland, Temall, and Merrell—as well as the Kandish cultures to the east and the Zorelli to the south.

And then there were the dreams—of murders, of rapes and killings and mutilations—most of which occurred in the slums beyond the Dredge. I sent out the Seekers when I could, just as I'd sent out Erick to find Corum. But a few of the dreams hadn't provided me with enough details—a face, a place, a name—to send someone searching. In those cases, there was nothing I could do except remember.

But this dream was different. I wasn't living someone else's life as it was ended or as they were hurt. This was a memory.

Except this last time, at the end, it hadn't even been that.

A few hours later, dawn's light just beginning to break the horizon behind me, I heard a cautious step on the balcony and turned to find Marielle holding out a cup of hot tea.

"Mistress."

I took the cup, shivering in my shift. Below, beyond the three stone walls that surrounded the palace, the streets of Amenkor were coming alive. I watched the movements of the people as I drank deeply, then sighed, turning away.

"I want to speak to Avrell."

"Shall I have him summoned?" Marielle asked as we stepped inside, motioning sharply to the other girls in the room. They began arranging my usual clothes, one moving to pull back the sheets on the bed. I watched intently as the sheets were stripped off, wadded up, and new sheets laid down. I suddenly realized I'd

never made a bed before, never even seen it being made by someone else, not even here at the palace since I'd taken the throne. At
Borund's manse, it had always been made when I'd returned, and
on the Dredge I'd never had a bed.

"No," I said, distracted, watching the servant work. "I'll go
to him."

"Very well, Mistress."

When I turned around, Marielle and the girl presenting my
clothes were trying to suppress smiles.

I growled and grabbed for my shirt.

†

I found Avrell in a section of the palace I'd never seen, hunched
over a table with a slanted top covered with parchment, Nathem at
his side. His hands were stained with ink, and his brow was furrowed in concentration. One hand trailed down a column of numbers, and he mumbled something to Nathem under his breath, the
creases in his brow deepening.

I hesitated a moment, then asked, "Where are the ships?"

Both Nathem and Avrell glanced up, Avrell's eyes darkening
briefly at the interruption before he recognized me. Leaning back,
he stood and stepped out from behind the desk with a small smile.

"Mistress, you did not need to come down here. If you needed
me, I could have come to you." He noticed the ink on his hands
and folded them together, hiding them in the sleeves of his robes.

But then you would have had time to prepare, I thought.

Behind him, Nathem began shuffling the papers, discreetly continuing whatever they'd been working on.

"I needed to get out of my rooms," I said, and began pacing
restlessly. "Regin said that most of the ships should return within
the month. We're already at the end of the third week and there are
only three ships at the docks. Where are the others?"

"I don't know."

I paused, hearing the undertone of concern in Avrell's voice. Concern that he was trying to hide.

He shifted back to the table, impatiently waving Nathem to the side, tapping the papers he'd been reading. I glanced down at them, but could only pick out a few letters and numbers. Marielle had been working with me on a daily basis, but I had no patience for such things. I fought back a surge of frustration. I didn't like having to rely on Avrell, didn't like having to rely on anyone for anything.

"These are the reports from the captains of the ships that have returned," Avrell said. "The first two are from Marlett and Dangren, both towns within a few days' sail north of here. The ship that returned yesterday came from Merrell, much farther up the coast, also north of Amenkor. All of the captains report rough water, and all three of the cities are in the same condition we are: short on food and supplies for the winter. However, none are worse off than we are. Most have sufficient grain and other essentials for the winter, and a few have some to spare. After some heavy bartering and with quite a few favors called in, all three ships managed to return with at least three quarters of their holds full."

"What of the other ships?"

Avrell shook his head. "Nothing, not even a message returned by land." He caught my gaze. "We should have heard back from them by now, even if it was to say they were caught in port by the seas or storms. But we aren't the only ones who've lost contact with their ships. Both of the captains from Merrell and Dangren said that ships have vanished from those cities. The most common explanation is piracy and early winter storms." His voice was tinged with doubt.

I began pacing the room again, Nathem shifting out of my way. "But you don't believe that."

"No."

"Why not?"

Avrell's eyes darkened. "Piracy rises when food is short, but not to this extent. And ships and their crews don't vanish completely without sign, by storm or by piracy. Wreckage or bodies would wash ashore somewhere. We've heard nothing from any of the small villages and towns along the coast concerning raiders or unexplained debris from destroyed ships."

I paced silently for a moment, Avrell watching.

"So where do we stand on resources for the winter with what Alendor and the consortium left behind and what these three ships have brought back? Along with what the fishing boats have harvested."

"With strict rationing, we can feed perhaps three quarters of the city now. No more."

I swore, Avrell raising an eyebrow at my vehemence. Even Nathem seemed surprised, coughing as he pulled out a second sheaf of papers and began working at another table.

"There is some good news," Avrell said. "Merrell has promised to send a shipment overland, but there's no telling when it might arrive. Perhaps not till spring. The roads between Amenkor and Merrell are not good even in the summer. But the grain they've already sent will be helpful."

"So," I said, halting. "What can we do?"

"Hope more ships arrive," Nathem deadpanned, without looking up from his own papers.

I frowned at him in annoyance, then bit my lip in thought.

Avrell straightened almost imperceptibly under my steady gaze. "What is it?" he said, voice guarded.

For a moment, I considered telling him about the dream. But then I recalled his face the night he and Borund and Erick had convinced me to attempt to kill the Mistress, saw his eyes.

I wondered if he was lying to me now, holding back supplies. But why? He had more invested in Amenkor then I did. He'd only be hurting himself. And I knew he wouldn't hesitate to replace me if he didn't like my decisions. He'd already attempted to assassinate Eryn, a woman he'd aided for years. He barely knew me.

Except that we both knew he would never succeed. He'd tried to place other Servants on the throne before resorting to me, and they'd all died. No one else could control the throne and survive.

And besides, I'd been trained as an assassin. He'd never get anyone close enough to kill me. The throne would warn me that they were coming, and I had my own skills, learned on the Dredge and now being expanded by Westen, to keep me alive after that.

I growled, shoved away the useless doubts and mistrust. "I need to get out of the palace."

The words came out more heartfelt than I'd intended.

Avrell hesitated, then said, "Of course. You've been inside the inner ward since you seized the throne. You're used to having the run of the city." He paused. He knew I was holding back something, but he couldn't determine what it was. "I'll arrange an escort."

He moved to the door, where my usual escort of four guardsmen waited outside. His hand had just fallen on the handle when I said, "I'd like you to come with me."

He stilled.

"Of course," he said in a neutral voice. Then he opened the door and said something to the guards outside.

An hour later, I stepped out of the main doors to the palace onto the wide stone steps of the promenade. They descended down to a circular courtyard where an escort of ten guardsmen and two Seekers waited on horseback, two other riderless horses saddled and ready near the front. The two Seekers nodded in my direction with cool smiles—I'd sparred against both of them under Westen's watchful eye—and the other guardsmen nodded as well, with obvious respect.

I frowned. Westen had said word that I'd disarmed him during our first match was spreading among the guard.

Avrell came up behind me, his blue-and-gold robes replaced with a fine blue shirt, leather breeches, and boots. He looked strange in the new clothes; I'd only ever seen him in the First's robes.

"Are we ready?" he asked.

"I don't know how to ride a horse," I said.

Avrell paused. "I see. Then I suppose we'll have to go on foot."

He motioned to the lead guardsman, who issued a curt order. All of the guardsmen hesitated, glancing at each other in confusion, then slowly began to dismount. When Avrell and I descended the last few steps of the promenade and headed for the gate, they formed up around us.

The first thing I noticed was that I was at least two hands shorter than any of the guardsmen or Avrell. The second was that they formed a tight group. I suddenly understood why Eryn had slipped away unnoticed on occasion, causing Avrell, Baill, and the guardsmen so much grief. They'd thought it was her madness, but I began to wonder. Having an armed escort all the time, even in the halls of the palace, became tiring.

We passed out through the inner gates into the middle ward, the entire group pausing just outside the gates.

I drew in a deep breath, smelled the sea salt on the air, a weight lifting away from my shoulders. I hadn't realized how confined I'd felt inside the palace. The sensation of openness enveloped me and I grinned. This was the Amenkor I knew: the streets, the alleys, the narrows.

The people.

A small crowd huddled around the gates waiting to get in, mainly servants and guardsmen, a few men and women that my gutterscum eye marked as easy, rich targets. They turned to look, curiosity mingled with suspicion lining their faces.

After a long moment, a few heads bent together and the suspicion faded, replaced with awe. A few pointed toward me, and I suddenly felt uncomfortable.

On the Dredge, and working as Borund's bodyguard, I'd always faded into the background, become gray. I'd depended on not being noticed, never being seen. But now . . .

I turned away from the gawking faces, from the sudden flurry of noise as word was passed down through the crowd, like a ripple on water.

Avrell grunted.

"What?" I asked, not looking toward the group.

Avrell glanced at me, then turned to survey the crowd, back straight, head held high. In the shirt and breeches he seemed somehow more . . . regal, more arrogant and severe. "News that there was a new Mistress flew quickly through the city," he said, turning back to me, "especially after you lifted the blockade. But no one knew who you were. It took them a moment to realize *you* were the new Mistress because the Mistress almost never leaves the palace. And when she does, she's always either ridden a horse or left by carriage. You'll have to learn to ride eventually." He glanced at me, scanning my clothes. "I'm certain they expected something . . . different."

I glowered at him, then turned back to look at the crowd. "Why are a few of them bowing?"

Avrell's eyebrows rose. "Because you are the Mistress, and most of the people of the city revere the Mistress. You are their liege, their protector . . . their god."

I shuddered, an emptiness opening up inside me. Uncomfortable, I turned away from the bowed heads.

"Let's go," I said, heading off to the right. The guard fell in smoothly around us.

"Where are we headed?" Avrell asked after a moment, his eyes darting down each street we passed, his brow furrowed in consternation.

"Wait." I didn't want to tell him, wanted to watch his reaction.

He sighed, but continued to scan the streets, perplexed.

I walked swiftly, turning down a few streets and alleys, but keeping the palace wall in sight. People moved out of our way, staring after us in confusion or awe once we'd passed, but I ignored them all, attention on where we were headed. I paused once, uncertain, but chose a street at random and reoriented myself once we'd reached the next cross street.

Twenty minutes later, the number of people on the streets dropped off. The buildings took on an empty air, windows blank, doors shut, some boarded up with signs in the window. The middle ward held all of the guild halls, housed some of the more influential merchants and their offices. But since the coming of the Second Fire six years ago—when the huge wall of White Fire had swept in from the ocean and burned its way through the city, leaving a small part of itself embedded inside me—the economy had slackened. Many of the buildings that had once held thriving businesses were vacant, the store owners and their employees now residing in the lower city.

Or the Dredge.

We rounded a corner and came upon the stable, the entire entourage halting.

"Do you recognize it?" I asked, watching Avrell's face closely.

Avrell nodded. "Yes. It's the building that houses the entrance to the tunnel beneath the palace wall. But why did you want to bring me here?"

"Who owns the building?" I thought I knew the answer already, but I had to be certain.

"The palace, of course."

I nodded. Avrell seemed as perplexed as when we'd left the gates behind. "Let's go inside."

I'd taken a few steps before I realized Avrell hadn't moved. "I don't understand what we're doing here," he said.

I sighed. "I have something to show you."

Avrell shook his head but followed.

The guardsmen pulled back the stable door and we stepped inside, the smell of old manure and fresh straw sharp on the musty air. Avrell covered his mouth with his hand and grimaced as he glanced around at the stacked crates that filled the building. A narrow path led down the center to the trapdoor and the tunnel.

"What did you want to show me?" Avrell asked, voice strained. He was trying to breathe through his mouth.

"Look," I said, moving up to the crates.

Avrell squinted at the markings on the sides. "Capthian red," he muttered, straightening abruptly. His eyes flashed. "We haven't had Capthian red in the palace in six months. It's been almost impossible to find."

I eyed him carefully, but he was scanning the crates in confusion, shoulders tight. I felt my suspicions begin to shift, turning away from Avrell, focusing on someone else. "Then who does all this belong to?"

Images of the lists provided by the merchants' guild flashed through Avrell's mind, I could see it in his eyes. Though his hand still clutched his nose and mouth, he no longer seemed annoyed about the forced outing, or the smell. Instead, his body was tense with concentration.

After a long moment, his gaze caught mine. "No one. None of the merchants reported owning any Capthian red." He glanced around at the number of crates, stacked to the ceiling. "Not in such quantities at any rate."

He thought for a moment, then stepped closer, inspected the markings on one of the crates. "There are no ownership markings on the crates either."

"Which means what?"

He stood, brow furrowed in confusion. "It means that this was smuggled into the city. But who would smuggle in this much wine? Alendor? One of the other merchants?"

I shook my head, a spark of anger igniting deep inside me, coloring my voice. "The building belongs to the palace. Alendor would never have hidden it here."

"Then who?"

I walked up to the nearest crate, glared at the markings on the side that were still gibberish to me, and said with utter certainty, "It was the Mistress."

I turned at Avrell's shocked silence, my face hard.

"It was Eryn."

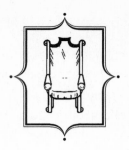

Chapter 3

"HOW?" AVRELL SPAT.

"What do you mean?" I asked. We were moving down the corridor leading toward Eryn's chambers, the guard escorting us—reduced to the usual four now that we were inside the palace—scrambling to keep up.

"How did she smuggle it into the city? How did she find the contacts? How did she get the wine into the defunct stablehouse without me knowing? She's barely left the palace for the last three years. She *can't* leave the city."

I pulled up short. I couldn't tell what bothered Avrell more: that Eryn had managed to smuggle the wine into the city, or that she'd done it without his knowledge. But that wasn't what had brought me to a halt.

"What do you mean she can't leave the city?"

For a moment, Avrell looked puzzled, too intent on Eryn's betrayal, but then he realized what he'd said and his eyes widened. "Nothing. It's not important now."

Some of the anger I felt toward Eryn shifted to Avrell. I took a small step forward, my hand dropping to my dagger.

Avrell flinched, then, with a small shudder, took control of himself. His back straightened and the poise he usually showed erased most of the rage from his face. He became the diplomat I'd seen when guarding Borund, except now that I knew him better I could see flickers of the rage he'd suppressed in his eyes.

"The Mistress is tied to the throne," he said stiffly, "and the throne is tied to the city. Because of this, the Mistress can never leave the city."

"What happens if I try?"

"You'll die."

I clenched my jaw, nostrils flaring. "Of course."

I didn't understand why being trapped in the city turned my stomach. I'd never been outside the city streets, had lived on or near the Dredge until I was fifteen, and after that I'd lived in the lower city, guarding Borund. I'd never even been close to the city's outskirts, had never considered what lay beyond except in a vague way. What lay outside the city couldn't help me on the Dredge. Even Avrell's discussions of other cities, other places, seemed unreal—nothing more than words or stories.

But now I couldn't escape, even if I wanted to.

I shoved the thought aside and spun, continuing down the corridor to Eryn's chambers. After a moment, I heard Avrell trying to catch up. At least now he was quiet.

Eryn had kept to the rooms Avrell had given her after I'd taken control of the throne, and I'd had no urge to seek her out. I still felt too unsettled around her, too off-balance. I didn't know if I could trust her after she'd manipulated me onto the throne, and so I'd ignored her, shoved her to the back of my mind, where she was a constant nagging threat. The only other time I'd seen her had been on the rooftop after I'd dreamed of Corum, and that confrontation had been strained.

I didn't slow as I came up to the outer doors to her chambers. I jerked them open before the guards could reach them, stalked into

the waiting room, scanning it with one swift glance. A forest of potted trees, a few scattered chairs and tables, a settee, a door to the
inner chambers.

With barely a pause, I headed toward the door. At some point,
I'd slid beneath the river.

"Varis, wait—" Avrell began, but with a surge of power I shoved
him back without turning, heard him grunt as the eddy struck, and
then I was through, into the inner bedroom, the door cracking
sharply into the wall.

A servant shrieked, dropped the linens she was holding with a
soft *fwump*.

"Where is she?" I asked.

With a trembling voice, the girl said, "The garden."

I frowned, but she pointed toward a curtained doorway, the
door open, a slight breeze pushing the curtain out into the room.

I shoved aside the curtain and stepped out onto an open veranda of white stone, a little larger than my own balcony, with a
small table and chairs. A wide stone balustrade lined with fat pots
separated the veranda from the small private garden beyond. In the
evening sunlight, the trees and trellised vines of the garden were vibrant, the white stone of the curving paths harsh to look at. I hesitated, let my eyes adjust, then stepped to the three stone steps
leading down to the garden.

I didn't feel the wall of force at the top of the steps until I ran
into it, too blinded by rage. I hit it hard, staggered back with a
barked curse, tasted blood on my lip.

"What is it?" Avrell asked, catching my elbow to steady me.
The guards fanned out behind us, eyes sharp, hands on swords.

I ran a hand across my mouth, grimaced at the smear of blood.
"Eryn."

"I felt you coming."

Everyone turned, the guards closing in tighter as Eryn stepped away from a trellis full of wide white flowers I'd scanned a moment before. I suddenly recalled the throne room, how she had hidden right in front of me, emerging only after I'd refused to play her games. Or rather, the throne's games. A trick of the river that I didn't know how to use . . . or see through.

Eryn stepped into direct sunlight, turned a hard gaze on the guardsmen. "You can leave now."

The guards turned, then hesitated, uncertain, confused. They'd taken orders from Eryn for years. The instinct to obey was automatic.

After a moment, Avrell gave them a short nod and they retreated to the inner rooms.

I frowned in annoyance. They should have waited for a signal from me, not Avrell.

As soon as they were gone, Eryn turned to me. "Why have you come here? This is my retreat, my private garden. I want nothing to do with the throne now. I don't want to be disturbed."

I stepped forward, halting at the edge of the wall of force. "Why didn't you tell me about the wine?"

Eryn frowned. "What wine?"

"The Capthian red you had smuggled into the city without my knowledge," Avrell said, his voice acidic. "The wine stored in the stablehouse in the middle ward."

Eryn didn't answer at first. "Are you certain it was me?"

"Who else could it have been?" Avrell countered. "None of the merchants would have dared hide illegally obtained wine in a building owned by the palace, let alone a building containing a passage beneath the palace walls!"

"Some would argue such a building would be the perfect place to hide goods," Eryn said. "Why would we search our own buildings?"

"But they wouldn't have known of the passage," I spat,

"wouldn't have stacked the wine so that the entrance to the tunnel would remain open. And if they had known of the passage, they wouldn't have risked the wine being found if the tunnel *were* used."

A troubled look passed through Eryn's eyes and her poise wavered, her gaze dropping to the stone of the garden's path. "I see."

Before me, the wall of force on the steps shuddered, then unraveled, rigid currents sliding back into their regular flows.

I relaxed, felt my pulse begin to throb in my cut lip now that my rage had been blunted. It hurt like all hells. "Why didn't you tell us about the wine?" I asked again, my voice calm but still laced with anger.

Eryn sighed and glanced back up, her eyes worried, watery and red, as if she were on the verge of tears. "Because," she said in a stern voice, "I don't remember smuggling in any wine."

Neither Avrell nor I moved.

"But you told me about the wine," I said, incredulous. "You showed it to me!"

"How?" Eryn said, stepping forward to the edge of the steps, so that Avrell and I were looking down at her. "How did I show you?"

"I dreamed I was coming to the palace with Borund, to meet with Avrell. We were following a dock boy, who led us to the stables and the tunnel. The first few times that was all it was, as if I were reliving the memory. But this last time, after we'd seen the crates of wine, the dock boy changed into you."

Both Avrell and Eryn seemed confused, staring at each other with furrowed brows.

"Could you have influenced her dream somehow?" Avrell asked, voice tinged with doubt. "Perhaps without knowing? We've never had two Mistresses alive at the same time before. Is that possible?"

But Eryn was already shaking her head. "No, I don't think so. The Sight doesn't work that way, and none of the previous Mistresses trapped in the throne had any knowledge of such a thing that I remember." She turned to me, frowning. "However . . ."

I shifted beneath her gaze. "What?"

Eryn sighed, her shoulders sagging in uncertainty. "It could be the throne itself. Or at least one of the personalities in the throne."

"What do you mean?" I asked, but I thought I already knew. The older woman who had smelled of oak and wine.

Eryn hesitated, glanced at Avrell, then moved up onto the veranda to the table and chairs, taking a seat. After a studied pause, Avrell moved to join her. I shifted to a place near the table, sitting back against the stone balustrade, arms crossed over my chest.

"The throne is a malevolent thing," Eryn said, her voice tired. She made a small motion toward the door and in the darkness behind the curtain I sensed the servant I'd startled before moving away. "All of those women—and a few men—all of whom at some point touched the throne and thus became a part of it, they all want the same thing: control. They know that they're dead—some of them have been dead since the throne's creation almost fifteen hundred years ago—but there is always the temptation to gain control, to seize it if necessary. If they can overpower whoever sits on the throne, then they can live again through that body. It's happened before. Someone ascends the throne, someone weak. Then the throne takes control, claims the power. In most cases, the person doesn't survive long after that. The throne itself overwhelms the inhabited person's body, destroys it."

I glanced toward Avrell, his mouth pressed into a tight, thin line. I had heard him talking to Nathem in the waiting room, had heard him describing how the women he'd tried to seat on the throne before me had died. I'd lived their deaths, in the moments when the throne threatened to overwhelm me, and I shuddered at the screams, at the memory of clawing my eyes out, of biting off my own tongue, of having my heart beat so hard and fast that it finally burst in a white-hot, searing explosion of pain.

And I remembered the meeting with the merchants, heard again the voice of the woman sliding through the currents of the river. She'd removed herself from the rest of the throne, fought her way free. And she'd wanted control, wanted me to give her control.

"But not all of those the throne took control of died," I said.

Eryn shook her head. "No. A few of them survived, overpowered by one or all of the personalities. In those cases, the new personality is subsumed, lost in the storm, and someone else takes over."

I thought of the throne room, recalled the voices echoing in its chambers the night I attempted to kill Eryn. A girl's voice, perhaps twelve, and an elder's voice, rough with spite and anger.

But in the end, Eryn had regained command. It was Eryn who had pushed me onto the seat of the throne. It was Eryn who gave me the choice to take control . . . or let the city die.

Eryn continued, "All of the women who have sat upon the throne before—and there have been at least two hundred—have had the Sight . . . what you call the river, Varis. And when the throne was first established, the Sight was enough. The Mistress could use it to build a barrier between her own personality and those within the throne. But as more and more people became part of the throne, that barrier had to be stronger and stronger, each new Mistress more powerful than the last. Not everyone who was seated on the throne had the power to master it, and those that didn't died. Close to a hundred have died in this way, most of them within the last few centuries. But we've reached an impasse. The throne has become too powerful for even the strongest of us with the Sight."

Eryn leaned forward, her eyes intent. "But there's something different about you, Varis."

I shifted uncomfortably.

"I sensed it in the throne room," Eryn went on, voice soft. "A Fire. A White Fire, like a small ember of the Fire that burned through the city six years ago. It burns inside you, protects you from the voices when the Sight cannot."

Avrell stirred. "Is that why you chose her to be the Mistress?"

Eryn shook her head, never taking her eyes off me. "No. I didn't know about the Fire until the throne room. I only knew that Varis was the only one with the Sight in the city strong enough to have a hope of controlling the throne. None of the Servants here would have survived, not even Marielle. You know. You tried the strongest—Beth, Arrielle, Cecille—" Her voice grew rough and she halted, swallowed hard. "You watched them die."

I suddenly understood the fear I'd sensed in Marielle weeks earlier. She was a true Servant. If Avrell had not shifted his attention to me, she might have been thrust on the throne herself . . . and killed.

No wonder Marielle feared him.

My gaze fell on Avrell. "So you knew," I said.

He looked at me blankly. "Knew what?"

My back straightened. "You knew that I was never supposed to kill Eryn, that it was a trap, the assassination just a ploy to get me into the throne room."

"Yes."

I snorted in contempt, even though part of me was relieved. At least now I knew he'd wanted me to be the Mistress, that my ascension to the throne wasn't a complete surprise.

"It wasn't his idea," Eryn said. "But he did bring your presence to my attention. He noticed you when he first met with you and Borund, told me of his suspicions that you used the Sight. It was my idea to have you attempt to kill me."

"Why not just have me brought to the throne room? Order me there?"

"Because of Captain Baill," Avrell answered, voice thick with derision. "He would never have allowed it. His position was too strong with Eryn on the edge of madness. He would never have given that up."

"And because you would never have accepted the throne unless you were forced to," Eryn added. "No one willingly takes the throne. Not now."

I thought about entering the throne room that night, of feeling the presence of the throne stalking me, hunting me as if I were prey, and shuddered. No. No one would willingly take the throne. Not once they came into the throne room and felt its presence anyway. Even those trained for it, like the Servants.

Silence settled, interrupted by Eryn's servant bringing a pitcher of chilled water and a set of glasses. As the girl poured three glasses from the pitcher, she glanced toward me and I sensed her relief.

Relief that someone else had assumed the throne.

I frowned as the girl bowed her head and left, slipping silently through the curtain to the darkness of the inner room. I wondered if she would have been next.

Avrell took a sip of water. "How does that explain your appearance in Varis' dream?"

Eryn sat back with a small sigh. "Everyone is vulnerable when they sleep. Our defenses are weakest, our protective barriers thin. I think that one of the personalities in the throne penetrated Varis' defenses, enough to influence her dreams. At first, whoever it was probably triggered her memory, hoping that would be enough for Varis to realize that the wine was in the stable. But when that didn't work, they used something more direct." She paused. "They put my image in the dream."

"But why your image?" Avrell asked. "Why use you?"

Eryn grimaced. "I don't know." She gave me a long, consider-ing look. "But maybe we can find out."

I straightened, a thin coil of unease uncurling inside me. "How?"

Eryn look a thoughtful sip of her water, set the glass down care-fully.

"You have an advantage that none of the previous Mistresses have had, Varis: me. I know how to use the throne, know how to manipulate *its* powers as well as the Sight. I could show you how to search for whomever is influencing your dreams, perhaps even show you how to protect yourself from them using the Sight. None of the previous Mistresses had a living Mistress to aid them, to guide them after they took the throne. We all had to rely on the voices, had to determine which voices we could trust to help us and which to ignore. All on our own. And there *are* voices within the throne that you can trust, Varis.

"Let me help you," Eryn said, her eyes imploring, a tinge of des-peration entering her voice. All signs of the regal, imperious woman I'd seen on the roof had vanished. "I could help you with the Sight, as well as the throne. Please."

Beside her, Avrell nodded to himself, his face intent, as if a problem he'd been wrestling with had been solved.

I hesitated, the coil of unease sliding deeper into my chest. If I allowed Eryn to get that close . . .

But I already knew my answer. I didn't want anyone influenc-ing my dreams. The thought itself sent shudders down my back. It made me vulnerable, weak. And I did need help protecting myself from the voices in the throne. The Fire wasn't enough. The woman who had smelled of oak and wine proved that.

"We can try," I said, and I saw relief flash in Eryn's eyes. She smiled. The first real smile I'd seen from her.

"Good," she said, relaxing back into her chair as she took a sip of water.

"But first," Avrell said, suddenly all business, "the wine. You said you don't remember smuggling in any wine, but obviously you did. Did you smuggle in anything else? And how did you do it without anyone knowing?"

Eryn glanced toward me, her smile widening. "Now, Avrell, you don't expect me to reveal all of the Mistress' secrets, do you?"

He grunted, not finding it humorous. "Of course not. However—"

"No." A trace of steel entered Eryn's voice. "I won't tell you everything, Avrell. You've learned enough about the Mistress' powers today."

Avrell drew breath to protest but caught himself, stiffening beneath Eryn's gaze. "Very well."

Eryn turned back to me, her face serious now, the smile gone. "I smuggled in some food and had it stored in various places throughout the city."

"What and where?" Avrell asked, leaning forward.

Obviously irritated, Eryn replied, "Some cured meats—pork and beef mainly—grain, potatoes . . . all staples. But not enough to feed the city for the entire winter."

"But it's more than we have now," I said.

Eryn frowned. "What of the ships you sent out?"

I shook my head, and Eryn sat back heavily and bit her lower lip.

"But if you don't remember smuggling in the wine," I said, "then maybe there are other goods you smuggled in that you don't remember."

She nodded. "Or worse. We may find that what I do remember is not, in fact, true. At the end, the throne was too powerful. What I think I remember may have been delusions, thoughts brought on by the other voices in the throne, or perhaps even their own memories that I've absorbed as my own. That's why I didn't come to you earlier. I don't know what I actually *did*, and what I only *wanted* to do, or attempted to do and failed." A forlorn look passed across Eryn's face, harsh with pain and loss. "For a time, I believe I actually was insane."

No one spoke for a long moment. Then Avrell turned to me, concern for Eryn clear in his eyes. "Perhaps whoever touched your dream to show you the wine knows where the other stores are hidden."

I nodded in agreement, but my mind had taken a different path.

I looked up at Eryn sharply. "Why did you blockade the harbor?"

When Eryn didn't answer, I continued. "You smuggled goods into the city, were preparing for a harsh winter . . . so why did you block the harbor and interrupt trade, keep ships with supplies from entering, and force our own ships to stay here, unable to get more?"

Eryn shook her head. "I don't know. Ever since that cursed Fire passed through the city, I've steadily lost control . . . of the throne, of my power, of my mind. I don't understand much of anything I did in the last few years. It's all mixed up, with large sections of it just . . . gone. As if I'd lost part of myself somehow. Just . . . gone."

Avrell shifted uncomfortably at the desolation in her voice, caught my attention meaningfully, then stood. "We should attempt to find some of these hidden stores," he said quietly. I pushed away from the balustrade I was leaning against. "Perhaps if you could tell us a place to begin searching?"

Eryn rose suddenly as well, suffused with new energy. The conversation had changed her. Instead of the morose woman I'd encountered on the tower or found wandering her garden moments before, she was now vibrant with purpose. "I can do better than that," she said with a grin and a lifted eyebrow. "I can show you."

†

Eryn burst out laughing at something Avrell said as we were escorted by the palace guardsmen through the market square in the lower city. We'd come from the outer ward, where Eryn had led us to an old building on Lirion Street stacked with barrels of salted fish. Avrell had been shocked, had sent one of the guardsmen back to the palace to retrieve paper, a quill and ink, and a small foldable table so that he could record what we'd found. Immediately after the guardsmen had left, he set the remaining escort to counting the stores.

Now we were heading down to some warehouses along the River, near the meat market and stockyards. Eryn and Avrell had been talking animatedly since we'd left the palace.

I watched them from behind as we moved through the crowds at the edge of the market and passed into the streets beyond. They were talking about the city, about things that had happened years ago, problems they had resolved together while Eryn was Mistress, people they had met. People I'd never heard of, and events that had only affected the upper city, the real Amenkor, that had never reached the slums beyond the Dredge.

I felt a pang of . . . jealousy? Loneliness? Something deep in my chest, vaguely familiar. Like the yearning I'd felt whenever the baker—the white-dusty man, I thought, and smiled tightly—had reached out to touch me.

I wanted to be part of the conversation, wanted to share in the laughter, in the memories. But I couldn't. I'd been gutterscum back then, nothing more than a girl dressed in tattered rags hunched protectively over a half-rotted apple.

My mouth twisted into a scowl.

Ahead, Eryn gasped and said, "Do you remember when Alden came to the fete with that frilly lace thing around his throat?"

Avrell grinned. "He claimed it was the highest fashion in Venitte at the time."

"That's right! I'd forgotten!" Eryn's hand gripped Avrell's upper arm, a casual gesture. Avrell didn't react. "It turned out he'd gotten the thing from some 'captain' at the wharf." She snorted, shaking her head. "Just punishment, I say."

We reached the edge of the River and Eryn's hand fell away from Avrell's arm.

"Here we are," she said, turning back to look at me. A smile still touched her lips, but she'd straightened, back to the business at hand. "There should be cured meats in here."

Avrell nodded, the guardsmen already at the wide doorway. When the leader of the escort motioned them forward, we stepped into the shadowed interior.

The place was smaller than the ones I'd visited in the warehouse district while acting as Borund's bodyguard, support pillars reaching to the ceiling, the rafters dusty and filled with cobwebs. A dry mustiness assaulted my nose, and one of the guardsmen sneezed. Avrell raised one hand to cover his mouth, as he'd done at the stablehouse.

Other than the cobwebs and a few traces of straw, the warehouse was empty.

"I don't understand," Eryn said, her voice tight, her brow creased in confusion. "I remember having cured meats shipped here. Unless . . ."

She halted, all of the confidence she'd shown since we'd left the garden trickling away.

Avrell motioned to the guardsmen, who scattered through the warehouse, checking the far corners, a few ascending the stairs against the back wall to see if there was anything in the rooms above. The floor creaked as they moved around, dust sifting down through cracks between the boards.

Stepping forward as we waited, I circled the bottom floor of the warehouse. In the far corner, the dust had been disturbed, as if something had been stored in the warehouse recently, but had been moved.

I frowned, began wandering back to where Avrell and Eryn stood.

Both Avrell and I knew what the guardsmen had found before they returned. We shared a look, Avrell's lips pressed thin with concern.

"I know I had cured meat stored here," Eryn said, back stiff, voice adamant.

"But you said yourself you weren't certain whether the memories were yours or not," Avrell said soothingly. "It could have been someone else's memory, one of the previous Mistresses."

"No! I stored meat here. I *remember*!"

The guardsmen had all returned. The leader of the escort shifted uneasily as we turned. "There's nothing here now, Mistress," he said to Eryn. He winced as he realized his mistake, shot a horrified glance at me. "I mean, Eryn."

An awkward silence fell. Then Avrell stirred. "Were there any other places where you thought you'd stored supplies?"

Still troubled, Eryn shook herself and frowned in thought. "Yes, a few other places. The closest would be on the other side of the River, on the Dredge."

A sharp pain lanced down into my stomach and I stilled, my mouth suddenly dry.

I hadn't been to the Dredge since I'd killed Bloodmark and fled the slums. I hadn't even been to the far side of the River since then.

All eyes were turned on me, Avrell's filled with an unspoken question.

I shrugged aside the queasy terror in my gut, met Avrell's gaze, and said, "Let's go."

We left the empty warehouse behind, Avrell and I falling into step behind Eryn, the guardsmen fanning out around us. Curt orders were passed as we neared the Dredge and the stone bridge that arched across the River and the guardsmen closed in tighter around us, but no one else spoke. Eryn was intent, focused on where we were headed; Avrell seemed on the verge of speaking, but I shot him a glare and he subsided.

As we crossed over the bridge, my stomach knotted and my hand fell to my dagger. Without thought, I slid beneath the river, slid into old, familiar patterns with an ease that was sickening.

The Dredge had changed in the two years since I'd last been here.

We moved through streets filled with people—more people than when I'd last been here—their clothes worn, spattered with dirt and grime, some with tattered shoes or bundled rags covering their feet, but most barefoot. They moved slowly, shoulders hunched, heads down, arms held listlessly at their sides or clutched tight to their chests. A few carried bundles. A significant portion of them were foreigners—dark-skinned Zorelli from the south, Kandish with scraggly feathers entwined in their hair, Taniecians from the north with the blue marking of the Tear of Taniece smudged on their right cheek.

But it wasn't their clothes or their postures that tightened the knot in my stomach, that pressed something hard into the base of my throat. It was their eyes. They were empty, without hope, desolate and beaten. A few were harsh with anger, or hard with desperation, but mostly they were like walking dead, already lost and forgotten. And everywhere there was a sense of darkness, of decay, of buildings crumbling and streets narrowing—a crushing sense of oppression, as if the very sky were closing in.

I felt the pressure creeping in on me, closing off my throat so that I couldn't breathe, settling over me like a smothering blanket. My pulse quickened, throbbing in my temple, thudding in my chest. I tasted the Dredge, the grit and refuse harsh against my tongue, the scents of dampness—of rot and shit and malignant growth—cloying, stronger than it should be. All of the memories of my life beyond the Dredge crashed down on me at once, heightening the sensations, making them more real, more vivid, and infinitely worse.

I turned toward Avrell in horror. His eyes widened, and he reached toward Eryn to stop her, to turn us back, but before he could say anything, Eryn halted and said, "Here."

I choked back the overwhelming sense of the Dredge, forced myself to focus on where Eryn had pointed, to ignore the prickling sensation crawling across my shoulders and up my neck.

It was a building like all the rest on the Dredge, edges worn, windows bricked shut, so that the only entrance was through a doorway half filled with shattered stone and debris.

"Are you certain?" Avrell said, doubt clear in his voice.

"Yes," Eryn said, more confidently. "I can see the ward I placed on the door. There's something here."

And as she spoke, I saw the ward as well, saw the subtle currents of the river where they twisted into a pattern I didn't recognize near the heap of stone around the door and around the base of the building and windows.

But the pattern's intent was obvious. As I moved closer to the building, I felt the river pushing me away. I resisted it, came to a stop before the door beside Eryn.

"Let's see what's here," I said.

Eryn reached forward with one hand and the ward fell away.

I scrambled up over the debris, stone and dirt shifting beneath my weight, and heard Avrell and the guardsmen protest behind me.

Three guardsmen followed me instantly, but I knew there was nothing dangerous inside the building. I'd already checked using the river.

"Is it empty?" Avrell asked, coming up to the opening.

"No," I said, and heard Eryn sigh with relief. "It's filled with crates. I can't tell what's in them."

Avrell climbed through the entrance, balancing carefully, grimacing in distaste. He brushed off his hands and eyed me carefully. "Are you all right?"

I nodded sharply. "I'm fine."

He shook his head at the obvious lie, then motioned toward the guardsmen, who began assessing the crates, one of them setting up the foldable table in the diffuse light coming through the doorway. "We don't need to stay here long."

I didn't respond, watched the guardsmen at work for a moment instead, then turned and crawled back out into the sunlight.

Eryn stood at the edge of the Dredge, a few of the guardsmen to either side. As I moved up beside her, she said, "We're attracting attention," and nodded toward the people on the street who were eyeing Eryn and the guardsmen warily. Most dropped their gazes and moved on quickly; others glared openly. One man with a clouded white eye hawked a ball of phlegm to the cracked stone cobbles before skirting those around us and disappearing down a darkened narrow.

"Guardsmen always attract attention on the Dredge," I said.

Eryn pressed her lips together tightly, and I felt the guardsmen to either side tense. Their hands fell to the pommels of their swords.

"Is this what it's like all the time?" Eryn asked.

I shrugged uncomfortably. "It's worse now than it was. It never used to be so . . . crowded. Or dirty this close to the River. The slums—the true slums—hadn't crept so far in this direction.

I would never have come this far up the Dredge back then. There wouldn't have been any reason to." Glancing down the street, I realized that we were close to Cobbler's Fountain, where I'd meet with Erick when I'd found one of his marks, where my mother had brought me to play when I was six, before the Dredge had taken her.

I frowned, focusing on the people before us again.

We *were* drawing a crowd. A restless crowd.

The back of my neck prickled with unease and my hand gripped my dagger.

Murmurs began to run through the group, low at first, people muttering under their breath, but nothing more. I suddenly recalled the man with the milky eye, saw the derision on his face as he spat, saw his hatred.

I shifted my weight, settled into a defensive stance. "Get the others."

"But the First is not done," one of the guardsmen protested.

Before us, the crowd seemed to ripple, the murmur rising.

Far down the Dredge, something on the river shuddered. Someone shouted. The tension in the air spiked.

"Get them now!" I spat, and stepped forward, in front of Eryn, two guardsmen following my lead, shoving Eryn behind them, the other scrambling up over the debris and vanishing into the building.

"What is it?" Eryn asked.

I didn't answer.

Down the street, the shouting intensified and the river recoiled, fear and anger and retribution mingling sharply with the scent of sweat. The crowd—no, it wasn't a crowd anymore—the *mob* before us shuddered again, the angry faces at the forefront surging forward as if pushed from behind, then receding like a tide.

And then Avrell was there, the rest of the guardsmen closing in

protectively on either side. At the same time the tidal surge of the
mob pushed forward again, threatened to overcome the guardsmen
at its edge, before pulling back and parting.

Into the opening left by the crowd strode a group of armed
men.

The palace guardsmen stiffened. The leader barked out an
order, and swords snicked from sheaths.

On the river I could taste the advent of blood, like copper. I
breathed it in through my nostrils, my hand kneading the hilt of
my dagger, and thought, *This is the Dredge. This is where I come from.*

But not where I belonged.

The group of men advanced, their makeshift weapons—half-rotted
boards, a few knives, stones—at the ready. Only the leader of the
mob carried a sword, his face twisted into a scowl of hatred, but the
blade wasn't drawn. Not yet. His hair hung in lanky brown chunks
below the shoulders, and his breeches and tunic were stained but
not crusted with dirt like the others. A scar marred the sharp line
of his jaw and his brown eyes blazed.

"What are you doing here?" he spat as he approached, halting
a few paces away. His voice was low and rough with rage. The
crowd's grumbling increased, a few men openly cursing. The old
man with the milky eyes spat on the ground again a few paces behind him. "Get out! You don't belong here!"

The guards bristled, stepped forward with swords raised, but
Avrell halted them with a barked order.

I drew in the copper taste of blood with flared nostrils, then
shifted forward, stepped clear of the guardsmen to face the leader,
my hand still on my dagger, the river tight around me.

"We're here," I said slowly, "to figure out how to feed you."

The man hesitated, the tension on the river wavering—

Then he burst into laughter. "Here to feed us!" he roared. He
turned to the crowd. "Did you hear that! They're here to feed us!"

The crowd responded with a roar of its own, half laughter, half angry derision. A roar that sent shudders through my spine.

Then the man with the lanky hair spun back. "And how do you intend to do that?" he hissed. All humor had left his eyes. There was nothing left but a deadly glint, cold and heated at the same time.

When I didn't respond, he snorted with contempt. "That's what I thought."

He'd already started to turn away when I asked, "What's your name?"

He halted. "Why?"

"Because I want to know."

He sneered, then hesitated, his eyes catching mine. The sneer faltered, became a frown.

Then he gave a mock bow and growled, "*Lord* Darryn, at your service," twisting the title with contempt.

My lips twitched and a few of those in the crowd chuckled, but when Darryn had straightened, I became deadly serious. I saw him jerk back as he caught my gaze again and I stepped into the opening, moving close enough to keep him off-balance.

"I am the Mistress of Amenkor," I said, loud enough so everyone could hear, and felt a surge of satisfaction as some of those gathered gasped, as Darryn himself blinked in surprise, "originally from the Dredge. And I *will* find a way to feed you."

Then I stepped back, turned to catch Eryn's eye, saw Avrell motion quickly to the guards, who began to force a way out through the crowd. The people of the Dredge refused to part at first, hesitant, their eyes on Darryn, but when he said nothing, did nothing, they grudgingly gave way.

When we'd worked most of the way free of the press of the bodies, Eryn moved up beside me.

"I replaced the warding on the building."

I nodded, afraid to speak. Tremors had begun to run through my arms and my hand trembled. I gripped the handle of my dagger to make it stop, turned my attention to Avrell.

"Did you get what you needed?"

He swallowed once, his face pale, his eyes wider than usual. "Yes. I think so."

"Good. Let's head back to the palace. I've had enough of the city for one day."

Eryn snorted, the sound weak.

I didn't stop trembling until we passed through the inner gates.

✝

When Erick returned from his hunt on the Dredge, I was working with Marielle, huddled over a padded board, a piece of chalk clutched tight in one hand.

"You're pressing too hard," Marielle said. "You don't need to force the chalk into the slate. And you're holding it too tightly. No wonder your hand hurts after each session. Just relax."

I growled with frustration, shot Marielle a hateful glare which she ignored, then focused again on the black stone.

Marielle had drawn a few lines at the top and written letters between them, the writing smooth and fluid. Beneath, she'd drawn more lines, with the same spacing.

I'd copied the first two letters onto the second set of lines, my script shaky and jagged. I frowned at the attempts. "I hate this."

"You're doing fine," Marielle said, but I could hear the strain in her voice. "Try the next one. And this time don't press so hard."

I sighed, took the chalk in a death grip, and scanned the next letter. I bit my lower lip and concentrated, the room fading away behind me as I touched the chalk to the slate. I began a slow, careful curve, but it began to waver almost immediately. I gripped the chalk harder, but that didn't help. I felt sweat beading on my fore-head.

When the chalk broke halfway through forming the letter, I barked in a half yell, half growl, "I can't do this!"

"Can't do what?"

Both Marielle and I shot a glance toward the door—Marielle's in relief, mine in irritation. Erick stood there, his Seeker's clothes stained with the Dredge, his eyes bright with laughter.

I grinned, then stood abruptly, shoving the slate behind me. "Nothing," I said.

Erick's brow furrowed and he stepped through the doorway. Eryn moved into the room behind him.

"I ran into her in the corridor and escorted her here," Erick said as he approached, voice low. He paused, caught my shoulders and held my gaze, expression suddenly serious. "It's done. Corum's dead."

I straightened, regret leaving a bitter taste in my mouth. Regret that I hadn't killed Corum myself, not regret that he was dead. But even that regret faded, washed away by the metallic taste of rain-water, leaving only a sense of rightness, of balance and satisfaction.

Erick watched me closely, then nodded in approval, letting his hands drop from my shoulders.

"What about those he had working for him?" I asked. "The other gutterscum he was using as slaves?"

Erick's face turned grim. "Most of them scattered when the guardsmen raided the building where he had them working. They're back in the slums beyond the Dredge. A few didn't have anywhere to go or were too weak to run. The guardsmen have them right now, down in the barracks. A healer is checking them for dis-ease and wounds."

"And what happens to them after that?"

Erick shrugged. "We let them go."

"Back to the slums," I said bitterly, "where they end up with someone else like Corum."

Erick shifted uncomfortably. "What else can we do with them?"

What could we do with them? I didn't know. But there must be something. I couldn't get Darryn's face—his contempt, his hatred—out of my mind.

But he'd let us go without harming us.

"So . . ." Erick said, his voice too casual, "I hear that you disarmed Westen in your first match."

I snorted. "And then he brought me to my knees, my arm twisted up behind my back. With one hand."

Erick didn't laugh. "No one's ever disarmed Westen in a bout before, not since he became captain of the Seekers."

I hesitated, hearing the serious note in Erick's voice. "I cheated," I said finally. "I used the river."

His eyebrows rose. "That's not cheating. And the Seekers have let the palace and city guardsmen know. You shouldn't have any problems with the guard after this. If they doubted your ascension as Mistress before, they don't now."

I didn't know what to say, a strange sense of exhilaration filling me at the pride I heard in Erick's voice.

"You're also the talk of the Dredge," Erick added. "I don't know what you did yesterday, but it certainly caused a stir."

There was a hint of disapproval in his voice—probably over the fact that I'd confronted Darryn personally—but before I could answer it, someone coughed lightly and Erick stepped aside, revealing Eryn, the moment broken. She had halted three steps into the room, her hands folded before her, her black hair loose, spilling down her shoulders, stark against her dress.

"If you're ready," she said. "I thought we could try to determine who is influencing your dreams today."

I frowned, stomach tightening into a knot. Setting aside the slate, facedown so that Erick wouldn't see it, I nodded to Eryn. "What do you need me to do?"

Eryn hesitated, then seemed to steel herself. "I think it would be best if we tried this in the throne room."

I froze, eyes going slightly wide. The tension in my stomach doubled and I swallowed, hard.

I hadn't been to the throne room since the night I'd taken control, had been avoiding it completely. My only concession had been to issue an order to have the damage done to the doors by Baill and his guardsmen that night repaired.

"Very well," I said weakly.

Eryn turned to lead the way into the hall.

I shifted, caught Erick's eye.

"I'll come with you," he said.

I felt better instantly.

The entrance to the throne room wasn't far from my chambers. The three of us halted before the iron-bound, wooden doors, the wood gleaming with an inner warmth. The soft curves of the ironwork were delicate yet formidable, newly wrought after Baill and the guardsmen had ripped the doors from the walls trying to gain entrance to the throne room almost a month before. I could still hear the iron hinges clanging to the marble floor inside, could hear the crack of the wood as it split under the battering ram. I remembered standing outside these doors that night, knowing that the Mistress waited for me inside, that the throne waited for me, and that it was a trap.

I felt sweat break out on my palms, felt nausea rising as Eryn hesitated. For a moment, we shared a look, and I saw in her eyes the same apprehension I felt.

Then Eryn nodded to the guardsmen who opened the doors with a ponderous creak of new wood and the faint squeal of new hinges.

Eryn and I stepped into the room together, Erick a pace behind. A long walkway led up to a tiered dais, thick columns rising to either side. Every torch and sconce of oil in the room had been lit. There were no darknesses, no places to hide. And at the end of the walkway, on the dais, sat the Skewed Throne, a white-and-gold banner covering the wall behind it.

It was just as I remembered. A twisted thing, its shape shifting before my eyes, at one moment a high-backed seat of stone with flat square arms, the next the stone warping, the seat molding itself to a new form: a simple chair, but with one leg shorter than the others. And then it would twist again, shifting fluidly, the motions sickening and silent, straining the eyes. A long divan; another square throne but with etched scrollwork and no arms; a river-worn rock.

But it was always stone. Cold, hard granite.

I shuddered, turned away. Before, I'd felt the power of the throne throughout the room, stalking me, a predator circling me, hunting me as I hunted for Eryn, my only protection the Fire inside me, and the river, holding it at bay. But now the voices were a part of me, and I felt them respond to the presence of the throne. Their shrieking increased, harsh with anticipation, with expectation.

With a conscious effort, I strengthened the Fire holding them back, felt a surge of hatred in return.

"You must sit on the throne," Eryn said, her voice steady but weak. We'd moved to the bottom of the dais, and I could see that she would not move closer, would not risk touching the throne again. Any qualms I'd had about having her there, so close to the throne, so close to seizing power again, faded. She feared the throne as much as I did; perhaps more, since she knew what it was capable of, knew what it could do.

I suddenly wondered what she'd felt when Avrell had tried to replace her with one of the other Servants. Had she felt them die? Had she died along with them?

Or had she helped kill them, however inadvertently?

I left her at the bottom of the dais, moved up the steps slowly, and stood before the twisting shape.

Then I turned, braced myself, and without further thought sat down.

I felt the throne move beneath me, revulsion prickling along my skin, shuddering up through my body as my breath caught, as my heart quickened. The voices surged higher, melding as one into a roar—

And then they relaxed, suddenly calm.

The throne stabilized, solidifying into a smooth curve of stone with two arms and no back. My hands curled around the edges of the arms and my back straightened, the pose completely natural. I felt suddenly heavier, the room before me more solid, more real. And through my pulse I could feel the city, could feel its heartbeat, could feel the people moving through the streets, the ships floating at the dock, the water of the harbor and the River slapping against the wharf and the riverbed. I throbbed with life, with emotion, an immense rush of sound and movement I could feel tingling in my skin.

I drew in a deep, steadying breath, let it out slowly as I submerged myself in the sensations of the city, and then I turned to gaze down on Eryn at the bottom of the dais, at Erick shifting uncomfortably a few paces beyond. Erick smelled of sweat and oranges, the scents more intense now. Eryn smelled of loam and leaves, like tea.

I focused on Eryn, felt the currents of the city shift around me. "What do I do?" I asked. My voice sounded thicker, more dense, as if it had the weight of all of the voices of the throne behind it, but neither Eryn nor Erick reacted.

Eryn licked her lips. "Focus on the voices, but don't try to pick out any words. Just listen to them as a whole. Think of them as . . ." her brow creased in thought, ". . . as people in a marketplace, all yelling and talking at once. You're just standing at the marketplace's edge, letting the roar wash over you, not really paying attention."

I frowned, closed my eyes on the throne room and focused on the pulse of the city around me, moving deeper into its life until I came to the edge of the White Fire that protected me. The voices reacted as I drew nearer, the stronger ones pushing forward, but I pushed them back, never let the Fire waver. I tried to imagine the marketplace in the middle ward outside the merchants' guild hall, tried to picture myself at the corner of a street, staring out over the white stone plaza at the rearing bronze statues of the horses at the fountain in its center, the voices of the throne individual people in the square. But the image wavered, grew ragged and torn at its edges, until I couldn't hold it anymore.

I grunted as it slipped away, clenched my hands tighter on the edges of the throne as I gathered my strength to try again.

Below, I could feel Eryn's expectant tension, could taste Erick's concern, like musty clothes.

I re-formed the image of the marketplace—the four horses, the gurgle of the fountain—tried to place the voices there . . . but the image began to slip again. I grasped at it in desperation—

And felt something pull.

The marketplace darkened, white stone growing grimy and gray, regular flagstone shifting to odd cobbles. The roar of the hawkers on the square became the raucous noise of a street.

Then, there was a gut-wrenching lurch.

Instead of standing at the corner of the guild hall's plaza, I found myself crouched at the mouth of an alley on the Dredge, the sound of the hundred voices of the throne now the familiar rushing background wind of the river.

My hands unclenched from the arms of the throne, and my breathing slowed.

After a long steadying moment, I said softly, "I've got it."

"Good." Eryn's voice seemed distant, as if coming from a far corridor, but I could still smell the scent of tea close by. "Now, think about the dream. But not what happened in the dream. Think about what the dream *felt* like. If someone was influencing the dream, changing it in some way, you should be able to feel them, like . . . like a shadow in the background."

Like gutterscum on the Dredge.

I began to replay the dream in my head, starting at the gates, moving swiftly through the streets to the stable, to the trapdoor and the tunnel. I let the dock boy's conversation seep past me, tried to focus on the movements, the tread of feet, the brush of clothes against the crates as we squeezed through the narrow opening to the tunnel's entrance. But there was nothing.

I tried again, slower, heard the rasp of our boots on the cobbles, felt the light from the oil lamp as Borund lit it from behind.

Nothing.

On the third try, as I lost track of the dock boy and Borund, as they melded into the smooth flow of motion, I caught the shadow. But it wasn't a feeling, it was a scent:

Loam and leaves. Like tea.

I jerked back, stumbled deeper into the alley, away from the Dredge, then caught myself.

In the depths of the throne room, I heard myself say, "It's you."

"What?" Eryn asked, voice still remote, but tinged with confusion.

"The shadow I sense behind the dream is you," I said more forcefully.

A pause, the noise of the Dredge still surrounding me.

"But that's not possible," Eryn said. "The Sight can't be used

that way. And besides, I didn't know about the wine! I don't remember hiding it in the stable!"

Ignoring Eryn's growing agitation, I edged back up to the alley's
mouth, crouched down behind a wagon half full of scabrous apples.
"Wait," I said.

On the eddies of the Dredge, where all of the voices of the
throne lay, I'd caught a scent. Faint, but there.

I drew in a breath, let the instincts I'd honed on the Dredge
take over . . . and caught the scent again.

I pushed forward, past the wagon and into the crowd, moving
swiftly. But unlike the real Dredge, the people on this Dredge didn't
ignore me. Instead, they turned, shouted in my face, grasped at my
tattered clothes, at my arms, thrust themselves in my path to catch
my attention. I struggled through them, noticed that they were almost all women, old and young, pockmarked and fair, with blonde
hair, black, a muddy brown with green eyes, in all manner of
clothes. All of the past Mistresses, and anyone else who had somehow touched the throne, all trying to gain my attention, hundreds
of them. I fought them, fought through their scents: tallow, ripened
melon, sea salt, and dead fish. I followed the scent of tea.

Until I rounded a corner at the edge of a narrow, where I halted.

Just inside the narrow, huddled in the darkness, was Eryn. But
unlike the voices of the throne behind me, this Eryn was somehow
less real, a shadow compared to the rest. A ghost.

The shade of the Eryn I knew raised her head, her eyes
haunted, darkened around the edges with fear and strain.

"Look," she murmured, then pointed down the narrow, away
from the Dredge, into the darkness.

I turned, brow creased, mouth set.

But instead of the narrow I expected, the darkness looked out
over the city of Amenkor.

With a start, I realized I was standing on the roof of the palace

tower at night, Eryn's shade beside me. The city lay spread out before me: the inner ward, the middle ward, the outer ward; the
wharf, the warehouse district, the lower city; and across the River,
the slums beyond the Dredge.

And the city was burning. All of it. Huge pillars of smoke
boiled into the air, tinged red from the fires beneath. On street
after street, husks of buildings stood out as fire ate at their foundations. Ships burned at the docks, a few blazing cold and harsh
in the water, flames reflected on the waves. Even as the full extent
of the scene began to register, to penetrate through the shock, I felt
a surge of power—a pulsing wave on the river—and one of the
guard towers at the entrance to the harbor exploded, stone and
wood debris flying up and out, arching over the water of the bay,
trailing flame and smoke and embers. The fire was a living thing,
hissing, spitting. A sizzling *fwump* rose up from the middle ward as
a guild hall collapsed, stone cracking, more embers rising high into
the night.

As I stepped to the edge of the rooftop, horror welling up inside
me, choking me, closing off my throat, the water of the harbor
caught my attention, rising on slow swells, dark and viscous.

The harbor water was red. Not with reflected firelight, but with
blood. And the waves were choked with bodies.

Eryn's shade drew up close behind me. "Do you see!" she
shrieked, her voice cracking with insanity. "Do you see!"

Then the winds shifted, blew smoke into my face so that I
squinted, blew Eryn's black hair back in streaming tangles. And the
smell from the city below hit, a noisome wave of smoke and ash
and blood, of salt and sea and death.

I turned away from the stench, doubled over as my gorge rose,
and in a panic I let the river go, shoved it aside with a wrench. I felt
the Fire inside me flare as if to protect me, felt part of it get caught
and tear free as I shoved the vision of the city away in desperation.

I heard Eryn scream in pain as the wave of power spread out on the river, as it tore through the vision of blood and water and fire.

Then I fell off the throne, collapsed to my hands and knees, trembling with weakness, and vomited onto the top step of the dais of the throne room.

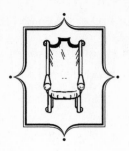

Chapter 4

"BUT SHE'S BEEN LIKE THIS for two days!"

The voice filtered through the darkness, followed swiftly by tremors throughout my body. But all of it was distant, coming from a farther shore, removed from me here, where I floated on the river. So I kept my eyes closed, let myself drift on the surface of the water, half submerged, and listened.

"I know, Borund." A familiar voice, hard and soothing, weary and comforting. Erick's voice. It made me want to open my eyes, to struggle from the river, but I felt too tired, the river currents too strong. "Remember what happened to her after the warehouse fire. You know it can take a while for her to recover."

Borund grunted. "I can still feel where she kicked me during one of the seizures then. But I'm not sure how much longer we can wait. Decisions have to be made about how to distribute the food. We can't just hand it out to whoever comes to the warehouses. And I have no idea how we're going to include the people of the Dredge."

Movement. Someone shifting closer.

"Are you certain this is the same as after the fire?" Borund asked, his voice concerned.

More movement. Then someone touched my forehead, brushed away a lock of my hair, the sensation faint and tingling, sending a shiver through me.

"Yes. She'll be fine."

Borund muttered a wordless agreement. "What about Eryn?"

The voices moved away.

"She's fine as well. She woke yesterday, according to Avrell."

"Did he say what happened? Did Eryn say?"

"No. Eryn refuses to discuss it. She's waiting for Varis to recover."

A pause. Then, in a softer voice, "You should get some sleep, Erick. How long have you been here?"

"Since it happened."

A subtle shift on the river. When Borund spoke, I could hear a more significant question hidden behind the simple words. "Watching over her?"

"Guarding her." Stiff and formal. Stubborn.

I smiled.

"If you insist," Borund said. I heard humor in his voice, a shared understanding. And also an acceptance, tinged with regret. Their attention returned to me. I could feel it, like sunlight against my skin. "You'll be a better . . . mentor to her than I will. You already have been."

Silence from Erick. I stilled, caught my breath, part of me confused, but part of me shivering with an unexpected need, hard and tight inside my gut. I'd never known my father, my mother nothing more than a wisp of memory, killed when I was six years old. I'd survived alone on the Dredge since then, after learning what I needed from a gutterscum street gang led by a boy called Dove. I'd had no one since then. At one point, I'd thought that the baker who'd taken pity on me and fed me on a regular basis would be something more than just a face I needn't fear. But no. He was dead now.

Which left Erick and Borund.

I'd never thought of either as being more than a trainer, or an employer.

Except that wasn't true, was it? I'd always wanted something more, but had never realized what it was. Not until now, when Borund put it into words.

Breath held, I reached out toward Erick, felt a bitterness inside him, felt his self-hatred. "I trained her to kill," he finally said, the words soft yet harsh.

"No," Borund said, his words just as harsh, refuting Erick as strongly as he could. "You taught her how to survive. You never wanted her to kill, like me. You always gave her the choice, killed for her if she said no. You trained her so she could protect herself from all of the dangers of the Dredge. No." Borund's voice was emphatic. "I ordered her to kill, to make my life easier. I *used* her, like a tool." He paused, a tremor of pain entering his voice. "She deserves more than that," he added, the words thick with suppressed emotion.

Erick didn't respond, but I could sense that the self-hatred he felt had been blunted, that he was watching me with a considering frown. The hard core of need inside me shuddered, and I relaxed, the held breath releasing in a slow sigh.

It was enough for now.

Borund stirred, his roiling emotions settled somewhat. I felt a surge of pity for him. He'd tried to think of me as more than a tool, especially at the end, when I'd returned from the fire in the warehouse district with seizures. But my usefulness as a weapon kept getting in the way, first with the merchant Charls, then Alendor, and finally with the Mistress. He'd never had the chance to think of me as anything else.

"I'll have the servants send in something to eat," he said.

"What are you going to do?"

A pause. "I'm not certain. We need her, Erick. Somehow, she keeps everything balanced: Avrell, Baill, the merchants."

"Eryn can help."

A sigh. "Perhaps. But not for long. She doesn't have the power of the throne behind her anymore. The merchants might listen to her for a time, out of remembered respect, but it won't last. We need Varis. She's more forceful than Eryn, more direct. And I think the merchants fear her."

"Because of the throne?"

Borund snorted. "No. They fear her for who she is, for what they know she can do with that dagger of hers. They've seen her in action, protecting me from Alendor and the consortium. And they've heard the rumors of what she did on the Dredge."

"Some of those rumors aren't true."

"But some of them are?"

A long, considering pause. A little of the self-hatred returned, but it was balanced by a shouldered responsibility. "Yes," Erick finally said, his voice somewhat defiant.

"Then the merchants have reason to fear her."

Silence, and then Borund heaved a heavy sigh. "I should return to my manse." Shuffling movement, growing more and more distant. "I left William in charge of organizing the storage—"

The voices faded. Where I floated on the river, eyes closed, I felt a pang deep inside, followed by sudden heat.

William. Borund's apprentice. I saw his tousled black hair, his eyes, green like the waters at the edge of the wharf, his smile, soft and tentative.

The heat in my gut turned fluid, spread to my chest. I smiled, stretched out in the sensation, arched my back.

Distantly, I heard the rustle of sheets as I moved, heard Erick returning alone to stand over me. I could feel him willing me to wake with a simple, direct stare. And I wanted to wake now, wanted to see him, wanted to see William. William must have recovered from the knife wound in his side if he was helping Borund at the warehouses.

But then I felt my own twinge of doubt, of regret and responsibility. William had been hurt because I'd failed to protect him, failed to anticipate the intent of the men who had ambushed us.

In my mind, William's smile faded. His eyes darkened with accusation, then shifted again, grew troubled. Fear bled into his features. His eyes flew wide open. Muscles tensed around his mouth and jaw.

This was how he had looked in the tavern when I'd gutted the assassin attempting to kill Borund. This was how he'd looked when I'd almost stabbed him on the wharf. Afraid. Terrified of me, of what I could do, of what I had already done. I could kill, without remorse, viciously and bloodily.

It was who I was. It was what made the other merchants fear me.

The heat in my center curdled and I curled in upon myself, drew away from Erick's presence hovering over me, away from the Mistress' bedchamber where I lay.

I didn't want to wake. Not yet. Not for Erick, nor for William. I was too tired.

Let Eryn deal with everything for now. All I wanted to do was sleep.

So I let the river pull me down into darkness.

†

I opened my eyes to bright sunlight filtered through drawn curtains and saw the simple white canopy above my bed. The folds of cloth rippled in a breeze.

I blinked, felt the grit around my eyes, the tightness of my skin caused by too much sleep, and heard a low murmur of voices.

I turned my head, wincing at the twinge of fading bruises and strained muscles, and saw Erick and Marielle sitting on the settee that I used to work on my writing, their heads bowed down over my slate.

The initial surge of contentment that slid through me on seeing Erick was cut short by a thread of anger and embarrassment. I didn't want Erick to see my work, my scratchings that were nothing like the smooth lines of Marielle's writing.

"I don't know what to do," Marielle said, her voice hushed but carrying easily. "She's trying so hard, but the letters don't come naturally to her. It's not a matter of her learning to read—she'll master that with little effort; she remembers everything—but the writing . . ." She shook her head.

Erick frowned down at the slate. "She's thinking about it too much," he said. Then he pointed to the board. "You can see the strain of it in the lines of each letter. Here. And here. She's trying too hard to do exactly what you do, to make the letters as smooth and flowing as yours are. But Varis isn't elegant and meticulous like you. She's blunt and direct. Forceful. You have to find a way to make the writing as blunt and forceful as she is."

Marielle's brow furrowed in thought. "How do I do that?"

I struggled up onto one elbow, tried to speak, the anger overtaking my exhaustion, but the words came out in a raspy cough instead. Both Erick and Marielle glanced up, then stood.

"Water," Erick said sharply, and as Marielle darted to the side table where she'd left the pitcher and glasses, he moved to the edge of the bed. The slate was left forgotten on the settee.

I glared at him as he helped me into a sitting position, then took the glass of water Marielle offered. I swallowed carefully, my throat raw, but the water washed the sour taste away and made my stomach rumble.

"I didn't want you to see," I said hoarsely, motioning toward the slate.

Marielle harrumphed. "He's been here for the last three days," she said, taking the glass of water away before I drank too much and made myself sick. "He was bound to see it eventually." She passed over a chunk of bread.

"You didn't have to show it to him." I switched my glare to Marielle, but she didn't flinch.

"I'll go tell the others you're awake," she said. "And get some soup from the kitchen. That's probably the best thing for you right now."

Erick waited until she was gone, then pulled a chair sitting next to the bed closer. He leaned back, made himself comfortable, then said, "She's trying to help."

I scowled and plucked at the sheets, ignoring the smile playing about Erick's lips.

But the smile faded and his attention shifted. "What happened?" he asked, voice serious.

My nervous hands stilled. I thought about the vision of the city on fire, of the blood and bodies in the harbor. I shuddered, felt a twist of nausea in my stomach that echoed what I'd felt while touching the throne, but fought it back. The image was too real, too . . . visceral. I couldn't keep it to myself.

I turned to Erick, frowned intently . . . and suddenly realized I wouldn't be sending him out in search of any more marks. The last few weeks without him had been too lonely, and I hadn't realized why until he'd returned, until I'd overheard Borund and Erick earlier. But now I knew what I wanted, without any doubt.

"I saw Amenkor," I said. "The city was on fire, everything burning: the palace, the docks, the Dredge. Even the ships in the harbor. And there were bodies in the water." My voice grew rough, cracked, but with effort I managed to control it. I swallowed down the horror, tasted its bitterness. "The harbor was filled with blood, a whole sea of it. And in the end it was too much to take, and so I shoved it all away. Hard.

"That's when I fell off the throne."

Erick nodded, his eyes thoughtful. "That's when Eryn screamed and collapsed as well."

I sat forward. I remembered the scream at the end, when the power I'd used to push the image away had rippled outward, a second before I'd fallen. I'd thought it had come from the shade of Eryn, since she'd been on the tower with me, witnessing the fire. But if it had truly been Eryn, not her shadow . . .

"Is she all right?"

Erick grunted. "She's fine. She was a little shaken, but she says there was no harm done. None that she can see." He stilled. "What do you think the vision means? Was it just an image, like in a dream, or was it something more?"

I thought back, tried to ignore the scent of smoke and ash, still sharp, making my nose itch and wrinkle in distaste. "I don't know." I thought about how I'd always used the river to see what *could* happen, to find the best time to snatch away the apple, or the easiest way to elude the guards. The vision had the same feel, viscerally real but also stretched somehow, not fully there.

I shook my head. "I need to ask Eryn. She has more experience with the throne. But I think I understand why she closed the harbor."

"Why?"

"Whatever destroyed the city in the vision . . . it came from the ocean. I could sense it."

We stared at each other for a long moment without speaking. Then Erick said in a tight voice, "So perhaps Eryn wasn't as insane as she seemed."

A hard lump closed off my throat as I realized that he was right. She'd had reason to close the harbor, reason perhaps to increase the guard in the city. I'd been sent to kill her—had agreed to kill her—on the assumption that she had gone mad. But what if that wasn't true? What if there *were* reasons for all her actions? Avrell himself had said that sometimes the Mistress' orders made no sense at the time, but were obvious in retrospect.

Then I shook my head, the lump in my throat easing. No. The vision still didn't explain her order to let the warehouse district burn, or her wandering the palace talking to herself, speaking in unknown languages, as the guards claimed. And I *knew* she had gone insane. I'd seen it in the throne room when I tried to kill her.

No. Eryn had been on the verge of total madness when I'd seized control. There was no doubting that. She'd admitted it herself.

But I didn't get a chance to explain to Erick. Someone knocked and a moment later opened the outer door. One of the guards outside leaned in.

"The First of the Mistress and a Master Borund are here to see you," he said when he saw I was sitting up in bed.

I sighed and leaned back into the pillows. Erick stood.

"I could send them away," he offered quietly.

I shook my head. "No, send them in."

Erick nodded to the guardsman, who stepped in to allow Avrell and Borund entry, then closed the door behind himself as he left. Both Avrell and Borund moved up to the bed, opposite Erick.

"Mistress," Avrell said with a formal bow of his head. "It is good to see you recovering."

"Yes, it is, Mistress," Borund said. "What happened?"

I glanced toward Erick, giving him a warning frown before turning back. "The throne was more powerful than I thought. I was too . . . *forceful* in my efforts to control it."

Erick shifted uncomfortably.

"What have you done while I was recovering?" I asked.

Avrell cleared his throat, catching everyone's attention. "We've managed to locate and secure the stockpiles of food that Eryn smuggled into the city, ten in all, by searching all of the buildings owned by the palace. There may be more, but Eryn couldn't have hidden anything outside the city by herself and we can't search every building in the city without rousing protests, so for now we've stopped looking."

"Now we need to decide how to store the goods we do have," Borund broke in, "and figure out how to distribute them among the populace over the coming months."

"I still argue for a single location that can be easily guarded," Avrell said.

Borund frowned. "And I still say it should be at a few separate locations in case something happens, like a fire."

As Avrell and Borund traded glares, I thought of the fires burning in the vision and sighed wearily.

"I've already decided," I said, cutting the two off before they could launch into a repeat of the argument they'd had a few weeks ago. "We'll put the food in separate locations." Borund smiled and nodded in triumph. "Avrell, choose the locations and let Baill and Captain Catrell know so they can assign guardsmen. There should be one in the middle ward, another in the outer, and at least one somewhere in the slums. Find an empty building in each area, something that Baill thinks will be easy to defend and control, and use that. There are plenty of empty buildings. The buildings that remain in the warehouse district can be used to cover the wharf and the upper city."

Avrell sighed disapprovingly. "Very well."

I caught him with a hard stare. "I have my reasons," I said sharply.

He frowned and straightened, looking questioningly at Erick, who didn't respond, his face blank.

I turned to Borund. "Once you have the locations, distribute them among the merchants and let them know where they're to store their goods. Some of it can stay in their own warehouses, of course, but any excess and anything from Alendor's or the consortium's supplies should be divided among the other locations. I expect the merchants to keep track of all of the supplies under their control, and to distribute them fairly when the time comes. Don't store all of the grain in one spot. We don't want to lose our entire supply of any one staple because of some accident."

Borund simply nodded.

"And how *are* we going to distribute this food as the winter progresses?" Avrell asked, his brow creased with honest concern.

I sighed and leaned back, feeling tired already. "I don't know yet. Just move the supplies for now."

Erick shifted forward, eyes worried. He searched my face and must have seen the exhaustion there. "I think that's enough for now," he said meaningfully.

Avrell seemed about to protest, but he subsided under Erick's flat stare and a quick look at me. "Of course. We'll continue this tomorrow, after you've had more time to rest."

I said nothing as they departed. Almost immediately after they'd left, Marielle returned with a tray containing a steaming bowl of soup and a small dish of fruit. She began to set it up next to the bed. I was already beginning to feel sleepy, but the thought of food kept me upright and awake. The smell from the soup made my stomach clench and growl.

Erick began to turn away, but I stopped him with a touch on his hand. He gave me a grave look, eyes intent.

"Thank you," I said.

I wasn't certain what I was thanking him for—wasn't certain he knew either—but his expression softened and he smiled, then reached up and flicked away a sweaty lock of hair from my forehead before settling into the chair to watch me eat.

✝

"So tell me," Eryn said, taking a slow sip of her tea, "what did you find when you were on the throne?"

We were sitting in chairs in the doorway of the balcony in my rooms, a small table with our cups and the pitcher of tea between us. Erick had dozed off in the chair next to my bed. Eryn had arrived almost an hour before, our initial conversation tense and meaningless, lapsing into thoughtful silence interrupted by Erick's snores as we stared up at the pale winter sky hazed with thin clouds. The afternoon light had just begun to fade toward evening.

I shifted uncomfortably. I'd been dreading this meeting since I'd seen Eryn's shade on the mock Dredge, since her shade had shown me the city burning. But Eryn hadn't come to see me, and I'd been too weak to go to her . . . and too angry.

But I hadn't hidden in my room doing nothing. I'd experimented with the throne's powers, searched the city for more of the wardings like the one she placed on the building in the Dredge. I hadn't found anything. I didn't think any of the other buildings hiding stored foods had wardings. Once I knew what to look for, the warding in the Dredge had been easy to spot.

I'd also tried other things, tested the throne's reach, tested my own reach. But I'd been careful, never letting the tenuous connection to my body break.

I just didn't want all of my knowledge about the throne to come from Eryn. I didn't trust her yet.

Eryn's gaze dropped to her cup. "You said that it was me."

I nodded, thinking back to the dream. I felt a surge of that anger now, but it was smothered by the sudden need to understand what had happened. "It was you behind the dreams. You were there, in the shadow as you said, nudging me to remember, and finally appearing yourself."

Eryn frowned. "That would explain why it was my image that appeared at the end of the dream," she said. "But it couldn't have been me. The Sight can't be used in that fashion. I know it! I've tried since then to influence Laurren's dreams, but it doesn't *work*!"

She set her cup down with a sharp clatter, tea spilling over one side, then stood and crossed her arms, moving stiffly toward the edge of the balcony.

My lips thinned, but my anger faltered. Her emotion was too raw to be faked, her distress too sincere. "Who's Laurren?"

Eryn huffed, then tensed in an effort to control herself. In a much calmer tone, she said, "Laurren is my principal servant, also one of the true Servants, one of the more powerful ones here. I've known her for years. If I could influence anyone's dreams with the Sight, it would be hers."

I hesitated, then stood and moved to Eryn's side, leaned against the iron railing as I stared down at the palace and city beneath us. "I don't think you used the Sight to influence my dreams."

Eryn flicked a glance toward me, confused and irritated. "How else could I have touched your dreams?"

I grimaced. "I think you used the throne."

Eryn straightened. "But that's impossible," she scoffed. "I'm not connected to the throne anymore. I can't feel it, can't hear it. When I reach for it, even out of habit, there's nothing there!" There was a tremor of loss beneath her voice.

"I know. I don't think you're connected to the throne anymore either. I can't sense any of the threads that bound you to it, the threads that I removed when I seized control."

"Then how could I have used the throne to touch your dreams!" Eryn said sharply.

I felt my shoulders tense. "I think part of you is still inside the throne," I said bluntly.

Eryn stilled, anger building tight and fast, like a storm cloud.

"What—?" she began. But then she stopped herself, forced herself to think instead of react.

I seized the opening. "There's a piece of you still inside the throne. I sensed it, found it hidden among the rest of the voices. A shadow of yourself, almost an echo, as if somehow, when I took control, when I cut the bonds between you and the throne, a memory of you got left behind. And I think that piece of you holds the memories that you've lost."

I halted, waited. I'd tried to connect with the shadow of Eryn in the throne itself, the one that had shown me the vision of the city burning. Tried to find out from her where some of the stores might have been hidden. But she refused to speak to me, didn't even appear to be sane.

The thought of a piece of myself being torn away, imprisoned outside of myself, sent a queasy shudder through my gut, made my mouth dry and tasteless. I expected Eryn to react the same way.

Instead, Eryn stared out across the harbor, her face unreadable, eyes pinched, skin taut.

"That's why I don't remember the wine," she said to herself, anger still evident in the curt words.

I felt the tension in my shoulders release. "And why the shadow of you does."

Eryn remained quiet, then said in a trembling, vulnerable voice, "I thought I'd escaped the throne."

I didn't know what to say, so I said nothing. The statement was at odds with the loss I'd heard in her words before. I wondered which emotion would eventually win out: yearning for the throne, or acceptance that it was lost.

Before us, the thin clouds became tinged with dark orange as the sun set. In the courtyard of the palace, a troop of guardsmen tramped in from the city and after a pause broke up, each guards-man going his separate way. On the wall of the inner ward, I saw the palace guardsmen changing shifts as well.

Eventually, the turmoil I felt from Eryn subsided. She turned to me. "But that doesn't explain your reaction at the end. Something else happened, something that startled you, frightened you." When I didn't respond immediately, she shifted closer, her voice harden-ing. "If you were better trained, you would have killed me with that blast of power."

I flinched, but straightened, my hand dropping to my dagger at the threat in her tone. "But I didn't kill you."

Eryn's face darkened, her head lifting. "No, you didn't. Instead, you knocked me unconscious and seriously overextended yourself."

"I've done it before and survived," I said, annoyance rising at the rebuke.

Eryn snorted. "Then you were lucky. You could have killed yourself as well, pushed yourself too far. All it takes is one careless mistake, and you could end up lost, your body nothing but a husk, your focus too scattered to bring you back. You need to be better trained in the use of the Sight."

I bristled, but Eryn halted, her lips pursed. She shook her head and let it drop, turning away as she asked, "So what happened?"

I felt an urge to confront her, my skin prickling, hand gripping tight on my dagger, but I forced my breathing to slow, forced the anger back. It didn't feel right, too sharp and quick and uncon-trolled. Too impulsive.

Once I'd calmed, I said, "The memory of you still inside the throne showed me a vision of the city burning, all of the people slaughtered. It was horrible, so I used the river to shove it away without thinking."

Eryn frowned. "I don't remember any such vision. But if the

Eryn inside the throne, my shadow, knew of it . . ." She trailed off, thinking. "Do you think it was a scrying, a vision of the future?"

I shuddered. "Yes."

Eryn's expression grew grim. "Then you must prepare."

I laughed, the sound short and humorless. "For what? There was nothing in the vision except fire and death, nothing but smoke and ruin."

"But it is still a warning. My shadow was trying to help you, with the wine and now with this. Think back to the image, look for details. What season was it? Winter? Spring? Summer?"

I thought about refusing, but under Eryn's harsh glare, I closed my eyes and concentrated. At first, I held the image still, just a memory of what I'd seen before, static and senseless.

But then I felt the vision twist, felt the power of the river surge through it.

The image enfolded me again, as real as it had been on the throne, full of sound and sensation, and I found myself back on the roof of the tower staring out over the city. My breath came in shorter gasps as I tried not to breathe the smoke, as I tried not to choke on the stench, even though I knew it didn't exist. Heat touched my skin, turned it waxy and slick, and from the city below I heard screams.

I pushed the horrible sound away, looked up at the sky clouded with plumes of smoke and ash. "I can't tell what season it is," I said, voice raised over the crackle of flame, the sucking roar of fire. "It's dark. Nighttime. I can only see smoke and flames in the streets. I can't even see the stars, or the moon."

Distantly, I heard the rustle of cloth as Eryn shifted closer, smelled the perfume she was wearing, the scent of the large white flowers from her garden warring with the reek of the smoke. "Look at the banners on the palace walls. What color are they?"

On the tower, stone cracked with a sharp retort and part of the palace wall fell away, slowly, but I ignored it and leaned out over the edge of the rooftop, hands pressed to the gritty stone. For a moment, the same dizziness that had overwhelmed me before sent the world spinning. A blast of heat hit my face, but I squinted, fought the vertigo long enough to see the banners, then lurched back with a gasp.

"They're yellow! A bright yellow!"

"Summer, then," Eryn said.

I continued to gasp, the raw stench becoming overpowering, then broke out in ragged coughing, the smoke invading my lungs. I doubled over, felt Eryn's hands on my shoulders, attempting to steady me.

"Look to the harbor," she commanded. "Look at the ships. What flags are flying on the masts?"

Still doubled over, coughing harshly, I forced myself to straighten and move to the edge of the tower, Eryn helping me to stand upright. I gagged, swallowed the sickening taste back, and scanned the ships burning in the water, trying not to see the bodies rolling in the movement of the waves.

"I can't see," I said. "I can't—"

The river suddenly gathered, and I drew in a harsh breath, felt the weight of the river coalesce into a focused thrust and release.

Far out on the edge of the harbor one of the watchtowers that guarded the bay exploded.

"They can use the river," I gasped, as the debris from the watchtower began to rain down into the bay, the realization sharp and horrifying, like a hand at my throat.

Then something else caught my eye. The warehouse district.

A plume of smoke drifted directly over the tower and I drew in a lungful of char and ash. Doubling over again, I lost my grip on the vision, felt it tatter and shred as I fell back into Eryn's arms. She guided me to my chair as tears streamed down my sweat-drenched face; reaction from the smoke. But of course there was no smoke, no fire.

Not yet.

"They can use the Sight," I managed between wheezing breaths, the sensation of heat and flame fading.

"Who?" Eryn snapped.

"The ones attacking Amenkor. The ones burning the city. They used the river to destroy one of the watchtowers."

Eryn's eyes flashed, then handed me my cup filled with tea. "Drink this."

I sipped as I shook my head, scrubbed the tears away from my face with the back of a trembling hand. My throat felt raw, my lungs dirty with soot. "Who else along the coast has Servants—true Servants?"

Eryn hesitated. "Everyone. There are men and women all along the coast that have and can use the Sight. Most don't realize what they are doing, using it in only mundane ways—to coax the fish into the net, to calm the deer's heart during a hunt, to smooth the escalating tensions in the tavern to avoid a fight." Her frown deepened and she turned away, moved toward the edge of the balcony. "There's only one other city that actually trains Servants as we do."

"Which city?"

"Venitte." Short and terse. "They have a school, almost exclusively male students. In fact, we have an agreement with them: they send any women proficient in the Sight here to be trained, we send the men down there. Anyone with sufficient power on the coast ends up here or there eventually."

"Why?"

Eryn shrugged. "It's always been that way. Venitte and Amenkor are sister cities, the ties between us old and strong. And we've always been the greatest powers on the Frigean coast."

"But if the people in the vision are using the Sight, then it must be Venitte that is attacking."

"I don't believe that." Eryn caught my gaze briefly, her eyes flaring, before returning to her scrutiny of the harbor, back stiff. "We've had good relations with Venitte for decades. There's no reason for Venitte to attack. It makes no sense."

I shifted in my seat, trying to recall everything that Avrell had told me regarding Venitte during the last month. But there was nothing. Nothing important anyway. Venitte had always aided Amenkor whenever possible, the Mistress and the Lord of Venitte always on good terms. There were occasional trade disputes, but Venitte was far enough south that these were rarely so serious that the merchants' guild couldn't handle it themselves. The rulers of the two cities almost never got involved.

Eryn suddenly sighed. "It doesn't matter," she said, turning away from the city to face me. "Whoever is attacking—Venitte or someone else—they are using the Sight. Which means we need to prepare."

"How?"

Eryn grimaced. "We need to begin training the remaining Servants. Marielle and Laurren have already had the minimal training required, so they can help. But if what you have Seen is true, then those that are attacking are extremely powerful. It takes effort to destroy a building as large as the watchtowers with one strike. It takes brute force. We'll have to start building on Marielle's and Laurren's abilities as well, and anyone else who shows early promise."

"When should we start?"

"As soon as possible. If the attack is coming this summer, that doesn't leave us much time."

I was already working with Avrell, learning about the political situation along the coast and the daily activities of the Mistress.

Then there was Marielle with the reading and writing and now numbers, Westen for dagger play and defense. . . .

I sighed.

Eryn placed a reassuring hand on my shoulder, misinterpreting my sigh. "Scrying, especially that far into the future, is always unreliable and difficult to control. There may not be an attack coming at all. And if it is coming, it may not be this summer. Right now, we have more pressing matters."

"Such as?"

Eryn didn't hear the sarcasm in my voice, or did and chose to ignore it. She settled herself into her seat. "Such as figuring out how to distribute all the food we have stored for the winter."

I scowled. "I don't see why we can't just hand it out."

Eryn laughed and shook her head. "And how would you go about doing that? Look at all the people in the city, Varis. Think of how many of them there are. How are you going to make certain everyone gets what they deserve? And what about the people that already have supplies of their own? We don't want to be giving food out to people who don't need it, and there are plenty of people in the city who would take advantage of something like that. Even if they don't have their own foodstocks, what's to stop them from going back twice? Or going to two different warehouses? Or three? No. Hoarding is going to be a serious problem, no matter how we distribute the food."

I thought about what she'd said, thought about how I'd lived on the Dredge, taking whatever I could, storing it for leaner times when necessary, especially during winter. On the Dredge I would have killed for food if I'd needed to. Most of those who lived in the warrens beyond the Dredge would. None of them would think twice about it.

I grunted in agreement, suddenly thankful the baker—the

white-dusty man—had been there to keep me from such desperation. "I didn't think it would be this difficult."

Eryn smiled in understanding but didn't say anything, sitting
back thoughtfully.

I tried to take another sip of the tea but found the cup empty.
"So, how are we going to distribute the food?"

Eryn glanced toward me. "I have a few ideas. Avrell seems to
think they'll work as well."

I frowned. I hadn't realized Eryn and Avrell had been discussing
it, and didn't understand why the thought bothered me so much.
"What ideas?"

Eryn hesitated. "I think we should make them work for it.
Have the women make bread from the grains at common ovens, or
curdle milk for cheese and butter. Have the men help to rebuild
the warehouse district, fish when they can, butcher the cattle.
Children can help with the hauling of wood and rock, or water for
the workers. Find something to do for everyone willing, something
constructive. For every day's work, they get an allowance of food."

Rebuild the warehouse district.

I felt my stomach clench. But not from regret over causing the
fire that had destroyed it. No. Not this time.

My stomach clenched because in the vision the warehouse district had been burning, just like the rest of the city. Because it had
been rebuilt.

Before I could respond to Eryn's suggestion, or tell her about
the warehouses burning in the vision, a horn began to sound from
the city below, followed closely by the sudden clamor of bells. The
noise grew as more and more bells were added, until it seemed
every bell in Amenkor was tolling.

Eryn and I shared a look, then rose and moved to the balcony's
edge.

At the docks below, men were scrambling to clear a mooring, others lining up along the wharf, crowding its edges in the last of the sun's light.

"Look," Eryn said.

I turned to where she pointed and saw, coming through the entrance to the harbor, a ship. One of its masts had been snapped off, and its sails were torn and ragged.

I felt Erick move up behind me. I hadn't even heard his snoring halt.

"What is it?" he asked, without a trace of sleepiness.

"It's one of the ships we sent out to search for supplies," I said, as it began a slow crawl toward the dock.

†

The wharf was thronged with people, all trying to see the ship as it pulled in to dock, their faces tense with worry in the torchlight. The entire wharf was ablaze with light, every torch, lantern, and wide bowl of oil lit.

I frowned as my escort of guardsmen began forcing a way through the crowd. The escort was led by Baill, who'd been waiting at the bottom of the steps of the promenade with twenty guardsmen behind him when I'd emerged from the palace. Without a word, Avrell had joined up with Eryn, Erick, and me inside the palace. It had taken us only thirty minutes to reach the wharf, the streets nearly empty.

"I can't see the captain of the ship," Avrell said, frustration clear as we ground to a halt.

"It's Mathew," I said. At his questioning look, I added, "It's Borund's ship, the first one to leave once the blockade was lifted. I can tell by the flags on the main mast."

He nodded. Ahead, Baill suddenly bellowed wordlessly and the crowd parted, startled.

We began moving forward again, tension rising as the crowd closed in behind us and crushed us together. I gasped as the escort was pressed up on all sides, started to panic when I realized I was too short to be noticed and could get trampled. Then a reassuring hand grabbed my shoulder, and I twisted to see Erick behind me. He smiled tightly, eyes darting to either side. Eryn and Avrell were close behind him.

"I wonder what happened," Erick said, shouting above the noise. "Did you see the mast had been broken?"

I shrugged, didn't try to answer as I was jostled sharply to the left, a piece of guardsman's armor digging into my side. I hissed in pain and irritation, fought the urge to shove back, to draw my own dagger in response.

Just when I felt the crowd becoming too much for me, even with Erick at my back, we broke through to the dock, spilling out into cleared space. A line of guardsmen held back the throng of people, the noise on this side almost deafening. People lined the wharf in both directions, those on the edge threatening to drop over into the dark water. A few hapless fools already had, bobbing in the swells as they fought their way back to shore cursing and spluttering. Others had mounted the wharf's supports, or were dangling out over the water, one foot on solid dock, held up by a grip on a rope. Those lucky enough to be on a ship moored close were packed at the railing or swung from the rigging. Almost everyone was shouting or whistling.

"They all know we're low on food for the winter," Avrell said grimly, scanning the mob. "And they know the ships were sent out to find more. It's going to be all kinds of hells getting this to a safe warehouse without the mob running off with it."

Baill turned from scowling at the crowd to look toward the end of the dock, where the battered ship was already moored. "Looks like the ship's already docked," he muttered.

"And Borund has already beaten us here," Avrell added.

Baill grunted.

I looked toward the end of the dock, saw Borund's red-and-gold coat, easy to pick out among the scrambling dockworker's drab grays and browns and bare skin. William stood at his side, and I felt myself straighten. They were both talking to Mathew, the ship's captain dressed in the same dark green coat he'd worn the first time I'd seen him, years before. But his face looked haggard, eyes dark with lack of sleep and shadowed in the flickering light.

"Let's find out what happened," I said grimly, thinking of the vision.

We headed down the dock, stepping over coils of ropes and around stacked crates, the wood creaking beneath us as the waves slapped against its supports. The closer we got to the ship, the more damaged it appeared. The sails were shredded, held together by hasty stitching and prayers. The foremast had been torn completely away, the splintered stump at the prow the only piece remaining. Rigging hung limp and useless, what was left working obviously repaired. The workers hastily unloading casks and cargo seemed shaken, eyes wide, movements sharp, even the few darker-skinned Zorelli workers from the far southern islands. And there weren't as many crew as there should have been.

My frown deepened.

"—found a good supply of dried fruits in Temall nonetheless," Mathew was saying as we approached. His voice was hollow, sounding aged and empty.

"Good, good," Borund muttered, motioning to William, who was keeping a running tally, marking papers beneath the lamps scattered along the end of the dock. "What else?"

Mathew drew breath, but then held it as he saw us approaching, his brow creasing.

Borund caught the look and turned, straightening. William scribbled down a last item, then glanced up, stilling when he saw me, eyes going wide before darting sharply away.

Something stabbed deep into my chest, thin and cold, like a dagger's blade. I winced, found I didn't want to be here anymore, but bit back the feeling and concentrated on Borund and Mathew.

"Mistress," Borund said, his voice happy, relieved, and pained at the same time. He bowed, Mathew and William doing the same a moment later. As he rose, he said, "Mathew has brought us back a full load of food for the winter."

"But at a cost," Mathew said. "We lost twenty crew to the storm."

"So this was done by a storm," Eryn said, voice sharp and commanding. The Mistress' voice.

"Yes," Mathew said, uncertain where to look, at Eryn or me. "We picked up our last cargo a week ago in Temall. We knew we were cutting it close—the sea was already rough—but thought the need for the food was worth the risk. We headed out to sea immediately." He drew in a steadying breath, wincing. I suddenly noticed his hands were bandaged and raw from working the ropes and wondered how many bruises were hidden by the clothes he wore. "The storm hit us only half a day out. We thought to skirt it, but got caught in the squall and were dragged out to deep ocean. By the time it ended, we were two days off course, our mast was broken, and we'd lost good men. We managed to limp back, but it wasn't certain we'd make it. The seas are the worst I've seen in years."

"But the cargo is intact?" Avrell demanded.

I glared at him, and he stiffened.

"I'm sorry, Mistress, but if he's brought back a full cargo, without spoilage, then we may have enough supplies for the city to survive the winter with tight rationing."

I wasn't about to let it go, but Mathew interceded by saying, "Then perhaps the loss of men was worth it."

I let the awkward silence hold for a moment, then turned to Mathew. "So a storm caused all this damage?"

"Yes," Mathew said again, and I traded a relieved glance with Eryn and Erick. "Why is that important?"

Before I could answer, Borund spoke, his tone serious. "Because most of the ships we sent out along with yours haven't returned. We've had no word of them. In fact, we'd assumed your ship was lost as well. We'd hoped you'd have word of the others' fate."

Mathew shook his head. "I heard nothing of the other ships at any port we stopped at, even on the return trip."

I swore silently to myself. What had happened to all of the ships? Where had they gone? And did it have anything to do with the city burning to the ground?

No one said anything for a long moment, faces taut with worry.

Finally, Borund said succinctly, "We should get these supplies off-loaded and to the warehouses."

"Of course," I said. I glanced toward William, but he refused to look at me, head lowered to the papers he clutched, white-knuckled, in one hand.

The dagger of pain I'd felt earlier inside me twisted, dug deeper.

I nodded to Mathew, not trusting myself to speak, then turned away, my escort enfolding me.

"So," Avrell said as we moved, "we know nothing new."

Trying to keep the bitterness over William's reaction out of my voice, I said, "But we have food."

Behind, I felt Erick's attention fix on me, concerned and troubled, but he said nothing.

"I'll have to bring down another brace of guardsmen from the palace in order to control this mob and help get the food safely to the warehouses," Baill said, voice all business. He turned to me for permission, his face harsh with scars in the firelight on the docks.

I wondered again if he'd had any dealings with Alendor and the consortium or whether he'd simply been following the Mistress' orders, but nodded. "Do it."

I sighed, pushed thoughts of William and Baill and the consortium into the background, and looked over the horde of people on the docks. I saw a riot of faces, mostly those from the coast, with dark hair and light skin. But there were others as well: the small, dark-skinned Zorelli from the south, of course; a few of the followers of the Tear of Taniece, their straw-colored hair vibrant in the torchlight, the blue mark of the Tear beneath the right eye appearing black in the night; even a few of the Kandish from the east, their hair braided and feathered, their clothes merely lengths of cloth wrapped and tied around them in intricate folds. All people we had to keep alive. There wouldn't be any more ships, any more food. Not until spring. I could feel it, an emptiness deep inside. Like hunger.

"Now all we have to do is survive."

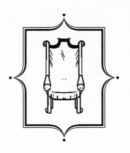

Chapter 5

"NOW HOLD ON TO THE THREADS, and I'll attempt to break through the barrier," Eryn said.

We were standing at opposite ends of a rectangular plot of winter-dead flowers in one of the palace's enclosed gardens. Ten Servants including Marielle and Laurren—a third of the total Servants in the palace—were arrayed around the edges of the garden, watching, their eyes intent, focused beneath the river on the eddies and currents. In a few moments, they'd be asked to do the same thing. Most of them were nervous, the river rippling around them, disturbed. Only Laurren appeared calm, her mouth turned down in a frown.

The stone of the path crunched under my feet as I shifted, but the noise was lost in the background sound of wind, the currents of the river flowing around me smoothly. I concentrated on the threads of the river I'd woven into a wall of force before me. Not as solid as the barrier that Eryn had constructed in her private garden, when I'd stormed in to confront her about the wine hidden in the stablehouse, it was still stronger than anything I'd constructed before. I'd improved steadily during each daily practice session, after Eryn had tested my strength the first week, determining what I had already learned by necessity on the Dredge and as Borund's body-guard. In the weeks since, she'd pushed me harder and harder, fo-cusing on the techniques I already knew, refining them, using me as an example to hone the Servants' skills. And I'd continued to ex-periment on my own.

"Are you ready?" Eryn asked, voice deceptively calm.

Tying the last threads of the wall together, I scanned the close-knit mesh of power for flaws, then glanced across the plot of dried leaves and spent flower stalks at Eryn. Her hair gleamed a shiny black in the winter sunlight, her face calm and expectant, hands folded before her.

My eyes narrowed. She expected me to fail. I could see it in her eyes. We'd worked on the barrier for the last two weeks, and each time I'd broken under her assault, the threads fraying as she beat at them relentlessly. And when the barrier failed, Eryn would send out a final punch that would knock me onto my ass.

But not this time. I was tired of picking myself up out of the dirt. Especially in front of all of the others.

"I'm ready," I said, and settled into a relaxed stance.

Eryn struck before I'd finished answering, a hard thrust hitting low, where she'd caught me unprepared once before. But I'd rein-forced the barrier there, and the thrust slid to one side, its power dispersing into the natural flow of the currents around me. Another lesson it had taken a week of bruising to master. I didn't need to stop the blows; that used up too much energy. All I had to do was turn them to one side, let the river itself take care of it once the danger was past.

Eryn nodded in approval, then followed the initial thrust with three hard punches directly at the center of the barrier. Unlike the first thrust, which had been edged like a sword thrust, these punches were blunt, with all the weight of Eryn's power behind them, like fists.

I grunted as they struck, twisted slightly as I let the threads bend and absorb some of the power before turning them aside. Immediately, I reset the barrier, slid back into the balanced stance I'd learned from Erick.

"Good," Eryn said. "Very good."

To either side, I heard the other Servants murmur, but I didn't relax, never let my gaze waver from Eryn, my jaw set.

Eryn's eyes hardened. "Now let's see how long you can hold it."

I barely had time to draw a breath to brace myself.

She struck high, a single thrust as thin and deadly as a rapier, followed almost simultaneously with two blunt punches near my midsection. Blows began to rain down on my left flank, hard, vicious cuts that made me gasp with the effort to turn them, while at the same time, macelike thuds landed to my right. I deflected them all, breath coming sharper as the attacks continued, slicing from the left, from above, dagger blades of power cutting in from below, scoring hard against the barrier. The wall flexed, allowed the heaviest thrusts to slip off to the sides, then firmed to allow the blade cuts to glance away. The attacks didn't cease, coming harder, faster, from all sides. I heaved short breaths through my nose, my stance shifting from the relaxed pose of a Seeker to the more familiar defensive half crouch of gutterscum on the Dredge. My breathing altered, coming in gasps now, and sweat broke out on my forehead, between my shoulder blades and breasts, in my armpits.

But the barrier held.

On the far side of the flower bed, Eryn's expression changed. Her mouth pressed into a thin line, lips whitening. Creases appeared in her forehead as she focused. The hands clasped so casually before her tightened.

I felt a surge of triumph. She'd broken through my barriers before without blinking, had barely even moved. I used the sudden

elation to shore up the barrier's edge, only to feel Eryn suddenly retreat, her energy pulling back, swirling around her as she regrouped.

I hesitated, uncertain whether the match had ended, began to
let the barrier go as I straightened, a tentative grin touching my
lips.

When my threads started to unravel, Eryn struck again.

The initial impact was stunning, and I cried out and fell back,
felt my barrier shudder beneath the assault, felt its edges fray before I could regroup. Stone bit into my hand as I stumbled and
caught my balance. Then I lurched forward with a sharp curse,
knelt down painfully on one knee, and poured energy into the wall.
A cruel smirk twisted Eryn's mouth, and I growled, thrusting the
barrier higher to match the intensity of her blows. Without pause,
she hammered at the wall on all sides, each blow shuddering with
force, beating at me mercilessly.

I found myself using every last bit of strength just to keep the
barrier erect, coherent and solid. I had nothing left to put into de-
flecting the thrusts, into shunting their power aside. I raised my
hands before me, fingers splayed, and braced myself against each
crashing blow, wincing at the sheer force Eryn put behind each one.

I wasn't certain how long I could hold out, but I gritted my
teeth and dug in. This was the longest I'd lasted against her since
the training had started. I wasn't about to yield.

It's a trick.

I hissed as the voice bled through the currents. A man's voice,
scented with a pungent incense I didn't recognize. Someone from
the throne.

Fear lanced through me. The Fire was weakening. But I couldn't
shore it up. All of my energy was pouring into the shield.

It's a trick, the man's voice repeated, more sharply this time,
stronger, full of authority, the accent strange, almost indecipher-

able. *She's distracting you with the heavy bludgeoning. She's undermining you somewhere else while you try to hold steady.*

A cold presence slid around me, ephemeral and heavily scented, like smoke. I could feel him as he paused before my barrier, could see a vague shape, a hint of clothes, of a wide face with a short, angled beard and shoulder-length hair. He scanned the shield, dark eyes darting left and right, examining the ripples on the barrier's surface as I repulsed each blow.

The shield was weakening. My strength was ebbing, draining away faster than I thought possible.

There! the man suddenly spat, turning toward me, the vague essence of an arm pointing to the left corner of the barrier. *Look! She's penetrated the shield there!*

I hissed and frowned, but scanned the area he'd indicated, crying out as Eryn struck again, the energy from the thrust seeping through the wall and hitting my shoulder with bruising force.

And then I saw it: a thin hole in the shield. As if someone had poked through with the tip of their knife. A thin ribbon curled out from the hole back to Eryn.

The cold presence of the man stepped closer, close enough so I could see the color of his eyes. Tawny brown, flecked with yellow. *She's stealing your strength, Varis,* he hissed. *Stop her.*

I shot the man a hateful glare, spat through clenched teeth, "How?"

His eyes narrowed in confusion, then cleared with sudden understanding. Shoulders straightening, he turned abruptly and said, *Like this.*

Something slid through me, shivering up through my body—

And then part of the shield let go, the threads parting like wisps.

On the river, Eryn's shoulders straightened with pure satisfac-

tion and the eddies around her gathered for another blow. She released the hammer blow. It contained enough force to shatter the
rest of the shield, to knock me flat, and it descended with horrible,
hideous grace.

A moment before it struck, the threads of the unraveled section
of the shield coalesced into a small ball of dense force and shot
through the needlelike hole, down the ribbon, and hit Eryn.

At the same time, the shivering presence inside me vanished.

Crying out, hearing an echoing cry of pain and surprise from
Eryn on the far side of the garden, I seized control of the fraying
barrier and threw it up in front of Eryn's final blow.

It landed. The barrier held for an instant, for a single indrawn
gasp, shunted part of the force aside . . . and then it shattered.

I was crushed to the ground with bruising force, stone cutting
into my hands, into my side and my face. I lay gasping, stunned,
vaguely aware of cries from the other Servants, of shouts from the
ever present guardsmen who'd been watching and waiting outside
the garden, unable to believe that Eryn would put that much energy into destroying my shield. Anger punched through the daze,
and I shoved myself up into a seated position before suddenly re-
membering the voice from the throne.

I thrust myself deep, heading for the barrier of Fire. I built up
a new barrier as I went, weaving the threads in a slightly different
pattern, one that Eryn had taught me for use against the personalities in the throne. I held it before me like a net as I came upon the
Fire, the mesh tight and not as flexible as for defense. I couldn't believe that the Fire had weakened so much that one of the personalities had escaped, had been freed enough that he could create a
semitangible form on the river, enough that he could seize control
of the river itself through me. Whoever the man was, he'd *used* me,
taken control of the shield I'd held long enough to rip a hole in it,
to shape that power into a stone to strike out at Eryn.

A frisson of fear for Eryn flashed through me, but I thrust it aside as I scanned the blazing white flames that contained the voices, listening to the raging cacophony on the far side. They seemed to be shrieking with laughter, the strongest close to the edge of the firewall, taunting me, belittling me. I stoked the Fire enough to send flames reaching toward them, scattered them like leaves before a wind, but they returned, the mocking laughter increasing.

I growled in frustration, keeping the net ready, and began a methodical scrutiny of the Fire, circling it, searching for weaknesses, for areas where the wall of the Fire had thinned.

But there was nothing. Nothing I could see anyway.

Something Erick had said while training me on the Dredge echoed up from memory: *No defense is perfect. There is always a flaw. You just have to be patient enough to find it.*

I'd used the advice on the Dredge and while guarding Borund in order to survive. But I'd always been the one searching for the flaw in someone else's defenses.

Now the blade was reversed.

I found I didn't like the feeling.

Frowning, I concentrated and traced the scent of pungent incense on the eddies, found it residing inside the sphere of Fire, as expected. Inside, even though somehow the man had penetrated the barrier enough to take control. I could feel him watching me, could sense that there were others around him, also watching, not taunting me or screaming or howling like those voices beating against the edge of the Fire. One of those with him was the woman who smelled of oak and wine.

Who are you? I asked, curt and demanding.

My name is Cerrin, he said, not reacting to my anger. Then he added, *Not all of the voices in the throne are your enemies, Varis.*

I glared at the seething wall in consternation, let the chaos of the voices inside roll over me, then spun and retreated. The net I'd formed unraveled around me as I went.

"Mistress!"

I surfaced from the river with a shudder, blinked up into the winter sunlight and the blurry faces of Marielle, another Servant, and a concerned guardsman until my eyes adjusted, then dragged myself to my knees and stood, glancing around, a pair of guardsmen reaching out to help steady me.

"Mistress," Marielle gasped again, eyes white with concern. "Are you all right?"

"I'm fine," I spat, fuming. "Where's Eryn?"

Marielle, the Servants, and the guardsmen stepped back.

Any anger I'd felt for Eryn evaporated when I saw her crumpled form on the far side of the dead garden, two other guardsmen leaning over her, Laurren and another Servant kneeling at her side. Laurren rolled her onto her back as I watched and Eryn moaned.

"What did he do to you?" I murmured to myself and I pushed through the concerned Servants and guardsmen and knelt down beside Laurren. I couldn't see any marks on Eryn, couldn't see any damage.

"What did you do to her?" Laurren spat, both fear and awe in her voice.

"I don't know," I said.

Eryn moaned again, and her eyelids fluttered open, wincing at the sunlight. She brought one arm up to shade her eyes. "What happened?" she asked, but then she seemed to remember, her eyes focusing sharply on me. "Where did you learn to do that?"

My stomach knotted. I didn't want to admit to her that it had been one of the voices. Didn't want to admit to myself what that might mean.

So I let the anger surface, let it color my voice. "I didn't *learn* to do *anything*. I did what I had to in order to survive, as I've always done." I sat back, giving her room to sit up, waving the uncertain Servants and guardsmen back. She reached out one arm for support. I caught it before Laurren could, helped her steady herself. "I was winning," I said, "but then you cheated."

"Cheated!"

"You started draining away my strength!"

"That's not cheating," Eryn huffed. She struggled up from where she sat on the stones, brushed the dust and dirt off her white dress. "In a true battle, do you think your opponents are going to show you all their tricks before they attack? Of course not! They're going to do whatever it takes to win."

I scowled, but there wasn't much force behind it. There had never been any rules on the Dredge, I didn't know why I expected rules here in the palace. "You almost killed me with that last blast."

Eryn's face suddenly paled. "Oh, gods! I never meant for the blow to fall, at least not with that much force behind it. I meant for it to frighten you, but at the last moment I was going to pull it back, hit you with enough to knock you off-balance. But then that . . . that dart of power punched me in the gut along my own conduit and I lost control." She paused, the corners of her eyes tightening in what I'd come to recognize as a sign she was using her Sight.

After scanning me thoroughly, she relaxed.

"I don't see any permanent damage. But I'm surprised you survived it so unscathed." She frowned, then added in a considering voice, "You must be much stronger than I initially suspected."

I grunted, trying to hide the satisfied grin that tugged at the corners of my mouth. "What *did* I do?" I asked.

Eryn didn't answer, seemed suddenly to become aware of the Servants and guardsmen watching and listening closely. She scowled. "Break up into pairs as usual," she barked, motioning toward the Servants. "Marielle and Laurren, walk among them and help out where necessary."

After a pause, the Servants began to drift away, animated conversations instantly breaking out in lowered voices, glances shooting toward me. Marielle gave me a tentative smile, then caught Laurren's arm. But Laurren refused to budge.

"I'm fine, Laurren," Eryn said. "Go help the others."

Grudgingly, Laurren allowed Marielle to pull her away.

I nodded to the attending guardsmen, who drifted back to their posts on the outskirts of the garden.

Eryn moved toward a stone bench in one corner, wincing as she went, one hand going to her side. I followed, sitting down heavily. I was hot and sweaty and covered with dirt. And I felt bruised from head to toe.

We watched the Servants as they practiced for a moment, Laurren barking out orders to strengthen an edge, to tighten those flows, Marielle pointing out weaknesses in a soft voice, smiling and nodding encouragement.

"So was it Cerrin? Or Atreus?"

Eryn turned when I stiffened in shock.

"I don't believe you just 'happened' to suddenly discover how to send that dart through my conduit. I'm surprised you found the conduit at all. Someone from the throne must have helped you. So who was it?"

My eyes narrowed defiantly, but Eryn's gaze never faltered. I could see her exhaustion in her face, her weariness, but she still had a core of stubborn strength remaining.

I forced myself to back down, took a deep, steadying breath. "It was Cerrin." When Eryn only nodded, I asked, "Who is he?"

"One of the Seven. They are the ones that created the Skewed Throne nearly fifteen hundred years ago. They are the heart of the throne, the force that binds it and holds it together. To some extent, they can control the other voices of the throne as well."

I thought about the group of voices I'd sensed surrounding Cerrin in the throne. The calm voices in the maelstrom. And I suddenly recalled, with horrid clarity, the creation of the throne. I'd been forced to relive it when Eryn had thrust me onto the throne months before, had felt one of the Seven's pain as they watched the others die as the two thrones consumed them.

I shuddered.

"Have you felt them before today? Have they . . . influenced you in any way?"

When I opened my eyes, I found Eryn watching me closely.

"No," I said, but then caught myself, thought back to that first meeting with Avrell, Nathem, Ireen, and the captains of the guards. I'd felt something then, as if I'd stepped back . . . or been pushed aside. And then there was the woman who smelled of oak and wine. "Yes. It's happened before. But not like today. A woman tried to seize control while I was meeting with the merchants. But she simply tried to convince me to let her have control. Cerrin slipped free even while I was trying to hold him back. He's the one who manipulated the river and sent the stone through the conduit."

Eryn's eyes grew grim. "The woman was most likely Liviann, another of the Seven. As long as the other Seven are with her, she's not a threat. But if she's alone . . ." She shook her head. "I'm more concerned about Cerrin being able to slip past the Fire enough to seize that much control of the river. Not to mention the protective net I showed you."

"Can I alter the net somehow to keep him contained?" I thought back to the transparent image of the man who'd taken control, recalled the faint outlines of the clothes he wore. A long, tapered coat, the cut archaic; a yellow silk shirt with a strange neckline; breeches of the same material as the coat. And boots, the leather sides high and flared wide, folded down in a style I'd never seen before. His voice had been accented as well, the words somehow clipped, the flow of the sentences not quite right.

"I don't know. I've shown you the strongest net I know of for containing the voices." A note of weariness had crept into her voice. She stood, began to make her way toward the open double doors to the garden, pausing only to allow the still practicing Servants to pass. "We'll have to experiment," Eryn continued. "Try to strengthen it somehow. Perhaps tomorrow."

"No," I said, too sharply.

Eryn glanced toward me, eyebrow raised.

I sighed, then grimaced. My muscles were already beginning to protest. "Avrell wants to show me the construction on the new warehouse district, and the setup of the kitchen and warehouse on the Dredge."

Eryn nodded, forced a smile through her exhaustion, her shoulders sagging slightly. "That's just as well," she said. "I think I'm going to be bruised after today. A day to recover would be welcome."

She halted as we entered the shaded interior of the palace, then grinned. "It appears that you're going to need the rest more than me, however."

Frowning, my eyes still adjusting to the shadows, I turned—

And groaned aloud when I saw Westen leaning patiently against the far wall.

"Ready to play?" he asked with a grin.

✝

I leaned down to pick up a stray mud-brick but halted halfway, jerking upright with a gasp and a blistering curse.

"Mistress?" Avrell asked, real concern in his voice. He'd halted a few steps ahead of me in his careful progress down the street on the edge of what used to be the warehouse district. The street was littered with stacked stone, lumber, loose rope, and mud-brick, and was coated with thick dust.

"I'm fine," I said through gritted teeth, silently sending Eryn and Westen to the deepest of hells while massaging the muscle screaming in protest in my lower back. But it wasn't just them. Avrell had gotten tired of walking everywhere within the city and forced Marielle to start giving me riding lessons. The first lesson had been excruciating, worse than one of Westen's training sessions. I'd hurt in places I hadn't even known existed.

And all of it was beginning to wear on my body.

Avrell hesitated, but moved on. Beside me, Erick scooped up the mud-brick I'd reached for and replaced it on the nearest heap.

"*Are* you all right?" he asked, pitched low so that none of the accompanying guards could hear.

I bit off another curse and nodded. "Fine. Just a little . . . weary."

Erick nodded as if that explained everything, face serious. But I could feel him silently laughing underneath.

Ahead, Avrell halted on the edge of a wide break in the buildings and streets. As we pulled up even with him, both Erick and I raised a hand to shade our eyes from the sunlight.

"Impressive," Erick said after a moment.

I had to agree.

Where the warehouse district had been reduced to charred support beams and soot-stained, crumbled stone in the fire two months before, Avrell and his labor crews had cleared a wide swath of flat land. Men, skin drenched with sweat, clothed only in breeches, were loading up carts with debris on all sides, keeping only what stone could still be used in the new construction. Everything else was being carted away, to the edges of the city, near the uninhabited northern jut of land that enclosed the harbor. I'd seen the work from my balcony and the roof of the tower over the last few weeks, but that had been from a distance, the sheer scope of the work being done somehow reduced. But here, where I could see the workers coated with char and dust from shifting the stones, hear the group leaders barking orders . . .

"We're just about finished sorting and clearing out the old stone, salvaging what we can from the lost buildings themselves," Avrell said. "Once we're done with that, we'll shift the workers to laying down new foundations, or shoring up the old ones where possible."

"How long do you think it will take to rebuild everything completely?" I asked.

Avrell scowled. "At this rate, all winter and most of the summer besides. But I expect that things will pick up shortly."

"Why's that?"

The First motioned toward the work crews loading up the carts. "Because we don't have many workers right now. It's early in the winter yet. Most people have put their own stores back and are using them now."

"So there's no need to send anyone to the work lines to get the credit chips for food," Erick said.

"Correct. But once people's personal stores begin to run dry . . ."

I grunted.

Captain Catrell had sent the city guardsmen out to warn people to ration, and that theft and hoarding of goods would be punished severely. Two houses had been raided in the first week after the announcement, the families arrested and confined, their food portioned and distributed among the warehouses being run by the merchants. At the same time, the guardsmen had announced the work policy. Men, women, and children could report to the warehouses for work details. In exchange for a day's labor, they'd receive enough rations for a meal, which they could get in one of the kitchens the servants from the palace had established near each of the warehouses. Most women were sent to grind grist into flour, or to the communal ovens to bake the bread that would be distributed at the end of the day to the kitchens, or to repair the fishing nets for the fishing fleets, or any of a hundred other similar tasks. Some worked in the kitchens themselves, along with the children, under the supervision of the palace servants. Most of the men were sent to the warehouse district or the fishing boats, or into the forests east of the city to hunt for game or cut down timber for the recon- struction. Some joined the city guard, if they could show some skill with a sword, then were used to police the makeshift warehouses, the kitchens, and the supplies.

Things had changed in the palace as well. A small stock of food had been kept inside the palace walls for use in the palace itself. The rest had been sent into the city. I'd insisted, despite protests from Avrell and Erick, who argued that the palace had to remain visibly stable and that the guards needed to be well fed to be effective. I'd relented somewhat regarding the guardsmen, but if the city was going to starve, then so would everyone in the palace.

I'd lived on the Dredge. I knew what it was to be hungry, knew that I would survive. Avrell and the others would learn they could survive on very little as well.

"Would you like to take a closer look?" Avrell asked, breaking into my thoughts. I glanced toward him, saw the look of appeal in his eyes, hidden behind his administrator's blank mask.

"Of course," I said.

Avrell grinned, then led us into the open space, pointing out piles of stone and stacked lumber as we moved. "This is the largest building that was lost. You can see the outline of the original foundation here and here. Nathem and I decided to start with that building first, then move on to the others later, since we can use this one's walls for supports for the others if necessary. We salvaged enough stone to get the entire building built, and I've got carpenters and masons from the guilds planning how to repair and relay the foundation, starting within the week."

Avrell's voice fell into the background as we continued, relating all the plans. The farther afield we moved, the more I began to orient myself, using the surrounding streets and the outlines of the lost buildings as reference points. A warm hand of dread began to close over my heart as I realized we were approaching the alley where I'd been ambushed by Alendor's son, Cristoph.

I halted in the spot where the alley had stood, kicked at the blackened dirt and the stone of the cobbles. All trace of the walls that had trapped me—of the crates that had hemmed me in and hampered my movements as Cristoph and his men surrounded me and beat me—were gone, cleared away by the fire and the workers.

Alendor had led me here, let me follow him and his own bodyguards from the tavern called the Splintered Bow so that his son and henchmen could trap me in the alley. All because Cristoph had tried to kill me earlier on the wharf and I'd managed to turn the blade against him and his friend instead. Cristoph had survived the encounter. His friend hadn't.

I glanced toward Erick, saw the grim expression on his face. He recognized the alley as well. I'd only survived the ambush because Erick had arrived and intervened. He'd almost died here, trying to save me.

I could see the same thought echoed in his eyes.

"Is there something wrong?" Avrell asked.

I suddenly realized his constant stream of information about the reconstruction had halted minutes before, and I turned toward him with a tight smile. "No. I was here once before. Before the fire. This is where Alendor's son ambushed me."

Avrell glanced down solemnly at the scuffed and fire-cracked cobbles. "I see."

We lapsed into an awkward silence, broken by a sharp yelp of pain and the sounds of a scuffle from the nearest line of men loading up the carts.

All three of us turned. The escort of guardsmen closed in around me, but I pushed forward, Erick and Avrell falling into step as we came up on the group of men. The gathering parted as soon as they saw us coming, revealing two men grappling with each other on the ground, cursing, dirt and dust flying. One of them was younger, leaner, only a boy, body writhing like a snake as the other, heavier man tried to force him to the ground.

"Bloody cursed gutterscum," the older man growled. Then he landed a sharp punch to the other's gut, the boy doubling over with a whoof of pain followed by a hiss of pure fury.

The heavier man thrust the boy to the ground, then staggered upright, panting heavily, eyes dark. He wiped a hand across his mouth, spat blood, lip curling up in a snarl. "This will teach ya."

He drew his foot back to kick the boy in the gut while he was down.

Rage flared inside me, hard and sharp, and without thought I lashed out, punching the heavyset man in the chest with the river.

The man staggered backward, eyes going wide in surprise, breath gushing from his lungs. The punch had come from nowhere, been landed by nothing that he could see. The ring of spectators caught him before he fell, as surprised as he was, then set him roughly on the ground as he tried to catch his breath.

The boy had dragged himself into a defensive crouch, watched me now with a feral, hateful gaze as I stepped forward between the two men. I could see the Dredge on the boy, like a dark cloak hanging over his shoulders. He was maybe fourteen years old, with sharp dark brown eyes and blond hair made muddy by layers of dirt and soot and sweat.

"What's going on here?" I asked, voice hard as stone. I glared at the heavyset man where he sat, legs still weak from my punch, breath still short. When he didn't answer, I turned my gaze on the rest of those gathered.

They shuffled where they stood, eyes not rising to meet mine. They'd recognized me, knew me as the Mistress.

I grunted with contempt, then turned to the boy.

He shifted backward, the movement hauntingly familiar. He was gutterscum, just like me. I could guess which way he'd bolt, could see the careful balance of options in his eyes.

The fact that he hadn't bolted already told me how desperate he was.

"What happened?" I asked, voice still hard. He wouldn't respond to anything else.

His gaze darted to the heavyset man, then returned. "He kicked me."

"Lying, filthy, fucking shit!" the man spat, face turning red as he tried to regain his feet. But I could read the truth in the men around him, the way they shifted away from the man, the way their eyes couldn't meet mine.

The boy scowled, and I could see him on the edge of fleeing. Back to the Dredge, back to the life he knew. His despair was clear: he'd taken a chance on the rumors of food for work, had risked coming out of the Dredge to find out if it were true, and this is what he'd found, what he'd expected to find.

It was more than I had risked at his age.

I shifted and the heavyset man halted where he'd struggled to his feet, eyes fearful.

I turned back to the boy. "Why did he kick you?"

Disbelief clouded the boy's eyes briefly as he realized I believed him, then he shot the man a deadly glare. "Because I'm gutter-scum."

Another man stepped forward, and the guardsmen behind me tensed. Erick motioned for them to wait as the man ducked his head.

"The boy's right. Hant's been after him all day, makin com-ments, flickin him with stones when he wasna lookin. I wouldna taken it as long as the boy did."

Behind, Avrell shifted closer and murmured, "The boy's one of the few we've had come to work for us from the Dredge."

Avrell's words were bland, but the meaning was clear. He ex-pected this type of condescension for those that came from the Dredge to continue.

Unless something were done now. Something significant.

I turned to Hant. The heavyset man was now uncertain. He could feel the shift in attitude among the men around him, could feel the blade now balanced against him.

"Erick," I said, and felt Erick step up beside me, motions pre-cise and formal.

"Yes, Mistress."

The boy gasped as he realized who I was. A low murmur ran through the gathered men as well. What they'd suspected had been confirmed.

"This kind of attitude can't continue. It *will not* continue." I pitched my voice loud enough so that all of those around us could hear. "No one in this city is better than any of the others. If those on the Dredge want to help us rebuild the warehouses, then they are welcome, and they will be treated exactly as everyone else is treated. There is only one city here: Amenkor." I turned back to Hant with pure contempt. "I want him punished. Do whatever you feel is necessary."

Avrell stepped forward, as if he'd been waiting for the opening. "I would suggest a public whipping."

I frowned, glanced toward Erick, who nodded minutely. "Do it," I said.

With a simple motion of his hand, Erick had the escorting guardsmen seize Hant and drag him, kicking, to one side. The rest of the workers stood silently, some with open shock, others with satisfaction or sympathy. I ignored them, turning to the man who'd stepped forward to defend the boy. "What's your name?"

The man seemed distracted by the scuffle Hant was raising behind me, but managed to say, "Danel, Mistress."

"And what do you do?"

Danel's attention began to focus more on me. "I'm a cobbler, Mistress."

I nodded, shot a questioning look toward Avrell.

The First must have read my intent on my face, for he said, "I believe we've been wasting your talents here hauling stone, Danel. We are always in need of people who can organize and lead the workers. Would you be interested?"

Danel nodded, too stunned to speak.

"Good," Avrell said. "Report to Nathem, the Second of the Mistress, tomorrow at the Priem warehouse in the upper city. He'll inform you as to what to do."

Danel nodded again, then stepped hesitantly back, where a few friends patted him on the back, eyes alight and excited.

I turned to the boy with a heavy frown, took in his relaxed stance—or as relaxed as anyone who lived on the Dredge ever got. "And your name?"

The boy frowned, the reaction automatic, then caught himself. Straightening slightly, burying his fear deep, so that most people wouldn't see it, he said defiantly, "Evander."

I waited until his defiance faltered slightly. "Tell those on the

Dredge that if they're willing to work, we can feed them. Not much, but more than they're likely to find on the Dredge this winter."

Then I turned away, retreating with Avrell, Erick, and the two remaining guardsmen who weren't dealing with Hant.

"You handled that well," Erick said, voice low enough only Avrell and I could hear.

I grunted. I wasn't so certain.

But Evander had done one thing: he'd reminded me of myself, of what the Dredge had been like.

"Do you think he'll spread the word on the Dredge?" Avrell asked. "Do you think he'll be believed?"

Memories churning up from the depths, I said with utter certainty, "He'll be believed. And he'll be more effective than the guardsmen."

"Why?"

I cast Avrell a knowing look. "Because gutterscum always recognizes gutterscum. Evander didn't see me as the Mistress. He saw me as Varis, from the Dredge."

I let Avrell think about that for a moment, then asked, "What about the kitchen and warehouse on the Dredge?"

"A shipment of food is being taken down there today. We're to meet up with Baill and the guards escorting the shipment near the bridge over the River."

Behind us, there was a sharp slap and a barked scream.

Someone had found a whip.

✝

We reached the bridge where the Dredge crossed the River and found Baill and the guardsmen already waiting, restless. Each of the three wagonloads of food was surrounded by twenty guardsmen, all with their hands on the hilts of their swords, all sweating nervously. They knew what had happened the last time we'd come to the Dredge. Only Baill seemed unconcerned, his bald head shining in the sunlight, his face fixed into a permanent frown.

"They know we're coming," the captain of the guard said as I approached. "We've seen at least three watching from the alleys and windows."

Which meant that there had probably been twenty. The entire slum would know by now.

"Are your men ready?" I asked. Baill grunted and nodded. "Then let's go."

He barked out an order and the first wagon lurched forward, two guardsmen in the seat. Avrell and Erick fell in beside me behind the first wagon, my escort staying close, drawing in tight, the other two wagons behind us. Baill remained in the lead.

As we passed over the arch of the bridge, the River flowing dark and smooth beneath us, I felt a niggling touch of the overwhelming dread I'd felt when we'd come the first time. But when the buildings closed in around us, the clean stone of the real Amenkor falling away to the decayed grit of the slums, that niggling sensation faded. Evander had helped me remember what I had been, and that I'd taken a chance and escaped.

Perhaps this winter, some of the others willing to take a chance could escape as well.

We were almost to the warehouse where Eryn had hidden the stores she'd smuggled into the city when Erick said suddenly, "Something's wrong."

"What?" Avrell asked.

I jerked out of my thoughts of Evander, of my old life, my hand settling onto my dagger. I glanced around in consternation, trying to pick up on what Erick had felt, then dove beneath the river. . . .

And felt it, too.

The Dredge was quiet.

But it wasn't empty.

I spun, tasting terror in the back of my throat as I darted forward past startled palace guardsmen, past the wagon, knowing even as I picked up speed that I was too late.

Behind, I heard Erick shout in warning, then curse under his breath as he started to follow. Ahead—

"What's the meaning of this?" Baill demanded, his voice loud, ringing out in the silence.

Too late, too late.

I rounded the front of the wagon, saw the street ahead blocked by a throng of men. No, not men. These were the dregs of the slums, the animals that hid in the deepest depths, that preyed on the gutterscum that were only trying to survive. Their grizzled faces, marked by scars and pockmarks and disease, were harsh in the sunlight, their mouths twisted into feral grins, their eyes insane with rage and death.

No wonder the Dredge was empty.

"We've come to take what's ours," the leader said.

And then a stone shot out of the crowd and found its mark, slamming into Baill's forehead with a sickening thud, and as he fell, as the scent of blood flooded the river, bitter and warm, the mob broke into a scream and roared forward.

The palace guardsmen surged forward to meet them. At my side, the horse pulling the first wagon screamed and reared up onto its hind legs, its eyes white with terror.

And then the mob collided with the guardsmen, and the world broke into a crush of bodies and sweat, of flickering blades and a hail of stone. I felt the initial impact of the two forces on the river, a pulsing wave rippling outward.

And then I was overwhelmed, men suddenly on all sides, the rearing horse thudding down into the mass of bodies with a sickening crunch. The scent of blood on the river became so thick I almost gagged.

"Varis!"

I spun, Erick's shout was almost lost in the tumult. Men crowded close on all sides, and my dagger was out, already blooded, although I didn't remember using it. A few palace guardsmen held my back for a moment, desperately trying to protect the wagonloads of food, before the thrust of the mob shoved them away and they were lost. The denizens of the slums closed in from all sides, coming from the alleys, from the narrows, crawling through the vacant windows of the buildings, through the darknesses that I'd always thought of as escapes. Through the press of bodies, I saw Erick lash out with his own dagger, saw a man scream in pain, blood flying, saw another lurch back before Erick's dagger took him in the throat. Thrusting the body aside, Erick stepped forward. But there were still too many men between us, all screaming, all intent on overwhelming the guards, on the food. Some had already reached the wagon, were smashing into the crates and barrels, clutching potatoes and squash and sacks of grain to their chests before leaping back into the mob. A sack of rice split and grains of white rained down, a few flicking my face, catching in my hair.

Rage enveloped me, sudden and intense, and pushing deep beneath the river, breath rushing out through flaring nostrils, I *pushed*, grunting with the effort.

Before me, men went flying, lifted forcibly up into the air and thrust away, and suddenly there was a clear path between Erick and me. Startled, he hesitated, then leaped into the opening, grabbing my arm.

"We have to get out of here!" he shouted.

I gave him a scathing, sarcastic glare and shot back, "Avrell! We have to find Avrell!"

He swore under his breath, scanned the mob, ducked as a piece of mud-brick shot past his head, then used his grip on my arm to shove me in a new direction. "This way!"

I stumbled forward, using my dagger and the river to force a path through the mob, Erick a steady presence at my back. As we angled away from the wagons, the press of bodies slackened.

And then suddenly we broke free, into the depths of an alley. Gasping, Erick drew up close to the wall, back brushing against the slick mud-brick. I settled into a crouch, breath harsh in my throat, heart thudding in my chest so hard it hurt, then jerked as someone else broke through the mob, streaking past us without a glance, a loaf of bread crushed to his chest, his expression ravenous.

I sucked in a haggard breath, then asked hoarsely, "Do you see Avrell?"

Erick shook his head. "No. Nor Baill. The mob's taken over all of the wagons now. The guardsmen have retreated to the kitchen. I don't think they can get into the warehouse. It's still warded. But I think they have Baill."

The roar of the mob was suddenly broken by a piercing animalistic scream.

Erick's face turned grim. "They must be running out of food on the wagons. They're after the horses now."

I stood up from my crouch, glanced over the seething morass of people, felt the wave of darkness it generated on the river and felt sick. "We have to find Avrell."

"I have him."

Both Erick and I spun, daggers raised, our movements almost exactly the same.

In the darkness of the alley behind us, Darryn stood, flanked by two other men and the elder with the milky eye. Darryn's face was blank, eyes centered on me. After a considering moment, he glanced toward the mob, then scowled before turning back to me.

"I can take you to him. You can stay with him under our protection until this dies down."

I almost spat in contempt, as the milky-eyed elder had done to me, but stopped myself.

Straightening, I nodded.

He led us deeper into the alley, back into the warrens that three years ago I had called home, the others falling in behind us, guarding our backs. As we slipped from narrow to narrow, passing through crumbled alleys and dead courtyards, the roar of the mob falling behind, I found the dread returning, not as powerful as before, but still there.

I shivered.

Then Darryn ducked through a low opening, nothing more than a hole in a wall.

I glanced back at Erick, saw him nod, and followed.

It opened up into a wide room, half sunk below ground, filled with tables, a few chairs, pallets against one wall. In the center of the room was a circular basin which must have once been a pool or fountain. A few chipped tiles remained at its edge, dirt ground so deep into them that there was nothing left of the pattern they must once have held.

Sitting on one of the chairs was Avrell, one hand clutching the opposite arm. Blood stained his shoulder, his dark blue shirt ripped aside. A man leaned over the wound.

"Mistress!" he said as I entered, then gasped as the man prodded the wound. "It was only a stray mud-brick," he finished weakly.

Darryn moved up to the man's side. "Well?"

The man grunted. "It needs a good cleaning and some stitches, but he'll live."

The rest of the men scattered throughout the room, one collapsing onto a pallet. The elder with the milky eye stayed behind at the rough opening, keeping watch.

Darryn turned back to me, ignoring Avrell's yelp of pain as the man I assumed was a healer began washing his wound. "And is this how you intend to feed the Dredge?" he asked acidly.

Erick's hand fell heavily onto my shoulder, restraining me. His grip was tight, the fingers flexing in warning as I tensed, trembling with rage.

I forced myself to relax, forced the hand that held my dagger to drop to my side. "You know how I intend to feed the Dredge," I said.

"Ah, yes. A day's work for a day's worth of food." He smirked. "How's that going to work if you can't even get the food to the kitchen?"

I gritted my teeth, jaw flexing, my hand kneading the handle of my dagger.

And then all the tension drained out of my body, and I smiled. "You're going to help me."

One of the other men barked out a short burst of laughter, but Darryn's face had gone completely blank. "What do you mean?"

I stepped forward, slipping out of Erick's grip. No one in the room moved, not even the healer. He held a needle in the air with a thin thread of gut running from its end down to Avrell's half-stitched wound, his face openly shocked.

"The crowd we drew on the Dredge when we first visited the warehouse didn't attack because you didn't want them to. They looked to you for permission. They obey you."

Darryn snorted. "Have you seen the Dredge today, Mistress? I don't control anyone."

I shook my head. "You don't control everyone. The ones ripping the wagons to pieces right now aren't the real people of the Dredge. The real people—the people I want to help survive this winter—are all cowering in their own niches right now, waiting for the animals to finish feeding so they can pick up the pieces. Just like you. Those are the people you control. And if you can get them organized, get them to cooperate . . ."

The man who'd laughed before began to chuckle.

"Shut up, Greag."

The room fell silent. I stared into Darryn's eyes, saw his age in the wrinkles around his eyes, saw the gray beginning in his hair. He watched me in turn, considering.

Then his gaze flicked to Erick. "Is she serious?"

"She's always serious."

Darryn frowned. "How do you expect to protect the food once it's here?"

"The warehouses will be warded by the Servants, who will also be present in the kitchen. And there will always be palace guards-men—" I halted. Darryn was shaking his head.

"That won't work. The Servants maybe, but not the guards-men. If you're truly from the Dredge, you'll know that."

And I did. The guardsmen wouldn't survive as a permanent presence on the Dredge. They were too feared, too hated.

"What do you suggest?"

Before Darryn could answer, Erick stepped to my side, mo-tioned toward the sword that hung at Darryn's waist. "Can you use that?"

Darryn stiffened. "Yes."

"What about these others?" Erick said, nodding toward the rest of the men hidden in the niche along with us.

Darryn shifted uncomfortably. "To varying degrees." Behind him, the healer grunted and returned to his stitching.

Erick turned to me. "Then have them protect their own ware-house and kitchen. Form a militia, made up of people from the Dredge, under Darryn's command."

I frowned, saw Avrell frowning as well but ignored him. "What do you think?"

He glanced around at the men in the room, asking a silent question and receiving silent answers—a nod, a shrug.

Then he turned back to me. "I think it might work."

†

"Mistress," Marielle said, her voice soft but strained. She winced as lightning flared through the open doorway leading out to the balcony, silver light flooding the room, followed a few seconds later by a harsh crack of thunder that shuddered through the air. "Come back to the settee, please! The storm is too close!"

I turned away from the balcony with a smile, felt the cold wind sweep into the room around me, tugging at my hair. Rain hissed onto the stone of the palace, harsh and relentless, a fine mist touching my face. The storm raged around me, prickled my skin, and with each flash of lightning I felt my heart respond with a quickened beat. Each roll of thunder shivered through my body, raised the little hairs on my arms, at the nape of my neck. I reveled in the sensation.

"Can't you feel it?" I said.

Marielle shuddered with terror. "Please! Come to the settee!"

Deeper inside the room, Erick shrugged, his expression as unconcerned as my own. We'd both been hardened to the weather. On the Dredge, there was little protection if you were caught in a storm.

Thinking of the Dredge brought a small surge of satisfaction. The kitchen and warehouse had finally been stocked with Darryn's and the Dredge militia's help. The militia only consisted of twenty men so far, and Baill was furious that the unit had been formed in the first place, but even now he and Captain Catrell were training more Dredge denizens who, when their training was complete, would be added to the force.

And more laborers were reporting to the warehouse district for work as well, a significant portion of them coming from the Dredge.

Lightning flared, the resultant thunder almost instantaneous. Marielle let out a small shriek. "Mistress, please!"

I sighed, closed the balcony door, but refused to draw the curtains, leaving the windows open. I moved to the settee, took the slate from Marielle's relieved hands. She stood and moved to pour me some tea to ease her own nerves.

I glanced down at the slate, picked up the chalk loosely in one hand. After her discussion with Erick, Marielle had given up trying to get me to draw elegant, curved letters. Instead, she'd had me think of the shapes as slashes, as if from a dagger—sharp and linear, with cutting, blunt edges. Forceful.

My letters had improved dramatically. We were working on words now, and simple sentences.

I stared down at the three-word sentence Marielle had scrawled on the top line, but as thunder shook the building again, Marielle casting a frightened glance toward the ceiling, I set the slate aside and stood.

"How long is the storm going to last, do you think?"

Erick cocked his head, listening to the wind, to the rain lashing against the stone. "It moved in swiftly from the ocean about midafternoon," he murmured, "but it doesn't sound like it's letting up any. I'd say not for another few hours."

I began pacing the room, too energized by the storm to remain still. "Then let's go see Avrell."

Erick nodded.

I stepped toward Marielle, who'd set my tea down. "Are you coming, Marielle?"

She turned. "If it's all right, I'll stay. I have . . . things I need to finish here." She cowered as more lightning flickered through the room.

I frowned, but nodded, turning toward Erick who held the door to the rest of the palace open for me.

We found Avrell in his office, poring over sheets of parchment with Nathem, Baill, and two masons I'd noticed leading labor crews at the warehouses.

"Avrell," I said.

All five men looked up, startled, their muttered argument cut short.

Avrell frowned, then stepped forward. "Yes, Mistress?"

Wondering what Baill was doing here, I asked, "What's happening with the warehouses?"

Avrell relaxed slightly. "We're progressing nicely, mainly due to the sudden influx of labor. The foundation to the main warehouse I showed you has now been finished and we've started on the walls, but of course we can't work on those today."

As if in answer, a rumble of thunder sounded, muffled by the stone of the palace this deep inside, but still audible.

Behind Avrell, one of the masons coughed meaningfully. Avrell's brow creased with annoyance.

I sighed. "What is it?"

Flashing his own glare of irritation at the mason, he said, "Two things actually. And at this point, neither of them have been investigated in any great detail."

I let my gaze narrow and Avrell stepped back behind his desk, pulling out a few sheets of paper. He still favored the shoulder that Darryn's healer had stitched up, moving the arm carefully as he shuffled through the pages. "The first is regarding the stone we need to rebuild the warehouses. As I said before, we have enough to rebuild the main warehouse, which is what we're working on now, but quite a bit of the stone used in the original buildings has been cracked by the heat of the fire and can't be reused in the new buildings."

Nathem spoke up. "We've been trying to figure out where to get stone from. We do have a quarry, but that is some distance away. Transporting the stone into the city during winter would be extremely difficult. Plus it would take time to cut the stone even before we begin to transport it."

"What about mud-brick?" I asked.

Glances were passed among everyone except Baill, who stood silently in the background, arms crossed, watching intently, his face the usual unreadable mask. Except that recently—since I'd forced him to initiate the militia on the Dredge—it had taken on an edge of bitterness.

"Mud-brick is possible," Avrell finally answered, "but it is somewhat unreliable, especially for the size of these buildings. And it is also labor-intensive. We'd still need to transport in the material used in the bricks, and then it would have to be mixed and fired. . . ." He shook his head.

"Why do you need to make it? There's tons of mud-brick from old buildings sitting unused in the Dredge."

Avrell and the masons looked momentarily stunned. Then Avrell turned to the masons. "Is that possible?"

The masons stared at each other a moment. "I don't see why not," one of them finally said. "We'd have to pick through it carefully, make certain it was sound. And we'd still need good stone from the quarry for the foundations and a significant portion of the walls. But . . ."

"Good," Avrell said. "Send some work crews down to the Dredge as soon as you can and check it out."

"Make certain they get in touch with Darryn," I said. "He'll want to warn the residents of the Dredge that you'll be there and what you'll be doing. And he'll want to escort the work crews while they're there, for their own protection."

I shifted my gaze toward Baill. An ugly red-and-purple scab marked where the stone had struck his head during the riot. He still hadn't spoken, and I couldn't see why he'd be involved in an argument over where to find usable stone for the warehouse construction. "What's the other problem?"

In an almost concerted move, the stonemasons and Nathem stepped back, eyes looking anywhere but at me. Avrell remained at the desk, but deferred to Baill.

A smile tugged at Baill's mouth, but it was fleeting.

Without moving, he said flatly, "We may have some stores missing from one of the warehouses."

I stilled. Missing supplies was a far more serious problem than where to find stone. "Is it missing from the Dredge?"

"No."

I almost heaved a sigh of relief. I wanted to believe Darryn could be trusted, *knew* he could be trusted if the river was any indication, but having supplies go missing almost immediately after I'd given him control . . .

I focused again on Baill. "Then how is that possible? I thought the city guard was watching over each warehouse on this side of the River, that the merchants were keeping track of the supplies under their care."

Baill nodded. "They are."

"Then how could some of the food have been taken?" Anger had begun to tighten my voice, and Baill reacted by straightening subtly, an answering flare of anger passing swiftly through his eyes.

"We don't know. As Avrell said, we don't even know for certain that the food is missing."

Avrell stepped forward cautiously. "According to our records, and the merchants' records, the Priem warehouse was supposed to have eighteen barrels of packed, salted fish. However, upon inspection, we couldn't find those barrels. It may just be a clerical error, or the barrels could have been taken to a different warehouse by mistake. It's too early to tell. I summoned Baill immediately and we were just beginning to discuss a course of action."

Baill nodded. "I think we should start with an inventory of the warehouses done by the guard, to verify that all of the supplies supposedly stored in each warehouse are actually present. If anything else is missing, we should find out now."

I considered for a moment, then said, "Do it."

Baill moved to the door. As he stepped outside and began to issue orders, I turned to Avrell.

"Which merchant has control of the Priem warehouse?"

Avrell's eyes never wavered. He'd been expecting the question. "Regin."

I bit off a curse, then forced myself to stop leaping to conclusions. Avrell admitted that perhaps the fish wasn't missing. Maybe it had simply been misplaced.

But somehow I didn't believe that.

In the corridor outside there was a sudden commotion, brief but loud enough to hear over the continuing thunder. I turned as the doors to Avrell's study opened and Baill stepped back through. His brow was creased with a frown, and his clothes were disheveled and damp in patches.

"There's someone here to see the Mistress," he said formally. "He wouldn't say what it concerned." Then he shifted to one side.

A boy stood behind him, surrounded by guardsmen, wide-eyed and breathing hard, splattered with mud and soaked to the bone, a puddle forming on the floor beneath him. He was dressed in a rough homespun tunic and breeches with no boots, his face pale, lips almost blue.

As I stepped forward, he shuddered with cold. "What is it?" I asked.

Teeth beginning to chatter, the boy sputtered, "There's been a shipwreck down in Colby."

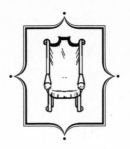

Chapter 6

"FROM WHAT I CAN GATHER from the boy," Avrell said, leaning back in his seat, wincing as he adjusted his shoulder, "the villagers didn't find an actual shipwreck. What they found was debris on the beach, large sections of a ship, just before the storm struck. They managed to haul the largest pieces of the debris up above the storm waters so that it wouldn't wash away, and then they sent the boy here."

After the boy's bald statement in Avrell's office, Avrell had taken him aside and questioned him, with my repeated assurances to the boy that it was safe to talk to the First. Servants were sent for dry clothes and food, while others were sent to inform the other captains, Eryn, and Borund. We'd convened in the same meeting room Avrell had used to introduce me to the captains of the guard.

"Were there any survivors?" I asked.

Avrell shook his head, mouth turned down with regret. "According to the boy, there weren't even any bodies washed ashore. Just wood and rigging, a large portion of the mast. . . ." He shrugged.

"But enough to identify the ship as coming from Amenkor?"

Borund asked. He was still damp from his brisk ride up to the palace in the rain after being summoned.

Avrell nodded.

At the far end of the table, Captain Catrell of the city guard leaned forward. "The question is, how did the ship founder?"

At his side, Westen nodded in agreement. "Was it by storm? But if so, what storm? The villagers found the wreckage *before* this hit." He glanced at the ceiling. The storm was moving off now, but the occasional rumble of thunder could still be heard through the thick stone walls. He leaned forward, eyeing Avrell. "How old was the wreckage?"

"The boy didn't know. The villagers sent him almost immediately after finding the debris. Aside from what I've told you already, he knew nothing."

Silence fell. Glances were exchanged between Eryn, Erick, and myself. We were the only ones in the room that knew of the vision of the city burning, and I could see in both Erick's and Eryn's eyes that I wasn't the only one thinking the wreckage could be from something other than a storm.

Straightening in my seat, the motion enough to draw everyone's attention, I said flatly, "I need to see the debris."

There was an awkward pause, and then Baill said tactfully, "Colby, the village where the wreckage was found, is outside of the city."

I frowned, confused, and then suddenly remembered.

I was trapped inside the city by the throne. I *couldn't* go see the wreckage.

I swore vehemently, startling both Captain Catrell and Baill. Catrell seemed shocked; Baill simply seemed intrigued.

"Someone has to go look at the wreckage," I said. "I need to know what ship the debris came from, how long it has been since it foundered, if possible, and how it was lost in the first place."

A few of those present seemed surprised at the force behind my voice. But then I realized: To them it was simply an unfortunate accident, a ship lost at sea, most likely by storm or from running onto a hidden shoal or perhaps piracy. They didn't have the vision haunting them. They couldn't see the bodies floating in the harbor, hadn't choked on the smoke of the fires.

Reacting to the intensity of my voice, Captain Catrell stood. "I'll send a contingent of the city guard immediately. We can leave tomorrow morning and be in Colby by late afternoon, with enough light left to investigate the wreckage so that we can return the following day."

Baill shifted forward. "I'll send a few palace guards along as well."

I shook my head, and Baill frowned, a flash of annoyance crossing his face. "No, Captain Baill. I want the palace guards to devote their energy to the food missing from the warehouse."

"Very well," Baill said.

It was clear he was unhappy I'd countermanded his suggestion.

But that still didn't solve the real problem. Captain Catrell didn't know about the vision. He and his men wouldn't look at the wreckage with alternative possibilities in mind. He'd probably already assumed it was from a storm, and that the debris had been lying on the beach for weeks. I needed someone who could factor in the warning given by the vision.

I glanced toward Erick, but hesitated.

Since he'd first returned from tracking down and killing Corum, he'd been a constant presence, my personal bodyguard, always near at hand, even if he wasn't always in the same room. I'd grown accustomed to having him there, for advice and for support.

He caught my gaze, gave me a slightly questioning look, as if to ask why I was waiting. He'd already assumed he would go.

But the thought of sending him filled me with sick dread. He was my only true ally in the palace. Marielle was beholden to Avrell; all the Servants were. And the guardsmen were under the control of Baill, even Captain Catrell. That left only Erick and the Seekers, and I'd discovered there weren't as many Seekers as I'd first thought. Westen had revealed that there were only about thirty Seekers in the palace—one Seeker for every ten guardsmen under Baill's and Catrell's control. So even though the Seekers swore their loyalty to the Mistress, and even though the Seekers were more deadly and skilled than the guardsmen, they were seriously outnumbered.

I didn't want to send Erick or Westen, not when there were so few I trusted.

Before either Erick or I could speak, there was a silken rustle of clothes and Eryn said, "Send me." She sat on the edge of her seat, her eyes wide in mute appeal.

I frowned, uncertain. Eryn was still an unknown, even after the hours we'd spent in training in the garden with the other Servants. Yet she'd done nothing but help me since I released her from the throne.

"Why?" I asked.

Eryn shifted slightly, and suddenly she was the woman who'd once sat on the throne, regal and composed. "Because until I was eight, I was raised on the rocky coastline, in a village much like Colby. I've seen debris from all kinds of shipwrecks. I know what to look for." She hesitated, then added in a much more emotional voice, "And also because I haven't been outside of the city for over twenty years."

My gaze narrowed. I'd heard what she'd not said, what she had really meant. She'd not been outside of the city because of the throne. This would be a good way to test whether she was truly free of its power. She was willing to risk death to make certain she was free, and this gave her an excuse to try.

And she did know what to look for. Like Erick, she knew of the vision, of what it foretold.

"Very well," I said, "but I'd like Borund to go, too." I turned toward him and saw his eyes widen slightly in surprise. "You know most of the ships we sent for supplies," I explained. "You'll have better luck identifying the ship."

Comprehension dawned, and he relaxed. "I believe William can manage for a few days while I'm away."

I suppressed a grimace at the mention of William's name, then stood. "Good. Then I'll leave you to your preparations."

Everyone stood, made short bows, and departed, Captain Catrell and Baill moving swiftly since they had orders to give, the rest at a more leisurely pace.

Once the others had left, Erick said quietly, "You could have sent me as well."

"I know," I said. I hesitated, almost added an explanation, but in the end said nothing. I didn't even turn to look at him, afraid he'd see the relief in my eyes that he was staying.

†

The party left an hour after dawn the next day. Along with Erick and my own escort, I accompanied Eryn, Borund, Captain Catrell, and a group of five other guardsmen to the edge of the city, all of us on horseback. One of the guardsmen carried the village's messenger boy behind him, the youth clutching tightly to his waist. Since it was the first time I'd been outside of the paddock on a horse, we took it slow, winding down from the palace and out the outer walls, then cutting east, passing through streets I wasn't familiar with. Following the River, we passed near the stockyards, the reek of slaughter washing over us on a faint breeze, even though fresh meat was scarce. The horses shied away from the smell, but we turned south before it became pervasive, moving parallel to the outer walls, the land dropping away from the palace and the hill that it sat upon. The buildings and streets thinned, until there was nothing but the southern road, rocky land, a few small bent trees, and scrub brush.

I glanced up at Eryn as the group paused on the rough road leading south from the city, the protective walls of the city above us, far up the steep slope of the southern part of the hill. Most of Amenkor lay north of the palace—on the edge of the harbor and along the northern jut of land that enclosed it—and east along the River. The openness here felt strange. I was used to buildings on all sides, or the waters of the River and harbor. I'd never ventured outside the Dredge or the lower city, wharf, and palace before becoming the Mistress. Here, where I could see the land to the east rising up to distant forested mountains and south along the dark rock of the jagged coastline, I felt exposed and vulnerable. But I quashed the sensation and turned to Eryn.

"Do you feel anything?" I asked, pitching my voice low so that only Eryn, Erick, and Borund could hear, brushing my hand along my mount's neck to keep it calm. I still hadn't grown comfortable astride the animal.

"No," Eryn said. "You?"

I shivered. "Yes." Deep in my gut, a gnawing sensation clawed at my stomach, like hunger but far worse. And it was steadily increasing the longer I stayed. I knew I was on the edge of the throne's reach. If I went much farther . . .

A look of pure wonder passed across Eryn's face. "Then it's true," she murmured, not hiding her disbelief. "I'm free of the throne."

She laughed, her joyful grin infectious. For a moment, I saw the young woman she had once been, carefree and mischievous.

Then she caught my eyes, saw my pained answering grin, and the Mistress in her took over, pushed her elation down, replacing it with a look of concern and pity. But not completely; there was still a smile on her lips. "Varis—" she began.

I halted her with a sharp shake of my head. With more force than I intended, I said, "It doesn't matter. I've lived my entire life inside the city. I don't need to go beyond its walls."

Eryn's face clouded with doubt, but she nodded. Perhaps she heard the lie. Now that I'd seen what lay outside the city, I wanted to see more. But that couldn't be helped.

"I'll be back tomorrow," Eryn said.

Then she turned and kneed her horse forward, the guardsmen starting out ahead of her at her signal. She rode gracefully, back straight, Borund falling in a few paces behind.

As she passed completely outside the throne's influence, the blissful smile relit her face.

I sighed, grimacing in pain as I placed a hand over my stomach. It felt as if someone had stabbed me and was now working the blade back and forth, slicing up my guts. "I need to get back to the city," I said, feeling suddenly flushed. And the horse was picking up on my discomfort.

Erick motioned sharply to my escort and we headed back, moving the horses as fast as the pain in my stomach would allow.

A hundred paces from the southern wall, the last of the sickening sensation faded.

I was home, I thought bitterly.

†

I spent the morning working with Nathem and Avrell on the rebuilding of the warehouse district, answering questions about what I wanted rebuilt where, settling disputes between workers and merchants. At my insistence, we visited one of the warehouses and kitchens so I could see how the merchants were organizing the work details and how they were handling the distribution of the food, then we headed toward the communal ovens, where the women and children were busy baking breads. But the smells of yeast and dough and flour reminded me too forcefully of the white-dusty man who'd helped me to survive on the Dredge before I met Erick—the baker who'd been killed because of me—and so I had Avrell take me back to the palace.

By then, Avrell had been put on edge. I'd never spent so much time with him before, had never asked him so many unimportant questions about how things were run, and my apprehension over the wreckage at Colby had transferred to him. I could see him casting suspicious looks at me, and so at midafternoon I released him. I didn't want him to think about Colby and what might be found there. His interest had already been piqued too much.

And perhaps there *was* nothing to find at Colby. Perhaps the debris was simply from the ship running aground on some hidden rocks, or breaking apart after being caught in a storm.

Or so I told myself as I paced my room.

In an effort to distract myself, I summoned Marielle and tried to pay attention to my lessons.

"Try to sound it out," Marielle said. We'd been working for two hours and her voice was frayed, her hair wild from running her hands through it in frustration. "You know all the letters."

"I know," I spat, a twinge of guilt stabbing through me even as I spoke.

Marielle tensed and in a hard voice said, "Just try."

I drew in a deep breath, closed my eyes, tried to gather my scattered wits, then opened my eyes and stared at the book in my lap. I focused on the word beneath my fingers. A long word, but one I knew, because I'd read through this page days ago.

But no matter how hard I tried, the letters wouldn't hold steady. My attention drifted. First to the uneasy fact that Marielle was one of the stronger Servants, that she could use the river if she wanted, that in fact I was training her to take my place. When I'd entered the palace to kill the Mistress, I'd run into one of the true Servants. But the only reason I'd known was that I'd touched her, had felt a thin slice of pain running up my arm, like the cut of a dagger. I'd always thought I'd know someone who could use the river just by looking at them. But no. I hadn't recognized that Eryn could use the river when I'd first met her in the throne room, not even after touching her. She'd actually used the river to block my attack before I'd figured out that she could control it. Was that because of the throne?

Marielle had never used the river in my presence except in the gardens while training. None of the Servants had. Was that because of Avrell? Had he ordered it?

I shoved the useless supposition aside, shook myself, and returned to the book. But I glanced toward the balcony to judge the time by the light.

It seemed the sun had barely moved since the last time I looked.

"Enough," I said, closing the book with a frustrated snap as I stood. "I can't do this now. We'll have to try again tomorrow."

A look of extreme relief passed over Marielle's face before she could suppress it. She stood, hands held carefully before her. "Is there anything else you wish to work on?" she asked.

I tried not to let the dread in her voice irritate me. "No. Just go." I waved her out, pacing to the balcony as she made her escape. Outside, she had a terse conversation with Erick, their voices too low for me to hear, and then Erick stepped into the room.

I glared up at the clouds scudding across the sky, then down at the city. From here, I could see the construction on the warehouses, the outlines of the walls now visible. The small figures of the men moved back and forth, and occasionally the breeze would bring the sounds of hammering and the bellows of the work leaders.

The activity somehow soothed me and the tension in my shoulders began to release.

"You're restless," Erick said.

I grunted. "You don't have to stay. I'm fine."

I heard movement and with a pang of regret thought he would actually leave, but he'd only shifted closer. "You've never been impatient before," he said, then added with a touch of humor, "except possibly when working with Marielle. On the Dredge, you had to wait often—for the mark to arrive, for the right moment to steal the apple. Why is waiting for Eryn to return and report any different?"

I shrugged. "Because then I knew what I was waiting for? I don't know. But it is different."

"You've changed in the last two months, since you became the Mistress," Erick said after a moment.

I didn't answer. Had it only been two months? It seemed like much longer than that.

Erick sighed. "So who do you want to harass now? Nathem? Baill? Westen? What about a little sparring lesson with me? I'm certain there's something I forgot to teach you on the Dredge that Westen hasn't already covered. He doesn't know everything you know."

I laughed and turned from the window, the offer to spar tempting. We hadn't fought each other since the Dredge, more than two years ago, and the thought that I might have learned something new on my own or from Westen, might have improved enough to actually beat him in a fair match, was almost too difficult to resist. But it was late, and if watching those working in the warehouse district could calm me, then maybe I could do something similar to calm my nerves even further. "No, I think I'll go to the throne room instead."

Erick's face grew somber, his stance tightening with disapproval. "Very well."

I shook my head, irritated again. "I just want to check on the city. Besides, I've been working with Eryn on controlling myself, and on protecting myself from the throne. I'll be fine." I knew from testing the throne on my own that I didn't need the throne to check on the city, that touching it wasn't required—I could sense the city even now—but touching it made sensing the emotions of the city as a whole easier. And right now all I wanted to do was relax.

Erick didn't look convinced.

In the throne room, at the sight of the amorphous throne shifting at the far end of the hall, my confidence faltered. But I straightened resolutely and walked down the central walkway, Erick at my back. He'd insisted on coming and, since the last time I'd used the throne I'd ended up unconscious on the dais steps in my own vomit, I couldn't argue with him.

At the base of the dais, I paused. Inside, I could feel the voices of the throne waiting, strangely quiet. I thought about Cerrin, who'd somehow escaped the Fire, and with careful deliberation I slid beneath the river and began to weave the protective net Eryn had drilled into me, trying a few of the alterations she'd proposed to help keep Cerrin and the rest of the Seven under control. Slipping deeper, I threw the net around the blazing sphere of White Fire that contained the voices at my core. The mostly quiet voices grew suddenly grim and disgusted and drew back from the wall of flame.

The net secured, I did another circuit around the sphere, searching for signs of the flaw that I knew must exist, but again I found nothing.

I turned to Erick. "I'm ready." I was surprised my voice was so steady.

He nodded, his stance alert.

Drawing a short breath, I moved up the steps and sat on the twisting stone.

Involuntarily, I winced, expecting the voices to come crashing down around me, smothering me as they had done before, now that they were close to their source of power. But while the same weighted blanket settled over, making the room feel more real, more dense, the voices barely stirred, only the intensity of their movements behind the Fire increasing.

I let my breath out slowly, let the pulse of the throne course through me. Taking another moment to check the security of the protective net, I smiled at Erick in reassurance, then sank myself in the sensations of the city.

For a long moment, I simply hovered, the city spread out before me, as if I stood on the rooftop of the palace's tower staring down over its sprawling streets and tightly packed buildings. The roiling flow of the people's emotions washed over me in rhythmic swells, like waves. The scent of the waves was cool and smooth with tentative contentment. Winter had set in, the ocean was turbulent outside the bay, but here, in the harbor, where the River met the sea, we'd survived. Where before there had been a riot of apprehension, concern over whether there was enough food, uncertainty about the sudden change of power in the palace, and fear about the repercussions of the madness everyone suspected in the old Mistress, now there was hope that everything would turn out all right. There was food. They'd seen it in the warehouses, seen it being offloaded from the ships, knew that if they were willing to work for it, the food could be theirs. Where before I'd sensed anxiety and despair, now I found industrious activity.

Not everywhere, of course. There was still a feeling of discontent near the Dredge. I focused on that part of the city, until I hovered over the Dredge itself, felt the people flowing down its streets and alleys.

Evander had done as I asked, had told those that lived on the Dredge of the work details, of how a man had been punished to protect him, even though he was from the Dredge. And Darryn had spread the word as well, had created the militia using people from the Dredge. Within the following week, Avrell's work force had doubled. Many were men and women who had simply fallen on hard times after the passing of the White Fire through the city six years before. People who had lived and worked in the lower city before the Fire, their only recourse to abandon the lower city for the Dredge after it had passed. In the fear and uncertainty it had left behind, trade had faltered. But a few were like Evander, like me—gutterscum that had known nothing else but the Dredge, that were willing to take a chance on something better.

I let the Dredge roll over me, then turned away. I'd done what I could for them. For now.

Next, I moved to the wharf, watched the workers packing fish in salt, rolling the barrels into storage. On the waters of the harbor, others were in small boats, hauling up crab traps, searching even though it was out of season. Still others were working in the rigging of the trading ships or on the decks, making repairs to rope and wood, pulleys and sails.

I stayed here the longest. The sailing ships had always intrigued me, even before I'd begun working as Borund's bodyguard. While hunting for easy marks on the wharf, I'd often sit for hours watching the dockworkers unloading cargo, dreaming about what strange foods the crates and barrels could carry, of what I could steal if given the chance.

It had been impossible then to imagine that I could have boarded one of the huge ships and left with it, escaped the city entirely. At that time, all I knew was Amenkor. There was nothing outside the warren of the Dredge, the streets and alleys of the wharf and the lower city. But I suddenly realized that I *could* have escaped on one of the ships back then. Perhaps not easily, but it could have been done. I could have traveled down the coast to the south, to the cities Avrell had told me about—to the cliffs of Venitte and the maze of caves and streets of that ancient sister city; to the rolling hills and vineyards of Marland; or even farther south, across the sea to the islands of the Zorelli.

But not now. I was bound to the throne now.

I drew back from the wharf and the activity on the docks reluctantly, then turned my attention to the warehouse district. But even with the sense of regret I now felt, watching the people of the city had worked. I no longer felt so tense, and for a brief moment I'd forgotten about Eryn and the group that had probably already arrived in Colby.

Unconsciously, I looked out over the city along the southern coastline. Where the influence of the throne ended, the undulating flow of the river became listless. The river still existed beyond the city, but it didn't have the same power without the throne behind it, its scents and tastes weren't as vibrant. It was just the river, the same power I'd used to survive on the Dredge.

Somehow, with the full power of the throne flowing through me, that now seemed paltry. Even with what I'd learned practicing with Eryn, who even without the throne's supporting power could do more with the river—or the Sight as she called it—than I'd managed to learn on my own on the Dredge.

Far down the coastline, outside of the influence of the throne, something flared.

I frowned, turned my full attention south.

And caught the flicker of light again. A white light, far enough away that it could barely be seen.

But now that I had seen it I realized I recognized it.

The White Fire.

Without thought, I reached for it, as I'd reached to find Corum on the Dredge that night on the tower, as I'd reached for Erick as he hunted. But then Eryn's warning brought me up short, like a slap.

Frowning, I withdrew to the palace's tower in my mind, began to pace its length, casting furtive glances out toward the tiny blinking white flame, Eryn's warning echoing through my head.

It's too dangerous, her voice whispered from memory. *Reaching like that, extending yourself out so far. . . . You could lose yourself, never find your way back.*

And that had been when I'd tried to reach out to the Dredge.

This looked much, much farther away.

I drew to a halt at the edge of the palace tower, facing the faint white light. I'd spent a lot of time pushing the boundaries of the throne recently, stretching farther and farther out over its influence without letting the connection to my own body break.

But if I reached for this Fire . . .

Don't.

I jumped, felt a tingle of guilt sweep through me as if I'd blushed, then steadied myself, the guilt hardening into anger and a trace of fear as I drew in the sharp scent of that strange incense, as I recognized Cerrin.

He stood next to me on the edge of the tower, the wind from the ocean flapping in the tails of his coat, his very presence more solid, more real. Here, the yellow of his shirt was vibrant, his coat a deep, rich brown. His short beard was trimmed to a sharp point and his tawny eyes glittered with a hard intelligence . . . and a deep melancholy.

Why not? I asked

He shook his head. *Because what Eryn said is correct. It is dangerous. It is foolhardy. It is stupid. More than you know have lost themselves by Reaching. But also because even if you can find your way back—which I doubt—you will be drained. And for what?*

I turned away. *How are you escaping the Fire? How are you escaping the net?*

We are the Seven. Almost fifteen hundred years ago we realized that we were the last of our kind, the last that had power—true power. The last that could wield all of the elemental magics. There was no one who would follow us. But we knew that someday there would be someone of true power again, and so we tried to preserve our knowledge. So we created the thrones—to preserve what we knew until it could be used again, and to protect the Frigean coast against those who would destroy it.

He looked out over the southern coastline. *There is more magic than just the Fire. Or the river. Don't Reach for the Fire. It's too dangerous.*

And then he vanished, his form tattering like a piece of cloth.

My jaw clenched. He hadn't answered my question.

Fuming, I stared out at the faint flicker on the horizon. I paced to the edge of the tower, arms folded across my chest, then paced back and bit my lower lip.

But the presence of another White Fire like the one that burned at my core was too tempting, too intriguing to resist.

And I knew I could find my way back, no matter what Eryn or Cerrin said.

Shoulders set, I reached for the distant flame.

For a fleeting instant, the world stretched out below, the sensation terrifying. Like the moment of total balance at the edge of a rooftop just before you jump, when you realize that what seemed like such a short distance down to the ground is really two stories, not one, but it's too late to turn back. But I could still feel my body, still feel the tenuous connections.

And then I leaped, letting my body go.

The coastline sped by below, too swift to see much more than white spray as ocean waves crashed into rocky cliffs, shooting up huge plumes in the late afternoon sunlight, the thunderclaps that followed muted. I barely spared a glance even for this, my heart thudding at twice normal, my gaze locked on the flickering White Fire ahead. Eryn's warning was sharp in my memory; I didn't dare look away, afraid I'd lose sight of the light. It blazed on the horizon, drew steadily closer. Heart pounding, I watched it pulse, like a beacon—

And then, suddenly, it was there.

I fell down into it, felt its flames envelop me without burning, just as the White Fire had on the night it passed through Amenkor six years before. In the instant before it claimed me, I saw the rocky coastline break into a stretch of beach strewn with pebbles and driftwood, saw a cluster of ramshackle buildings a little farther inland over a crest of scrub grass and dunes, smelled smoke from a real fire, mixed with the scents of stew.

And then there was only the Fire.

†

"Would you like something to eat?"

The woman's voice, rough and uncertain with nervousness and awe, filtered through the white wall of flame that surrounded me, that held me suspended at its center. For a moment, my heart thudded with panic at the thought that I was trapped, like the voices were trapped inside the Fire at my core. I flailed at the wall before me, shoved at it hard, and felt it give way.

I found myself staring out at a bare cottage and an older man seated at a rickety table, face in a tight scowl that appeared permanent, scarred with the sun and covered with a grizzled, patchy beard. Wisps of thinning white hair drifted above his head, his eyebrows the same ancient, steely gray but heavy and thick. A dark mole the size of my thumbprint marred his forehead over his left eye.

He was watching me intently, his light gray eyes sharp.

Beside him, stooped over the pot steaming above the fire, the woman who had spoken—as thin as the man and just as wizened, her long wiry hair kept back from her face by a kerchief—lifted a ladle of the thin stew. "It's rabbit. Not much, but . . ."

I tried to shake my head, raise a hand to ward away the soup since it was obvious these people had little to eat, but instead I heard myself say, "Thank you, just a cup," and felt my hand reach out to accept the small steaming cup that was proffered.

Except it wasn't my hand that grabbed the hot cup and raised the thin stew to my lips to sip. It was Eryn's hand, Eryn's fingers that got burned, Eryn's tongue that was scalded, and Eryn's voice that spoke. But I felt it all, tasted the salty broth of the stew, smelled the steam.

And suddenly I realized that the Fire I had searched out was inside Eryn, that I was looking through her eyes, feeling what she felt, tasting what she tasted as if I were actually there.

"It's delicious," I heard myself say, but the contradiction of hearing Eryn's voice muttering the words, of feeling Eryn turn her head so that her gaze fell on Borund and Captain Catrell, both huddled inside the small hovel, of Eryn acting without any control by me, was too much. I drew back, isolated myself from Eryn's actions so that there was a clear distinction between her and me, between what I wanted and what she wanted. I sensed that if I didn't remove myself, if I remained, I'd eventually get confused between what was her and what was me. And I also sensed that with a little effort I could actually make myself be felt, that I could actually seize control of Eryn.

This must be what it felt like for the voices inside the throne: always present, able to feel what I felt, see what I saw, smell what I smelled. Except they were all dead.

No wonder they wanted control, fought so hard against the Fire I caged them with. Behind the Fire, they couldn't truly feel me, couldn't taste and smell and touch. Couldn't act, not of their own volition. But the temptation to take control was always there, just out of reach.

And no wonder the Mistress couldn't retain control once the voices were let free. If one of them were let loose, remained loose for too long, the distinction between that personality and the Mistress herself would begin to blur. They'd begin to overlap, until neither remembered where their own personality ended and the other's began.

Or as Eryn had suggested earlier, until one of the personalities dominated the other.

I shuddered, withdrew even further, not certain whether Eryn could sense me, not wanting her to sense me. I didn't think she had, but then there'd been no outward sign that the soup was too hot. She'd hidden the pain behind her smile, not wanting to offend the woman of the house. Perhaps she'd hidden her reaction to my presence as well. She'd been the Mistress for almost twenty years; she was practiced at deception.

But how had this happened? How did the Fire get inside her? I hadn't noticed it in anyone else, had worked with Eryn closely during my training and hadn't seen it then.

And how would I get back?

Cerrin's warning about the risks of Reaching too far afield suddenly assailed me and I shot a glance toward Amenkor, realizing only then that I was still beneath the river. But Eryn was inside the cottage and I couldn't see through the walls of driftwood and lumber. Not without the power of the throne behind me. I'd have to wait until Eryn moved outside.

Uncertain now, wishing I'd listened to Cerrin's advice and not reached for the white flame on the horizon, I settled back to wait.

Borund and Captain Catrell both took steaming cups of the stew at a stern glance from Eryn, Borund sipping politely, Catrell swallowing in gulps. After a brief pause, Eryn lowered her cup to her lap and turned toward the old man, meeting his gaze squarely. "You sent the boy?"

"Ayu," he said, his accent thick. He leaned back and crossed his arms over his chest, the chair creaking beneath his weight.

Eryn nodded. "We'd like to see the wreckage."

"Why?"

Eryn frowned. "I don't understand."

He sat forward abruptly. "We's found parts of wrecked ships afore, and none's come to see it. Always too busy. Why's this un different?"

Eryn shot a startled glance toward Borund, who shrugged, then turned back to the fisherman. "Because we sent out quite a few ships recently, and only a few of them returned. We'd like to know what happened to the other ships. If this is one of them . . ."

"Ayu," the man grunted. He cast a dark eye on Borund, who shifted beneath the glare and took a hasty sip of his stew. He took in Borund's red-and-gold coat, the clean-cut breeches, and white shirt so out of place in this barren cottage, and his scowl deepened.

He turned back to Eryn. "I ken show ya the wreckage," he said, but he made no move to rise from his seat, the woman ladling out a much larger portion of the stew and setting it in front of him. As if the matter were settled, he turned to the stew, completely ignoring everyone else in the room except the woman, who began ladling out a bowl for herself.

Eryn stiffened and said tightly, "We'd like to see it before the sun sets, if that's possible. We want to return to the city early tomorrow."

The man acted as if she hadn't spoken, scooping out a chunk of meat from the stew with two fingers and slurping it up. The old woman sniffed in disapproval, thunked her own stew down on the table with force, and gave him a glare.

The old man caught her gaze and for a moment they warred, his scowl deepening, her hands settling on her hips.

Finally, the man snorted, slammed his stew down to the table, and stood. Without glancing at Eryn, Borund, or Catrell, he stalked from the hovel with a curt, "Folla me."

"Excuse Gellin," the woman said, her eyes casting daggers at his retreating back. "We don't see people from the city often."

Eryn gave her a reassuring smile, then stood, setting the stew to one side. "The stew was wonderful," she said, then bowed her head and followed Gellin. Borund and Catrell followed close behind, Catrell motioning the other guardsmen waiting outside the cottage to their side.

"He doesn't seem too happy to see us," Borund said as they moved past the few ramshackle houses that made up the entire village. All were built of wood and all had a long, thin boat turned upside down outside, traps and thick nets heaped underneath the boats or stored in small hutches next to each house. Through open doorways, faces peered out cautiously. "None of them are very welcoming."

"Can you blame them?" Eryn said, maintaining her smile. "As Gellin's wife said, they don't see people from the city often. I'm certain that when they do see us, they take it as a sign that there's trouble ahead. I know the elders in the village where I was raised did. Men from the cities were an omen, a harbinger of bad times. The last time the guard arrived in my village, they took me away kicking and screaming and brought me to the palace. I was only eight at the time."

The heat in Eryn's voice caused Borund's stride to falter.

"Whatever for?" he asked.

"To become the Mistress, of course," she said, voice blunt and filled with long-held hatred.

Borund backed off, his brow furrowed in consideration.

The old man led them through the village, out across the dune that protected the inland from the waves, toward a rocky rise to the south. They climbed over the granite, using scrub brush and small, twisted trees with long needles and rough bark to help them over the steepest parts. The guardsmen cursed the terrain, their armor clattering against the stone when they stumbled or fell while Gellin smirked, but Eryn climbed the stone smoothly, the stone rough enough to provide plenty of hand- and footholds.

When they crested the rise, they looked down into another stretch of beach, another plinth of rocky outcropping on the far side, the stone biting into the sea. Waves crashed into the rock and hissed onto the stone of the beach. Well above the cove's waterline lay three large pieces of what had once been one of the merchant ships: a section of mast as thick as my waist and twice my height, the wood scarred and pitted; a large section of the prow; and a flat section of deck, part of the square hole that would have led down into the hold cutting into one of its sides.

"There," the old man said. His biting tone had mellowed, as if the sight of the crushed ship had sobered him somewhat.

Captain Catrell and a few of the guardsmen began the climb down the far side. Eryn stood silently for a long moment, searching the wreckage, but from this distance it appeared that the ship had been torn apart, perhaps against the rocks of the shoreline.

Eryn pursed her lips, then turned and began a careful descent to the beach, Gellin watching her closely.

"You fisherfolk," he said, as Eryn jumped the last stretch, landing in the loose rounded rock of the beach.

"Yes," Eryn said. "I grew up in Tallern, on the coast."

Gellin nodded succinctly, his eyes no longer so hostile.

Stones rattled against each other as they began to make their way to the wreckage. The guardsmen scattered out along the beach to search for more debris, some heading farther inland to scout, to where the beach gave way to overhanging needled trees and grassy underbrush. Borund and Catrell headed straight for the wreckage, Borund struggling to maneuver among the driftwood and dried seaweed at the waterline. He swore as he slid off of a piece of wood into a patch of dried, crusted seaweed, sand fleas and flies hopping and swarming around him as he danced away, yelping.

Eryn grinned, and even Gellin chuckled, but the mood sobered instantly as Eryn came up onto the wreckage.

She knelt down beside the piece of decking. The edges away from the opening to the hold were jagged with splinters, the boards ripped forcibly away, as if a giant had grabbed both ends of the deck and simply snapped it in half. But Eryn ignored the obvious signs of breakage and looked more closely at the wood, sitting forward to run her hands over its surface.

"You pulled this off the beach before the storm hit?" Eryn asked.

"Ayu."

"And when was the last storm around here?"

Gellin squinched his face up in thought. "Last howler come two hands before."

"Ten days," Eryn muttered under her breath. Then, louder, "And this wasn't here then?"

"Boy come here ever odd day," Gellin said. "Not here two days back."

"It could have been caught in the last storm, offshore, and just now found its way onto the beach."

Eryn looked up at Captain Catrell's voice. She hadn't heard him approach, too busy examining the deck before her. "This piece is heavily pitted and waterlogged," she said, shaking her head. "It's been in the water a long time. And look at these markings." She pointed to where the wood of the deck had been scarred black, a thick line running toward the opening to the hull, then angling sharply off to one side.

Catrell frowned. "Looks like the deck caught fire. I found some gouges in the mast that could have come from swords or axes. Perhaps it was piracy."

"Perhaps." I edged forward, hearing the doubt in Eryn's voice. She didn't believe it was piracy at all.

She ran her hand over the scorch marks in the wood, her frown deepening, then stood, moving across the sand and jumble of driftwood to Borund's side at the piece of the bow of the ship. The merchant was leaning over the jagged end of the bowsprit where it had been snapped off and now jutted out of the sand. Only a section of the bow had survived where the bowsprit joined the hull. But enough of the hull to either side remained intact for Eryn to pick out the roughly carved shape of a naked woman's head and upper body, her back arched at the junction as if supporting the weight of the ship.

As Eryn, Catrell, and Gellin approached, Borund stepped back from the largest section of the hull. "It's definitely from Amenkor," he said, brushing sand off of his hands and coat. "The Amenkor sigil is clear along the hull. And based on what's left of the bowsprit and the coloration of the hull, I'd say this was the *Tempest*." He turned to look at Eryn, his face mournful. "One of my ships. It was headed south, to Verano."

"South again," Catrell said.

Eryn nodded. "Only one of the ships that returned was from the south, and from what I could gather, that ship never strayed far from the coast. It hopped between towns on the way back, trying to trade for as much as possible in the smaller ports."

Borund nodded. "Captain Mathew has always understood what needed to be done. And been willing to do it."

"But he also didn't travel that far south. Since he was entering more ports, he had to sacrifice distance. The rest of the ships were traveling farther. They had to catch the currents farther offshore."

Borund grunted agreement.

"Then we *are* dealing with pirates," Catrell surmised. "They're hitting the trade routes off the southern coastline."

Eryn said nothing. I could feel her disagreement though and thought of the scorch marks. The ship had clearly been attacked. The marks of a fight that Catrell had found on the remains of the mast confirmed that. Then the ship had most likely been set adrift, left to be torn apart by the storm. Or it had foundered during the attack itself.

But something wasn't right. Eryn felt it. For now though, she seemed willing to let Borund and Catrell think it was piracy.

She turned toward the fading sunlight, shadows beginning to edge along the beach. "It's getting dark. We should head back to the village."

Catrell nodded, then whistled sharply, the guardsmen congregating around them as they headed back to the rocky rise and began to climb. The few clouds above were just beginning to burn a deep gold when Eryn reached the top of the rise and looked north, one hand raised to shade her eyes.

Seizing the opportunity, I edged forward, scanned the horizon and saw a blazing white light to the north, like another setting sun, much larger than the flickering flame I'd focused in on to find Eryn. Without hesitation, I gathered myself tight and as I did so I realized the Fire that lay within Eryn had a scent: old blood and freshly turned earth. An undertone, like the shadow scent Eryn had left behind after manipulating my dream.

But old blood and freshly turned earth was my scent.

The Fire in Eryn had come from me.

Startled, I paused. But Eryn dropped her hand, began to turn away. And so, without thought, I leaped for the white light on the horizon, leaving Eryn and the mystery of the White Flame inside her behind. The darkening landscape rushed past, waves edged in brittle sunlight like the clouds above, dense trees softening the edges of the rocky defiles and hidden coves below.

Then I saw the edge of the city of Amenkor, felt the presence of the throne grip me as I entered its influence, saw the throne room crowded now with guardsmen and a few Seekers at the doors, at the side entrances, Avrell and Erick on the dais talking animatedly, shouting at each other—

And I fell into my body, drew in a halting, rough gasp that hurt my chest, my heart stuttering before finding its beat.

"—don't know what's happening," Avrell said, voice tightly restrained but loud.

"Bloody hells you don't," Erick growled. "You're the First of the Mistress! You—"

He cut off sharply at my gasp, almost lurched forward to touch me, but Avrell clamped a hand roughly onto his arm and held him back, his knuckles white with the effort.

"Don't touch her," the First ordered, voice like stone. "Let her recover. I don't know what the throne will do." Real fear pinched his face, and I suddenly realized what he meant.

He wasn't certain it would be me that returned.

And he was right. For all he knew, one of the voices of the throne had taken over.

Swiftly, I dove to the Fire, checked the net I'd put in place, checked the wall of Fire. The voices were seething with confusion, the maelstrom turbulent and enraged, all of them trying to gain my attention, but I ignored them all. The barriers—both the net I'd woven and the Fire itself—were intact as far as I could tell.

Not that it mattered against the Seven it seemed.

I turned my attention to Erick and Avrell, slowed my breathing, calmed my heart.

"It's me, Varis," I said, and then demanded, "What happened?"

Erick broke in first, voice rough and heated with emotion. "You went rigid, stopped breathing. I didn't dare touch you, so I summoned Avrell."

Avrell scoffed. "She was still breathing, just very slowly."

"You weren't so certain an hour ago," Erick spat.

Avrell seemed ready to rise to the bait, so I cut in. "Enough. Why are there so many guardsmen?"

Avrell answered. "When the trance lasted more than an hour, I decided it was prudent to secure the throne room. I summoned the guardsmen, to make certain you were safe. With only Erick here, and your escort outside, you were completely vulnerable in that state."

Meaning Avrell didn't trust Erick, knew he wasn't under anyone's control like the other guardsmen. And I didn't quite believe Avrell's explanation that they'd been summoned for my safety. He'd called them in case one of the other voices had returned, rather than me.

Even as the thought crossed my mind, I noticed the two guardsmen to either side of the dais, hands resting casually on the pommels of their swords. Behind each, standing too close and too tense for comfort, were two Seekers, their eyes intent on me, on Erick, waiting for a sign from either of us to attack the guardsmen to protect their Mistress.

The guardsmen and the Seekers were on the verge of an all-out fight in the middle of the throne room. The tension on the river tasted slick and metallic.

I shot a hard glance at Avrell. "Call them off."

Avrell's gaze hardened.

"Call them off!"

With a subtle hand gesture, the two guardsmen shuddered and fell back. But they didn't go far. The two Seekers who'd been threatening them shifted casually, placing themselves near the first set of columns, still within a few deadly steps of either guard.

Taking a small step forward, Avrell demanded, "What happened?"

I tensed. A day before I would have answered him, told him the truth, or at least most of the truth. But I could still feel the presence of the guardsmen at my back, could still taste the edge of the blades, could feel Erick enraged at Avrell's side now that he realized Avrell's true intent behind summoning them to the throne room.

I also realized that Avrell had spoken the truth earlier. He really didn't know what had happened.

Drawing in a steadying breath, I said, "I was keeping an eye on Eryn. They found the wreckage. They should be returning tomorrow, as expected."

Confusion crossed Avrell's face. "How—?" he began, but cut himself off.

I raised a questioning eyebrow in challenge, my displeasure clear.

Avrell backed off, disgruntled.

I glared out at the guardsmen and the few Seekers spread throughout the hall. "The extra guards are no longer necessary," I said.

After a hesitant moment, they began to file out. Outside, I saw my usual escort of palace guardsmen frowning as they passed.

As the last of the summoned guardsmen departed, I turned my glare on Avrell. "You may go as well. I'll send for you tomorrow, after Eryn returns."

He bristled, jaw working, but said nothing, bowing low before stalking down the hall.

Releasing the throne, I stood and stepped down from the dais, watching his retreating back with a frown.

"I didn't realize what he'd summoned them for," Erick said, "or

I would never have let them into the throne room. I thought they could be trusted. Then, when nothing changed, when you were still . . . gone, I summoned the Seekers."

"Some of the guardsmen can be trusted," I said. "We'll have to find out which ones."

Erick nodded. "I'll take care of it." He hesitated, then asked, "So what did happen?"

"Exactly what I said. I followed Eryn, saw the debris from the ship."

"And was it lost because of a storm?"

I shook my head. "No. Eryn doesn't think it's piracy either, but I don't know why yet. Someone attacked the ship. Even Catrell agrees with that."

"Who could it be? One of the other cities? Venitte? Verano? But we've had good relations with them all for the last twenty years, since Eryn took the throne, since before that. And as far as we know, none of them has any kind of war fleet. Nothing fit for the open ocean anyway."

"I don't know. But I think Eryn does. It has something to do with the marks of the fire they found on the debris." I turned to Erick. "We'll just have to wait and ask her."

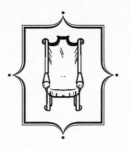

Chapter 7

"WE HAVE TO BLOCKADE the harbor," Eryn said as soon as she swung herself down off of her horse and handed the reins to the waiting stableboy. She was covered with dust from the road, her mount lathered with sweat from the hard ride from Colby, its muscles shuddering from the exertion.

"Where are Captain Catrell and the other guardsmen?" Erick asked. We had been waiting for Eryn at the outer gates to the palace since I'd felt her enter the city and the influence of the throne.

"Still a few hours outside of Amenkor. They couldn't keep up, and I needed to talk to you as soon as possible," Eryn said, shooting me a sharp warning glance. "In private."

"Why?" Erick said. His voice was hard, eyes intent.

"Because of the fire on the deck," I said.

That brought Eryn up short. She drew breath to say something, then noticed the array of palace guardsmen that surrounded us. Grunting, she said sharply, "The gardens."

Eryn led the way, clearly puzzled as to how I knew about the fire on the shipwreck in Colby, but willing to wait until there was no one able to overhear. When we passed through an archway out into open sunlight and the gardens, I motioned the escorting guardsmen back and proceeded with Erick to a small section of the garden flanked by a few trees surrounding two stone benches, Eryn in front of us.

The moment the guardsmen were out of earshot, Eryn straightened, brow creased in a frown, her stance imperious. "How did you know?"

I hesitated. But I had to trust someone. If Eryn had wanted the throne back, she could have taken it by now. She could have killed me "accidentally" during one of our private training sessions here in the gardens, could have touched the throne while I was searching for the presence behind the dream, or at any other time for that matter since she knew how to conceal herself from the guardsmen using the Sight. But all I'd seen whenever she was in the presence of the throne was terror.

No. Eryn didn't want the throne. But she was having a hard time giving up being the Mistress.

I drew in a deep breath. "I saw the wreckage on the beach. I saw the mast, the deck, the broken bowsprit. I saw it all through your eyes."

Eryn's eyes clouded with confusion. "You Reached even after I warned you not to? You Reached all the way to Colby? How is that even possible? How could you even see that far beyond Amenkor, when the throne has no influence there?"

"I had something to focus on, to guide the Reaching," I answered, then continued before Eryn could respond. "It's the White Fire. There's a small flame of it burning inside you, which is what caught my attention in the first place. I used that to Reach out toward you. After that it was like watching everything through your eyes. I saw everything you saw, tasted everything, touched it." I halted, on the verge of telling her that for a moment I had almost seized control, knew that I could if necessary.

But trust only went so far. And there was no way to tell how she'd react to that after fighting the voices within the throne for so long.

Eryn didn't believe me. I could see it in her eyes.

"What were we served by the fisherwoman when we arrived in Colby?" she asked.

I sighed. "Rabbit stew. You didn't want to take it because you knew they had little enough to eat—you know what life is like in a fishing village—but thought it would be polite to accept a small cup. You forced Captain Catrell and Borund to eat some as well. The village's elder, Gellin, was a little rude, but his wife put him in his place before he took you to the wreckage."

Eryn's eyes widened as I spoke. Now she whispered, under her breath, "Mistress' tits! You really were there."

Erick seemed startled by the curse.

"Oh, please," Eryn said, waving a hand dismissively at his raised eyebrows. "I grew up in a fishing village. I knew worse curses than that before I was five." Then she turned to me, her eyes narrowing down to slits. "Is the Fire still there? Can you see it now?"

I slid beneath the river, felt the throne augment my power, felt the guards at the two main entrances to the gardens, felt the stronger eddies of the city waiting outside . . . but drew myself away from those currents reluctantly, turning my attention on Eryn instead. I could sense the voices of the throne watching intently, somehow more focused and calm than usual.

"Yes," I said. "But it's harder to see it now. When I was looking from the top of the tower before, when you were in Colby, it seemed much brighter, like a beacon."

I withdrew from the river. Eryn began pacing, deep in thought.

"It must be the throne. The power here in Amenkor is so dense, almost like a weight, a cloak. The currents must be masking the Fire. But that still doesn't explain how the Fire got there in the first place. Could it have been left behind when the Fire passed through the city six years ago, as happened to you? But why didn't I sense it then, as you did? Why can't I sense it now?"

I suddenly remembered that moment in the throne room, after the shadow Eryn, still trapped inside the throne, had shown me the vision of the city burning to the ground. I'd shoved the vision away, felt something tear in the process, heard Eryn scream. . . .

"The Fire came from me," I said. "It has my scent—old blood and fresh earth."

Eryn stopped pacing, a hundred questions in her eyes.

But Erick cleared his throat and said curtly, "The pattern of fire on the wreckage?"

Eryn frowned in annoyance. "Of course. We can discuss the Fire later." She motioned to the stone benches along the garden path. Eryn and I sat; Erick remained standing.

"Tell me what you saw in the wreckage," Eryn said curtly.

I drew in a deep breath, then halted, not certain what to say. I'd been thinking about the remains of the ship since I'd seen it through Eryn's eyes, had scrutinized the damage over and over in my mind, but I couldn't figure out what had made Eryn so certain that the ship hadn't been attacked by pirates.

I looked at Eryn, then sighed. "I don't know. I saw what you saw: the deck had been broken, the wood splintered as if the ship had been snapped in two. Captain Catrell reported that there were signs of a battle. Borund verified that it was a ship from Amenkor, one of his ships actually, the *Tempest*. And I saw the marks made by the fire on the deck. I know that's what concerned you the most, but not why."

Eryn nodded, placed her hands in her lap and leaned forward

intently. "The fire *is* the problem. If it hadn't been for those mark-ings, I would have concluded piracy as well, just as Captain Catrell did. But the fire . . . it wasn't made naturally."

I frowned in consternation. Behind me, I felt Erick shift closer, grow more tense. "What do you mean?"

"I mean, the fire that helped to destroy that ship was con-trolled by the Sight. Think back on the markings. The scorch marks on the deck are too focused, the damage confined to a nar-row path. And that path isn't even linear. The markings on the deck ran straight and true, and then veered off sharply in another direction. Fire doesn't behave that way naturally. This fire was guided." Eryn sighed. "My guess is that whoever attacked the ship had the help of someone with the Sight. That person used the fire to target people."

I thought back to the shattered decking Eryn had leaned over on the beach, saw her tracing out the path of the fire with one hand, the way that path angled sharply away from the opening that would have led down to the hold.

In my mind's eye, I saw one of the deckhands on the ship run-ning, terrified, fire scorching along the deck behind him. I saw him turn when he reached the opening in the deck in an attempt to es-cape, saw the fire turn to follow.

There would be no escape from such an attack.

I shuddered, looked up into Eryn's eyes again with an expres-sion of horror.

Erick stepped forward. "How does that rule out piracy? Couldn't the pirates have someone like Varis with them? Someone who learned to control the Sight on her own?"

Eryn's brow creased in thought. "It's possible, but unlikely. Controlling fire in such a specific way . . . that requires training. It's not something most of the Servants in the palace could do even after training. You have to have power, and you have to have an extreme force of will, a focus that doesn't typically come naturally to anyone with the Sight."

"Could you do it?"

Eryn turned toward me, thought for a moment, then nodded. "Yes. I'm not sure how, precisely. I've never seen it done before, never even really thought about trying it. Fire isn't solid, rigid, like stone. It's too flexible. And because it's so amorphous, it would require much more power to mold, to shape and control it in a precise way. But with enough time I think I could figure out how."

Short, succinct, matter-of-fact. It was a small reminder that Eryn was powerful, even without the throne behind her. And it sent a shudder down into my core.

I shifted uncomfortably on the stone bench.

Erick had begun pacing. "How can we be certain that it isn't pirates? And if it isn't, who else could it be?"

Eryn shifted. "The only other possibility along the coast is Venitte. The men at their school would have the training necessary to direct fire, but I don't think they'd have anyone with enough power to actually do it."

"We keep coming back to Venitte," I murmured.

Eryn frowned. "I know. It's becoming harder and harder for me to convince myself that somehow, in some way, March isn't behind this."

"March?"

"The Lord of Venitte. He rules our sister city, much as the Mistress rules here, except he has no throne—at least nothing like the Skewed Throne. He is . . . a very old friend." She smiled, but it was filled with sadness and regret, tremulous and hurt at the same time.

"Does Lord March have the means to build ships of war?" Erick asked into the silence. "Would he have ordered an attack on Amenkor's trading ships?"

Eryn shot him a glare, back stiffening, then faltered.

Looking down at her hands clasped in her lap, she said, "Yes. He has the means to build ships of war. But," she said, turning blazing eyes on Erick, "there have been no reports of any type of ship construction in the last few years. Nothing of this significance. Ask Avrell. He has agents in all of the key ports along the Frigean coast."

"I don't want Avrell to know," I said.

Eryn seemed startled. "Why not?"

I bit off a sharp retort, realized she didn't know about the incident in the throne room, when I'd Reached toward Eryn and Colby. She hadn't been back in the city long enough to find out.

I straightened. "I'm not so certain I trust him completely yet." At Eryn's confused look, I added, "I'll let Erick explain. For now, let Captain Catrell spread the rumor that it was pirates who destroyed the ship until we know otherwise."

"He's going to be suspicious that it's something else," Eryn warned. "I wouldn't have abandoned the escort on the return from Colby if I thought the ship had been attacked by pirates."

Erick grunted. "That's even better. If the ship was attacked by someone else, having a little doubt spicing the rumor of piracy should make it that much less of a shock when we reveal who it really was."

Eryn didn't respond, but it was obvious she didn't agree. "And what about the harbor? Are you going to reestablish the blockade?"

I considered a moment, then shook my head. "No. I don't see any reason to."

Eryn's expression darkened. "Even after the warning vision of the city burning? Even after seeing the scorch marks on the deck?"

"No. Whoever is attacking the ships hasn't made any attempt at our harbor—"

"Yet," Eryn cut in.

"—yet," I added with a glare. "Until we know who the attackers are, and what they want, I'm not going to risk causing a panic in the city, not when the people are already concerned about starving this winter."

And I didn't want to give Avrell a reason to think I needed replacement either.

I rose from my seat. Eryn followed suit.

"And how are we going to find out who the attackers really are?" she asked as we made our way out of the garden.

"I don't know," I said.

But I had an idea.

✝

"Good," Marielle said as she passed behind me and glanced over my shoulder at the slate. I was working on my sentences on the settee in my chambers, sunlight streaming through the balcony doorway. A breeze blew in through the opening, cold with the edge of winter, but not cold enough to keep the doorway closed. "Now try to construct something more complex. Then I think we'll shift to mathematics."

I growled. I hated mathematics, and Marielle knew it. Out of the corner of my eye, I caught her smile.

I turned my attention back to the slate, wiped off the simple sentence I'd written with a damp cloth, then began a new one. I grinned maliciously as I began to write, the letters coming easily now.

"Let me see," Marielle said when I finished.

I held up the slate.

Marielle gasped, brought a hand up to cover her smile even as her expression grew stern. "Mistress! I didn't teach you such language! Where did you learn that?"

I laughed and set the slate to one side, then paused with a frown.

Where had I learned those words?

Marielle picked up the slate and sat down on the settee beside me, shaking her head. "You did misspell 'horsefucker,' though. We'll have to work on that."

She said it in such a serious tone that I burst out laughing. Marielle joined me a moment later.

When the laughter had died down, Marielle wiping tears from her face, she asked, "Who is Bloodmark anyway?"

I grew quiet instantly, turned away. "Someone I killed on the Dredge."

Marielle stilled. I thought she'd pull away, horrified, as William had always done, realized that I'd already tensed myself in preparation for that reaction and how it would hurt.

But instead, Marielle placed a hand on my forearm. I turned toward her, startled, saw the sympathy in her eyes, an attempt at understanding, even though she couldn't possibly relate. She'd been raised in the palace since she was six.

Before I could respond, someone knocked on the outer door.

"That's probably Erick," I said as Marielle rose to answer it. I stood as well and moved to the entrance to the balcony without stepping out to its edge, my mind shifting from sentences and Bloodmark and death to my idea on how to determine who was attacking the trade ships. From the balcony doorway, I could see one side of the jut of land that enclosed the bay and the stone tower that guarded the entrance.

I didn't want to have to blockade the harbor unless it was absolutely necessary. When Eryn had done it, it had thrown the city into a panic. I could still remember the mob thronging the palace gates within minutes of the bells tolling, issuing the orders.

Behind, I heard Marielle lead Erick into the room, then turn to leave.

"Marielle," I said, heard her halt. I turned. "I think you should stay."

"As you wish," she said, although her brow creased as she frowned. She clasped her hands in front of her and stood, waiting.

"You wanted to see me?" Erick asked formally. He'd come as a guardsman, a Seeker, not as a mentor.

"Yes." I motioned to the settee, but he shook his head, preferring to stand, his gaze intent. "I wanted to talk about how to find out who has been attacking the trading ships."

Erick grunted. "I thought you were going to talk to Avrell about it eventually. As Eryn suggested."

My nose squinched up in annoyance. "Maybe. But by talking to Avrell we'd only be guessing. Avrell has already said he hasn't received word from his contacts in the other cities regarding the missing trade ships. I want to know who's attacking us, without any doubts, even if in the end it is only pirates."

"What did you have in mind?"

I hesitated, biting my lip as I moved away from the balcony window back into the room. "I want to use the Fire."

Erick frowned. "I don't understand."

Behind him, Marielle shifted uncomfortably as well. She'd never been asked to stay behind during any discussions between me and Erick, or any of the others for that matter. It was obvious she felt she shouldn't be overhearing this conversation. But for the moment I ignored her, focused on Erick.

"You know that I saw what Eryn saw in Colby," I said, beginning to pace. Now that it came down to explaining my idea, it didn't seem as solid as it had before. "What you don't know is that I think that during the first use of the throne, when Eryn was trying to explain how I could find out who had been manipulating my dreams, somehow I placed a portion of the White Fire inside her in the process. At the end, when the vision of the city burning became too horrifying, I shoved it away. I think I tore a piece of the Fire inside me off in the process and it attached itself to Eryn."

Erick remained standing, eyes narrowed as he watched me pace. "How is that going to help us find out who's attacking our ships?"

I halted. "I want to send out more ships. I want to try to tag some of the people on those ships with the Fire as I accidentally tagged Eryn, and then I want to use the ships as bait. Hopefully, whoever is attacking the ships will seize the opportunity and attack again. Only this time, I can be watching using the Fire, as I watched what Eryn did in Colby."

"And what about the people on that ship? The one that gets attacked?"

I grimaced. I'd already thought of that. "They'll be prepared. They'll know what to expect."

"No, they won't. Not if what Eryn says is true and they have someone who can use the Sight participating in the attack. They won't be able to defend against that."

My shoulders tightened at the rebuke in his voice, but I said nothing. Erick watched my reaction, then lowered his head as he thought.

I glanced toward Marielle. She'd gone still, was staring at me with a slight look of bewilderment and fear. Then she glanced away, as if ashamed.

I wondered what she was thinking, but then Erick grunted and looked up.

"It has possibilities, but I don't think you've thought everything out yet."

"Like what?"

"Like the fact that you'll be sending out a ship in the middle of winter. Have you seen the waves out beyond the harbor? They're high and strong. The seas won't be kind. It's possible that the ship will founder simply because of the weather. You'll have to find captains and crews willing to take that risk. Because of that, you won't be able to send out more than one or two ships at best. Most won't go, even if it is the Mistress ordering it. The captains and their crews aren't stupid." He began pacing.

"So let's say you get one ship, with a crew crazy enough to try this. There will have to be a contingent of guardsmen on board in case they do actually get attacked. You won't be able to get the crew to go unless they feel they have a fair chance of surviving the attack. That requires even more men agreeing to the plan. But that shouldn't be a problem. You *can* order the guardsmen to go and expect them to obey. As long as we choose the right men. We'd have to pick men familiar with ships and the way they operate.

"Then there's this idea of 'tagging' one of the crew members. From what happened in the throne room when you Reached for Eryn, I'd say you have to be in contact with this person in order to witness the events. But what if the attack comes when you aren't connected? You won't be able to watch them continuously. You *are* the Mistress. Amenkor is relying on you to get everyone through the winter. They have *faith* that you'll get them through. That faith will falter if you vanish for a week or more while you deal with the ship. Even if you aren't actively doing anything, just your presence out in the city—down in the slums, out at the communal ovens, on site at the rebuilding of the warehouses—is enough to keep the people going. I've *seen* the change in the people since you started visiting the construction sites and the warehouses, since you set up the kitchens and the Servants have been seen more outside the palace. You won't be able to continue that if you're tied to the throne watching the ship."

"He's right," Marielle broke in. She swallowed when we both turned toward her. "The people *talk*, Mistress. And for the first time since the Fire swept through the city six years ago, they're speaking with hope. Even though it's winter, even though food is scarce. All

of the Servants have noticed it while working in the kitchens, handing out food. The people *need* you."

I shifted uncomfortably at the intensity in Marielle's voice. I
hadn't realized people were paying such close attention to me,
hadn't realized that what I did mattered. Not to that extent.

"So let's review," Erick said, voice tight. He began ticking off
points on his fingers. "You need a ship. You need a captain. You
need a crew. You need guardsmen. And you need the gods' own luck
to be in contact when the ship gets attacked."

"But we need to know who's attacking the trade routes," I
countered, a defensive note creeping into my voice. "If it were simply a matter of a few lost ships, then I'd wait until spring. But it
isn't! More than a few ships have been lost, and according to Avrell,
it isn't just Amenkor that's lost ships. And then there's the vision."

Erick scowled. "I thought Eryn said that what happened in the
vision didn't occur until summer. And she couldn't even guarantee
that it was this summer."

"But she also said that the visions weren't always accurate."

"Which means that there may not be an attack on the city
coming at all!"

Now it was my turn to scowl. "Can you think of any other way
to find out who has been attacking the ships? Besides using Avrell
for educated guesses."

Erick, who'd drawn breath to speak, subsided, then shook his
head. "No."

I sighed. "All this speculation won't matter much if I can't tag
someone with the Fire in the first place."

"True," he said. "Who do you—" He halted in mid-sentence,
eyes narrowing suspiciously. "You want to try to tag me, don't
you?"

I nodded. "If it doesn't work, then we'll go speak to Avrell, even
if I don't completely trust him. If it does work . . ."

Erick seemed about to say no, but then his shoulders sagged. "What do you want me to do?"

I motioned to an empty chair. "Have a seat, get comfortable."

As he moved to the chair, grudgingly and somewhat nervously, I turned to Marielle, who jumped as if goosed by one of the guardsmen.

"Yes, Mistress?"

"I want you to watch us," I said, "that's all. Put a protective shield around us both, as we've done during training, something that will contain . . . whatever it is that might happen. If something goes wrong, I want you to find Eryn." If something did go wrong, there probably wouldn't be anything Eryn could do, but still. . . .

Marielle nodded, tension draining out of her in a rush. "Of course, Mistress. I thought—" but she cut herself off. She seemed extremely relieved. "Never mind. Where do you want me to sit?"

I placed Marielle on the settee and watched her draw a few deep breaths before she relaxed and went still. A moment later, she murmured in a distant voice, "I'm ready."

I moved a chair a few paces in front of Erick and sat down.

Erick looked at me across the short distance between us. His eyes had hardened, as if he'd steeled himself for some horrible task and wasn't expecting to survive. "Are you certain this will work?"

I dove beneath the river, felt Erick's true fear—fear that he was hiding behind a mask of bravado—wash over me, felt Marielle's more exposed fear behind me. Where Marielle sat, the river felt more dense, as if the eddies and currents had gathered there more closely. She hadn't constructed the shield yet, was waiting for me to define the boundaries where I would work.

I smiled at Erick in encouragement, then said, "No."

He frowned in annoyance and darkened his glare, but I felt his amusement.

Shifting my position on the chair, I pushed myself deeper into the river, dove down to the sphere of White Fire at my core, and held there. The voices of the throne behind the Fire were animated, pushing up as close as possible to the flames, but they didn't feel malevolent, weren't screaming and thrashing and trying to break free. Instead, they were thronged together like a crowd of gutterscum children surrounding a street-talker telling stories on the Dredge, shoving each other aside for a better position. And they were talking, arguing with each other, scoffing at and berating each other's ideas. I could smell the unfamiliar spice of Cerrin, could feel his presence at the back of the crowd, standing with five others. Liviann, the older woman who smelled of oak and wine, stood at the forefront, close to the Fire, watching intently but not participating in the conversations of the other voices around her.

These were the Seven I'd witnessed create the thrones when I'd claimed the Skewed Throne. The Seven who had poured their energy—and in the end, their souls—into their creation. I'd felt them die, the demands of the thrones too great to withstand.

The other voices in the throne made way for them, deferred to them. For these other voices, what I was attempting was something new, something the majority of them had never seen before. Some of them wanted me to succeed; others wanted me to fail. I could feel their shifting intents. For now they were mostly curious.

But from the Seven . . .

From the back, I felt Cerrin nod encouragement, felt the same from the rest of the Seven as well.

I shrugged aside their attention, focused on the Fire, on the presence on the river that was Erick. Then I halted.

I wasn't certain how to do this.

I felt the Fire pulse, felt some of the voices chuckling as they sensed my hesitation. Angry, I reached out and forced the Fire higher, forced the voices to retreat slightly. They hissed in irritation.

I focused again. "I'm ready," I said, and the river responded as Marielle drew its currents tight, weaving them into a strong shield that enveloped Erick and me where we sat.

Concentrating, I tried to slice a portion of the flame off of the main barrier, tried to use the river as I would my dagger, a sharp blade that could sever and cut. But the Fire bent away from the blade, as if pushed away by the blade-eddy I'd created. The Fire wasn't rigid enough for the blade to slice into it, too amorphous and flexible for such an attack.

Eryn had been right.

I tried a few more times, using various thrusts and stabs Erick had taught me during my training in the slums, then newer techniques taught by Westen, but none of them worked. The Fire was too resistant.

A few of the voices snorted in contempt and began to wander away, their attention shifting elsewhere. Those that remained began calling out suggestions, some of them trying to help, others jeering and making crude comments.

Cerrin shifted forward as the crowd thinned, coming up to stand behind Liviann, who remained close to the front, still watching intently.

I frowned, let the blade-eddy dissipate back into the general currents of the river.

"What's wrong?" Erick asked, an edge of tension in his voice. I could taste his sweat, salty and pungent. The inactivity was making him more nervous. His cold, calm bravado had begun to fray.

"Nothing," I said. "My first attempt didn't work. I'm going to try again."

I thought about what had happened when I'd tagged Eryn. Then, I'd been terrified. I'd shoved at the river, pushed it hard, with enough violence that I'd torn a piece of the Fire away. It hadn't had time to react, to bend and adjust to the currents. And I'd shoved everything away, in a wide wave, with no focus.

Maybe the blade-eddy was too focused.

I shifted so that both Erick and the Fire were in view, then began gathering the river before me, tightening it so I could punch it outward. I could feel the pressure build as I channeled more and more of the river into the punch, heard Eryn's voice from the training sessions as she explained how to tighten the flows, how to make them more intricate and thus more dense.

"Get ready," I said, and heard the strain in my voice.

Erick heard it too. "Is this going to hurt?" he asked suddenly.

"Perhaps."

I was just about to release the energy, felt it pulsing under my control, when Cerrin barked, *Don't!*

I staggered, barely kept hold of the pent-up energy before me, then snapped, "What!"

Through the river, I sensed Erick's confusion, felt Marielle shift forward on the settee in concern.

That won't accomplish anything. It will only hurt the Seeker.

I pulled back on the energy, allowed some of it to disperse back into the river. "It worked once before."

I could feel Cerrin's contempt radiating from behind the Fire. *You were lucky before. And Eryn had her own defenses from the Sight. This Seeker has nothing.*

His contempt and condescension sparked an anger deep down inside me. Cerrin sounded like Bloodmark, his words harsh and bitter with ridicule.

And yet he'd stopped me from harming Erick. Bloodmark would never have done that.

I let some of my own anger tinge my voice as I asked, "Do you know how to do this?"

I felt his presence pause behind the Fire, felt the oak-and-wine-scented woman's attention focus on him.

You were always more talented with Fire than the rest of us, she said.

The other members of the Seven had shifted forward as well, the other voices in the throne crowding around them.

She does have more Talent than any of the previous Mistresses . . . at least within the last few hundred years. This from a woman, younger than Liviann, her hair long and black and straight. I remembered her from the creation of the throne, remembered her struggling to get free.

Yes, Atreus, another man said, his voice sharp, his eyes like flint, *but she is certainly no Adept.*

She's not an Adept, no, Garus, Cerrin said. *But she does have the Talent.*

Do we trust her? Liviann asked.

The silence stretched. I began to think Cerrin wouldn't answer, began to grow irritated, but then:

Yes.

He shifted forward, ahead of the others, moving to the edge of the Fire.

"How do you know how to do this?" I demanded, my irritation at being excluded from their conversation, at only being given half answers both here and on the tower before I Reached for Eryn, coloring my voice.

Because before the Seven created the two thrones, I worked with Fire. That was my strength. That's why I can escape the net you have placed over the voices, why I could help you earlier when you sparred with Eryn. The net can't hold me because I can slip through the Fire instead, bypass it.

I drew breath to ask him about the Talent, about being an Adept, about how he could use the Fire to bypass the net—

But I let the breath go with a shudder.

"So how do I tag Erick with the Fire?"

Cerrin hesitated, than said, *Like this.*

I felt him reach out across the net Eryn had shown me how to use to contain the voices, slip through the protective barrier of the Fire itself, and heard the other voices within the throne gasp. A few tried to take advantage, tried to stretch the same way the man had, reach out from their prison, but they screamed when their reach touched the Fire. The oak-and-wine-scented woman stepped forward but halted, watched carefully but did nothing.

The man's essence stayed behind the Fire, but as I watched, the river between the Fire and Erick began to change beneath his direction. A whirlpool formed, swirling like a funnel, the mouth at the edge of the Fire, the tail trailing away, snaking back and forth slightly as it elongated, extending out until it reached Erick. I heard Erick gasp as it touched him. But not with pain. In surprise, his body tensing, then relaxing.

Now push the Fire along the conduit, Cerrin said. When I hesitated, he added, *Now! I can't hold the conduit forever.*

I let the ball of energy I'd been holding in reserve release, turned toward the Fire and pushed it outward, not with the sharp edge of a blade but like a shield. It flared higher, and a tendril of it coursed out along the conduit, down the funnel.

As soon as it reached the end, touching Erick, who sucked in another shocked breath, Cerrin closed off the mouth of the funnel, neatly cutting through the tendril of Fire. What had been contained in the conduit surged down along the collapsing length until it settled into a steady flame near Erick's heart.

I felt Cerrin's reach draw back behind the barrier, felt him beginning to withdraw.

"Wait!" I said, no anger or irritation in my voice now. When he paused, I said, "Thank you."

He seemed surprised. Then he nodded, eyes closed, the gesture somehow intensely formal, and turned away. As he retreated, the rest of the Seven closed in around him, the other voices surging forward in animated discussion.

I turned to Erick, verified the Fire still burned inside him, although muted as it had been with Eryn here in the city, then pulled myself up out of the river.

Marielle had moved and now stood behind me uncertainly. She'd let her protective barrier drop. "Is everything all right?" she asked when I looked over my shoulder. "Who were you talking to?"

I shuddered, felt exhaustion settle into my muscles. "I had some help from one of the voices in the throne."

"Something definitely happened," Erick said. "I felt a tingling sensation, and a bitter cold. But I don't feel anything now."

I smiled. "I think it worked. We'll have to test it tomorrow. Send you out of the city, perhaps to check up on the timber operation to the east."

"And then what?"

Erick rose when I stood, touching his chest over his heart as if looking for damage.

"Then we talk to Borund about a ship," I answered.

†

Trees. I'd never seen so many, so close together.

They closed in around Erick and his escort of guardsmen as they entered the forest east of the city. As he rode beneath the canopy into the forest's shadow, I felt the heat of the sun drop, the shadows closing in, and drew in the spicy scent of pine as Erick breathed in deeply and held it. The air was cool and sharp and dark, laced with greenery, with lush earth and sunlit dust motes.

It was a scent I recognized. Cerrin. The elusive incense that I had not been able to recognize before was the scent of the shade of the forest.

Something stung the back of Erick's neck and he swore, swat-
ting at it. He slowed his horse to a walk, patted its neck as he murmured to it, its ears flicking back in answer. Behind him, I heard
the two other guardsmen's mounts slow as well.

Then, reluctantly, I let the protective Fire within Erick go,
pushed myself up on the currents of the river—reduced here so far
away from the presence of the throne—until I broke through the
tops of the pine trees and could look west, toward Amenkor and
the white blaze that would guide me back to myself.

I'd experimented as Erick rode east, before he'd reached the
confines of the forest. I found that I didn't need to see the Fire itself as long as I was willing to risk Reaching outward into unknown
territory, as I'd tried to do on the tower when searching for Corum,
before Eryn pulled me back. All I had to do was Reach out until I
had the Fire within sight, then I could find my way back.

I streaked toward Amenkor, the world blurring below me,
slowed as I entered the city, and felt the power of the throne settling back around me.

As I flew toward the throne room, I spotted another Fire, in the
gardens of the palace.

Eryn.

I halted, hovered high over the stone path. Below, Eryn was
speaking with Avrell as they moved sedately across the garden, her
voice low. Avrell was frowning, his expression dark.

I hesitated a moment. But only a moment.

I dove down and settled into the Fire inside Eryn.

"—she needs to blockade the harbor!" Eryn said. "I don't understand why she's not doing anything."

"Perhaps because she doesn't feel a few burn marks on a ship-
wrecked deck is enough to warrant such a course of action," Avrell
answered.

Inside my cocoon of Fire, I stilled, shocked.

Eryn had gone to Avrell after all, even after I'd asked—no, *ordered*—her not to.

"But it's more than that," Eryn continued. "Look at all the ships that have gone missing from Amenkor and the surrounding cities over the last year. Almost a dozen, if your sources can be believed. That's more than mere piracy and weather. And then there's the vision."

Avrell halted. "What vision?"

I hissed, shock changing over into anger. I pushed to the edge of the Fire, willed Eryn not to speak, almost reached out to seize control, to force her not to speak.

"There's a portion of me still trapped inside the throne," Eryn said. "That shadow of me showed Varis a vision of the city totally destroyed after an attack." Eryn turned to face Avrell. "The attack came from the ocean, Avrell. That, along with the missing ships, the fire on the deck, the fact that she sensed the people attacking in the vision were using the Sight. . . . We need to protect ourselves from whatever is out there. That must be why I blockaded the harbor before, to protect the city from an attack."

Conflicting emotions raced across Avrell's face. Fear, doubt, suspicion.

In the end, he settled on almost no expression at all, his stance reserved.

"Why hasn't Varis come to see me about this?" he asked.

Eryn snorted. "Because she's afraid you're trying to replace her just as you replaced me."

"Why would she think that?"

"You had the guardsmen waiting for her inside the throne room before, didn't you?"

"That was because I didn't know what was happening!" he spat. "If I've learned anything over the last few years it's that when it comes to the throne you can never be too careful. As soon as I realized that Varis was still in control, I called the guardsmen off!"

"Not soon enough for Varis."

I drew back from the Fire as the two halted, Avrell's eyes hard with anger. I felt Eryn force herself to relax, her voice to calm.

Avrell suddenly turned, moving swiftly across the garden, back toward its main entrance.

"Where are you going?" Eryn called after him.

Avrell halted, looked back over his shoulder. "To see the Mistress."

Eryn stilled, her breath held, her heart stuttering. A moment of panic shivered through her.

Then the anger kicked back in, the certainty that she was right, honed by over twenty years of being the Mistress herself.

She moved to follow.

I pulled myself up out of the Fire, catching one last glimpse of Avrell passing through the archway of the garden into the palace before I sped back to the throne room, the White Fire blazing up around me. I gasped as I reentered my body, felt Marielle's presence in the throne room, along with the usual four guardsmen. I'd had them wait inside the throne room this time, since Erick wasn't present.

Marielle took one hesitant step up to the dais where the throne sat, reached a hand out unconsciously before stopping herself. "Mistress? Is everything all right? Did it work?"

"Yes," I said, my voice surprisingly calm, even though it vibrated with underlying anger, with the power of the throne. "Everything worked fine. Erick's inside the forest."

I motioned to the guardsmen, the one in charge stepping forward. Before he'd left, Erick had introduced him, had told me he could be trusted.

"Keven."

"Yes, Mistress?"

"The First of the Mistress will be arriving in a moment, along with the *former* Mistress, Eryn. I want your men to be on either side of the throne."

Keven hesitated at the emphasis on "former," frowned, then said, "Yes, Mistress." He motioned to the other three guardsmen, ordering two to one side of the throne, the third taking his place beside Keven on the other.

I nodded in approval.

"Marielle."

"Yes?"

"Stay where you are."

Marielle turned as the main doors on the far side of the throne room swung open, a guardsman stepping hesitantly inside. He'd been ordered to keep everyone out.

Before he could speak, I said, "Let them in."

He nodded, then pushed the doors open wider to let them pass.

Avrell came in first, followed almost immediately by Eryn. They moved down the central walkway quickly, coming to a halt just before the dais.

"Forgive me, Mistress," Avrell said, nodding his head slightly.

"She told you about the shipwreck," I said without preamble.

Avrell appeared momentarily shocked, but recovered quickly.

I did not watch him. I stared at Eryn, did not try to hide the anger I felt coiling inside me.

"And about the vision of the city burning," Avrell added.

I stood. The moment my fingers left the throne I felt it begin to twist behind me, reshaping itself into another form. But the sensation no longer crawled across my shoulders, no longer prickled against my skin.

The room fell silent. I felt the guards at my back tense, felt Marielle stiffen at my side.

"I told you not to talk to Avrell about this."

"I thought that—"

"No!" I barked, and anger sparked in Eryn's eyes. Her back straightened and her nostrils flared briefly. Beside her, Avrell flinched, then drew himself upright, back stiff, face expressionless— the face of a diplomat, a politician. "There is no excuse," I said. "I told you not to speak to him, and you did."

"You weren't *doing* anything," Eryn protested, her voice cold, hard, strained.

"You aren't the Mistress anymore," I said flatly. "I am."

Eryn drew in a sharp breath, held it, but said nothing. I glared at her from beside the throne, felt it flowing smoothly from one shape to another behind me.

We held each other's gazes for a long moment, then I stepped down from the dais purposefully, motioning to Keven. "Get an escort ready. We're heading into the city."

"All of us?" Avrell's voice was neutral, without any inflection whatsoever.

I glanced toward him. "All of us."

"And where, may I ask, are we going?" Avrell asked as he fell into step beside and slightly behind me. I motioned Marielle to my other side; Eryn followed behind.

"To see Borund about a ship."

†

We found Borund at the warehouse that had been set up on the Dredge, the kitchen next door bustling with activity, a few members of the Dredge's militia standing at the doors to both the warehouse and the kitchen, their faces hard and serious, their hands on the pommels of their swords.

The escort paused outside the warehouse—blocked by the activity on the street because I'd refused to bring horses down to the slums after the mob attack—and I nodded to the Dredge guardsmen. As I stood there, I glanced down the Dredge, slid beneath the river unconsciously, felt the pulse of the street, the eddies and flows. I stared at the people, at their torn clothing, at the dirt on their faces, and beneath the river I could feel their hope. A living thing, passing through them and around the streets, seeping into the narrows and alleys that made up the deepest part of the slums. I thought of Evander, working stone in the warehouse district, thought of all the men and women he'd brought with him since I'd had the abusive work leader Hant whipped. I thought of Darryn and his militia, of the order he had imposed. And I thought of what Marielle and Erick had said before I'd placed the Fire inside of him, of how the people had hope again.

A few of the gutterscum and denizens of the Dredge paused at the sight of so many nonmilitia guardsmen, then caught my eye. A couple of the younger boys sneered, made rude gestures. One woman slapped one of the boys on his head, spoke to him harshly, as he glared at her.

Then the woman smiled and bowed toward me, making the sign of the Skewed Throne across her chest before moving on.

I turned back, away from the Dredge, saw Avrell watching me closely, face still expressionless. But he was gray beneath the river. So were Eryn and all of the rest of the escort.

The guardsmen moved forward.

"What can I do for you?" Borund asked as soon as my escort allowed me into the building. Behind him, women were hauling large sacks of bread still warm from the bakeries and ovens along the Dredge into the adjacent kitchen. A few came inside the warehouse and placed some of the bread on long tables before retreating back out into the streets. Behind the tables, crates were stacked almost to the ceiling, straw poking out from between the wooden slats. Dangling from the ceiling were strings of onions and garlic and smoked dried meats that would keep well in the cool, dry air of the building. From where I stood, I could see barrels labeled salted fish and on the far side of the room—

William.

I turned my attention back to Borund. "I need a ship and a crew to man it."

Borund's eyes widened and he turned his full attention on me. "What for?"

My entourage of guardsmen had finally caught William's eye. He moved up behind Borund as I answered.

A day or two ago, William's presence would have flustered me, forced me to back off. But not now, not today.

"I want to send it out as a trap," I said, then I outlined my plan, what Erick and I had discussed. I told him about the shipwreck in Colby, about the fire, about how I could keep in contact with the ship, about the vision. I told him everything.

Through it all, I kept my eyes on Borund. He listened intently, didn't interrupt. His only reaction was to rub his hand across his bald head, smooth down the hair that still grew in a half circle around his ears and in the back. The movement jostled the wire glasses askew on his nose, but he didn't adjust them.

At the end, he grunted. "It's a suicide mission for the ship, even with the guardsmen on board," he said. "You realize that?"

I nodded grimly.

He frowned, then said, "Give me three days. I'll find you a ship, and a captain and crew to man it."

I nodded. "I'll be ready."

Borund turned back to the warehouse. For a moment, William watched me uncertainly, as if he wanted to say something, then he turned to catch up to Borund.

My gaze followed William as he paused to snatch up a sheaf of paper from a desk set against one wall, but then he ducked into the depths of the warehouse.

When I turned around, I met Avrell's gaze.

"An interesting plan," he said. "Let's hope Borund can find a ship."

I didn't answer.

As the escort moved out onto the Dredge, Eryn came up beside me.

"You could have told me," she said, too low for anyone else to hear.

Without looking toward her, I said harshly, "I would have. You didn't give me enough time to figure it all out."

Then I stepped away, leaving Eryn behind.

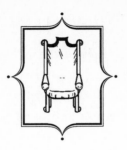

Chapter 8

"BORUND FOUND A SHIP," I said. "And a captain
and crew to man it."

It had taken him five days, not three. I'd called
together the captains of the various guardsmen—Baill, Catrell, and
Westen—as well as Avrell, Nathem, Eryn, and Erick, to discuss who
else should be sent. We were in the same conference room Avrell
had used to introduce me to everyone after I'd taken the throne,
but this time the room felt different. Before it had been closed in,
confined, and crowded. The few potted trees and small tables in the
corners, the Skewed Throne banner against the back wall, had all
been threatening. And over two months before, in these people's
eyes, I'd been nothing but an unknown, a nervous and somehow
dangerous girl who'd managed to steal the throne from beneath
them.

Today, I'd barely noticed the potted plants, the banner, the tables. And the men who had thought they ruled the city were hesitant, wary, and uncertain around me. Before, I'd been someone
they could sidestep if they needed to, a ruler only in name, too
young and inexperienced to be truly dealt with.

But almost a week ago, I'd truly claimed the throne. Not just in

name, but in action. I'd become the Mistress. They'd heard from
their guardsmen what had happened in the throne room. Suddenly,
they didn't feel as secure in their positions and it showed. In the
way they sat in their seats, in the way a few of them wouldn't meet
my gaze.

"And what is it that you need from us?" Baill asked. He looked
tired, the skin around his eyes pinched and strained. But his gaze
was as penetrating as ever. He sat in his usual place at my right side,
Eryn on my left, the rest of them arrayed down the length of the
table on either side. Erick stood behind my seat at the head of the
table. "We're guardsmen, not sailors."

I frowned at the curtness in his voice. "I need a small force of
guardsmen to man the ship, since the intention is for it to be attacked. I asked you here to help me select the number of men on
that force, as well as someone to lead them."

"You could have done that without us," Westen said. "You are
the Mistress."

"I know," I said, bristling. Then I caught Westen's eye.

He had not meant it as a challenge.

I let some of the tension I felt ease from my shoulders,
cursed silently. Baill had put me on the defensive with a single
question. "I'm asking you for your advice," I said in a much
calmer voice.

Westen's eyes narrowed in consideration. Then he nodded, as
if satisfied. "Then I suggest you send at least twenty guardsmen
with the crew. That should be sufficient."

Baill snorted. "Twenty? The crew of the ship will be stumbling
all over them the entire journey. And what do you expect these men
to do if the ship *is* attacked? They're guardsmen. They traipse
around the city and stop street fights. What can they do on a
ship?"

Captain Catrell's eyes darkened at the condescension in Baill's

tone. "With all due respect," he said, not looking in Baill's direction, "the city guardsmen would be better on a ship than the palace
guardsmen. They're used to fighting in close quarters and in
strange and varied locations. Sir."

Baill shook his head. "But the palace guardsmen have their own
ships."

"That they barely take out of the harbor!" Catrell protested. "A
trading ship is completely different."

As the argument continued, I glanced toward Avrell, shot him
a questioning look. The first time we'd had such a meeting, the
guardsmen had been united, a single front in opposition to Avrell
and his manipulations to get me onto the throne, Baill in control,
backed by Catrell. They'd only relented when it became clear that
Eryn herself had wanted me to become the next Mistress, that
Avrell was simply doing what she'd intended.

But now it appeared that there was some friction between
Catrell and Baill. They were both clearly on edge.

Avrell caught my glance, frowned and shook his head slightly,
uncertain.

I slid beneath the river, watched the confrontation through the
currents.

Catrell had set himself up in firm opposition to Baill, but I
could not tell why. He seemed agitated, the flows around him harsh
and swift, more gray than red, as if he were being torn between two
opposing forces, being forced to choose. Baill seemed irritated that
Catrell was arguing with him, but implacable, the river more focused and intent. He expected Catrell to relent, was getting frustrated that he hadn't yet.

And Baill was completely red.

Westen, gray and harmless, was watching the entire confrontation with interest.

"But ten men isn't going to be sufficient if they do get attacked," Catrell said. "That wouldn't be sufficient against a band of pirates! If this is something more—"

"If this is something more," Baill interrupted, words forced out through gritted teeth, "it's not going to matter if there are ten men or thirty! They're all going to die!"

Catrell drew breath to continue, eyes flaring, but I cut them both short.

"That's enough." They both turned toward me, Catrell still agitated, face slightly red. I frowned at Baill, at the closed expression on his face. "I think it best to send as many guardsmen on the ship as they can handle, to give them the best chance of survival."

Baill's face closed off even more. He leaned back in his chair, crossed his arms over his chest. He became a silent wall of disagreement, of discontent.

I didn't turn away, didn't back down. "And," I continued, "I think the force should be mixed. The palace guardsmen that have experience on the patrol ships in the harbor will make up the majority of the force. Select twelve men from those forces, Captain Baill." I shifted my gaze. "I want another eight from you, Captain Catrell. Try to get men who've worked on the docks before, or worked on ships or come from fishing villages. Guardsmen who may be used to the ocean."

Catrell nodded sharply, satisfied, his shoulders relaxing. He cast Baill a dark look before shifting his gaze to the table.

I turned to Westen. "Would you like to send some of the Seekers as well?"

Westen seemed surprised I'd asked. "Unless you wish to, I don't see how they would be any more effective than the regular guardsmen on a ship."

I nodded, then turned to the room as a whole. "Then who should lead them."

There was a moment of suspended silence, and then Avrell

shifted forward. "It should be someone you trust," he said, "and someone who trusts you. After all, this person is going to be your link to the ship."

I frowned, glanced toward Baill and Catrell and Westen. Out of the three of them, I trusted Westen the most, simply because I'd dealt with him and his Seekers more than any of the others, calling on them whenever I'd dreamed of someone that needed to be dealt with, someone like Corum. Catrell I knew from the excursion to Colby and the wrecked ship. Outside of that, I'd only had contact with him on a few excursions to the city, when he'd been part of my escort. No other direct contact was necessary. And Baill . . .

Baill had been busy organizing the patrols that protected the supplies in the various buildings that had been converted into warehouses and kitchens now scattered throughout the city. With Catrell's help, since the city guard made up the majority of the force guarding each warehouse. Baill had barely been in the palace over the last few months.

So which of the three did I trust the most?

Behind me, I heard Erick shift forward, stepping up to my right side. "It has to be me," he announced to the room.

My heart dropped. Cold fear tightened in my chest, coursed through my body like ice, tingling in my arms and fingers. "No," I said without thinking, even as inside the cold fear shifted into an even colder acceptance.

I'd known I would be sending Erick on the ship for days, practically since the moment I'd successfully placed the White Fire next to his heart with Cerrin's help.

I'd known, but I still didn't want to accept it.

I caught Erick's eyes, saw the determination there, the intent. His face was hard, his stance rigid. It was a stance I recognized instantly from the Dredge. He'd already made up his mind, and nothing was going to sway him.

On the Dredge, it would have worked. I would have backed down, as I'd done when he'd decided to recruit Bloodmark as one of his trackers. I'd known that was a mistake, but I'd relented. Because I was young, and I didn't want to lose the only chance I had to escape the slums.

Now I was the Mistress. I didn't have to relent. I *could* deny him, could *order* him to stay—

But I knew I wouldn't.

Feeling the coldness deep inside, a coldness of the heart that left me feeling empty, I drew breath to agree—

But someone touched my arm.

I snapped my head around, letting anger fill my eyes. I expected the person to flinch back, to retreat.

But it was Eryn. The stern expression on her face never faltered. "It's the best choice," she said, her grip on my arm tightening slightly. "Out of everyone here, you trust him the most. Who else can you send?"

"I know," I said, letting the coldness touch my voice. We'd barely spoken over the last week, since I'd confronted her in the throne room; we'd been avoiding each other as much as possible. But I still respected her advice, and so in a softer voice, repeated, "I know."

Suddenly, twenty guardsmen didn't seem like enough. Suddenly, the entire plan seemed flawed.

Eryn's grip on my arm relaxed. A knowing sympathy tightened the corners of her eyes.

I turned back to the table. The coldness inside had grown, now spread to my arms, numbing them. "Does anyone want to argue?"

No one said anything. Of course, I thought bitterly, trying to shove the coldness away. Erick's departure weakened my position, and strengthened theirs. Baill actually shifted forward, his obstinate wall relaxing with a hint of approval.

"Then Erick will lead the expedition," I said, and felt something stab deep down inside me, something more than a political consideration.

Nathem leaned forward, shuffled a few pieces of parchment before him. "Then we need to discuss the allocation of provisions for the ship," he said, and began a litany of supplies that would be needed and which warehouses those supplies could be found in.

I barely listened. His voice faded away into nothing but a dull roar, the sound like wind in my ears. The world faded to gray. But I hadn't slipped beneath the river. This was something different. This had no focus, no intent, no currents. This was simply nothing. No feeling, no emotion. Nothing but a quiet, cold numbness, throbbing with the slow beat of my heart.

I don't know how long the numbness held, how long I hovered in silent shock, listening to my heart. It felt like eternity, but it couldn't have been long. When the world began to fade back in, the numbness retreating, I heard Nathem say, "—although we have enough stores. I just don't understand how we could have misplaced those crates."

"What crates?" Avrell asked.

Beside me, I felt Baill straighten in his seat, suddenly attentive.

Nathem shook his head, face perplexed. "There were supposed to be ten crates of Capthian wine in the warehouse on Havel Street near the wharf. Instead there were only seven when we counted."

"Weren't supplies missing from the Priem warehouse a few weeks ago?" I asked. The words felt distant, the coldness still enveloping me. But even as Avrell answered, the last of the numbness faded.

"Yes." Avrell glared across the table. "Captain Baill was supposed to look into it."

Baill shifted in his seat, the motion careful and considered. "We searched the entire Priem warehouse, using Master Regin's master list. We found that indeed a few barrels of salted fish were missing. However, we have yet to determine if they were simply misplaced or were actually stolen."

"But now more supplies are missing?" I asked. "From a different warehouse?"

"Yes. But I'm not surprised. We're far enough into winter that the people have begun to feel the effects of the rationing. Those that aren't willing to work for their fair share are becoming more desperate. And we all know what people are capable of when they're desperate." His steady gaze fell on me as he spoke. I felt my stomach tighten, felt my hand slide toward my dagger, still always within reach.

"But I thought it was the guardsmen's job to keep the supplies safe from such . . . desperation," Avrell interceded. His glare had darkened at Baill's veiled slight; now Baill's eyes hardened at Avrell's implied insult.

"Enough," I said. "What matters is that we find out what's happened to these missing supplies. What do you suggest?"

Avrell thought for a moment. "We need to do a complete inventory. All of the merchants need to check the supplies in their warehouses against the master lists at the same time. Once we know what's missing, perhaps we can find out how it's being stolen from the warehouses without the guardsmen's knowledge, and where it's being taken afterward."

I nodded. "We'll deal with that later. Right now, I want to get the ship's expedition organized and away." I turned to Catrell and Baill. "Have your guardsmen meet me at the docks by noon. Nathem, work with Borund to get the supplies for the ship loaded by then. The ship's name is *The Maiden*. The captain is Mathew."

Baill and the rest of the captains rose and left, Captain Catrell giving me a short bow before departing. Nathem did the same. Avrell, Erick, and Eryn stayed, Eryn deep in thought.

"Mathew is the one who survived the storm and brought in the last shipment from the south, isn't he?" she asked.

I nodded, recalling his haggard look on the docks as his crew was greeted by the mob of townspeople on the wharf. "Yes."

She caught my gaze. I saw a mute apology in her eyes. It was the closest she'd come to acknowledging that she had overstepped her bounds by talking to Avrell about the shipwreck in Colby and the vision of the city burning.

"Have you given any more thought to the fact that if the ship is attacked there will more than likely be someone using the Sight on the enemy's side?" she asked.

I hadn't, but I didn't see what could be done about it. "They'll have to rely on the guardsmen to protect them."

Eryn hesitated, then nodded, stood, and departed with Avrell.

Which left me and Erick alone.

I didn't look toward him, felt him shift his weight from one foot to the other behind me, his clothes rustling.

The silence between us stretched. Until it became too uncomfortable for me to bear.

I stood.

"It had to be me," he said, his voice rough.

I spun, the coldness I'd felt earlier returning with a bitter taste in the back of my throat, like metallic water. "It *could* have been someone else. It could have been *anyone* else."

He shook his head. "No. You've already tagged me with the Fire. You already trust me. You know how I'll react. And I can't be your personal bodyguard forever."

My stomach constricted. I wanted to tell him he was more than a personal bodyguard. I wanted to tell him that I felt relaxed around him, more confident, more certain. I wanted to tell him I was afraid of losing him, that he was a mentor to me. No. More than that. That he was a father to me.

I wanted to tell him many things, but all I said was, "I don't want you to go," my voice tight and ragged.

He smiled, and in his eyes I saw that he knew why I didn't want him to go, that he understood all of the things that I couldn't bring myself to say. And he knew why I couldn't say them as well.

He reached out, pushed a few loose strands of hair from my forehead.

I took the single step between us and hugged him tight, head against his shoulder, tears I refused to shed burning in my eyes. He stiffened for a moment, then enfolded me in his arms, one hand stroking my hair.

I closed my eyes, drew in a deep breath to remind myself of his scent: the sharp tang of oranges. And something else, something subtle, that I hadn't noticed on the Dredge, that I could only smell with the power of the throne behind me. Lavender.

I sighed.

"I'll be fine," he said, his chest rumbling beneath my face, his voice thick and coarse.

And even though I knew it was a lie, I felt better.

†

"Where in hells is he?" I growled.

At my side, Erick scanned the raucous crowds on the wharf, men and women going about their usual business, a few of them pausing to stare at the activity surrounding *The Maiden* and the large group of guardsmen and soldiers that surrounded me, Erick, and Avrell on the dock. Captain Catrell was already here with his group of eight city guardsmen, all dressed in armor, the metal glinting dully in the pale winter sunlight. All eight men were bristling with confidence, all in their mid-twenties or early thirties, all with unforgiving eyes and an impressive array of scars in visible places. On the Dredge, I would have given them all a wide berth.

"Your directions were clear," Avrell muttered from my other side. "He's doing this on purpose. I think—"

"Here he comes," Erick cut in. Then his voice darkened with contempt. "With his twelve guardsmen."

I scanned down the wharf, saw the usual eddies of the crowd interrupted near the end of the dock a moment before Captain Baill emerged, twelve palace guardsmen trailing behind him.

Avrell hissed, stiffened in outrage. I felt my body tense as well, my jaw clenching.

I placed a hand on Avrell's arm to restrain him as Baill and his men came to a halt before us all. The loading of the ship continued around us unabated.

"Mistress," Baill said.

"Captain Baill." I scanned the group of men behind him. "And are these the men you've chosen for this venture?"

They were a ragtag group dressed in armor and with swords in sheaths. At least half of the men were my age or younger, inexperienced youths with excitement in their eyes, nervously shifting from foot to foot. The majority of the rest were old, at least in their forties, their hair mostly gray, their eyes tired, grudging but willing. They didn't fidget like the younger men, but it was questionable whether some of them could draw their own swords. Only three of them were of the same strain as the men chosen by Captain Catrell. But these had a shifty look in their eyes, their expressions dark, eyes flicking toward every movement. They reeked of trouble and my nostrils flared.

Gutterscum always recognizes gutterscum.

"Twelve palace guardsmen," Baill said, "as you requested."

I turned my gaze on him.

He met the gaze evenly, a hint of challenge in his eyes.

"Then let's get them on the ship," I said in answer, turning toward Erick.

His eyes blazed with anger, but he said nothing.

Catrell barked out a command and his eight men gathered together their small packs and marched up the lowered plank onto
the deck of the ship, where the ship's crew—men from Amenkor
mixed with the usual darker-skinned and slighter forms of Zorelli
men from the south—scrambled to prepare the sails and rigging for
departure. Captain Baill motioned his contingent aboard as well.
They sidled up the plank, the younger men chattering, the older
ones and the troublemakers looking on in contempt, or with no expression at all.

"Not a very impressive command," Erick murmured, so low
that only Avrell and I could hear.

"He meant it as a slight," Avrell spat.

"I meant it as a warning," Baill said behind us. All three of us
turned. "This is a fool's errand. There's nothing to be gained here,
nothing to be learned. I'll not waste good men on an expedition
bound to fail."

With that, he moved down the dock and vanished into the
crowds.

"He gave us his least experienced and most feeble fighters,"
Avrell said.

"And his troublemakers," Erick added.

"Will you be able to handle them?"

Erick nodded. "I shouldn't have any problems. Catrell gave us
some of his best men. That should be sufficient."

As he spoke, Captain Catrell approached and nodded. "All of
the guardsmen are aboard, Mistress."

"Good."

He nodded again, then retreated toward my usual escort of
guardsmen, led by Keven, keeping themselves out of the way of the
dockworkers to one side.

Erick watched Catrell silently. Then his stance shifted, became more formal. "I put Keven in charge of your escort while I'm gone. We went through our training together, at least until I was chosen to become a Seeker. He'll guard you with his life. I trust him, and his advice. Listen to him. I've also chosen all of the guardsmen in his contingent, so you should be surrounded by those you can trust implicitly."

I tried to speak, but something hard had lodged in my throat. I stared up into his face instead, saw him start to smile.

Then his gaze shifted to something over my head.

I turned and saw Eryn, her personal Servant Laurren, and an escort of guardsmen making their way down the dock. Laurren was carrying a satchel.

Eryn's movements were stiff with purpose. "Good, the ship hasn't left yet," she said as she came to a halt in front of us.

"You didn't need to come down here," I said.

"Yes, I did." She met my gaze, held it steadily. "I want to go on the expedition."

I stilled, felt my face go slack, devoid of expression. "Why?"

Eryn lifted her head. "Because we know that whoever is attacking these ships is using some form of the Sight, a form we've never seen before if they can truly control fire. If there's to be *any* hope of the ship surviving, it needs some form of protection from that. I'm the best chance they've got."

Hope flared inside my chest. If Eryn were on the ship, if she could protect them from someone else using the Sight. . . .

It might give the men on the ship a fighting chance.

"You can't send her," Erick said flatly.

Both Eryn and I sent him a scathing glare. "Why in hells not?" Eryn spat.

"Because Varis needs you here. For training, for advice on how to rule, for any of a hundred reasons. You can't be spared for a suicide mission."

Eryn frowned, her glare growing heated. Then she growled in exasperation, turned to me and spat, "Then take Laurren. She knows almost as much as I do. She can help."

In Eryn's eyes, I saw the real reason she'd wanted to go. She'd wanted to atone for speaking to Avrell. But Erick was right. I couldn't spare her. There was still too much I needed to learn.

I shifted to Laurren. She straightened as my gaze fell on her. Her short-cropped brown hair caught in a breeze from the harbor and the freckles on her cheeks stood out sharply in the sunlight, somehow in opposition to the hardness in her eyes. She knew the risks of the mission. The knowledge had pulled the skin around her mouth taut. "And do you want to do this?"

Her rounded face tightened, eyes flashing. "Of course," she said with conviction. "I live to serve the throne."

I grunted. "Do you need to get your own clothes?"

"No, Mistress. I'm about the same size as Eryn, I can use hers."

I nodded, was about to motion her toward the ship when Erick said sharply, "You should tag her with the Fire as well. It will give you another advantage . . . in case something happens to me."

I frowned, chose to ignore his last statement. "Are you willing?"

Laurren glanced once toward Eryn, but nodded.

I dove beneath the river, felt the Fire that surrounded the throne, felt the voices, sensed Cerrin, Liviann, Atreus, and the rest of Seven watching.

Do you want help? Cerrin asked.

No, I said, not speaking out loud.

I plied the river, created the funnel as Cerrin had done earlier, conscious of the Seven watching, of all of the voices watching behind them. The eddies only wavered once, but then I steadied myself, let the Fire course down the tendril after it attached to Laurren.

Distantly, I heard her gasp, heard Erick say, "Don't worry. It doesn't hurt . . . much."

Then I sliced the Fire at the mouth of the funnel, felt the funnel collapse, a small flame of the Fire settling near Laurren's heart.

The Seven murmured with approval as I let the river go.

"I can't feel anything," Laurren said, her voice detached.

"It's there," Eryn said. "If I concentrate hard enough, I can feel it. I can't see it, but I can sense that it's there."

I nodded toward the ship. After a momentary hesitation, Laurren stalked up the plank, halted at the top to scan the deck, then strode purposefully toward the foredeck.

"That may make a significant difference if we do run into trouble," Erick said.

Eryn snorted, then bit her lip with worry. "I hope so. It's a huge sacrifice on my part. She's the only Servant who knows how to make a proper cup of tea."

I laughed, a short sharp sound, a horrible nausea twisting my stomach as I lost sight of Laurren in the frenzy of activity on the deck. The realization that I'd most likely sent Laurren to her death along with Erick had just sunk in.

Borund and Mathew appeared at the top of the plank, began to make their way down. On the dock, the last of the crates were being hoisted up into the hold, or hauled up other planks to the deck. Activity was shifting from the dock to the ship itself, men clambering up the rigging, ropes tied off. The sense of excitement began to climb.

"We shouldn't have any troubles outside the harbor," Mathew was saying as he and Borund approached. He glanced up toward the sky. "Weather is holding steady today. But farther south . . ." He shrugged.

"Do the best you can," Borund said. He made a deep bow as they drew near. "Mistress."

"Borund. And Captain Mathew. Is everything ready?"

"Yes, Mistress. All provisions have been loaded, the guardsmen are aboard. We're ready to set sail."

I nodded, the lump returning to the back of my throat. I tried not to look at Erick. "Then good luck."

Mathew grinned. "I have a good crew. We don't need luck."

He turned back to his ship, stepped away with a barked command, the men at the railings darting away, repeating the order all along the ship. Lines tethering the ship to the dock began to be unwound. More men scrambled up into the rigging. Mathew stepped to the plank, began to make his way aboard.

Erick stepped away from the group, back rigid. He followed Mathew up the plank without a word, without glancing back.

I swallowed hard, closed my eyes briefly, then forced myself to draw in a deep breath and steady myself.

When I opened my eyes, Borund was watching me. He smiled, grasped my shoulder, and squeezed once.

The plank was withdrawn. Sails began to unfurl, and the ship pulled away from the dock. Slow at first, then picking up speed as the wind caught, the limp sails filling out with small muffled *whumphs*.

We watched the ship as it made its way across the harbor, smaller fishing craft skimming out of its way. No one spoke.

Then it passed out between the two juts of rocky land that enclosed the harbor, the two small guard towers on either side silhouetted against the skyline. I felt it fade from the throne's senses.

I dove beneath the river, reached up and out to search for the White Fires I'd used to tag Erick and Laurren. Without the full power of the throne behind me, I could barely sense them, didn't dare Reach for either one.

I sighed, found Eryn, Avrell, Borund, and Catrell watching me with mixed expressions of concern and sympathy. Keven and the escorting guardsmen had moved up behind them.

"Now all we do is wait," I said.

†

I huddled inside the White Fire within Erick and tried not to let the motion of the ship make me sick.

Through Erick's eyes, I watched the deck roll, saw a wave of water approaching hard and fast from the right and felt Erick grip the handrail of the deck a moment before the wave hit. Wood shuddered beneath the onslaught, spray kicked up high over the bow, pattering down on the deck like rain. It pelted Erick's face, sharp and stinging, and then he dragged himself toward the bow of the ship, using the handrail and a rope for support. Overhead, black clouds boiled, the sea on the horizon a cold slate gray with wind churning the tops of the waves into whitecaps. Far off to the left, sunlight pierced down through the clouds, the rays vibrant against the receding blue sky.

"How long until the storm hits!" Erick shouted as he reached the bow of the ship.

Mathew turned to glare at him, face deadly serious. "Not much longer!"

Another wave crashed into the ship, sending a sheet of water over Mathew and Erick. I tasted the sea salt on my lips, felt the water seep down through my clothes, instantly soaked.

"You should get down below!" Mathew bellowed, his voice almost lost on the wind. He motioned with his hands, then physically shoved Erick back along the deck, following behind.

Erick hunched down, the ship lurching to the right. As he moved, I could see the black ocean now on the left, where the heart of the storm lay.

I shuddered. Even as I watched, a thin bolt of lightning pierced down out of the clouds and struck the water, a frigid crackling blue.

A moment before Erick reached the hatch leading down to the guardsmen's quarters in the hold, a torrential sheet of rain fell from the sky without warning. He gasped as it stung his face, struggled to find the ladder rungs as the ship lurched and creaked beneath another wave, and then Mathew slammed the hatch closed in his face.

I gathered myself together, then withdrew from the Fire, leaving Erick soaked, chilled, and dripping on the lower deck of *The Maiden*. I drew myself up into the roiling forces of the storm over the ship, fought their violent flows, then searched the horizon to the north until I'd found the white beacon of Amenkor. I sped away, leaving the ship to the storm.

There was nothing more to see there. The ship wouldn't be attacked in the middle of the storm. All I could do was hope that Borund's confidence in Mathew as a shipmaster wasn't misplaced.

I sank back into myself and opened my eyes to the throne room with a gasp. A harsh tremor of weakness sank into my arms, my legs, holding me tight for a breath, for two, and then it began to fade.

"How was the weakness this time?" Marielle asked. Marielle was waiting a few paces away with a blanket, Keven and his guardsmen arranged around the throne. He refused to wait outside. He'd become overly protective of me since Erick had left.

"Worse than the last time, but it's passed now." I stepped down from the throne and Marielle enfolded me in the blanket.

"You're shivering," she said in a scolding tone.

"The ship's headed into a storm," I said, teeth chattering. The blanket felt warm and dry. I couldn't shake the feeling that I was soaked to the skin, as Erick had been. "The rain was bitter cold. I don't think we have to worry about them encountering an attack any time soon."

Marielle simply nodded. I'd been checking up on Erick, Laurren, and the ship on a regular basis over the last few days and she'd grown accustomed to odd reactions, such as me feeling bitterly cold or wet . . . or nauseous. I didn't react well to the movements of the deck. Marielle had started bringing blankets and hot tea to the throne room.

And then there was the weakness. The longer I Reached, and the longer I stayed out, the more my body reacted when I returned. At first, it hadn't been anything more than a sense of fatigue, as if I hadn't slept in days. But the farther Erick and Laurren traveled from Amenkor, the more exhausted I'd felt, until now when I returned my limbs trembled, as if my muscles had been abused, as if I'd just spent the last few hours working with Westen instead of sitting on the throne.

Marielle handed me a steaming cup and I sipped, letting the warm, soothing liquid and hot steam take away the chills as I recovered, ignoring the tremors in my hands.

"How far south are they?" Keven asked. He was broader of shoulder than Erick, heftier, and held himself more relaxed than most of the guardsmen of higher ranking in the palace. He didn't exude the same sense of dangerous calm that enveloped Erick, since he hadn't been trained as a Seeker, but like Erick he felt solid, immovable, and always alert.

"Somewhere near Urral."

Keven grunted. "That's a third of the way to Venitte. They're entering the prime target area now. Most of the ships that have vanished have done so there."

Which meant I'd have to keep a closer eye on the ship from now on. I sighed. Using the throne in this manner was exhausting.

No longer feeling so cold and wet, I handed the cup of tea back to Marielle and nodded to Keven and his men.

"Avrell, Nathem, and the rest of the merchants are meeting in the upper city shortly to begin the inventory of the warehouses. Get an escort ready."

Keven bowed, then motioned to one of his men, who immediately headed toward the throne room doors.

Marielle came to retrieve the blanket.

We met another five guardsmen at the gates to the middle ward, effectively doubling my guard, then headed on foot toward the merchants' guild hall. As we passed through the middle ward, the people on the street stepped out of our way, most with a short bow of respect or a quick tracing of the Skewed Throne across their chest. I watched them all closely, saw the signs of the rationing in their faces, a look of haggardness. But most of these people had their own stores put back and were living off of that. They had no need of what was stored in the warehouses or came from the kitchens yet.

When we reached the merchants' guild, Keven led Marielle and me through an arched entryway into the back courtyard, then into the hall itself through a back entrance. I couldn't help thinking that this was how I'd entered the guild hall the first time, as Borund's personal bodyguard. Borund had just discovered that the merchant Charls was the one attempting to kill him. He'd wanted Charls to know he knew, had brought me along for protection . . . and as a warning. It hadn't worked.

We entered the main hall and I almost gasped.

When I came as a bodyguard to Borund, the hall had been crowded with merchants and ship captains chatting, trading, doing business. It had bustled with activity, the roar of conversation loud, almost overwhelming.

Now, the hall was almost empty. The huge support pillars and

tall ceilings only made the emptiness more pronounced. Light
streamed down through thin windows, revealing a marble floor,
scattered rugs, and a few chairs on the edges of the room for more
private and relaxed conversations. Tapestries and banners hung
from the walls or in between the support pillars, limp and forlorn.
The entire room smelled musty with disuse.

On the far side of the room, near a set of stairs leading up to a
second level, Avrell and Nathem were gathered together with
Borund, Regin, Yvan, and a few lesser merchants. Their conversation echoed in the open hall, the sounds strangely intrusive.

"—rather simple, Yvan," Avrell was saying as we approached,
his voice tight. "Some of the stores have gone missing. We want to
know why and who's been taking them. In order to do that, we
need to know about everything that's missing. So the Mistress has
ordered that an inventory be done of all of the warehouses. *All* of
the warehouses. To be inventoried *today*. Is that understood?"

Yvan snatched the master list that Avrell was holding out
toward him, almost ripping the paper in the process. His eyes shot
daggers. "Yes. Perfectly."

"Good. I want a comprehensive list of everything that's missing
by this evening."

Grumbling, most of the merchants took their lists and began
to filter out, the majority giving orders to apprentices as they left.
Yvan passed his list to his apprentice without looking at it, then
began a slow, awkward walk to the exit, his heavy form lumbering
along. He was breathing hard before he made it halfway across
the room.

Regin stayed behind. "Some of us have more than one warehouse under our control," he said, "as well as our personal estates."

"I know." Avrell handed him a list. "Nathem is going to oversee
the Priem warehouse while you handle the Duncet warehouse and
your own estates. I'll be taking care of Yvan's second warehouse."

"And the warehouse on Lirion Street?"

"Borund is handling that, as well as the warehouse on the Dredge."

Regin nodded. "Very well. I'll have the list ready by this evening." He followed Yvan, moving swiftly.

Avrell sighed heavily as he left, then caught sight of me. He visibly gathered himself together, but his face looked weary. "Mistress. I didn't expect to see you here."

"I thought perhaps I could help," I said, as the escort came to a halt.

Avrell relaxed slightly. "Of course. In fact, I can have you deal with Borund's warehouse on the Dredge, while he handles the one on Lirion Street, if that's all right with him?"

Borund grunted. "Be my guest. I've got enough to do at Lirion."

Avrell handed over the appropriate list, then asked quietly, "The ship?"

"Heading into a storm." I couldn't keep a note of worry from my voice.

Borund nodded. "Mathew knows what he's doing. They'll be fine."

The group broke, Avrell and Nathem setting off for the lower city, Borund turning toward Lirion Street in the middle ward. I headed toward the Dredge, Keven, Marielle, and the escort in tow.

When we reached the warehouse, it was bustling with activity. I paused to watch the flow of workers, then caught the arm of one of them as he passed.

"Who's in charge here now?"

The man looked annoyed until he noticed the escort and realized who I was. He immediately knelt and bowed down, almost reverentially. "William, Mistress." He pointed toward the left side of the warehouse without looking up.

My heart sank, and I suddenly regretted offering to help. I

should have stayed up in the palace, working on mathematics or something.

As I hesitated, I caught Marielle's eye. She glared at me, then motioned toward the kneeling man with her head.

"Oh!" I said. Then I frowned, reaching down to touch the man's head awkwardly. "Thank you."

The man ducked his head, then backed away in a half crouch before turning and fleeing back into the warehouse with a stunned look of awe.

I shook my head, glanced down at the sheet of paper in my hand, then sighed. Gathering myself together, I went in search of William.

He was working in the back section of the building, ordering workers around while consulting a list of his own. His hair was as wild as I remembered it from the first time I'd seen him on the dock, but he'd changed. He stood straight, shoulders back, head high, gestured with his arms as he spoke. He seemed taller somehow, more visible. Before, he'd always been a part of Borund's shadow, but here, in the warehouse, without Borund around . . .

"No, no, no!" he said, waving his arms to catch the worker's attention and stop him. "I said put that in the second section, not the third. It should be stacked with the dried peas."

The worker had stopped, but he wasn't paying any attention to William. He was gawking at me and my entourage.

"Well?" William said, frowning in exasperation. "Why aren't you moving?"

The worker nodded in my direction.

William turned, then froze, a look of terrified shock passing across his face before he composed it into a blank expression. He fumbled briefly with his papers, then forced his hands to stop moving, and drew in a deep breath. "Mistress, what can I do for you?"

"I'm here to take inventory."

"Ah," William said, then paused. A look of confusion crossed his face. "I thought Borund was going to do that?"

"He was. I volunteered to help, and they gave me this warehouse."

"Ah," William said again.

Another pause, this one long enough to become awkward.

I glanced around the warehouse, at the stacked crates and barrels. "Shouldn't we get started?"

William jumped as if I'd pinched him, then nervously turned around. "Of course, of course. Let me just . . ." He spotted the worker, who still stood gawking. "Harold! Take that to section two!"

The worker jerked, mumbled something indistinct, then vanished behind a stack of crates.

William turned again. "Let me just . . . get rid of these papers. Yes. And then we can get started." He started to put the papers back into some type of order, but they became even more disorganized. Finally, he gave up, shoved them into a heap, and said, "Follow me."

He led us back to the front of the warehouse where he had a table set up with extra paper, ink, and a chair set up like a desk. He put the loose papers down on the desk, then turned. He seemed to have composed himself on the way to the desk.

"How do you want to proceed?" he asked.

I shrugged. "However you want. You're in charge of the warehouse."

He hesitated again, looked at me as if he thought I was trying to trick him somehow, then he straightened. "First, we'll have to keep everyone not doing inventory out of the warehouse."

"Very well."

William called all of the workers to the front of the building, then sent the majority of them away on other tasks on the Dredge, or transferred them to the communal ovens or the docks. Those that remained were men and women who could count and a few who could read. He broke these up into teams and dispatched them to various places in the building to count crates. Only two of those present could write. These he kept near the front of the warehouse to record the amounts and types of food and supplies each team had counted.

Once the teams were dispatched, he turned to me.

"How long do you expect this to take?" I asked.

William shrugged. "A couple of hours at most. We have quite a few teams."

"I see."

From the back of the warehouse, I could hear the teams beginning to call out numbers and foodstocks.

I frowned at William. "I can count, you know."

He stared at me in incomprehension.

I sighed. "I came down here to help. Why don't we form a team and start counting?"

Light dawned. "Of course! I didn't think. . . ." He trailed off, then shook himself. "Of course. Follow me, we'll start on the second floor."

He headed toward the back of the warehouse again. Before following, I motioned to Keven. "Have the escort watch the warehouse. I don't think I'll need an entourage to help me count boxes."

"I'll stay with you," he said, with a tone that suggested I'd better not argue. I gave him an irritated glare, but he only smiled.

As he sent the other guardsmen to patrol the warehouse, Marielle shifted closer, grinning hugely, her eyes sparkling.

"What?"

She leaned in close and whispered, "He likes you."

"Who, Keven?"

"No," Marielle said, rolling her eyes in disgust. "William."

I shot her a dark frown, but deep inside something surged upward—hope and dread and a queasy excitement that warmed my
blood and tightened my chest, making it harder to breathe.

Then I remembered William's look in the tavern after I'd gutted the assassin that had tried to kill Borund. Horror and revulsion
had contorted his face, obvious through the shock. He'd had the
same look when he realized I was going to kill Alendor.

"No," I said, trying to crush the roiling hope in my chest. "He
despises me."

Marielle seemed surprised at the harshness in my voice, taking
a small step backward. But then the knowing grin returned, somewhat subdued.

"I don't think so," she said. Then she swept past me, following
William.

I glanced toward Keven, who pretended he hadn't heard. But
the twitch at the corner of his mouth gave him away.

I snorted, then headed for the stairs.

We began at the southern corner of the floor. I clambered up to
the top of the stacked crates, Marielle following, surprising both
William and Keven. Then we began working our way northward,
Marielle and I counting as we went, calling down numbers to
William below. Keven dealt with the crates closer to the floor,
William reading the labels. The tops of the stacks were dusty and
filled with cobwebs, and both Marielle and I were covered and
sneezing in fits by the time we reached the end of the first stack.
Crouching and straddling the crates as we moved down the line was
also hard work, and soon we were drenched in sweat. But it was the
first time that either of us had done anything outside of attend
meetings in the palace or train using the Sight in the gardens—or
the dagger under Westen's eye for me—in a long while. The sheer
novelty of manual labor was exhilarating.

We climbed down from the first stack and burst out laughing as we saw each other in the full light. Both Keven and William were grinning as well. Dusting ourselves off, we moved to the second section.

The hours went by quickly. At one point, Marielle claimed exhaustion, and so William climbed up to the top as she took over recording the results. At first, having William that close, in such a confined area, felt uncomfortable. But as soon as we began counting, that awkwardness faded. For the first time since we'd known each other, I was not a bodyguard or assassin or the Mistress. I was simply Varis.

As we reached the end of the last stack, I shifted to the edge of the crates and sat, legs dangling. I was breathing heavily, my white shirt stained a drab gray, my breeches caked a uniform brown with the combined sweat and dust. William moved to sit down beside me, breathing hard as well. He had cobwebs caught in his hair, his face smeared with dust and grit and sweat. But his eyes were bright.

He turned toward me and the strange exhilaration I thought I had crushed came back, pounding in my chest.

He smiled and I grinned in return.

"You should come up to the palace more often," I said, and instantly cursed myself.

His smile faltered, then steadied. "Perhaps I will from now on."

Down below, Marielle shouted, "We're all done down here. What are you two doing up there?"

We leaned over the edge, peering down at Marielle's and Keven's upturned faces. Marielle was smiling. A little twisted smile. She raised her eyebrows suggestively, and I replied with a heated glare.

Leaning back, I sighed. "I suppose we should climb back down, see how the rest of the teams are doing." But I realized I didn't want to go. Not yet. I wanted to stay there, with William, covered in dust and cobwebs, the taste of grit in my mouth, the scent of my own sweat and his sharp in my nostrils.

William grunted, hesitated a moment, then twisted and began climbing down.

I watched the top of his head for a moment, strangely disappointed, then followed.

All of the other teams were finished. William collected all of the lists and sat down at his desk to begin comparing them to the master list. My stomach growled, and I realized I hadn't eaten anything since that morning. The inventory had taken up most of the day. It was almost dusk. But looking around at all of the exhausted faces of the workers from the Dredge, all beginning to take on the edges of strict rationing, I found I didn't mind. I'd gone days in the slums without eating, knew I would survive a little hunger now.

I turned back to William when he grunted. He leaned back from his lists, held them up to scan them again, then turned, surprised.

"Well?" I asked.

He shook his head in disbelief. "There's nothing missing. Everything that's supposed to be here . . . is here."

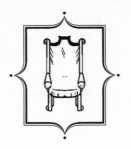

Chapter 9

"WELL, THAT'S CERTAINLY NOT TRUE at the rest of the warehouses." Avrell paced back and forth on the garden path as he fumed, his hands tucked in the sleeves of his dark blue robes, his head bowed forward.

I glanced toward Eryn, seated on the stone bench beside me. I'd never seen Avrell so agitated, so angry; not even when he'd thought Eryn had tricked him somehow by smuggling in the Capthian wine without his knowledge. I seethed with anger myself, but unlike Avrell, I found myself retreating into myself, reverting to old habits: I'd become deceptively calm, my hand itching for my dagger. But Avrell and Eryn weren't the ones responsible for the missing food, and so I waited, the anger held tight and controlled inside me.

"How bad is it?" Eryn asked.

Avrell paused in his pacing, looked up at her, at me, then spat in irritation and waved the question toward me before continuing.

I straightened, thought about the reports from the individual warehouses that had come in throughout the evening and night yesterday, then began.

"It's bad," I said grimly. "The worst warehouse hit was the one on Havel Street, near the wharf. Twenty casks of wine and almost forty crates and barrels of assorted food—pickles, beans, and dried meats—were missing. The Priem warehouse had thirty barrels missing, including the salted fish we knew about earlier. Both warehouses on Lirion Street and Tempest Row were missing foodstocks as well. In fact, all of the warehouses established after the fire in the warehouse district have something missing, except the warehouse we set up on the Dredge."

Avrell snorted. "The one warehouse you would have thought would have been robbed blind by now."

I shot him a glare of mixed anger and irritation. He grimaced and had the grace to look embarrassed.

"That is rather curious," Eryn said.

I turned the glare on her.

She shrugged. "Why is it that the warehouse on the Dredge isn't missing anything? Whoever is taking the food is obviously not afraid, nor stupid. And they must be well organized. Look at how much has gone missing already, and we've just now noticed. Why is it that they've left the Dredge stores alone?"

"Probably because they would have been seen," I said bitterly.

Avrell frowned. "They should have been seen no matter what warehouse they chose. We have guardsmen posted at all of them. And Darryn is watching the warehouse on the Dredge with his militia."

Eryn shook her head. "But not all the time. And besides, guardsmen can be paid to look the other way, bribed with money or perhaps even some of the food that's being taken. The guardsmen aren't all reliable."

"I didn't mean they'd be seen by the guardsmen," I said, annoyed that they didn't understand. "I meant that nothing goes unnoticed in the slums. There's always someone watching, whether you can see them or not. The streets are never empty, even when

Darryn and his militia aren't there. If someone had tried to take something from the warehouse, they wouldn't have lasted ten minutes. Someone else would have seen them and reported it, or killed them and run off with the food themselves. We'd have found bodies. And someone would have seen *that* as well. And eventually someone would have told Darryn." I shook my head. "No, whoever is taking the food knows that they'd never get away with stealing from the Dredge. They'd find themselves with their throat slit, their body dumped in a back alley somewhere, probably with Darryn's permission." I sighed. "Besides, the people of the slums have too much invested in that food. It's the only chance they have of surviving the winter. Most of them won't be willing to risk that, and they won't be willing to let anyone else steal it from them either. The warehouse on the Dredge is probably the safest warehouse in the city."

Avrell and Eryn mulled this over quietly. Finally, Avrell sighed and settled down beside Eryn on the stone bench. He picked at invisible dirt on his robe.

"So how are they getting the food out?" he asked. "It's not like they're lifting a few loaves of bread or an apple. They're taking entire crates. That requires wagons, and men to do the work."

"Some of the guardsmen must be involved," Eryn added. "More than a few, since more than one warehouse has been hit."

Avrell shifted in his seat. "We can't compare the lists of which guardsmen were working which warehouses, because we don't know when the food was taken. And at least one of each of the merchants' warehouses was hit, so we can't narrow it down that way. None of their personal estates reported anything missing either, probably because most of the merchants have manses behind enclosed walls."

I stared across the gardens, through the few denuded branches of the trees and shrubs, to where Keven stood watching us from a discreet distance. "Erick said I could trust Keven and the guardsmen he chose for my personal guard before he left," I said. "I'll ask them to question some of the other guardsmen quietly—both palace and city guardsmen—and see what they can find out. Maybe some of the other guardsmen have seen something suspicious."

Avrell nodded. "That may give us somewhere to start looking."

I felt my tightly controlled anger slip a little. "So who did it? I don't care how they did it, I just want to know who it was. And where the food is now. I want that food back."

Avrell looked up at the sharpness in my tone. "My guess would be one of the merchants. Regin, Yvan, Borund, and the lesser merchants all have unquestioned access to the warehouses. All they have to do is show up with a cart and tell the guardsmen they're there to move some of the food to a different warehouse. They could even have papers. It wouldn't matter. Most of the guardsmen can't read, and there's no reason for them to doubt the merchants in the first place. We've moved hundreds of supplies that way already, almost on a daily basis. So even if we find some guardsman who thinks he saw something suspicious, we can't prove anything."

"But she doesn't need to prove anything," Eryn said, one eyebrow rising slightly. "She's the Mistress."

I thought about that for a moment, then shook my head. "I'm not going to raid every merchant's estate looking for the missing food. Especially since we don't even know it was a merchant in the first place."

Eryn's eyes darkened. "You may have to," she said. "Not everything you'll be forced to do as Mistress will be fair, Varis."

I stiffened in defiance, then realized Eryn wasn't trying to force me to change my mind. She was simply offering advice.

And she was deadly serious.

I forced the tension in my shoulders to relax. "I'd rather have some type of reason before I act right now," I said. "But I will act when I have to." It wasn't a concession, but it let her know I'd heard what she meant.

Eryn held my gaze a moment more, then nodded.

All three of us lapsed into thoughtful silence, a cloud drifting over the sun high above.

Eryn's shoulders tightened. "What if you used the throne?"

I frowned. "What do you mean?"

She straightened up even more, her eyes alight. "I mean use the throne. It's connected to the city. You can use it to see individual streets, the people on those streets, get a feel for their emotions. Why not use it to search out each of the merchant's estates individually. They'd never know."

"Then what?" Avrell asked.

Eryn snorted as if the answer were obvious.

"You raid that merchant's estate," she said.

The anger I'd been holding in check leaped forward at the idea. I stood up abruptly, the weight of my dagger pressing into my back where it was tucked into my belt. Energy seemed to bleed off me, the same sensation I'd felt working in the warehouse the day before. I'd been trapped in the palace and in politics too long, inactive. I needed to move, to hunt, and here was my opportunity.

"Where are you going?" Avrell called from behind me. I was already halfway across the garden.

Without slowing, I said, "To the throne room."

†

The city's life pulsed around me and for a long moment I let myself simply float in it, the eddies and currents soothing. The black despair I'd felt in the slums immediately after assuming the role of Mistress had lifted with the stationing of a warehouse and kitchen in that area, with the creation of the Dredge militia, and with the work force that traveled daily from the slums to the burned-out warehouse district. Construction there had slowed since the readily available stone had run out, but now teams of carts and workers streamed from the city to the northern quarry and the Dredge, so the building continued. The roiling fear that had hovered over the city since the coming of the White Fire had abated.

I gathered myself and pushed higher above the city, turned south to where the flickering Fires that I'd placed inside Erick and Laurren could be seen. At this distance, they appeared as a single flame, with no way to distinguish between them. I thought about taking a moment to check up on the ship, but my anger over the missing stores pulled me back down to the city.

I wanted to know who had stolen that food.

I started with Borund's estates. Not because I didn't trust him—I didn't think he'd taken anything—but because I was more familiar with them. As his bodyguard, I'd escorted him everywhere, to all of his warehouses, all of his buildings in the city. He'd lost a significant portion of his warehouses near the wharf in the fire, but there were still a few left. I started with those.

Skimming over the wharf, over the flow of the people on the docks and working on the ships, I slid down and down and slowed until I'd settled into the currents on the main thoroughfare. Weaving in and out among the people, I came swiftly to the first warehouse, slipped through the half-open doorway and inside.

A few men and women were moving among the boxes and crates, but I soon decided they were doing nothing suspicious and so I drifted down among the stacks of supplies, the crates closing in overhead, muting the sounds of the other workers. After a few feet, weaving in and out amongst the crates, the stacks reaching almost to the ceiling, I felt totally isolated and a little claustrophobic. The scent of straw struck me, and I shuddered, felt sweat break out on my forehead and in my armpits. Unconsciously, I gripped my dagger tighter. Then I realized why.

I'd chased Cristoph into a warehouse exactly like this after his ambush had failed, had killed him among the warren of paths among the crates. In his attempt to stop me, he'd flung his oil lantern at me and started the fire that consumed over half of the warehouse district. All to keep me from killing his father, Alendor; and to avenge his friend, who I'd killed earlier on the wharf when Cristoph tried to rape me.

I halted in the middle of the crates at the memory, but shook myself and shoved the memory aside. It was useless to dwell on it. Alendor was gone, had fled the city according to Avrell's network of spies; and Cristoph was dead. Pushing forward, I continued my scouting of the warehouse, ignoring the pungent scent of straw and oil.

When I'd completed a circuit of the warehouse, I'd found nothing out of place. I scanned it again once, watched the workers a moment more, then shrugged and pushed up out of the building and down the street to the next warehouse.

It was the same as the first. When I finished with Borund's warehouses near the wharf, I moved to his personal estate.

The manse was just as I remembered it. Gerrold manned the estate with the help of Lizbeth and Gart, the stableboy. I paused to watch Gerrold let Borund in at the gates, Borund dismounting and handing the reins of his horse off to Gart. Then I went inside, scanned the rooms downstairs, ducked into the kitchens and down the back staircase to the cellar where rough-woven sacks of the essentials—rice and barley—and strings of vegetables hung from the rafters. I scanned through all of the food stores, but found nothing that seemed out of the ordinary. No hidden crates of wine, no stacked barrels of salted fish.

I moved back upstairs, then to the second floor. I paused in my old room, stared at the bed, the dresser, the table and chair. Nothing much had changed. I found Lizbeth in Borund's room, fussing with the bedcovers, folding them over just so before moving on to pull the curtains back from the windows to let in the midmorning sunlight.

I stayed the longest in William's rooms. Lizbeth had already been there, the bed already made, the curtains pulled back so that sunlight lit the entire space. I edged up to the desk, stared down at the sheets of paper scattered over its surface. Lists of goods and prices, with sources written in tight, legible script in neat columns. I smiled as I remember Borund telling me how much William had hated keeping track of everything when he'd first arrived as the merchant's apprentice. Now, he kept everything more organized than Borund himself.

A piece of paper that seemed out of place caught my eye and I shifted to the back corner of the desk. It was a sketch of some sort, a drawing.

I frowned, leaned forward for a closer look—

Then jerked back with a gasp of surprise, my heart thudding in my chest.

It was a sketch of me, of my face.

Guilt surged through me, and I quickly scanned the room to see if anyone had noticed, unconsciously sinking into a defensive stance. But of course no one was there, and they couldn't have seen me even if they were. I wasn't actually in William's room, I was back in the palace, sitting on the throne, Avrell, Eryn, and Keven watching over me.

My heart settling a little, I turned back to the sketch, reached out to touch it, but then withdrew my hand.

I hadn't known William could draw, even after living in the same house with him for almost two years. All I'd ever seen him do was work on lists for Borund—inventories and sales records.

I looked more closely at the face. It was definitely me. Straight dark hair cropped about shoulder length on either side of a narrow face. A few tendrils fell over my eyes even though my bangs were trimmed short, and I felt an urge to reach forward and brush them out of the way, as Erick always did to me. My head was tilted a little to one side, my eyes questioning, a few creases between my eyebrows. I had the faintest hint of a smile, the entire expression on my face making it seem as if I was uncertain whether I was supposed to be laughing or not.

I leaned back. Was this what William saw when he looked at me? It wasn't what I expected. It wasn't hard, or cold, or angry. I didn't see the edges I saw in Erick's face, the edges I associated with being a Seeker. I didn't see the calculated deadliness of a Seeker either.

I withdrew from the manse, paused on the street outside, watched the people walking by without really seeing them.

Perhaps Marielle was right. Perhaps William didn't look at me and see a disgusting, cold-blooded killer, someone who'd hunted for marks as a Seeker on the Dredge, someone who'd killed on command for Borund and Avrell later on.

On the street, a man almost walked into me, but before I could react he stepped to one side for no apparent reason, the flows on the river forcing him around me. I watched him as he continued on, his sudden deviation not even registering on his face. But he'd interrupted my thoughts on William, and I suddenly remembered what I was here for.

Borund was cleared as far as I was concerned. Time to move on to the other merchants.

I spent the next few hours scouring warehouses and buildings that had been converted into warehouses after the fire, as well as the personal estates of each of the merchants. Most of the warehouses were uninteresting, workers shifting goods or handing them off to the kitchens. At one warehouse, goods were being loaded onto a cart. I waited until all of the sacks of grain were loaded, then followed the cart, hoping that it would lead me to the thief, but it halted at the mill, the grain they unloaded to be ground into flour for use at the communal ovens.

I sighed and continued searching.

The estates were more interesting, servants moving out and about at various tasks, the merchants in meetings. I saw stableboys snoring, shovels dropped forgotten at their feet; maids giggling as they worked, passing along gossip; cooks bellowing out orders in stifling kitchens. Once, I intruded on a guardsman and a maid in a tryst on the second floor of a manse, the guardsman hissing for quiet when the woman squealed and giggled in delight.

Toward dusk, the sun beginning to set on the mountains far to the east, exhaustion lying heavy on my shoulders, I slid down the back stairs of the last manse and pushed through the door at the bottom.

I blinked into the darkness of the cellar, noticed the sharp scent of freshly turned dirt before my eyes adjusted. As soon as I could see, I stepped into the earthen room, past a sack of walnuts, a bushel of dried apples, a string of garlic.

Nothing out of the ordinary. Except I could still smell the scent of fresh earth.

All of the other cellars had smelled of old earth, dry and packed down with use.

I scanned the room, breathing in deeply, then moved to the right, where the scent seemed strongest.

I halted before a stack of barrels and glanced down at the earthen floor.

The barrels had recently been shifted. There was a gouge in the floor, and a pile of loose dirt on the hard-packed earth of the cellar floor.

I stepped toward the barrels, slid along one side and behind—

And entered a narrow tunnel.

The scent of new earth was dense here, almost overpowering.

Crouching down instinctively, even though the roof was high enough for me to walk upright, I moved down the tunnel, emerging into another room after only ten paces.

A room packed with crates and sacks stacked to head-height in the narrow space.

The anger I'd felt since I'd learned that someone was stealing from the warehouses—an anger that had died down during the course of the day and the long hours of fruitless searching—resurfaced with a rush of heat to my chest. My jaw tightened; my nostrils flared.

Without thought, I pushed myself out of the manse, up above the city, and rushed back to the throne room. I had a moment to notice that Eryn had left, that only Avrell and Keven remained, and that someone had brought in a tray of food, and then I settled back into my body and pushed myself up off of the throne.

Both Avrell and Keven gave a start at the sudden movement, Keven reaching for his sword before settling back down. Avrell lurched up from his seat on the stone steps of the dais.

"What did you find? Do you know who's taken the food?"

I caught both his and Keven's gaze.

"It's Yvan," I said, and the contempt in my voice made Avrell step back a pace.

†

It took Baill almost a full day to organize enough men for the raid on Yvan's estates. When I'd told him, he'd seemed surprised, but then his face had gone blank, the same expressionless facade he'd worn when I'd first seen him as Borund's bodyguard and he had barred our entrance into the palace.

Except he still seemed exhausted.

Noticing the dark smudges around his eyes, I'd said, "You should get some rest. I can have Captain Catrell plan the raid."

"No!" he'd barked, his eyes glinting. As I raised my eyebrows at the harshness of his tone, he scrubbed at his face with both hands, then placed them flat on the desk before him. "I mean, no, Mistress. Captain Catrell is currently busy elsewhere. I'll have the men ready by this evening."

Now Avrell, Baill, myself, Keven, and an entourage of twenty palace guardsmen hid in an alley in the outer ward where most of the merchants lived. At the entrance to the alley, Baill peered around the corner, his hand resting lightly on the pommel of his sword, searching the darkness. The sky overhead was cloudless, the night lit by an almost full moon. Baill no longer acted exhausted, although the dark smudges remained.

I watched him quietly, already beneath the river, the currents surging around me. All of the men were tense, their emotions wild and erratic. Armor clinked and clothing rustled as they shifted nervously. We'd been waiting for over an hour as the rest of the guardsmen moved into place on the remaining sides of the wall that surrounded Yvan's manse. We already knew he was in residence; he'd been driven through the main gates in his carriage a few moments after we'd entered the alley, and the rest of the group broke off for their own positions.

Baill nodded at a signal from someone I couldn't see, then pulled back from the alley's entrance. The rest of the guardsmen edged closer to listen in.

"Everyone is in position," he said. "They've closed and locked the main gates, so we'll have to batter those down."

"Leave the gates to me," I said, voice hard. Without conscious thought, I'd slipped back into my role as a Seeker, a bodyguard.

Baill frowned and glanced down to where I idly swung my dagger through various moves with one hand. I hadn't even realized I'd drawn it. "Mistress?"

I caught and held his gaze. "I'll handle the gate," I repeated. "It won't be a problem as long as you put me in the lead."

He suddenly realized that I meant to be part of the party entering the walls, that I didn't intend to wait in the alley until everything was over. He shifted uncomfortably, seemed about to protest but sucked in a breath instead, trapped between my intense gaze and the fact that I was the Mistress, someone he should be protecting at all costs. He shot a hopeful glance at Keven, expecting him to intercede as my personal bodyguard, but Keven only shrugged.

Finally, Baill grunted in disgust and nodded toward Avrell. "And you?"

Avrell shook his head. "I'll come in after everything has settled down."

"Very well. I don't expect much resistance."

"He might have a few bodyguards," I said. "Most of the merchants had them by the time we ended Alendor's consortium. But that's all. They shouldn't be a problem."

"Very well," Baill said again, looking over the rest of the guardsmen, catching their eyes, making certain they were ready. He didn't glance at Keven or Avrell, his gaze ending on me. "After you."

I nodded in acknowledgment, then stepped out from the alley.

Yvan's manse stood at the end of the street, the main gates opening directly onto the cobblestone road. Stone walls ran parallel to the cross street in both directions from the large arch of the wooden doors of the entranceway. As I came out of the alley, dagger clutched in one hand, I paused, did a quick scan of the area using the river, but sensed no one other than the guardsmen in Baill's force. Satisfied, I started walking to the gate.

As I moved, I pulled the waters of the river tight before me, gathered it into a solid wall of power. I felt Keven immediately behind me to my right, his sword drawn. He smelled of earth and dew. Baill moved to the left, radiating calm intent. The rest of the guardsmen came up behind.

When we were ten paces from the closed wooden gates, I paused. Jaw clenching, all of the fury I felt toward Yvan pounding in my blood, I punched the gathered power of the river forward.

The gates exploded inward with a rending shriek of twisted metal and splintering wood. A sharp crack followed as the stone surrounding the hinges shattered, debris pattering to the cobbles of the street, the gates crashing to the ground in the garden beyond the wall. All of the guardsmen jumped—one cried out—but neither Keven nor Baill faltered.

Then we were through the gate, into the outer garden, picking our way over the broken debris, a loose stone path running from the street up to the front door of the manse. Candlelight burned in most of the downstairs windows. As soon as we entered the garden, Baill's men scattered to the left and right, streaking toward the other entrances, where the rest of the group were waiting for the doors to be unlatched. Only seven guardsmen remained with Baill, Keven, and me.

Shouts began to filter through the night, coming from the back of the manse, where the carriage house and stables would be.

"He'll try to make a break for it as soon as he realizes what's going on," Keven said.

I nodded. I didn't intend to give him the chance.

We reached the stone steps that led to the double doors of the manse. Someone—a servant—opened the front door and peered out into the darkness, lantern raised high. His eyes widened as he saw me, and he jerked back.

Before he could react, Baill's guardsmen leaped up the steps, shoved through the half-open door and dragged him out onto the porch. He cried out, dropped the lantern, which shattered on the ground and went out, and then one of the guardsmen thumped the struggling man over the head with the pommel of his sword.

Guardsmen held the doors open as Baill, Keven, and I entered, both escorting guardsmen on edge, swords drawn. The foyer opened onto two flights of stairs leading upward, and two doors to the left and right. A layout similar to Borund's manse, but larger. And filled with ostentatious and elegant furniture, rugs and tapestries and urns.

I frowned at the extravagant display of wealth.

"Where is he?" Baill asked.

I stood in the middle of the foyer, glanced up, to the left. With the power of the throne and the river, I could sense the fear of the servants as the guardsmen worked their way through the manse. The men in the stable and carriage house had already been taken, were being held outside behind the manse. The servants in the kitchen had been cornered as well. A few others were scattered throughout the house, mainly on the second floor, some still asleep.

But there was a small group of people off to the left.

"There are a few servants still left upstairs," I said. Three guardsmen broke off and headed up the stairs. "Yvan is down here."

I led the way, Keven and Baill a step behind. When we reached the closed door, I halted, let the guardsmen shift into position on either side, swords drawn.

The scent of sweat and fear lay thick on the river. I caught Baill's eye, then nodded.

He stepped back, kicked the door in with a grunt. It burst open with a sharp crack, the doorframe splintering. Inside, someone gasped, and something shattered. Someone swore, followed by a flurry of activity and the sound of swords being drawn.

Then everything went quiet.

Baill, Keven, and the remaining guardsmen slid into the room, stepping to either side of the open door.

Then I entered.

It was a dining room, the table almost fifteen feet in length, running from the door to the far side of the long room. It was lined with empty chairs and platter upon platter of food. Candles stood in candelabra on all sides and down the center of the table. At the far end of the room, Yvan sat at the head of the table, a cloth napkin tucked into the front of his shirt, stained with grease and sauce. He held the greasy leg of a chicken in his hands, staring down the table at Baill and the guardsmen in horrified shock. Two bodyguards, swords drawn, bodies tense, stood to either side of him, protecting his flanks. A servant trembled to one side, the remains of a broken platter of what looked like sauced strips of pork staining the rug at his feet.

Yvan recovered quickly. Tossing the chicken leg down on the heaping plate before him, he shifted forward, his face suffused with anger, grunting with effort as he tried to stand. The servant leaped forward to help, staggering under Yvan's weight.

Gasping, breath short, Yvan bellowed, "What is the meaning of this?"

I glared at him in disgust, felt my anger triple as I breathed in the heady scent of all of the food—more food than had been served in the palace in the last three days, more food than most of the people of Amenkor would see in a week. I felt myself trembling with rage.

"Take him," I said, surprised at how calm my voice sounded.

Baill's guardsmen moved down the length of the table. For a moment, Yvan's bodyguards hesitated, swords raised, and the river thickened with resistance. But the bodyguards knew me, knew Baill. Glowering, they relaxed, sheathed their swords and stepped aside, allowing the guardsmen to surround Yvan. His servant moved swiftly out of the way.

When the guardsmen attempted to grab Yvan's arms, he jerked out of their grip.

"How dare you touch me!" he shrieked.

"How dare you pretend you've done nothing when you're gorging yourself on enough food to feed half the barracks!" I barked, my restraint finally broken. I felt Avrell enter the room behind me, heard him gasp at the sight of the food on the table.

In a much deadlier tone, I asked, "Where did you get all of this?"

"It comes from my personal estate—"

"You stole it from the warehouses!" I shouted, cutting him off, taking a step forward, my hand slamming down on the table. "You stole it from Amenkor!"

Yvan spluttered, face shocked. "I did no such thing!"

I snorted in disgust and motioned to Baill, who stood to one side, his eye on the bodyguards. "Bring him with me."

I led the group down the hall into the kitchen, where even more food was being prepared. Behind, Baill and the guardsmen herded Yvan along as fast as his bulk would allow. Avrell and Keven kept up with me.

We descended into the cellars, Yvan's servants scurrying to find lanterns at Keven's direction.

"I don't see anything out of place here," Avrell said cautiously.

Keven sniffed the air. "What's that smell?"

"Freshly dug earth," I said. I headed straight for the barrels that covered the entrance to the second room.

With Keven's help, I shoved aside the barrels covering the tunnel.

One of the servants gasped. Keven ducked down into the tunnel, emerged a second later, his face grim.

Avrell frowned, then ducked into the tunnel as well.

Baill, Yvan being forced down the stair ahead of him at sword point, appeared in the cellar.

I glared at Yvan. "Now tell me you haven't robbed Amenkor blind," I growled.

Yvan straightened where he stood, his mouth clamped shut. But his eyes blazed raw hatred.

I shifted my gaze to Baill. "Take him back to the palace and hold him. I'll deal with him later."

Baill jerked Yvan back, and for the first time a flicker of fear appeared in Yvan's eyes. But before he could protest, Baill shoved him up the stairs.

I heaved a sigh of relief, felt pent-up anger and tension release from my shoulders in a wave. I let the river go.

Avrell reappeared, a worried frown creasing his forehead.

Before he could speak, I said, "Seize everything. And search the rest of his estate as well. I want to know everything that he's taken."

Avrell nodded, but the concern remained.

I caught Keven's gaze, exhaustion settling onto my shoulders like a blanket. I'd sustained myself by sheer rage for the last two hours. All I wanted to do was crawl into bed. "Let's head back to the palace."

Keven gathered a few of the other guardsmen as an escort, and we began to wind our way through the outer ward. The streets were quiet, only a few windows still lit with the faint glow of lanterns or candles. Most of the buildings were dark, hidden behind their own low walls, everyone asleep.

I moved slowly, too weary from the day's activities to pick up the pace. As we reached the gate to the middle ward and began the trudge up the hill toward the gates of the palace, I turned to stare

at the inner walls, at the parts of the palace that could be seen beyond them.

The walls of the palace seemed to glow in the moonlight, the
white stone almost silver. Large bowls of flaming oil were lit at intervals, and at various spots on the palace—along the promenade,
on the tower—the fire flapped fitfully in the breeze coming off of
the harbor.

A sudden sense of the surreal stole over me and I paused, the
guardsmen drawing to a halt. Keven moved to my side, face creased
with concern. "Mistress?"

I shook my head, gave him a withered smile. "It's nothing. I'm
just tired."

"We could send for a horse, perhaps a carriage."

I shook my head. "No. I'm fine."

I took one last look at the palace, then continued on.

We passed through the inner gates into the courtyard, proceeded
up the steps of the promenade and into the palace. Here there were
more people, servants preparing for the coming day's activities,
guardsmen on the walls, page boys and Servants moving about at
odd tasks. We passed through the heavy set of double doors guarded
by a phalanx of silent guardsmen into the Mistress' inner sanctum—
doors that had once been the outer gates of the original gray stone
palace—and turned toward my personal chambers.

As we passed by the throne room, I paused again, then bowed
my head.

"What is it?" Keven asked.

"I haven't checked in on Erick since yesterday morning."

I hesitated, weariness dragging my shoulders down, but eventually I sighed.

"Just a quick look, to make sure he's safe," I said.

The guardsmen drew back the double doors and I made my way

down the aisle, past the stone columns, then up the steps to the throne where it twisted and warped itself on the dais. As I settled into it, I almost changed my mind, almost decided I was too tired. But then the throne settled down into the familiar curved shape, my hands coming to rest on the front of the arms, and I felt the power rush through me, the voices surrounding me, the sound now almost soothing.

I drew strength from them, then lifted myself up, searched out the White Fires far, far to the south, and leaped.

I skimmed over water, the waves undulating beneath me, almost totally black in the night, the moon like a cold silver coin on the darkness. I focused in on the two White Fires ahead of me—one scented with oranges, the other like lilies—both rushing toward me as I Reached, and then I saw a streaking flash of fire, real fire, saw the fleeting outline of three other ships . . . no four! . . . in the fiery afterglow of an explosion, felt a moment of confusion, of disorientation—

And then I dove into the orange-scented Fire.

I heard a scream, a bellow of rage, heard swords clash and then suddenly a man's body fell backward before me, blood flying up to spatter my face. I shoved the dead guardsman—one of Baill's men—aside with a grunt, raised my own sword, felt the descending blow shudder through my arm as I caught it and thrust it back with a heave, sending the attacker stumbling over another body, and then suddenly I was in the clear.

I gasped, wiped my face free of the blinding blood, and spun.

The entire ship was being overtaken. One of the attacking ships had come up alongside, had tethered itself to *The Maiden*, men pouring over the side.

But not ordinary men.

Within the Fire, I lurched back in shock, withdrew even further as I realized I was too entwined with Erick, with his emotions.

Then I turned my attention back to the attack, fear shuddering through my body.

Someone stumbled into Erick from the side, grabbed his arm to steady himself. Erick jerked back, startled, raised his sword, then halted.

"In the Mistress' name," Mathew swore, voice thick with horror, "who are they?"

And deep inside, I heard one of the voices—one of the Seven, I thought, perhaps Cerrin—gasp, *Gods, not them.*

Erick drew in a deep breath, tried to steady the dread and adrenaline that coursed through him. He shook his head. "I don't know."

"They're sea-demons," one of the crew gasped behind them, blood running down his face from a cut in his scalp. His eyes were wide with terror. "Sea-demons, from the tales!"

Erick watched as more of them poured off the sleek ship tethered to *The Maiden.* They were short, dressed in loose clothing, almost like silk, in a riot of colors, with armor underneath. They screamed as they struck—high, piercing ululations, black hair flying as they jumped from one ship to the other, strangely curved swords glinting in the fires all along the deck. Most were covered with tattoos, along their arms, on their faces. A few wore necklaces of shells.

But the most telling feature, the thing that struck horror into Erick's gut, into *my* gut, was their skin. It was a pale, pale blue, like a winter sky.

Deep in the White Fire at Erick's core, one of the voices in the throne writhed in recognition, radiating shock and disbelief. *It can't be them.* A sob, almost a wail.

Who are they? I screamed at the voices, screamed at the Seven, choking on the scent of blood and fire.

But before anyone could answer, another ball of fire lanced out from the second ship, arced out over the water that separated the two, and crashed into the mast high above, flames shattering and raining down on the deck. Erick and Mathew ducked, lurched out of the way, moving swiftly up the foredeck.

"Where in hells is Laurren?" Erick hissed under his breath. He shot a glance out toward the half-seen ships that circled the trader ship. He thought there were three others, aside from the one tethered to the trader ship, but he couldn't be certain.

"I saw her on the aft deck," Mathew said, "but then I was cut off from her."

Erick grunted. "Head down the port side," he said, motioning with his hand. "Have everyone move in this direction. We can't defend ourselves if we're scattered all over the ship!"

Mathew nodded, broke away from Erick, clambering down the deck over dead bodies and broken shards of the rigging. Erick turned, caught another blade with his sword, then drove the dagger in his left hand up under the makeshift armor into the gut of the attacking blue-skinned man. The attacker gasped, blood pouring from the wound in his chest, and then Erick thrust him aside.

"At least they die like ordinary men," he muttered to himself.

Someone screamed, a bloodcurdling death cry, and he glanced down the deck. Part of the crew huddled together, swords and axes flailing, two guardsmen with them, but they were surrounded, backed up against the railing of the deck.

Erick leaped forward, body slipping into old rhythms. Within a heartbeat, three of the attackers had fallen. The rest turned to face him, two more dying as the guardsmen cut them down from behind, and then the group was free.

"To the foredeck!" Erick shouted, shoving them along toward the prow of the ship. They stumbled forward, eyes wide in shock.

Erick glanced toward the second ship, noticed another that circled farther out in the glow of the firelight on the ocean. He spat a curse.

On the second ship, a ball of fire flew up into the air. In the backwash of light, he saw a woman standing on the prow, her black hair flying wildly about her in the wind, her hands lifted before her. Her face was twisted with concentration, her eyes cold and deadly with intent. She wore loose clothing, like the warriors, but her ears were pierced with gold rings, three on each side.

Then, before the aft deck, the thrown fireball struck something in midair and exploded, fire raining down an invisible wall of force to the surging ocean below. In the fiery light, Erick saw Laurren, her face screwed up in a scowl of hatred. A sharp gust of air followed the explosion of the fireball, but before Erick could react, another ball of fire arched out from the ship circling farther out, striking the same invisible wall.

A bright ball of light exploded across the ocean, illuminating the other circling ships clearly, flashing hot on the surface of the ocean. In the near-blinding explosion, Erick saw two other women, one each on the other two ships, both dressed like the first, both with gold earrings.

Then he was hit by a concussive force of wind that shoved him back. Everyone on the ship staggered, some crying out in shock. The sheet of fire winked out.

The next ball of fire slid past Laurren's shield, shuddered into the side of the ship, exploded and rained down the side into the water, the pungent scent of smoke prickling in his nose. Erick heard wood creak with strain, felt the ship rock up on a swell and thud hard into the ship already tethered to the port side. As they separated, some-one fell down between the two ships into the water with a scream.

On the aft deck, Laurren raised her hands, drew back, and flung her arms forward as if throwing a spear out into the darkness of the ocean.

Wood planking shattered on the nearest ship, chunks flying out from its side.

A weak shout of triumph went up from *The Maiden*'s crew.

Erick pressed his lips together grimly.

Three against one. He didn't like Laurren's odds.

I didn't either.

Gathering myself, I leaped out of Erick, sped across the deck, fire dripping down from the burning sails, rigging collapsing to the body-strewn deck, and sank into the Fire at Laurren's core.

Laurren, I'm here.

"Mistress," Laurren gasped, her face already covered in sweat, her eyes wide, her heart thudding so hard it hurt. "They're so strong!" Her voice was nothing more than a whisper.

Another fireball struck her shield and I felt the force rippling as Laurren staggered backward, her hands raised before her. Gritting her teeth, she spat, "And there are so many of them."

Anger boiling up from inside me, I said, *Give the shield to me. Use your strength to strike back at them. Try to take out the women.*

Laurren nodded, flinched back as two fireballs struck almost simultaneously, the force shuddering through her arms, down into her chest. Jaw clenched, she released the flows of the river, the shield collapsing—

And at the same moment I reached forward—through the Fire, as Cerrin had reached through the Fire to help me guide the river so many times before—grabbed the disintegrating edges and pulled the shield tight.

Laurren cried out in relief and staggered forward, her hands coming up to her face, trembling with the effort.

Grappling with the shield, a fireball hitting it with a glancing blow and shuddering down its length to strike the ship, I spat, *Laurren! You have to fight back! I can't hold the shield and strike back at the same time!*

With an effort, Laurren drew herself upright, breath harsh, choking as smoke drifted across her face.

Then she gathered the river into a focused rod of power, like a spear, and with a grunt of effort and pure hatred, she hurled it toward the nearest ship.

It struck with a rending of wood and the bowsprit of the circling ship sheared off, splinters flying up into the face of the woman at the prow. She screamed in fury, arms flung up to protect her face, and then ducked out of sight.

Laurren chuckled, the sound somehow dead.

Don't stop. There are at least two others like her.

Laurren nodded, sucked in a deep breath, and began to send spear after spear out into the darkness, targeting the three circling ships. The first, naked with the lance of the bowsprit missing, turned back and the attacking Servant appeared again, fireballs shooting out from its side now. The first hit the mast, *The Maiden* shuddering as it exploded, fire raining down in tatters; the second caught my shield. More fire arched out of the darkness, pummeling the shield, the mast, and Laurren answered, each spear sent with a gut-wrenching growl.

Then the fireballs shifted. I saw three arch out of the night, had a moment to realize they weren't aimed at the ship itself, had time to say, *Laurren*—

But the warning came too late.

Even as I strengthened the shield before us, the first fireball hit, followed instantly by the second, the third a breath behind. Laurren cried out, flung her arms up to ward herself as each exploded, fire coruscating out from my shield in all directions, surrounding us in a wash of hellish light. I grunted, pulled the shield in tighter, sacrificing the protection of the ship in order to keep the fire at bay. Heat seared Laurren's upraised arms, scorched away her eyebrows, turned her skin waxy. I felt the shield shudder again, felt another barrage of fire strike it before the first had even faded, felt the heat intensify, felt Laurren's hair catch fire. Three different attacks, from three different directions, all with the same purpose.

It was too much. I couldn't hold the shield, could feel it shredding even as I gasped in a broken, ragged voice, *Laurren! I can't hold it! I can't—*

And then it collapsed.

Fire roared into the opening, enveloped Laurren in a seething mass of flames that flung her back. Fire raced up her arms—my arms—seared into flesh, crackling and spitting like a roast thrust onto a spit on the hearth. I screamed, Laurren's voice rending the night, shrieking, and flames scorched down into my lungs, burning inside and out, choking me, charring deeper into skin, into bone—

And then I flung myself out of Laurren's body, still screaming, in pain, in hatred, in denial, my gut clenching and twisting because I couldn't save her, because I hadn't been able to hold the shield.

Laurren staggered across the aft deck, her scream dying, her body a pillar of flame reaching high into the night, and then she came up against the wheel, hard, back twisted. She spun, arms trailing fire, gripped the wheel in desperation, as if trying to hold herself upright.

And then collapsed to the side and lay there, not moving, not even twitching.

A fireball arched past where I hovered on the river, my own scream dying as the sensation of being burned to death faded. I gasped, choked on smoke, on fire itself, felt as if I were weeping, sobs hitching in my throat even though my body was over a thousand miles distant.

The fireball struck the mast, and I suddenly heard the screams of the other men on the ship.

Thrusting Laurren's pain aside, I dove down into Erick again. "Erick!"

Erick spun, saw Mathew and a group of men hacking their way down the starboard side. He leaped forward, joined the fray, sword used mainly to guard as his dagger slashed in and out. All horror vanished as calm settled over him, the skills he'd been drilled in as a Seeker coming to the fore, taking over.

One of the curved rapiers snicked in and sliced along his jaw, nothing but a nick, but the blue-skinned man fell back as Erick's dagger cut across his throat. Two more of the attackers took the man's place, black eyes seething with rage. They let out a piercing shriek, but Erick didn't flinch, cutting in sharply. A blade slashed along Erick's side, the pain like white-hot fire cutting across his ribs, and he hissed, punching his dagger hard through the leather armor into the man's heart, and then the entire ship lurched and everyone stumbled to the side, the remaining attacker falling away.

Erick suddenly found himself among Mathew's men. He gasped, slapped a hand tight across his side, felt blood—his own blood—coat his fingers.

"They've brought another ship up alongside," Mathew yelled over the fight. He grimaced as a blow landed hard on his shoulder, then brought his own blade down hard, slicing through the man's wrist. The blue-tinged man screamed. Blood fountained from the stump as he lurched away, splashing the man next to Mathew before the handless man fell to the deck and was trampled underfoot. "And we've lost Laurren."

Erick shot a glance toward the aft deck, saw the billowing flames where Laurren's body had fallen, and grimaced. His stomach twisted with regret, with actual pain. The cut along his side was worse than he'd thought. But there wasn't time to deal with it.

He drew breath to order everyone to the foredeck, but another ball of fire roared out of the night and landed squarely on the deck, at the base of the mast.

Erick expected it to explode into fragments, like the other ones. Instead, this one's flames spread outward like a pool of oil . . . and then began snaking along the deck, tendrils of fire shooting out toward the feet of the men all around it. I could see the forces at work on the river, could see it being guided. . . .

It caught one of the crew almost instantly.

Before Erick could yell out a warning, the man's clothes erupted like a torch, fire seething upward. The man screamed, the sound sending shivers down Erick's spine. Arms flailing, the man stumbled, hit the mast with his back, then staggered toward the side of the ship, hitting the railing with his hips, then rolling over the top.

He struck the side of the tethered ship once before vanishing from sight.

"Shit!" Mathew breathed. He wiped his mouth with the back of one hand as their gazes met, and in Mathew's eyes Erick saw hopelessness.

They weren't going to survive this battle.

Erick felt the realization settle over him with a strange sense of calm, interrupted only by the pain in his side.

"Get the men to the foredeck," he said, voice steady. "We'll take as many of the damn blue-skinned demons as we can with us."

Mathew hesitated. Then his face hardened, grew grim, and he nodded.

Turning, he bellowed out an order and shoved the men closest to him forward. On the deck, the eerie fire continued to spread, flames streaking out and engulfing men as they ran, swerving around the blue-skinned warriors as they drove Mathew, Erick, and the rest back. I tried to watch, tried to reach out with the river to disrupt the flows that controlled the fire, but Erick was moving too much, dodging and retreating, all in fluid motion, his side screaming at the abuse. Another fireball streaked out of the night and hit the mast, the entire ship shuddering, and then another. Erick fought back, dagger slicking in and out, sword cutting through skin, striking bone, getting tangled in the clothing the warriors wore. And still the men came, pouring in from the starboard side as grapples were thrown from the third ship and the two were tethered together on that side.

The Maiden's crew and the few remaining guardsmen, mostly those provided by Captain Catrell, were driven into the prow of the ship, the group tightening up, the guardsmen shoving the regular crew into the back to defend them as the spacing narrowed. Fire resumed arcing over from the outer ships, striking the deck, the mast, flames now roaring along the port railing, eating away at the aft deck. Most of the sails had been consumed; only tatters remained. Rigging dangled down from the crosspieces of the mast.

Then a ponderous groan shuddered through the ship.

Erick stepped back from the edge of the fighting, caught Mathew's gaze from across the group of crewmen.

The captain of *The Maiden* nodded toward the mast.

Another groan, and this time the majority of those still fighting paused and turned.

Erick heard wood beginning to splinter, a soft, insidious sound, then noticed that fire still roared at the base of the mast.

With a heartrending groan, the mast listed. Wood cracked, the retort hard and sharp and reverberating in Erick's chest, and with a slow, ponderous grace the mast began to fall, trailing fiery sails and rigging behind it.

It struck the aft deck of *The Maiden,* the decking splintering upward at the force, the shudder running through the ship and vibrating in Erick's teeth. He clenched his jaw tight, turned back to the surrounding blue-skinned men—

And then threw down his sword, wincing. It clattered on the

deck, the sound small compared to the crash of the mast. His free hand went to the cut along his side. He pressed hard, trying to staunch the flow.

To either side, the guardsmen tossed their own weapons to the deck, their eyes hard and angry.

The tension on the ship didn't decrease. Instead, one of the blue-skinned men stepped forward from the crowd, pointed his curved sword at Erick.

He spat something in a language Erick didn't recognize, eyes blazing with anger. His face was covered with tattoos, swirled, like waves, and the lower half of one ear was sliced off.

The blue-skinned man eyed Erick, then snorted in contempt. His blade retreated.

Movement came from the back of the attackers, and then a woman stepped out from the crowd. Back straight, head held high, she advanced on Erick and the crew, and the blue-skinned men around her retreated, giving her a wide berth.

She was dressed in the strange silklike cloth of all the others, but her dress had lengths of cloth attached at the waist and wrists, and her ears were pierced with more of the gold rings than the women on the other ships—seven on each side. Her long black hair was held back with a band of gold on her head. Her blue skin was flawless, her eyes black and hardened like stone.

She halted a few paces before Erick. The man who'd spoken to Erick drew back another step, but his eyes never left Erick's face.

The woman spoke, and again the voice in the throne responded—a roar of rage. But I couldn't distinguish who it was amid the chaos. I couldn't catch the scent.

Erick shook his head, frowning in confusion. The woman glared at him, then scanned the rest of the guardsmen, the crew, her eyes falling on Mathew before finally returning to Erick.

She waved her hand in dismissal, said something low, and the man who'd threatened Erick nodded, smiling tightly, a look of anticipation in his eyes. She began to turn away. The blue-skinned men around her stepped forward, swords raised.

I suddenly realized what she intended.

She meant to kill them all.

I leaped forward, horror causing the Fire around me to flare higher. Seizing control of Erick's body, I screamed, "No!" using his voice. I reached for the river using the Fire at Erick's core, wound it tight and flicked it outward like a lash.

It licked across the front rank of blue-skinned men and they shrieked, thrust backward by the force of the invisible blow, and then the whip slid across the woman.

And there it met a wall of force, as tightly woven and dense as anything I'd ever seen Eryn wield. The whip struck the wall and leaped back, recoiling, almost snapping into Erick and the rest of the crew before I brought it back under control.

The woman spun, eyes flashing, and then she moved, so fast I barely saw her, too fast for me to react.

The wall of force surged forward, shoved everyone back from Erick, and then snapped in hard around his throat, crushing into his neck like a hand and lifting him up. He choked, feet dangling off of the deck, pain screaming up from his side with its own white fire, and then the woman stepped forward, peered up into his eyes.

I felt more lines of force reaching out, probing. I withdrew behind the wall of Fire, let my control of Erick slip, suddenly afraid, cursing myself for losing control, for lashing out.

The woman frowned and I suddenly realized she sensed the Fire. She could taste it, as Eryn had tasted it when I'd tried to kill her in the throne room. She could sense it.

And she recognized it.

She frowned, the probing tendrils retreating. Erick continued to

choke, his vision beginning to blur, to narrow, but then the invisible hand holding him relaxed, lowered him to the deck.

He gasped as it loosened enough for him to breathe. But it
didn't release him. Instead, it pressed him farther downward, forced
him to his knees.

The woman stared down at him, her eyes narrowed, her frown
deepening.

Behind her, the man who'd threatened Erick earlier took a tentative step forward, said something.

The woman didn't answer at first. Then she motioned to the
rest of the guardsmen and crew and repeated her earlier command.

Hatred seized me, and as the crew screamed, guardsmen cursing and diving for their dropped weapons, the blue-skinned men attacked. Blades fell, the night filled with the sounds of death.

I surged from the Fire again, reached for the river in desperation
to stop the slaughter, to save Erick, to save someone—

But the grip on Erick tightened. With horror, I felt the river
gather around the woman, felt it harden into blunt force.

Before I could react, before I could begin to form a wall to protect myself, to protect Erick, the woman struck.

I saw the hammer of force fall, felt it shudder through Erick's
body, heard him scream as a horrifying pressure built up behind his
eyes, throbbing with his heart. Blood fountained down onto his
forehead, ran down into his eyes, filled his ears, his mouth, as he
arched back at the pain, as the pressure inside his head increased,
as it escalated, until it streamed from his body like sweat, soaked
into his clothing like blood—

Then the world exploded.

And everything went dark.

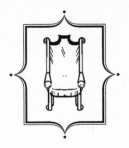

Chapter 10

VARIS.

I moaned, the pounding in my head somehow more intense than usual. I could feel it radiating outward, sending pain away in waves. I felt as if I were adrift, lost and directionless, tugged here and there by invisible currents, the sensation soothing, like sleep or the sigh of wind through the leaves of a tree.

Varis. You need to wake up.

I winced at the voice, tried to shove it away, tried to ignore it. But it was more than a voice, it was a presence, permeating me, surrounding me. It persisted, nudging me, prodding me, the movements becoming more desperate.

Varis. You're dying.

I woke with a gasp. But that wasn't correct. I became *aware* with a gasp, as if I'd struggled through water, almost out of air, lungs aching, and had finally reached the surface. I flailed around, felt the comforting eddies and currents of the river surrounding me, felt the presence of the voice—of many voices—hovering just out of reach, watching me carefully, subdued and sad and concerned. Not all of them. A few still wailed at the edge of the Fire, but the majority of the voices were quiet.

And then I calmed, abruptly, forced myself to remain still, to focus on my surroundings.

Ocean. Beneath where my consciousness drifted, I could see the slow undulation of waves, lit by fractured early morning sunlight, golden and soft. I could smell it, sharp with salt, damp and heavy, like syrup. It rolled silently below me, a breeze drifting out of the west.

Where am I? I asked.

The voices conferred, but it was the voice that had woken me that spoke. Cerrin's voice.

You've been adrift on the river, he said, his voice still tinged with his usual self-pitying sadness, but with a hint of energy now as well, of renewed purpose. It hurt when he spoke, my head throbbing with a steady pulse, in sync with my heartbeat. *The Ochean severed your link to Erick, and in the process knocked you unconscious. You've drifted wherever the currents of the river have taken you for the last eight hours.*

Erick! Everything that had happened on the ship came back with the blunt force of a hammer. I suddenly felt his searing pain, felt again the pressure building inside his head, felt the blood pouring down his face as he arched back, mouth open in a blood-chilling inhuman scream.

I lurched up on the river, sent myself high, began scanning the ocean in all directions. There was no land in sight, nothing but black water rising and falling, the sun a blazing gold on the horizon, the sky a pale cloudless blue above. I spun around again, grew more focused, more frantic, and then I spotted a cold flare of White Fire on the horizon, faint and far away.

I sped toward it, heart shuddering. Erick's pain lashed through me again, the river around me roiling at the memory.

I had to find Erick. I had to save him. He'd gone on the mission under my orders, had risked everything because of me, because of my plan, my idea.

The White Fire began to draw nearer, but slowly. To distract myself, I asked, *The Ochean? I've never heard that name before.*

Another whispered conference.

The blue-skinned woman on the ship who has the Sight, the one who attacked Erick, the one with seven gold earrings in each ear. She's the leader of those people. They call themselves the Chorl.

I frowned. I'd never heard of the Chorl, never heard of any blue-skinned people. The Zorelli who manned most of the trading ships were dark-skinned—a deep brown—but they came from the islands to the south. Everyone knew that. The rest of the people I'd seen in Amenkor or had ever heard of had pale skin, white that had been tanned to various shades of light brown. Aside from the Zorelli, everyone on the Frigean coast was pale.

No one could even remotely be called blue-skinned.

The memory of the warriors streaming up over the side of the ship, their cries piercing the night, sent shivers of horror and revulsion through my skin. Their tattoos, their clothes, their rounded, flattened faces—everything about them was too strange, too inhuman, almost unreal.

How do you know this? I asked harshly, the horror already edging into hatred. *How do you know who they are?*

I felt Cerrin's presence hesitate. Another voice, a woman's voice, Liviann's or perhaps Atreus', hissed at him sharply, and he grew grim.

Because we fought them once before when they came to the Frigean coast. We fought them. And when we defeated them, we banished them, sent them back to the ocean from which they came, sent them west. They decimated the coast for the span of five years. We thought we'd never see them again, thought perhaps that they'd died out, but we prepared nonetheless. That's one of the reasons we created the thrones: to protect the coast from attack.

Who is this "we?"

The Seven, Cerrin said, his voice sad again.

He fell silent, withdrew back into the maelstrom of the voices, back into a pain I didn't understand.

I felt a surge of anger, thought about demanding that he answer more questions, but beneath me the color of the ocean had changed, no longer a deep dense blue verging on black. It had lightened.

Ahead, the White Fire blazed. My heart raced, pulse quickening. Perhaps I wasn't too late. Perhaps I could still save Erick.

And then I saw the coastline, saw the rocky shore, saw the arms of land reaching out to embrace the harbor.

Amenkor.

The blaze of Fire wasn't Erick. It was the Fire inside me.

The revelation was staggering, and I shuddered to a halt outside the influence of the throne, outside the entrance to the harbor, waves crashing into the stone arms of land, spray sheeting up toward the two stone watchtowers at their ends. I spun, searched the horizon to the south and west, desperate. I soared higher, higher still, until the air began to feel thin, until the river itself felt thin, diluted, like the air, and still the horizon was empty.

Damn it! I screamed, frantic. *Help me!*

The voices remained silent, withdrew even further, unnaturally quiet. A somber quiet, filled with pain and loss and understanding. A quiet that somehow smothered those that still fought to escape their prison, to seize control. Because those that still fought to escape were so few.

But I barely noticed, pushed myself higher still. There was no Fire. No tag for me to follow. No way for me to link up with Erick. Which meant—

I halted, a cold certainty seeping down into my gut.

I drew in a harsh, trembling breath, held it.

I scanned the horizon one more time, knowing I would find nothing.

I felt a pain begin to build inside me, begin to sting at the corners of my eyes. A pain totally unlike that which had racked Erick's body, had seethed in his veins and shuddered in his heart, had built and built behind his skull. This pain started deep in my chest, swelled and seeped outward, a hot, visceral pain that felt fluid and sick and left me drained and weak and useless. This pain closed off my throat with a hard, nauseating lump. I tried desperately to hold the pain in, the stinging in my eyes increasing, tears beginning to stream down my face. I felt myself shudder with the effort—

Until I couldn't hold it in any longer.

I screamed. A raw scream of rage and pain and loss. Of guilt and regret and unfairness. And when that breath had died, strangled into nothingness, I gasped in another breath, the sound ragged and harsh and broken, and I screamed again, so hard it felt like my throat had torn.

The voices responded. The Seven—as well as those that were now calm, now quiet—shifted forward, reached out through the protective Fire under Cerrin's guidance, surrounding me, holding me, comforting me. I shut off all consciousness of the river, closed myself off from the world, and surrendered to the fluid pain, let it sear through me. I let the voices protect me as my screams descended into racking sobs and twisted guilt.

I curled in upon myself.

And I let myself drift again.

†

The pain receded like the slow ebb of the tide and my awareness of the river returned. First nothing more than a sound: ocean waves crashing up against a rocky shoreline. It took me a moment to recognize it, for it to seep through the numbness left behind by the pain. But once I did recognize it, my awareness spread, like a drop of oil on the surface of water, or blood seeping into cloth. I smelled

the shore, sand and wind and stone. And seaweed drying in the
sun.

I opened my eyes, breathed in deeply, and stared down the
length of beach to a rocky crag jutting out into the ocean, the
surf pounding into the stone with crashing spray and sparkling
mist. I stared at the beach a long moment without thinking,
barely aware of the afternoon sun against my face, until I noticed
movement.

A crab scuttled across the sand, heading for the rocky plinth.

I glanced around, noticed the beach running up to a layer of
rocks and driftwood, then a dune with wisps of grass that merged
into a bank of pine trees. Behind me, another rocky crag cut off the
view of the beach to the north.

It reminded me of the little cove near Colby, where Eryn had
investigated the remains of the shipwreck.

I turned back to the water, looked out over the waves, to where
the sea darkened into true ocean.

Erick.

The ache in my chest returned, but it was dull, nothing more
than a throb of grief. I was too numbed, too exhausted.

I reached for the voices of the throne, felt their presences in the
background behind the wall of Fire, but none of them came forward. They'd changed. For the first time, that realization sank in.
They were no longer fighting among themselves, no longer bickering and biting and seething in a maelstrom of hatred. Instead, they
were calm, intent, and focused.

Except for a few still screaming at the edges, they'd banded together, had united with a purpose. The Seven were keeping those
that had not joined them under control themselves, and now they
were simply waiting.

I should have been concerned, should have used the river to

renew the net that protected me from them, should have thrown up a second net for additional safety. I shifted uneasily. . . .

And then I let the concern go. It didn't matter. Nothing mattered now.

Time passed, the sunlight overhead shifting. I did nothing, said nothing, felt nothing.

And then:

Varis.

It was the woman with straight black hair. Atreus. She stood with the rest of the Seven arrayed behind her, Cerrin in the back, his form shifting restlessly, his presence troubled.

Varis, we need to speak to you. About the Chorl. About the Ochean.

What? I said.

You have to understand how dangerous they are, Atreus said. *You have to warn Amenkor, warn the entire Frigean coast. If they have returned—*

Garus snorted. *They have returned! Open your damned eyes!*

Garus!

What!

I focused on the man who'd cut Garus short. He was younger than Garus, had no neatly trimmed beard, was thin where Garus was broad. And I recognized him. I'd witnessed the creation of the thrones through his eyes, felt his pain as the rest of the Seven fell around him, consumed by the raw energies they'd called into existence.

He leveled a stern gaze on Garus, and the older man backed down with a grumble.

Thank you, Seth, Atreus said.

But Garus is right, another woman said. She had straight black hair, just like Atreus, had the same facial features as well—thin face, high cheekbones, fine nose. An older version of Atreus, harsher, her mouth set into a perpetual frown. *The Chorl have re-*

turned, and you need to know how dangerous they can be. And Cerrin is going to show you.

All of the voices in the throne turned to Cerrin. He glanced up. *Why me, Alleryn?*

Alleryn's frown deepened. *Because yours is the more powerful, more convincing story. And because your story was the beginning.*

Cerrin grimaced, then steeled himself. Without shifting forward, he said, *For Olivia, then, and my daughters.*

He reached through the Fire and grabbed me, and before I could draw breath, I was trapped.

✝

Wind blew across the veranda, rustling in the long, thin leaves of the potted plants in urns on the edges of the stonework lining the edge of the patio. The air was raucous with the cries of seagulls and other birds. I moved to the edge of the balustrade, stared down over the cliff into the bay far below.

Venitte lay spread out before me, the wide bay filled with ships of all kinds, birds wheeling both above and beneath my position, horns and bells joining their cries occasionally. Sails bellied out in the wind, drawing the ships out to one or the other of the two channels that branched north and south around the island that protected the bay from the worst of the winds and the storms. Other boats streamed toward the main wharf farther inland and the domed buildings on the hills behind, or toward the hundreds of jetties and piers that lanced out into the water beneath the cliffs on either side of the bay. On the opposite cliff, white stone buildings with red clay-tiled roofs and lush inner gardens formed a bright mosaic in the sunlight.

"Do you have to go in to Council?"

I turned, smiling even before I saw Olivia, her skin dark and vibrant as she exited the shade of the house and came to my side. Behind her, Jaer and Pallin scampered out into the sunlight, laughing. Pallin, seven, reached out to grab her sister, but Jaer—two years younger and much smaller—eluded her, ducking and screaming with delight as Pallin gave chase.

"You know I do," I said, taking Olivia into my arms. I kissed the top of her head, breathed in the scent of her hair. "The Council has many important decisions to make."

"More important than me?" She said it lightly, mocking me.

"Hmm . . . you ask dangerous questions. More dangerous than the Council."

She laughed.

Down on the water, there was a muffled sound, like an explosion, echoing against the cliffs.

"What was that?" Olivia said. Pulling free from my grasp, she moved closer to the stone balustrade, leaned on it.

Frowning, I joined her.

Another muffled *whumph,* and another, the sound distorted as it bounced against one of the stone walls of the channel.

Olivia shook her head. "I don't see anything."

"It's coming from the channel," I said. I glanced toward the wharf, toward the Council chambers, the largest stone building in Venitte, its spire reaching into the sky, then back toward my wife.

Olivia turned at the tone of my voice, her eyes flicking toward the children. "Should I . . . ?"

Before I could answer the unasked question, ships began pouring through the mouth of the channel. Black ships, their hulls glistening in the sunlight as they threw up spume before them. They lanced into the bay, sails all unfurled, bellied out with the wind, moving at a fast clip. First five appeared, then ten, then twenty, spreading out on the bay as they breached the channel. And still more came.

"Cerrin?" Voice taut, strained, worried. "Who are they?"

"I don't know."

The lead ships encountered the first Venittian, and fire leaped out, arched across the water in a sizzling ball and exploded in the Venittian's sails. Olivia gave a startled cry, the fear tight and hideous in her voice—

And then suddenly there was fire everywhere, arching up and out from every ship, searing through the sky trailing smoke, striking ship after ship as bells and horns began to blow, as birds scattered with harsh cries, fleeing, the ships in the harbor doing the same, turning ponderously and skimming back toward the inland wharf, toward the city, the Council and the walls that could protect them.

But the fire wasn't restricted to the ships. Great sheets of it flew high, bursting with deadly intent in the bright mosaic of houses on the cliffs on the far side of the bay.

"Cerrin!"

I spun, anger boiling like acid in the back of my throat, curling tight about my fear. "Get Jaer and Pallin. Now!"

Behind, I heard fire sizzling close, felt a wash of heat across my back and glanced up in time to see a huge fireball roaring overhead, heard it explode in a house higher up the cliff above us. Olivia cried out, her eyes wide with fear now, and Jaer screamed.

"Olivia!"

She turned from where smoke and fire leaped into the sky behind our house, and in her eyes I saw the fear drain away. "Pallin," she snapped. "Get your sister. We're leaving."

I turned back toward the bay, moved up to the stone railing as three more fireballs arched into the houses to either side. Screams came from the left, and a body fell from the cliff, trailing flames and smoke.

Real fear began to boil in my gut. The bay was choked with black ships.

I shoved away from the veranda, stalked across the patio to where Olivia waited with the girls inside the arched doorway. "Come on," I said. "We have to get to the Wall."

Behind, the veranda exploded into flame.

Ducking, Pallin trembling in my grip, we raced through the house. Olivia screamed at the servants as we ran, ordered them to get to the Wall. We spilled out onto the street, smoke blowing across the stone paving, people shrieking on all sides, a few stumbling with blood drenching their faces, others staggering, arms burned. A body lay in the gutter, facedown. The house two buildings down was a blazing inferno, flames leaping high into the air.

"Go!" I yelled through the roar when Olivia hesitated. "Go now! Head down—"

A fireball exploded in the street not ten paces away, the sound deafening, heat searing outward, a concussive wave that sucked my breath away, that knocked all of us flat, Olivia's form slamming into my stomach and chest, her arms still around Jaer. Pallin was wrenched out of my grasp and pain scorched its way up my arm. I heard a muffled scream, smelled the sickening stench of roasted flesh, felt the hair on my arms singe, my face turn waxy with heat, blister—

And then I crashed into the stone of the street, the rounded cobbles gouging into my back. A form landed on top of me, crushed the breath from my lungs, but I lay stunned, unable to breathe, unable to think. I stared up into a blue sky interrupted by trails of heavy, dense smoke, the world reduced to a muted roar, to the scent of burned cloth and hair.

My breath returned with a startled gasp, my throat tearing as I sucked in air, then coughed. I fought the urge to vomit, tasted the bile at the back of my throat but swallowed convulsively, then tried to shift.

The weight holding me down didn't move.

I glanced down, saw the blackened flesh of an arm clutched tight to a smaller body.

I screamed, lurched up onto my elbows, kicked out sharply, and then I saw the glint of gold on the child's arm.

The bracelet. The bracelet I'd given her for her fourth birthday.

My heart stopped, caught in my chest for a breath, for an eternity—

And when it resumed, it brought with it a devastating calm.

I sat upright, clutched the two bodies close, ignoring the crackle of charred skin, ignoring the pain from my own damaged arm, saw the third body crumpled on the cobbles beside me, twisted in upon itself. I held Olivia and Jaer close, tears coursing down my face as panicked citizens of Venitte swept past, screaming, as fire scorched the sky above, exploding on all sides.

Then, still unnaturally calm, I stood, carried the two bodies— so light, so fragile—back into the house, returning a moment later to retrieve Pallin's body. Calm, careful, my motions slow and methodical. I laid them in the cool shade of the inner sanctum, where the household fountain gurgled playfully, cooling the air. I arranged their arms across their chests as best I could, stroked the distorted metal of Jaer's bracelet, still weeping, the tears coming in a flood, burning in the heat blisters on my face, then I drifted back out to the veranda, where the fireball that had struck as we fled had left a scorch mark on the stone, had eaten away a chunk of the balustrade itself.

I stood at the edge of the cliff and watched the ships burn their way down the bay, listened to the shriek of voices on all sides, listened to the spitting hiss of fire.

I watched the city of Venitte go up in flames.

†

I sat on the ground and let the rhythmic sound of the waves wash over me, breathed in the heady scent of the beach and let it clear my lungs of char and smoke and death.

Those are the Chorl, Cerrin said, and I suddenly understood the melancholy that always surrounded him, understood the self-pity, the self-hatred that sometimes flared up as anger, the vacant desolation of his voice.

And that was only the first assault, Liviann said, her own voice full of righteous anger, *the first of the devastation. After the attack on Venitte, which we managed to halt at Deranian's Wall and then repulse after two months of siege, they began marauding the coast, attacking ports, villages, setting up camps in inlets and coves. And their Adepts—*

No, Garus barked. *They were not Adepts. They could not control all branches of magic.*

But they were *powerful,* Atreus intervened. *And there were many of them.*

So many it seemed we would never prevail. This from Silicia, a slight woman who usually remained quiet in the background. I remembered her death when the thrones were created, remembered the blood trailing from her mouth after she'd collapsed.

That is why we created the thrones, Cerrin said. *We managed to drive them away, mainly by focusing on their . . . on their Servants. We targeted them, because that was their edge in battle. We Seven could not protect the armies against so many, and so we began hunting them, assassinating the Chorl Servants in their own camps, killing them in their sleep, focusing on them in battle.*

Exterminating them, Garus said.

Silicia shuddered, her essence twisting with distaste. Atreus grew grim.

And it worked, Liviann said, her voice matter-of-fact. *When their Servants dwindled, when we began to turn back their armies with ease, both on land and sea, they withdrew, back to the ocean, back to its depths.*

But the coast was decimated. Cerrin shifted forward, his voice intent. *Amenkor, Venitte, all of the major cities had been hurt or destroyed. We might have pursued them, wiped them out completely if possible, but winter approached. Most of the cities retreated behind their walls, concentrated on survival.*

We sent out ships in the spring, Seth said, *tried to find the lands they originated from, but we found nothing.*

And we knew that there were no Adepts being born, that there was no one to replace us. Atreus again.

And so we created the thrones. Back to Cerrin. *To help those that did survive after us, those that had some of the Talent, if not all.*

We didn't realize the thrones would destroy us, Alleryn said, her mouth pressed into a thin line. *We underestimated the power that would be required in their creation.*

You have to warn Amenkor, Varis. You have to prepare. Determination had entered Cerrin's voice. *And we can help you. All of the voices of the throne can help you. We have them under control now.*

Let me think, I said, felt the majority of the Seven straining forward, ready to argue more. But Cerrin gave them all a stern look, ushered them back.

I sat on the beach, in the cove, and watched the sun descend toward the ocean. I thought of Erick, of Laurren, of Mathew and the entire crew of *The Maiden.* I thought of Cerrin's memory, of Olivia and Jaer and Pallin, of him clutching their charred bodies to his chest. I thought of Venitte, reduced to burning buildings, columns of black smoke billowing into the blue sky, and thought of the vision of Amenkor itself burning, fire orange and pulsing in the night.

And when the sun began to set, when the first stars began to appear on the horizon behind me, above the trees, I stirred.

I rose up above the seclusion of the cove and looked for the White Fire. It blazed to the south. Without rushing, I Reached for it, felt the world blur beneath me, felt it grow more dense as I entered the influence of the throne, felt the life of the city fall over me like a mantle as I settled into myself in the throne room. As I settled, I felt people in the throne room, most removed toward the far end near the doors, but two others stood closer: Eryn, pacing in front of the throne, and Marielle, seated on the steps of the dais.

I gasped in a deep breath of air, the sensation sharp and painful, as if my body had grown accustomed to not breathing, then choked on the air and bent over in a fit of coughing.

"Thank the heavens!" Eryn murmured. And then, in a louder voice, "She's back! Keven, send someone for Avrell. And get that healer back in here!"

The coughing fit ended.

I stood, stepped away from the throne, stumbled as tremors coursed through my body, worse than at any other time before, my legs so weak I could barely stand. I was suddenly surrounded— Eryn, Marielle, Keven—all talking at once, demanding explanations, demanding to know if I was all right, voices tinged with worry. Someone grabbed my arm, held me upright, helped me step down from the dais. Someone else tried to present me with a cup of tea, the scent of earth and leaves sharp, biting through the smell of the stone and tallow of the throne room, the bitter scent of fear beneath the stone, and suddenly it was all too much.

"Stop," I said, too weakly to be heard. I tried to shove the helping hands away, but when no one retreated, when someone pressed a damp cloth against my forehead, fury flared sharp and fast.

"Just stop!" I shouted, my voice cracking through the throne room, bringing everyone up short.

Into the new silence, Avrell and a man I didn't recognize hurried into the hall. Avrell, eyes wide, face as open and readable as I'd ever seen it, came to an abrupt halt as he saw me, the other man halting beside him. He stared at me, met my eyes, his own full of fear and worry, and then he bowed his head, murmured something I couldn't hear, a prayer of some sort, and then he signed himself with the Skewed Throne across his chest.

When he glanced back up, there were tears in his eyes. "Mistress," he began, but halted. He struggled to continue, but couldn't.

Instead, he straightened, cleared his throat uncomfortably, then motioned the man beside him toward me.

"This man is a healer," he said. Thin, with gray hair and kind eyes, the healer hurried forward.

"I'm fine," I said, the tremors still shuddering through my arms, through my legs. I realized Keven was the one keeping me upright, and I leaned into his solid weight.

The healer took my hand and placed two fingers on the inside of my wrist as he began to scan my face, his lips moving, as if he were counting beneath his breath.

"I said, I'm fine." I glared at him as I tried to pull my hand out of his, but I was too weak. He returned the glare and refused to let go, his count never faltering.

Avrell had moved forward and now stood directly behind him. In a calm but warning tone, he said, "Let him check you." He glanced toward the waiting guardsmen, who stood hovering at the edges of the throne room, toward Marielle, who stood to one side in obvious distress. Eryn and Keven were also concerned, although they hid it better.

I tensed, ready to argue, but then relented.

The healer felt my muscles relax and nodded. Satisfied with whatever he'd found with my wrist, he laid a hand on my forehead briefly, then began probing beneath my neck.

As I waited, I felt something on my upper lip. With my free hand, I reached up and rubbed it, my fingers coming away with flakes of dried blood.

I shot a questioning glance at Avrell, but it was Eryn who answered.

"That happened late last night, about an hour after you sat down on the throne." Her voice was grim. "That's when we first sent for the healer. But he couldn't help you, not while you were sitting on the throne. We couldn't let anyone get close, and we didn't dare take you off the throne. We didn't know what it would do to you."

I nodded.

The healer finished with my neck, then stepped back. "I don't see anything wrong with her aside from the obvious trembling and the bloody nose. And the nose stopped bleeding hours ago. Some rest should handle the trembling."

Everyone heaved a sigh of relief, the tense guardsmen in the background relaxing, Marielle signing herself with one hand.

"Satisfied?" I asked curtly.

Avrell frowned, assumed a more formal pose, then nodded. "Yes."

I grunted, straightened, feeling more steady on my feet, and pushed past him, moving toward the doors, Keven remaining at my side. I felt everyone hesitate behind me, the other guardsmen in the room coming to attention and forming up near the door. Eryn, Marielle, Avrell, and the healer remained in the throne room.

"Where are you going?" Avrell asked.

"To my chambers," I said, voice still harsh. "I need to rest."

"What about Erick and the ship?" Eryn called after.

I halted, felt a stab of pain deep inside, felt my anger flinch.

But then I hardened and continued toward the doors. "He's dead," I said. "They're all dead."

†

They left me alone for two days, under the careful watch of Keven and his guardsmen. I stayed in my chambers for the most part, pacing my bedroom, or staring out at the city from the balcony. I watched the progress in the warehouse district while sipping tea and nibbling food brought by Marielle, although I wasn't hungry. She'd enter, set the trays down on the various tables, her eyes lowered, her head bowed. But I could see her biting her lower lip with worry, could feel her wanting to reach out to talk to me, to comfort me, but not daring. Then she'd pick up the tray containing the used dishes and leftover food I couldn't eat from the meal she'd left before and leave, Keven closing the door behind her.

I had Keven escort me to the rooftop twice, where I stood at the stone half wall at the edge and stared out at the sea or frowned down at the entrance to the harbor. Keven stood a short distance away, ready to leap forward and grab me if I showed any inclination to jump. I could feel the tension radiating from him, could taste his worry and smell him berating himself for not knowing what to do or say to make me feel better, all mixed in with his own grief.

They all thought I was grieving. For those lost on the ship. For Laurren. For Erick. But I'd already done my grieving, on the river and in that cove. On the Dredge, there was no time for grief. Not if you wanted to survive. The palace was no different. But the seclusion it allowed me was necessary. I needed to think. And learn—about the Chorl, about the Ochean. And I needed to plan. With the help of all of the voices of the throne, but in particular, the Seven—Cerrin, Liviann, Atreus, Alleryn, Silicia, Seth, and Garus.

They *had* been waiting . . . for me to be ready to hear them, to *listen* to them.

When Avrell and Eryn finally did send someone to speak to me, it wasn't who I expected.

†

Keven knocked on the door, then looked in. "There's someone here to see you, Mistress."

I glanced up from the slate I held with a frown. If it had been Marielle, he would have simply let her in. I sighed and set the slate aside. "Send them in."

Keven hesitated. "Are you certain?"

"Yes."

He withdrew and a moment later William stepped through the door.

I rose with a start, thought immediately of the sketch I'd seen of myself on his desk, and felt myself blush. "William," I blurted, then caught myself. The blush grew hotter.

He halted inside the door, scanned the room with nervous curiosity as if he had wandered somewhere he didn't feel he should be, but then his gaze fell on me. He smiled awkwardly, still nervous—but not about being in the Mistress' chambers anymore—and asked, "Do you want me to leave?"

"No. I was expecting . . . someone else."

He nodded. "They almost sent Borund, but then Marielle convinced them to send me instead."

Marielle. My eyes narrowed as I remembered her comments at the warehouse.

The silence grew. My gaze flicked around the room and fell on the slate on the settee.

The blush faded. William wasn't here to see me. Not really. He'd been sent because Avrell and Eryn and the others wanted to know what had happened. They needed to know.

Because I couldn't do everything necessary myself.

I sighed. "They want me to come out and speak to them, don't they?"

I caught William's grimace. "Yes."

I nodded. He'd wanted this to be something more than just a summons from the First and the former Mistress. He'd wanted it to be about us. I could see it in his face. But something always seemed to come between us: the assassin after Borund, the ambush when William had been stabbed, my intent to kill Alendor. And now the threat of the Chorl and the Ochean.

I moved a few steps toward him, felt him tense, and stopped. I wasn't certain what I should do, and so I fell back on what I did know. "Tell them to get everyone together in the throne room in an hour. All of the merchants and their apprentices, the captains of the guard, and whoever else with the guard they feel should be brought along, plus Avrell, Eryn, Nathem, and the Servants."

William nodded solemnly, then turned to leave.

"And William."

He paused at the door.

"I'm glad you came."

His shoulders relaxed a little as he left.

✝

I entered the throne room from one of the two side entrances near the dais and the throne itself, Keven and two other guardsmen entering a few steps ahead of me, the rest of my escort coming in behind. Conversation filled the room with a dull roar, the aisle before the throne and the spaces between the four massive columns on either side packed with guards in various forms of armor, Servants in white robes, Avrell and Nathem in dark blue, and a few multicolored, gold-embroidered merchant jackets and the plainly dressed apprentices. As soon as Keven appeared, his men fanning out along the dais of the throne, the conversation stilled, the room falling mostly silent. Only the faint sounds of rustling cloth and scuffing feet remained as people shifted nervously.

I mounted the three steps of the dais without looking out into the faces of those gathered, my palms sweaty, and not from the heat of all of the candles that had been lit or the bodies in the room. I'd worn my whitest shirt, my cleanest pair of breeches, and my newest pair of soft leather shoes. My dagger was tucked into my belt at my waist and I'd allowed Marielle to cut and comb my shoulder-length hair. I could feel everyone's eyes upon me, could sense their expectation, their curiosity, their fear. I'd never called them all into the throne room like this, never spoken to many of them directly at all. They didn't know what to expect.

I hesitated a moment before the throne, stared down at it as it shifted from one shape into the next: narrow and thin, rectangular then round; a simple slab of stone, then a gaudy ornamented chair. The first time I'd seen it, the motion—the very feel of it, prowling around the room like a wild cat—had made me nauseous and sent shudders down my back. But not anymore.

I reached out and touched it, felt it recognize me, felt the stone tremble beneath my fingers . . . and then the throne twisted one last time and settled into the shape I knew so well now: a simple curved seat with no back, the armrests curled under.

I turned and sat, and the entire room seemed to sigh.

I stared down at those assembled, noted Avrell, Eryn, Baill, Catrell, Westen, Borund, and Regin at the forefront, near the base of the dais. Darryn was with them, shifting uncomfortably. I wondered who'd thought to summon him, then saw Westen's casual nod. I caught each of their gazes, then scanned the rest of the men and women in the room, felt them fidget with nervousness, some glancing at their neighbors, others craning their necks to get a better view of me and the throne. The room was tense, as if everyone had held their breath.

I glanced down toward Avrell and Eryn and announced, "We have a new enemy. A people called the Chorl."

A moment of confused silence, people drawing back, brows creasing in confusion—

But not everyone. I saw Avrell cast a horrified glance toward Eryn, saw her own shocked look before she controlled herself, her eyes devoid of any emotion. Avrell took his cue from her, but I saw him shudder.

Everyone else began speaking at once.

I let them talk, knew that it would not last long. Aside from Avrell and Eryn, no one here knew anything about the Chorl, about who they were or where they came from, except perhaps a few of the ship captains, who might recognize the Chorl as the sea-demons from the tales they were raised on as children. But the tales did not mention the Chorl by name. It had been too long, the tales too distorted. The sea-demons had been reduced to creatures of the deep, not a race of blue-skinned men and women who bled as we did, who fought with swords and ships and magic.

The sense of confusion that permeated the room escalated as the crowd quieted, and then Avrell stepped forward, in the space just before the throne.

"And who are the Chorl?" he asked. Only I heard the tremor in his voice.

I stared down at him, saw that he'd asked the question purposefully, even though he already knew the answer, and smiled. It was not a nice smile. It was twisted with the pain of Erick's and Laurren's deaths and the lives of all of the rest of the crew of *The Maiden*. It caused Avrell to take an uncertain step backward.

"Let me show you," I said.

I reached out on the river, threw a net wide, so that it encompassed everyone in the room. A different net than the one that Eryn had shown me to keep the voices of the throne in check. This one I'd learned from Cerrin while secluded in my chambers. Even as I set it into place, I felt Cerrin's nod of approval. It bound everyone in the room to me temporarily and as it did so, I felt all of the Servants in the room gasp, heard Eryn suck in a sharp breath at the base of the throne. No one else felt anything, turned in consternation to frown at the Servants, some taking a tentative step away.

Before anyone could react further, I sank myself down into memory, placed myself back on the ship, inside of Erick . . . and then I pushed the memory out along the strands of the net and forced everyone to relive Erick's last moments on the ship.

Blood flew up into their faces and the entire room gasped, some hissing in shock, lurching back, hands raised. A few guardsmen started to draw their swords, but halted as Erick thrust aside the dead body of the guardsman, as he raised his sword to block the descending sword. The blade jarred into Erick's upraised sword, pain shivering down into his shoulder, and the room gasped again, but the initial shock and babble of voices subsided.

Then Erick spun, and those in the room got their first sight of the Chorl.

Someone screamed. A few others fainted dead away, their bodies hitting the floor with slithering thuds since no one moved to catch them, all still caught in the grip of the memory. Guardsmen cursed, merchants and Servants cringed, and somewhere in the back of the room someone was violently sick.

"Enough!" someone shouted, the sound intervening on the memory. I frowned, recognized the panicked voice as Regin's, but I didn't relent. Concentrating harder, I focused the net, made the memory more real, more visceral, until everyone in the room could smell the blood, could taste the fear as Erick surged forward to save the crew, as he began the retreat to the prow.

And then I shifted the memory, slid into Laurren's head. I heightened her fear, her desperation, her determination to inflict as much damage as possible on the Chorl Servants and their ships with her spears as I held the shield. I sent my horror through the net as my grasp of the shield failed, intensified the sensation of being burned alive, fire drawn down into my lungs, scorching my body, as Laurren writhed in agony

And then I pulled back, returned to Erick as he dodged into the melee surrounding Mathew and retreated, horrified, from the fire as it snaked across the decking, engulfing man after man like human torches. The reactions in the room intensified, someone screaming continuously, unable to stop, more sounds of retching as guardsmen and Chorl died, bellies slit open, throats cut, and still I pushed harder. I wanted them to feel the pain of the crew, to live their sacrifice. I wanted them to understand what knowledge of the Chorl had cost.

Erick's death would mean something. Laurren's death would mean something. Not like the murder of the white-dusty man, killed by Bloodmark for no reason other than to hurt me.

Another horrified, awed gasp from those caught in the net as the mast groaned and cracked and shattered into the deck, seeming to shudder through the stone of the throne room beneath their feet. Utter silence—nothing but indrawn, held breaths—as the fighting halted, as the man threatened Erick and the Ochean shifted through the blue-skinned warriors.

She ordered the deaths of *The Maiden*'s crew, turned back when I lashed out with the river . . . and then she killed Erick.

I held nothing back. I let everyone in the room feel his torment, forced everyone to shudder with his pain as the screams of the rest of the crew sounded all around him as they were butchered by the Chorl.

But I cut the memory short a moment before the pressure inside Erick—before the pain—knocked me unconscious.

When I let the net release and the memory faded, there were ten people in the room who had fainted, another twenty who had bent over or collapsed to the floor, moaning or vomiting in a corner. Everyone looked pale, eyes wide with shock, limbs weak and trembling. Avrell was holding Eryn by the arm to support her, her face utterly exposed, and I suddenly realized with regret that I'd forced her to witness—no, worse, I'd forced her to *live*—Laurren's death.

Even Baill and the guardsmen were shaken. The purple bruise on Baill's bald head from the rock thrown in the Dredge stood out, livid, against his pale skin.

I waited a moment to let everyone catch their breath, to let the scent of blood and smoke and ocean clear from their senses.

Then I said, "Those are the Chorl."

"What . . ." Avrell began, but his voice cracked. He licked his lips and cleared his throat, his gaze wandering about the room as if uncertain where to look, where to focus. "What . . . do you intend to do?"

I leaned forward, caught his wandering gaze, held it. "I intend to fight them."

A stunned silence, interrupted by a bark of laughter.

Everyone turned their eyes on Baill. "You expect to fight them?" His voice seethed with disdain. "How?"

"All work on the warehouse district will cease. Everyone will shift to fortifying the encircling juts of land that surround the harbor and rebuilding the two guard towers at their ends. There was once a wall there. We'll rebuild it. That will be the first line of defense, because when they come, they will come from the sea."

Baill seemed shocked that I had a ready answer.

Catrell stepped forward. "How do you know this? How do you know they will come here, to Amenkor?"

Because the Ochean recognized the Fire inside of Erick, I thought. Because she recognized the power there. She didn't know what it was, but she'd seen it before, tasted it before.

And she wanted it for her own.

But that was not what those in the hall would believe.

"Because I've seen it," I said instead. "The Skewed Throne has shown me."

I didn't want to show them the vision of the city burning, of the harbor filled with blood, didn't want to show them the destruction. It would be too disheartening, too horrifying.

I didn't have to. Eryn stepped forward, faced the throne room. "I saw it as well, before Varis replaced me as Mistress. They *will* come here. But we can prepare for them. We *will* prepare for them."

Murmurs filled the room, laced with fear. One of the fears found a voice.

"What about those fires? How can we defend against those?"

I couldn't see who'd spoken, but it didn't matter. "The fires were produced by women like the Servants of the Throne, women who have power. Since I ascended the throne, Eryn and I have been training the Servants of the palace. They will defend the city from the Chorl Servants."

"The Servant on the ship didn't last long," someone grumbled, loudly enough to be heard by everyone. Others nodded.

Eryn flinched, her eyes going tight with grief.

I felt a surge of anger. "Laurren was overwhelmed by three of those women! She sacrificed everything to protect that crew! It won't be one against three when the Chorl arrive."

No one responded. No one questioned how I knew this. Which was good because I had no idea how many of the Chorl had the Sight.

Westen stepped forward. "You said the watchtowers at the entrance to the harbor were the *first* line of defense. What else do you have planned?"

All eyes turned to me and I settled back into the throne. The despair I'd seen on the faces of those gathered after I'd shown them

The Maiden's death had faded, had begun to slip from shock into wary hope. All I had to do now was convince them that they had a chance. I had to convince them when I had not convinced myself yet.

"Here's what I intend to do. . . ." I began.

And everyone in the room shifted forward to hear.

†

It took three hours to discuss and argue the rest of my plans with those gathered in the throne room, and by the end, most of their faces were tense but filled with determination and hope.

As they began to file out of the room, I stood up from the throne, stepped partway down the steps of the dais. Keven shifted forward to stand beside me, and at the bottom of the dais, Avrell, Eryn, and, surprisingly, Captain Catrell stepped forward. Baill gave Catrell a sharp frown, but after a moment turned to push his way through the crowd of people at the door, guardsmen falling in around him.

No one said anything until the majority of the Servants, guardsmen, and merchants had left. Then Avrell turned toward me, his face grim. "Do you think it will work?"

I shrugged, exhausted, drained by the arguing, by the tension that still gripped my shoulders. "It has to. It's all that we've got."

He nodded.

"You already knew about the Chorl. I saw it on your face." I let anger touch my voice, directed it at both Avrell and Eryn, unconcerned that Catrell and Keven would overhear. "Why didn't you tell me about them?"

Eryn answered. "Because they never crossed my mind as a possibility."

"They haven't been seen on the Frigean coast in almost fifteen hundred years," Avrell said. "They're . . . a history lesson, something I read about as part of my duties as the First of the Mistress, nothing more."

Keven frowned. "They aren't history anymore. How long do we have to prepare?"

"According to the throne, they won't attack until the summer. That gives us a little less than four months." Even as I said it, I felt a twinge of uneasiness in my gut. My hand drifted to the hilt of my dagger for reassurance.

Keven grunted with satisfaction, eyes widening. "That should be plenty of time."

Eryn's lips were pursed, her brow creased. She looked as uneasy as I felt. "We should still move quickly. The more training the regular citizens that will form the militias have, the better. The Servants will need more extensive training. They've made significant progress so far, but nothing like what they'll need to defend against the Chorl. And the walls and towers won't go up overnight. There will be unforeseen problems."

Her words didn't seem to lessen Keven's optimism.

Out of the corner of my eye, I could see Captain Catrell shifting his weight as he waited, unwilling to interrupt. But before I could turn to him, Avrell said, "Then we should all get busy. There's plenty for all of us to do."

"No," I said, my eyes narrowing. "There's one more thing that needs to be handled before we direct our energies to the walls and preparing the citizens and Servants." In answer to their perplexed looks, I added, "Yvan."

Avrell straightened abruptly. "There's something you need to know about Yvan and the raid on his manse."

I didn't like the sudden formal tone. "What?"

He grimaced. "Yvan was indeed hoarding food. Everything in the second cellar you found had not been reported to the guild or to you at your request. However . . ."

I felt a spike of irritation at Avrell's hesitation. "However what?"

"Yvan isn't the one who took the food from the warehouses."

Dead silence. No one moved, all eyes on Avrell.

"What do you mean?" I asked finally, my voice sharper than intended. Avrell flinched.

"I compared the food we found in Yvan's cellar with the report of what was missing . . . and it doesn't match. There's not enough food in his cellar to account for all that's missing . . . not even after making allowances for what Yvan may have already eaten. And there are stores in his cellar that we aren't missing at all." He took a deep breath. "I think Yvan hid stores that he already owned when you demanded an inventory at the end of the fall. I don't think he's stolen anything from the warehouses at all. It's someone else."

"But who?" When Avrell shook his head, I turned to Keven. "What did you find out by questioning the guardsmen?"

Keven shrugged. "We stopped checking around once we caught Yvan, but before that, we had a few tentative leads. Some guardsmen had seen a group of other guardsmen leading some wagons near the stockyards, on the edge of the city, as if they were escorting cargo. Except it was late at night. They thought it was odd, but nothing in the city has been normal in the last few months. A few others have gotten sudden changes in orders at the last minute, mainly a change in what warehouse they were assigned to guard. Other than that, we hadn't found out much."

I frowned, irritation turning to anger. "So who is it? Who's been stealing from the warehouses if it isn't Yvan?"

At that, Captain Catrell stepped forward with a stiff, nervous bow. "It's Captain Baill. I know. I've seen him."

†

I was still fuming over what Captain Catrell had revealed when I met my escort at the palace gates. My anger was like lightning, white-hot and snapping out from me on the river in sharp jagged lines, making everyone around me jittery. But, for the moment, I was holding the anger in check. There was nothing that could be done about Catrell's suspicions, not at the moment anyway.

But there *was* still Yvan to deal with.

I reached the last steps of the promenade and checked on the covey of guards Keven had assembled and the entourage of people that were lined up to follow us down to the main market square. Avrell was there, of course, along with Eryn and Nathem, the two administrators dressed in their finest dark blue robes, Eryn in a brilliant white dress. Behind them were Masters Borund and Regin, both in their merchant robes and both with appropriately somber faces. They were mounted, their horses dancing impatiently at the wait, tossing their heads. William and Regin's apprentice rode be-hind them, backs stiff, mouths pressed tight.

Behind them was another group of guardsmen, leading a team of horses at the head of a cart. But this wasn't a normal cart. This had been modified into a rough metal cage on wheels, the vertical bars only four feet high, so that the prisoner inside had to stand hunched over or sit with his legs drawn up to his chin or dangling through the bars outside the cart. Yvan was fat enough he was forced to sit, his legs dangling. He still wore his merchant's coat, but the material was filthy, the usually immaculate cream-colored material now stained a dull brown-gray, the black embroidery al-most impossible to see. As soon as he saw me his face twisted with hatred, and he seized the bars of the cage, screaming obscenities across the courtyard.

I watched him for a moment, saw Borund wince as he began to yell, Regin's face tightening as if in pain. Then I turned away and approached Keven, who held my mount.

Yvan's yelling escalated, then dropped away into heated murmuring as the guardsmen surrounded the cart.

"Is everything in the market ready?" I asked. A sense of nervous tension had slid into the anger and I felt the palms of my hands go sweaty.

Keven nodded sharply. "Yes, Mistress. Everything is set."

"Then open the gates."

Keven motioned toward the gates. As they began to creak open, I mounted, Keven doing likewise beside me, and everyone in the entourage came to attention, straightening their clothing or calming their own mounts. My horse—a relatively calm dusk-colored mare—shifted beneath me and I felt my stomach twist. Yvan fell silent, but I could feel the anger radiating outward from him on the river, like a slowly pulsing sun.

It wasn't until Keven, the escort, and I rode through the gates that I noticed the crowd.

I shot a questioning glance toward Keven.

"I told the guardsmen to spread the word," he said. He caught my confused frown. "The people of Amenkor need to know that the wealthy get punished as swiftly and as harshly as the poor. They've come to expect it from you after you had that man Hant whipped on the construction site. They'll want to see justice done with Yvan as well, especially after what he's done. His crime hurt them as much as it did the power of the Skewed Throne."

I didn't respond, wasn't certain I really understood. As we emerged out into the street, the crowd of townspeople shifted out of our way, a murmur rippling from the front ranks to the back as they saw me. But unlike that first time I'd appeared outside the palace, when I'd forced Avrell to accompany me to the stablehouse where we'd discovered the Capthian wine hidden away, this murmur was one of excited awe, not frowning curiosity. Women leaned

their heads together, pointed, eyes alight. Men craned their necks
to see, and children elbowed their way to the front. A number of
those gathered signed themselves across the chest with the Skewed
Throne symbol.

I looked toward Keven again, who held himself proud, back
straight and rigid, his attention on what lay ahead. His men fanned
out around us without any evident order given and kept the townspeople at bay, even though they weren't being unruly. I saw a smile
touch the corner of Keven's mouth, a flicker of movement, there
and then gone, the deadly serious expression returning.

Straightening, I turned my attention back to the street ahead,
noticed that people lined the entire route, blocking the cross
streets and alleys, some hanging out of the windows of the second
floor.

The farther we moved, the louder the murmur grew.

Then Yvan and the cage emerged. The awed murmur turned to
a hiss, anger welling up like an ocean wave on the river, rippling out
as word spread down the street faster than we were moving.

Keven picked up on the sudden change, his stolid poise slipping
as he frowned. "We'd better move a little faster. I'm not sure the
guardsmen will be able to hold the people back if we don't pick up
the pace."

I nodded, feeling the rage swell, and then Keven motioned
sharply to the guardsmen on either side. Our horses began to walk
faster.

We passed through the middle ward gates into the outer ward,
the crowd content to hiss, shifting in agitation as the cage drew up
alongside them. Once it had passed, the men, women, and children
fell in behind the entourage, until we trailed a large contingent of
townspeople behind us. And the more people that joined the entourage, the more agitated the crowd became.

We passed out into the lower city, through the gates of the

inner ward, and the temper of the crowd changed. In the upper city, it had been composed of businessmen, lesser merchants, guildsmen, the wealthier citizens and their families, but once we reached the lower city. . . . Dockworkers and sailors and servants to the wealthy mixed with those from the Dredge who had come to the warehouse district to help with the construction. Hawkers and farmers shouted out cruel obscenities alongside gutterscum and whores. The noise grew to a roar as we descended down through the streets, past alley and narrow, courtyard and tavern, escalating as the crowd behind Yvan's cage tripled.

As we entered the edge of the marketplace and began to shove our way through the hundreds gathered there toward the pillory at the center, Keven kneed his horse forward and leaned in close. "This is uglier than I thought it would be!" he shouted over the cacophony as those already in the marketplace caught sight of the cage. "We'd better get done with this quickly and get out, before it gets out of hand!"

Not able to answer, the guardsmen pressed in close, the crowd shoving in from all sides, I nodded. Keven's hand latched onto my arm as we were crushed together, then pulled apart, our horses snorting and tossing their heads, until we burst into the center of the marketplace where the guardsmen had cleared a wide area around the pillory itself.

I gasped, drew in a few steadying breaths as Avrell, Eryn, Nathem, and the merchants cleared the crowd. The cart carrying Yvan was having more trouble, the crowd closing in tightly, threatening to overwhelm the guardsmen set to protect it.

Dismounting, all of us watched, stunned, as it inched forward, until it finally reached the edge of the cleared area.

Keven heaved a sigh of relief. As we turned, I saw Baill approaching, his gaze sweeping the mob as he drew to a halt. "Do this quick," he growled, then caught my gaze.

I tried not to flinch, felt myself tense instead, felt my fury escalate, supported by the roiling hatred of the crowd.

He hesitated, as if he saw something in my eyes, in my stance, then he spun and bellowed out an order to pull the cart up onto the raised platform of the pillory. I watched him as he retreated, snorted in contempt.

"We'll deal with him later," Keven murmured, his voice unnaturally calm. He turned toward me, and I saw in his dark eyes the same hatred and sense of betrayal I felt deep down inside myself. There was a promise there—a promise he'd made to Erick, a promise he meant to keep.

I nodded, and set my feelings aside, focused on Yvan. The guardsmen had managed to haul the cage up onto the pillory's platform, were ready to pull him out and clamp him into the pillory.

But there was one last thing that needed to be done . . . and it needed to be done by me.

I walked up the ramp leading to the platform, my attention entirely on Yvan, not even noticing that Keven and a select group of guardsmen had followed me until I'd reached the edge of the pillory and halted before Yvan. Only then did I become aware of something else as well.

The entire market had gone silent.

The silence sent an itching sensation across my shoulders and down my back, but I didn't let the prickling touch my face. Eyes as hard as I could make them, anger as blatant in my frown as possible, I stared at Yvan.

He smelled. Of sweat and piss and grime. The smell of terror. All of the hatred, all of the vituperative obscenities he'd flung at me, all of the haughty arrogance of the wealthy merchant elite, was gone. He stood in front of the pillory, held by guardsmen, eyes wide, shaking.

I sighed, saw a faint flare of hope wash over him, then I reached for the river, cast out another net, also passed on to me by Cerrin, that encompassed the entire market square.

"You are guilty of hoarding food," I said in a quiet voice, but because of the net everyone in the market heard it clearly. There was a rustle of reaction from the crowd, but it subsided. "Do you deny it?"

Yvan flared with defiance, the scent sharp and bitter, like dandelion milk, but then his shoulders sagged and he hung his head. "No, I don't deny it."

A grumble rolled around the square, the crowd shifting, uncertain, their anger blunted.

Yvan lifted his head slightly, enough so he could see me, so that he could judge my reaction.

It was a look of sly cunning, of buried deceit.

It reminded me of Bloodmark.

Anger flared, sharp and acidic and I turned toward the crowd, drew my dagger, and held my arms up to the sky. Yvan jerked back from the movement, startled.

"People of Amenkor," I said, raising my voice even though I still held the net in place. "Merchant Yvan has declared his guilt. As Mistress of the Skewed Throne, I pronounce the following sentence."

A hush fell, and I turned back to Yvan.

"Yvan will be stripped of all of his possessions except for the clothing he currently wears. All of his estates, all of his goods, belong to the Skewed Throne. His license from the merchants' guild is revoked. All of the rights and protections, given to him as a citizen of Amenkor, are removed." I took a careful step forward, my grip tightening and loosening on my dagger. Yvan tried to pull away, but the guardsmen held him tight. "He is no longer under the protection of the Skewed Throne. He is a traitor and will be branded as one."

I didn't give him a chance to react. Without hesitation, with a
smoothness and quickness that Erick would have been proud of, I
raised the dagger, placed the tip on the side of Yvan's forehead, one
hand behind his neck to hold him steady, and with three quick
slashes I carved the Skewed Throne into his forehead.

Yvan screamed and jerked back, a short, high-pitched bark of
sound that cut off and sank into panting whimpers as the guardsmen caught him and shoved him forward again. The sly look of
cunning was gone, cut away. Blood welled in the three slashes,
began to slide down between his brows, past his nose, and into his
mouth.

I let the net go, leaned forward into his stench, caught his wild
eyes and held them. "You're gutterscum now."

Then I stepped away, motioned with one hand to the pillory.
The guardsmen shoved Yvan forward, thrust him down to his knees
and over the open block of wood. He struggled, cried out, and
kicked, but there were too many guardsmen. Three held his head in
place, two each for each arm, and then the top of the pillory was
slammed down over his neck and wrists and the lock slid into place.

The guardsmen stepped away as I reached the end of the ramp.
Keven and my escort formed up around me, leading our horses, the
rest of the entourage—Avrell, Eryn, Nathem, and the merchants—
hastily mounting and filing in behind them.

The mob surged forward, streaming around us and our mounts
as if we were boulders in a river. The first stone was thrown before
we'd made it halfway to the edge of the market square. A small
stone, nothing more than a pebble.

Yvan screamed like a stuck pig. The mob burst into vicious
laughter. Someone started a chant, others applauded, more stones
sailed through the air, no longer just pebbles.

"He won't last the night," Keven said, his voice grim. "They
won't be satisfied with small stones for long."

My eyes narrowed. "We have more important things to worry about."

"Like Baill?"

I shook my head. "We'll get Baill eventually. I meant the Chorl."

Chapter 11

THE WIND GUSTED SHARPLY on the top of the tower overlooking Amenkor, catching in the loose folds of my shirt and tugging at my hair. The banners attached to the outside of the tower walls snapped and whuffled. The wind brought with it the scent of the ocean and a hint of warmer weather. Winter was ending, spring officially only a few days away.

My stomach growled and I pressed a hand against it to quiet it. I wasn't the only one hungry. In the last three weeks, since Yvan had been stoned to death on the pillory, rations had been cut back severely. Winter might be ending, but we still needed enough supplies to last us another month, until the first spring harvest. Farmers were already out on the surrounding land plowing fields and planting in hopes that the weather would hold and an early harvest would be possible. But it wouldn't come soon enough. There were already deaths reported in the Dredge.

I sighed, drew the power of the throne in tight around me, and Reached for the Dredge, slipping into the flows, drifting on them, then directing them until I stood on the broken cobbles near Cobbler's Fountain, where once I'd gone to meet Erick, to tell him I'd found a mark . . . or killed one.

The memory, the sight of the dry, dead fountain, brought a sharp pain, one that I thought would have been blunted by now. I suppressed it as best I could, stared up into the cracked and pitted face of the woman who stood at the center of the fountain, as I'd once seen Erick do. He'd been searching for something in her face then, didn't know that I'd followed him, that I was watching. I hadn't completely trusted him yet.

But seeing the doubt in his face, the mute appeal for something I couldn't understand back then, had felt wrong, had made my stomach queasy. It had been too personal.

It was the last time I'd followed him.

The stone statue of the woman—one arm holding an urn on her shoulder that had once poured water into the fountain, the other on her hip, only a stump at her shoulder and a few fingers remaining—revealed nothing, so I turned away. There was a flash of bright sunlight, a faint echo of a giggling child splashing in the pool of water at its base, but these faded quickly. That part of my life was over. I'd survived it and moved on.

I turned to the warren of alleys and narrows beyond the Dredge instead, moved down the old familiar paths, into buildings where people huddled or slept, their faces gaunt, haggard, but still alive. I saw families, saw children roving in gangs, saw a cat that had managed to survive instead of being eaten, its ribs sticking out through its matted, mud-caked fur.

I moved deeper, not bothering to creep from shadow to shadow as I once would have done. I wasn't really here, was only observing. So I stalked down the middle of the alleys, ducked and slid through impossibly small holes into niches and alcoves, into secluded rooms, using the throne and the river to seek out those that still survived.

Until I found a woman and child tucked away in a crumbling courtyard. The woman, hair thin, face pale and sweaty in the sunlight seeping down from the opening above, gasped in short, irregular, phlegmy breaths where she lay on a twisted, tattered blanket on the ground. The skin around her eyes was blackened with sickness, her eyes staring off into nothing.

The child, a girl of no more than six, dressed in a makeshift dress, played with a doll with no arms or legs in the dirt of the courtyard to one side.

The woman coughed, the sound horrible, tearing at her throat, and the girl looked up. "Mommy?"

She stood, motions careful and ponderous, doll clutched tightly in one arm, and moved to her mother's side. The woman had rolled onto her side, and the girl halted a few small steps from her and stared down.

"Mommy?"

With a supreme effort, she rolled her head to one side, eyes finding her daughter. She couldn't move her arms. She was too weak. It was obvious any food she'd had had gone to her daughter.

"Ana," she gasped, voice nothing more than a whisper.

Ana crouched down on her knees and elbows in the dirt, doll still tucked tight to her chest, and leaned in close so she could hear.

The woman's eyes closed and her panting breath halted. For a horrified moment, I thought she'd died. But then she gasped, eyes flying wide. She focused again, licked cracked, dry lips.

"Ana, go to the kitchen. Go . . . to the guardsmen."

Ana frowned, eyes squinched tight. "Can't leave you, Mommy."

The woman snorted, the sound defeated, lost.

She knew she was dying.

"Just . . . go. Bring them back."

The words exhausted her. Her head rolled back into place, and her eyes closed. Her breaths panted, her form shaking with each one. Her skin took on a waxy, feverish quality.

Ana hesitated, stood and watched her mother's trembling form a long moment, one hand petting the top of her doll's head where it was clutched to her chest.

Then she turned and walked to the edge of the courtyard, mouth set in a pouty, uncertain frown. She paused once, turned back, then dashed out into the narrow.

I could sense her terror as she ran, followed it with one part of my mind as I turned back to the woman, as I knelt down beside her.

Her breathing was coming faster now, and on the river I could sense her fever, could sense the sickness in her, like a splotch of darkness in the sunlight.

I reached out to touch it, but her breath caught. Her eyes flew open again, latched onto mine.

"Oh," she breathed. A light suffused her face, a smile touched her lips. "It's you."

And then she died.

My hand fell to my side.

I stayed with her a moment, then followed Ana until she made it to the kitchens, until Darryn had been summoned. He'd take care of her.

Then I returned to the palace, to the tower, knowing that people like the woman were dying all over the Dredge, succumbing to sicknesses they would normally survive if they had enough food, some dying of exposure, or starvation. Mostly the old and the young, but a few like this woman, who'd sacrificed everything to save her daughter.

And there was nothing more I could do.

My stomach growled again, but I ignored it.

I heard Eryn approach from behind. She halted beside me, stared out over the harbor, face to the wind. Her white dress and long black hair hissed and flapped in the breeze, but she didn't seem to mind.

"Any word from Captain Catrell?" she asked. It had become a daily question, something I asked Keven every morning upon waking, to the point where all I needed to do was send him a questioning look.

I shook my head, lips pressed grimly together, Keven's usual response. "And no word from the guardsmen Keven has set to keep a lookout either."

Eryn bit her lower lip. "Baill is laying low. He managed to keep Catrell busy and distant until your summons to the throne room to tell us about the threat from the Chorl. He must have known Catrell was suspicious of something. But he couldn't order him to disobey a direct summons."

I nodded, but said nothing. There was nothing to say. Catrell had told us he'd seen Baill with a group of guardsmen escorting a cart away from the warehouse on Lirion Street almost a month before. He'd approached Baill without thought, had chatted with him—

Then noticed later, as he looked at the roster, that there had been no scheduled transport of goods from Lirion Street. That, in fact, the guardsmen that had formed the escort were supposed to be watching various other warehouses.

After checking the assignments and speaking to a few of the other guardsmen on duty that day, he'd discovered that Baill had ordered replacements for those in his escort at each of the warehouses and had reassigned them to Lirion.

It was within Baill's rights as captain of the guard to rearrange the guardsmen as he saw fit, but it had felt . . . wrong to Catrell.

He'd almost revealed what he'd seen at the meeting I'd called about forming a garrison for the ship. But as far as he could tell, nothing was wrong. He hadn't heard of the missing food until later, after Yvan had been caught and he thought the problem resolved.

And before that, Baill had kept him busy, out of touch with what was happening in the palace.

As Catrell spoke to me, Avrell, Eryn, and Keven listening in, he'd cursed himself for being a fool, for not realizing that Baill was distracting him, keeping him away. His guilt and regret had flooded the river, tinged with outrage at the betrayal.

But in the end, it was only a suspicion. Catrell hadn't seen where Baill had taken the wagon and its supplies, and Keven hadn't been able to learn anything from discreet inquiries with the guardsmen involved. No one knew anything; no one had seen anything.

If Baill was stealing the supplies, he'd chosen his cohorts well.

In my gut, I knew Baill was guilty. I could see the same betrayal in everyone else's eyes as well, knew that they wanted him caught and punished as much as I did.

"You should just arrest him," Eryn said, as if she'd read my thoughts. Her voice was low, her eyes hooded, staring out at the two watchtowers and the newly rebuilt walls. "You should confront him in the throne room, force him to touch the throne. It would kill him, but you'd know for certain he was guilty."

A shudder of horror passed through me at the thought of forcing Baill to touch the throne. A reaction more from the horror that passed through the voices in the throne than from myself.

Some of them had used the throne in such a way, as a last resort. But the death of the person who touched the throne . . .

I repressed another shudder, forced the thought away.

But then I thought of the woman dying in the slums, of her daughter, Ana, and felt anger spark.

"But what if he's not guilty?" I asked.

Eryn snorted. "He's guilty. You know it, and I know it. That's why the Dredge warehouse didn't have any missing food. Baill never had control of the guardsmen there; he couldn't get past Darryn and the militia."

"Knowing it and proving it are two different things." I shook my head. "No. We'll do what we originally planned: wait until he tries to steal more, then catch him in the act, force him to tell us where he's taking it so we can get it back. We just have to be patient."

"It's been three weeks. I'm running out of patience. What if he doesn't try again? What if he decides he's taken enough, now that he thinks we know?"

Now my expression darkened. "He'll try again."

Eryn wasn't convinced, but she didn't argue further. Instead, she took another step closer to the edge of the tower, motioned out toward the watchtowers and the walls. "Those went up faster than I expected," she said.

I moved up beside her. "Avrell said that the masons were surprised by how well the old wall had held up. The watchtowers, too. It was only a matter of repairing a few sections that had crumbled, shoring up the supports inside the towers and finishing off the one side that had collapsed. They've turned their attention to the defenses inside the city now and left the watchtowers to the guardsmen." I'd ventured out along the juts of land on the wall myself once, gone to visit those keeping an eye on the ocean in the watchtowers and to see the massive signal fires that would be lit if they caught sight of the Chorl. But the wall and the towers were close enough to the edge of the throne's influence that it made me uncomfortable. Not sick, like the sensation of knives shifting around in my stomach I'd gotten when escorting Eryn's envoy to Colby, but queasy enough that I hadn't gone back.

I shifted my attention from the watchtowers to the wharf and the lower city. I could see carpenters and other workers crawling over the trading ships in the harbor, altering them so that they had at least minimal defenses. The palace's sleek patrol ships that had sealed the harbor while Eryn was the Mistress were circling the water near the entrance to the harbor. And deeper within the city, in the streets that led up to the wall surrounding the outer ward, others were working on barricades and other defenses, some suggested by the guardsmen, most by the voices in the throne— Mistresses who had been forced to defend the city in the past, both successfully and unsuccessfully. Voices that were cooperating with each other for the first time in decades.

If the Chorl got past the watchtowers, the ships, and the lower city, they'd hit the three walls that surrounded the palace, separating it from the middle ward, the outer ward, and the lower city itself. And all along the way they'd be fighting the guard and the militia, the citizens currently training in the courtyard below and the marketplaces in the city, the Servants who were training in the palace gardens even now. I could sense them plying the currents of the river behind me, Marielle leading the lesson today.

Amenkor would not fall lightly.

Eryn pressed her lips tightly together. "Is it enough?" she asked.

I didn't answer.

She turned toward me, caught my gaze. "Have you tried to use the throne to scry, as I did when I was Mistress? Have you tried to see the future?"

I hesitated, not certain she'd want to hear. But she'd been the Mistress once before. She deserved to know.

"I've tried. Twice. Both times it was the same as before: the city on fire, ships in the harbor burning, the water filled with bodies and red with blood."

Eryn growled, slapped her palm down flat on the stone of the tower's edge in frustration. "It should have changed!" she spat out over the wall, into the wind. "It should be different!"

My eyes narrowed. The vision had changed: the warehouse district was no longer completely rebuilt. Because we'd abandoned it to work on the watchtowers and the other defenses. And now the watchtowers were destroyed first, rather than after the city had mostly fallen.

But I saw no reason to tell Eryn. It didn't change the outcome of the vision at all. In fact, it verified that the vision wasn't of some long distant future attack, but of something imminent.

I felt Eryn's frustration as well, crawling across my skin. But we were doing everything we could think of to prepare. All that was left was to wait.

I felt someone enter the spiral stairwell to the roof, felt his tension, his excitement, his panic. The guards at the top of the tower straightened as they heard the boy's pounding footsteps echoing up from below—

Then he burst out onto the tower. I'd already turned, already taken a step forward in anticipation.

"Mistress!" the boy shouted, then gasped and pounded his chest, trying to catch his breath. His eyes were wide, his face flushed red with exertion. "Mistress! Captain Catrell says he's done it."

I felt a surge of satisfaction as Eryn asked, "Who's done what?"

The boy glanced at her. Still breathing hard, he grinned. "Baill's rearranged the guard on the warehouses."

†

I crouched down at the edge of an alley and glanced out into the night-darkened, cobbled street in both directions, listening to the rustle of Keven and his guardsmen settling into place in the alley's depths behind me. Armor clanked, someone splashed in an unseen puddle, and someone else cursed.

Then everyone fell silent.

Keven crouched down beside me. "Anything?"

I shook my head. "The street's empty."

We'd chosen to ambush Baill in a circular market with a fountain at its center where three major streets intersected. One street provided a direct route from the Tempest Row warehouse to the fountain square. Captain Catrell had insisted on covering that route. He was to wait until Baill had passed him, then close off that escape route. The street Keven and I covered was Baill's most likely choice once he reached the fountain—it led south, past the stockyards and out of Amenkor, meeting up with the southern trade route. Captain Westen covered the third street away from the fountain. He'd been as enraged as Catrell at Baill's betrayal, but—unlike Catrell—he hadn't voiced it. His stance had shifted, had become deadly, a motion that reminded me painfully of Erick.

He'd offered to send the Seekers after Baill, as they'd been sent after the murderers and rapists on the Dredge, but I'd said no.

We needed the food Baill had stolen—all of it. We needed to take him alive, so he could be questioned, so we could get that food back.

A muscle in my leg began to cramp, and I winced and shifted uncomfortably, then grimaced. I'd been Mistress too long. I'd never have cramped this early in a watch when I'd been on the Dredge. Not even after being a bodyguard for Borund.

I began massaging the muscle, caught Keven's eye. "Now we wait," I said.

He nodded, signaled his guardsmen, then leaned back against the wall and stared up at the stars overhead. The moon was already out, everything cast in a faint gray light.

I sighed and settled in as well.

Old habits asserted themselves. I checked out the rough stone of the alley, noted the deeper darknesses of alcoves and doorways and windows. All possible escape paths. But unlike the Dredge, these darknesses weren't wide open and crumbling, with empty rooms and corridors beyond. This was east of the city, Amenkor's

River only a few streets north. This stone wasn't falling into ruin and slicked with sludge and ground-in mud.

And the people here weren't starving. Not like those on the Dredge, like Ana's mother.

Yet.

I sighed, saw Keven glance toward me out of the corner of my eye, then I slid beneath the river, pushed myself deep enough so I could feel the city of Amenkor pulsing around me. For a moment, I held myself in the alley with Keven and the guardsmen, felt their boredom mixed with tension, then I turned my attention out into the street. I could see it clearly now; no darknesses, no escapes. To the left a rat paused, beady eyes looking in my direction as if he sensed I was watching, then he skittered away.

My stomach growled. On the Dredge, he would have been dinner. On the Dredge, his fellows had already been dinner, Darryn sending out rat patrols like hunting parties on a regular basis now, hoping to bring back fresh meat.

I turned to the right, leaned out from the alley far enough I could see the water of the fountain dancing in the moonlight, then focused and *pushed* at the river, the same way I'd pushed to see the vision of the city burning. But this was limited to a small area—the fountain—and a short period of time.

I grunted, then pulled back into the alley. At Keven's questioning look, I said, "Baill will be here in an hour."

Keven frowned, then motioned to a page boy, who sped off deeper into the alley with the news. He'd inform Catrell and Westen.

The men shared a few glances, then shrugged.

A little less than an hour later, everyone just beginning to get restless, Keven's page boy returned.

"Baill passed Catrell's position a few moments ago," he reported breathlessly.

Everyone in the alley tensed. I drew my dagger, felt its handle slip into a familiar grip, and edged closer to the alley's entrance.

To the right I heard low voices, too distant to make out, and the creak of a wagon. But I still couldn't see anything.

Then Baill appeared. He glanced down the street and I pulled back out of view slowly. All of my instincts were screaming, but I forced myself to wait, to allow Catrell and Westen time to move into position. The sounds of the wagons grew louder, the voices clearer, cutting off the splashing sounds of water from the fountain—

And then, at a barked command from Baill, the wagons halted.

I froze, muscles tensing, shot a quick frown at Keven.

He shrugged, motioned that we should head out into the street, reveal ourselves.

I shook my head. Something was wrong.

And then I heard the sound of horses, of shod feet clopping onto cobblestones.

Coming from the left.

With horror, I realized that someone was coming to meet Baill.

I shoved Keven toward the darkness at the other end of the alley, his massive bulk resisting a moment, until he heard the horses. With a sharp gesture, he ordered the men back, everyone scrambling to move, fast, without making a sound. Armor scraped against stone, and boots dragged across the cobbles. Someone splashed through the puddle again. I followed, Keven a step in front of me.

And then suddenly Keven motioned everyone down, halting as the sounds of the horses drew even with the alley's entrance.

I spun, my butt on my heels, my back pressed flat against the wall, dagger tight to my side as sweat dripped down my back and between my breasts, and watched as a group of horses passed in front of the alley.

Thirty horses in all, each mounted by a man dressed in armor like the guardsmen. But they weren't guardsmen. These were gut-terscum. Bodyguards. Mercenaries.

My heart sank. They were here to guard the food Baill had stolen, here to take control of it, to smuggle it out of the city and transport it somewhere else.

Which meant we'd never get back the food he'd already taken.

Despair seized me, but then, in the few moments it took the thirty mercenaries to pass by the alley door, it transformed into hard cold fury. Fury solid as a stone, sitting in the center of my chest.

Someone touched my shoulder and I spun, recognized Keven a moment before I would have struck with the dagger. He didn't flinch, his eyes boring into mine. "This is going to be harder than we anticipated," he said.

I heard what he hadn't said, what he hadn't asked. But I wasn't going to let Baill escape now. Not after this, and not with any more of Amenkor's food. Not after witnessing Ana's mother's death. Not after seeing how everyone else was suffering on the Dredge.

Keven must have seen the answer in my eyes, for he straight-ened where he crouched, then motioned toward his men, the ges-tures short and sharp.

The alley grew suddenly grim as men shifted, loosened clasps on swords, checked their armor. I crept to the end of the alley, scanned the dark street in both directions again.

The mercenaries had just made it to the end of the street, were entering the fountain's circle. One of them broke away, horse trot-ting forward to meet Baill, who stood before a cart loaded with crates and surrounded by palace guardsmen.

I almost darted across the street to the opposite side,

crouched low and moving swiftly, as I would have done on the Dredge, but I caught myself. Straightening, I let the anger slide through me, drew it around me like a cloak, felt the guardsmen behind me respond with their own anger, their formation tightening, stances solidifying.

I stepped out of the alley, Keven at my side, his sword drawn, the rest of the guardsmen close behind. We walked to the mouth of the street where it emptied out onto the circular plaza and halted, Keven's men shifting to block off any escape.

Someone in Baill's group saw us, barked out a warning.

The guardsmen and mercenaries reacted instantly. With a sharp cry, the guardsmen abandoned the cart and food, scattering toward the other two entrances to the plaza. The mercenaries cursed, kicked their horses into a milling confusion of rattling metal and frightened animals.

I lost sight of Baill. The guardsmen at my back tensed but held firm.

Baill's guardsmen had almost escaped to Tempest Row when Catrell's party appeared. Shouts of despair filled the circle and Baill's guardsmen turned, ran blindly toward the last remaining escape. But Westen appeared before they'd made it halfway across the plaza.

Baill's men ground to a halt, wavered at the edge of the fountain. The stench of fear flooded the river, mixed with the smell of horse and dung.

Silence descended, interrupted only by the snort of a horse, the stamp of a hoof. The mercenaries had formed up in a wall around Baill and the man who'd gone to meet him.

I took a step forward. "It's over, Baill!" I said, loud enough so that everyone in the plaza could hear.

I watched the crowd of horses.

No one emerged.

I felt my anger spike. "Come out! All of your escape routes have been cut off!"

Silence. No one moved. I glared at the mercenaries, their faces tight, eyes dangerous, their unshaven jaws clenched tight. A few had drawn their swords and they watched me balefully from their saddles.

Then, with no warning at all, the mercenaries charged.

I slid into a defensive crouch without thinking, heard the guardsmen behind me gasp, then surge forward and tighten up, Keven bellowing orders. The mercenaries roared, an unintelligible battle cry of pure sound, the pounding of hooves on cobbles descending upon us like the crash of an ocean's wave. I breathed in the scent of desperation, almost overwhelmed by horse sweat, and then the first mercenary reached me.

I lashed out with the river, a solid punch of force that slammed into the massive chest of the horse bearing down on me. The animal screamed, tossed its head, tried to lurch backward, and ended up rearing high, hooves kicking down at me as the mercenary attempted to regain control. I punched out again, shoved the river forward hard in a solid wall as the horse twisted sideways and began to fall.

I grunted as animal and rider crashed into the shield, the mercenary screaming as his leg was crushed between his horse and the shield he couldn't see. Heart thundering, I shunted man and horse aside, stepping to the left as they came shuddering to the ground beside me. The man screamed again as the horse rolled onto his chest, and then the scream cut abruptly into a gurgle and died.

The scent of blood flooded the river.

The horse flailed, eyes wild, kicked out sharply, head twisted back by the reins in the dead man's hands. Its hooves connected with another horse, the rest of the mercenary's charge grinding to a halt as they hit Keven's guardsmen hard. The line gave, the horses

parting around their fallen brother, then held, the entrance to the
street collapsing into a melee of mercenaries, guardsmen, and
horseflesh.

Gripping my dagger in one fist, I dove deep into the river, settled into its flows—

And then I slid into the melee.

My dagger slicked across flesh, cut into legs and hands and
arms, anything that became exposed. I growled as I fought, felt
blood spatter against my face, but continued on. I plunged my dagger into a thigh, heard the mercenary shriek even as I reached up
and jerked him from the saddle to be trampled underfoot. Swords
flailed and I ducked, tasting the metal as it snicked by my head,
then dodged as the horse on my left staggered, almost crushing me
into the one on my right. I stepped on something soft, felt it roll
beneath my foot, and lurched forward, grabbing onto a saddle for
support. A mercenary glared down at me, eyes like flint, raised his
sword for a thrust, but another blade punched hard into his armpit
and back out again through his shoulder and he screamed, his arm
half-severed from his shoulder. Blood poured down on me, blinding
me for a moment and then the horse surged forward, out of my
grip, the man's scream fading.

I wiped the blood from my eyes with the back of my arm
and found myself surrounded by Keven's guardsmen in a protective circle. He stepped back from the edge of the fighting, the
last mercenary threatening us falling, and said, "The attack is
faltering."

He pointed to the far side of the fountain, where Westen and
Catrell's men had seized the wagons of food. As we watched, the
last of the mercenaries that had attacked Westen and Catrell's men
broke off, galloping toward the open street Westen had abandoned
in order to protect the food.

"Shit!" I swore, seeing the open street. "Where's Baill?"

"I never saw him," Keven said.

"Shit, shit, shit!" I shouted. I began checking the faces of the bodies that surrounded us, turning those facedown over. A few groaned, but I left those for Keven, searching frantically.

I wanted Baill. I *needed* Baill. I could feel Ana's mother's eyes burning into me, could hear the awe and hope in her voice as she whispered, *"Oh, it's you,"* before dying.

Keven and his guardsmen began searching as well, stumbling among the dead horses and pools of blood in a widening circle.

I'd almost reached the street where the attack had started when one of the guardsmen cried out.

I spun, was halfway to the man before anyone else reacted. "Is it Baill? Is he alive?"

The man shook his head. "He's alive, but it's not Baill."

He kicked the body over. I heard the mercenary moan, had begun to turn away in disgust, when something clicked.

The man was familiar.

I crouched down next to the man's side, his breaths coming in short little gasps, stared intently into his face, looking beneath the black blood, the long, lanky hair, the mercenary's clothing. I looked close . . . and then I sat back on my heels and scowled.

"Hello, Alendor," I said, my voice cold and deadly, twisted with sarcasm. "Welcome back to Amenkor."

Then I reached down, grabbed the neck of his shirt, and hauled him upright.

He screamed.

†

Avrell and Eryn were waiting on the steps of the promenade with torches flapping in the breeze when Keven and I emerged from the gates of the inner wall, my escort dragging the bound, gagged, and fuming Alendor behind us. Captains Catrell and Westen came in last, their guardsmen hauling the remaining mercenaries that hadn't died in the attack off to the cells.

I wanted to deal with Alendor now.

"Baill escaped," I said as I approached Avrell and Eryn. Avrell's face fell, Eryn's grew grim.

"But how?" Avrell asked. "He should never have had a chance in that plaza—"

"He wasn't just stealing food and storing it elsewhere in the city," I said, cutting Avrell off, my voice tight. "He was smuggling it *out* of the city. The men sent to meet him to take the food were there—mercenaries on horseback. Once they attacked, it was chaos. He slipped away during the fighting."

They considered the implications of that in silence. Eryn nodded toward the man Keven and his guardsmen were holding. "Then who is that?"

"That," I said, drawing in a deep breath to steady myself, "is Alendor."

"What!" Avrell blurted, his shock evident, but he quickly regained control. "How did he get back into the city? Why is he here?"

"I don't know," I said, turning to move up the steps to the palace. "But it's obvious he was working with Baill. I want to know why, and to what purpose."

"But how are you going to find out?" Avrell asked as he and Eryn fell into step behind me, Keven, Alendor, and the rest of the escort following.

I didn't answer, shot a glance toward Eryn. She'd already guessed how, and I saw her give an imperceptible nod of agreement. Her lips were pressed tightly together, her eyes, her stance, deadly serious.

Because if Alendor was involved, then the missing food took on a much greater import than some of Amenkor's citizens starving. It meant there was much more going on, something much bigger. Alendor didn't work for trivial ends. When I'd been hired to kill him before, he'd been trying to take over all trade within Amenkor itself by forming a consortium of merchants, killing those merchants that refused to join or that were in the way. With Baill's help, he would have had control over the palace guardsmen as well. He could have controlled all of Amenkor.

The implications of Alendor and Baill working together . . .

I felt an empty pit open in my stomach, making my mouth dry. Because something else was going on here, something I couldn't quite see. Something that threatened the entire city of Amenkor.

And I needed to know what, needed to know *now*.

We entered the palace, Eryn sending servants hurrying ahead of us to light sconces and candles. It was the dead of night, but the palace came suddenly alive with activity.

"Where are we going?" Avrell asked.

"The throne room."

We passed down the long corridor leading to the doors to the inner sanctum, the phalanx of guardsmen stepping to the side as we moved through what once had been gates in an outer wall but were now at the heart of the palace. Then we were outside the double doors of the throne room.

A couple of guardsmen moved forward and pulled the doors outward, and I entered, walking down the long aisle between the massive columns, my eyes on the throne as it twisted and warped from shape to shape. I felt its presence sifting through the entire room, draped that power around me as I mounted the dais, the others—Avrell, Eryn, Keven, the guardsmen—arraying themselves around the room. But I did not sit. At the top of the dais, standing to the left of the throne, I halted, turned around and stared down at Alendor. Keven had forced him to his knees at the bottom of the dais. The guardsman looked as if he wanted to slit Alendor's throat now, his face hard and angry. But he only held the ex-merchant in place, hands on his shoulders.

I could sense terror in Alendor, but his eyes smoldered with hatred. Not the petty hatred of Yvan. This went deeper, had burned longer. I studied his face. I remembered seeing him in Charls' manse, plotting with the other merchants to kill Borund. He'd had a mustache, gray-streaked hair pulled back in a ponytail. His face had been shaven, the mustache trimmed neatly.

Now, he had a bristly, gray-shot beard, and his mustache was ragged beneath his long nose. His skin was tanned and dry with the exposure to the elements, and still flecked with dried spots of blood from the attack in the circle. His mercenary armor and tattered, bloodstained clothing clashed with the mental image I held of his always pristine mustard-colored merchant's coat.

But the eyes were the same. Cold. Sharp. Calculating. Even here, bound and gagged before the Skewed Throne.

"Remove the gag," I said.

Keven jerked the knot in the back free, Alendor wincing, and when it fell to the floor, Keven stepped back a pace, drawing his sword. Alendor coughed, then worked his mouth as if he'd tasted bitter ash and spat onto the throne room floor. He stayed on his knees, but drew himself upright, back straight and defiant, stance as poised as possible. His jaw clenched as he glowered at me.

I'd hoped that the presence of the Skewed Throne stalking on the dais like a caged animal would cow him as it had me when I'd first entered the throne room, before I'd become the Mistress. But as a merchant of Amenkor, he'd been to the throne room before. He knew what the Skewed Throne felt like.

"Avrell told me you'd left Amenkor, gone to the southern cities," I said. "Why have you come back?"

Alendor's glower intensified, but he said nothing.

"Where are you taking the food? Who are you giving it to?"

"I'll tell you nothing, bitch."

Keven growled, and, with a move so swift I barely saw it, he backhanded Alendor so hard the ex-merchant toppled to the floor with a cut-off cry followed by a stifled groan. Two guardsmen rushed forward and jerked him upright again, Keven circling around behind him as Alendor used his tongue to probe his split lip. Blood dripped from the cut, on his chin, but he only sneered.

For a moment, I felt a stab of pity.

But then I remembered him leading me into an ambush, re-membered the gutterscum he'd hired as bodyguards as they kicked and punched and beat me into a bloody pulp in a back alley of the warehouse district. He'd meant for them to kill me, meant for his son to eliminate me because I was in the way, screwing up his plans for the consortium by protecting Borund, keeping him alive. The only reason I'd survived was because Erick had intervened, had dis-tracted them long enough for me to regroup.

The thought of Erick sent a spike through my anger. I'd come out of that with more than just a bloody lip. So had Erick.

And I thought of Ana, of her mother, of all the other people I'd seen that morning as I wandered the slums. I saw their gaunt faces, their ribs standing out, their sallow skin. And as each face flickered before me, I felt my anger surge higher, felt it spill over into rage.

"Where are you taking the food?" I shouted, voice echoing in the chamber, throbbing with the power of the throne behind it. I saw a few of the guardsmen flinch, saw both Avrell and Eryn stiffen in surprise.

Alendor spat blood. Then he smiled, his eyes smug. "You'll have to do better than roughing me up with your pet guardsmen," he hissed.

Keven stepped forward, hand raised again, and for all his blus-ter Alendor flinched back, but I halted Keven with a raised hand.

"Very well," I said.

Then I reached out with the river, with the power of the throne, and as the Ochean had done with Erick, I seized Alendor about the throat with an invisible hand, squeezed it tight as I jerked him upright, lifted him completely off of the floor, and threw him down onto the dais steps before the throne.

As soon as I let the hand of force go, Alendor heaved in a sucking breath, his legs kicking out as he tried to roll himself onto his back. His breath came in shortened, ragged gasps of terror as he managed to get himself onto his side, but before he could begin to roll off the dais steps, I punched him hard in the gut with the river.

His eyes flew wide, grew round as he tried to breathe but couldn't, and then something broke, and he coughed and contorted into a protective curl around his stomach, blood splattering onto the steps from his cut lip. He sucked in another breath, the sound torturous, as if his throat had been torn, and he coughed again.

I moved down the few steps to where he lay in a fetal position.

"Where are you taking the food?" I repeated, my voice calm once again.

He gasped, shifted enough that he could look up at me, his body angled across the steps of the dais, the throne behind him. Blood and snot covered the lower half of his face, and a bruise was beginning to form on his temple where he'd struck stone after I threw him.

But his eyes still blazed with hatred. "Fuck you."

I took a single step forward, and he kicked out, forced himself up another step, then another, trying to get away from me. He shoved himself up onto the top of the dais, the Skewed Throne directly behind him, the stone sliding smoothly from shape to shape.

"Fuck you, Varis," he repeated, my name twisted into a curse. He gasped with pain, but was still defiant enough to attempt a grin. "I'm not going to tell you anything."

Silence settled over the throne room. Behind me, I could feel Avrell and Eryn tensing. They knew what was coming, had seen it before, had suffered through it in Eryn's case. But the guardsmen were only confused, most a little afraid, uncertain what was happening.

"No," I said, and I could hear the sadness in my voice, heard the voices inside the throne grow quiet. I reached out, grasped the front of his mercenary's clothes with the river, and lifted him upright. "You're going to tell me *everything*."

A look of confusion crossed Alendor's face, and then I shoved him onto the throne.

For a moment, nothing happened. The throne solidified, its constant motion shuddering to a halt halfway between transformations. A look of awe crossed Alendor's face.

Then, both he and I gasped, the sound sharp, reverberating through the room. I felt something stab deep down inside my gut, the sensation cold and visceral and twisting inside me. Alendor sucked in a hissing breath, teeth clenched tight against the sensation—

And suddenly I was looking out over the throne room through Alendor's eyes, could feel the ties binding his hands cutting into his flesh, could taste the sick slickness of blood on his lips. The knife in my gut—in Alendor's gut—sank deeper, grew colder, and I hissed again at the pain, and a moment before I closed my eyes, the pain escalating sharply, I saw my own body collapse to the throne room floor, saw Avrell and Eryn step forward, both their faces grim.

And then the frigid pain in Alendor's gut exploded outward and he screamed, a bloodcurdling masculine shriek that rose and rose as the knifing cold stabbed into his chest, into his lungs, seared down his arms and legs and sliced through every vein and nerve in his body.

When it reached his head, jabbing through his eyes, everything went mind-numbingly, blindingly white.

And the screaming stopped.

†

We have him.

I shuddered as Cerrin's voice intruded on the whiteness, then felt the voices of the throne surrounding me, the same maelstrom I'd felt before, when Eryn had forced me onto the throne. Except this time the voices weren't screaming at me, battering at my defenses in an attempt to seize control, shrieking with the winds of a hurricane and trying to tear me apart. This time the maelstrom was the roar of a thousand voices talking among themselves in a crowded marketplace. A few madmen were still shrieking at the edge of the plaza, but the other voices had surrounded them, were keeping them in check.

Cerrin's presence, smelling of the sharp scent of pine, shifted forward in the crowd, followed by Liviann, Atreus, and the rest of the Seven.

"We have him," Cerrin repeated.

"Where?"

Cerrin drifted away and I followed. We worked our way through the crowded marketplace, Liviann and the rest of the Seven trailing behind us. As before, when I'd thought of the throne as a crowd on the Dredge, the women interspersed with a few men jostled into me, reached out and touched me. But this time they weren't trying to overwhelm me, to crush me. This time, the touches were reverent, supportive, most giving me a small nod, a quick smile, before stepping aside to let me pass.

Cerrin led me to the center of the marketplace. When we emerged from the bustling crowd, I halted.

In the center of the marketplace sat a pillory, Alendor already on his knees and locked into place. He struggled, spitting curses, his neck and wrists bloody where he'd already scraped them raw. He ceased as soon as I stepped forward to where he could see me.

"You fucking bitch," he gasped, his face red with rage. "What have you done?"

"I forced you to touch the throne."

He heaved, eyes squeezing shut as he strained to break free of the pillory, hands flapping in their restraints.

Finally he stopped, breath heaving. "Release me!"

I shook my head. "I can't. You're already dead. You've become part of the throne."

He stared at me in horror, refusing to understand even though deep down inside he knew it was true.

I reached forward, felt him flinch as I touched his forehead and closed my eyes. "Now, tell me where you were taking the food."

He tried to resist, flailed as I concentrated, but it was futile. This is what the throne had been created for: storage of knowledge, of memory, so that the Mistress could access it, use it, learn from it. It had just done a little bit more than that as well, storing personalities, . . . and storing souls.

I felt a rush of wind against my face, tilted my head up and drew in the deep scent of the ocean and sand, and then opened my eyes.

†

Alendor rode on the back of a horse, the animal walking slowly down a rocky road toward an abandoned village. It was dusk, the light beginning to fade. I heard the rumbling roar of ocean waves against a rocky beach through the trees, heard the creak of wagons and the dull thuds of horses behind him.

He turned. Behind, a group of mercenaries surrounded two

wagons loaded down with sacks and crates. Amenkor's mark stood out clearly on the nearest crates.

The food Baill had stolen.

I felt a flare of anger, but then we entered the village.

The buildings were nothing more than shacks, the wood bleached white by the sun, most ready to collapse at the slightest touch. A few broken crab traps lay about, some caught in torn netting. There were no doors, no windows, only gaping openings no longer even covered by cloth. Outside a few of the hovels were small boats with jagged holes punched into the bottoms.

Alendor led the mercenaries and the wagons down to the edge of the village, where the dunes rose above the high tide marked by heaps of driftwood and tufts of saw grass. The wind blew sharper once Alendor reached the top of the dunes, catching hold of the horse's mane and tugging at his ponytail.

Without a word, the mercenaries began pitching a camp, a few trotting off to gather wood, others breaking out tents and organizing a campfire, still others setting up a watch. As they worked, Alendor shaded his eyes against the setting sun and stared out at the ocean. As soon as the smoke of the cook fire drifted across his senses, he dismounted, one of the mercenaries taking the reins of his horse and leading it away.

The men settled in. Someone returned with a brace of hares, which were quickly skinned and set to roasting on the fire. Three men started a game involving thrown dice and runes, curses and laughter punctuating the darkness. Alendor kept to himself, a mercenary presenting him with one of the charred, roasted hares. A sense of quiet expectation fell over the group as the night progressed.

Then, as the moon rose over the treetops, one of the sentries cried out and everyone around the campfire looked out across the dune toward the cove.

Torches bobbed above the water.

Alendor stood, straightened his mercenary outfit with a frown, then motioned to the men.

The mercenaries jumped up and began hauling the sacks and crates down to the edge of the water. Alendor followed, a few of the huskier, deadlier-looking men at his side.

He halted and watched the torches on the cove move closer. When three boats rowed into view from the darkness, he muttered to the two men at his side, "Be careful. Don't antagonize them like last time. Let me do the talking."

The men grunted and shifted uncomfortably.

The boats ground into the sand and figures jumped out, most moving toward the pile of crates and sacks to one side, the mercenaries backing off as the others began to load them. Three of the figures moved toward Alendor.

As they came into view, their torches guttering in the wind from the ocean, I gasped.

The Chorl.

The leader, face set in a permanent scowl, spat something to his two escorts, then stepped forward, glaring at Alendor and then the two mercenaries. He was short, dressed in the same silky cloth as those who had attacked Mathew's ship. A series of dark blue tattoos lined both cheeks from ear to jaw, and one of his ears—

The lower half of one of his ears had been sliced off.

It was the same man who had attacked Mathew's ship, the same man who had held Erick at sword point, who had ordered the crew's death.

"You brought shipment," the blue-skinned man spat, the words sharp and halting and unfamiliar in his mouth.

Alendor nodded. "And I expect to be paid."

The blue-skinned Chorl watched him with cold, black beady eyes. Then he shrugged, pulled a sack that had been tied to his belt,

and tossed it onto the sand. It clinked, but Alendor did not move
to pick it up.

"Another shipment in one month?" Alendor asked instead,
never taking his eyes off of the leader of the Chorl.

"No!"

Alendor froze, a frisson of fear trembling through his arms. He
knew their agreement was tenuous, that at any moment the Chorl
could turn on him. He was only useful as long as he could provide
them with food.

"Attack move," the man said haltingly, sneering. "Now first day
spring."

The two Chorl behind him chuckled, and the blue-skinned man
grinned, then burst out laughing before turning and sauntering
back toward the boats, now loaded. His strangely curved sword ran
silver in the moonlight at his side. When he reached the boats, he
turned back and spat into the sand in contempt.

A shiver shuddered through Alendor, then he cursed as he
reached for the sack on the sand, the boats slipping back out into
the cove, vanishing in the darkness.

"What was that all about?" one of the mercenaries asked as
they headed back to the campsite.

"Amenkor," Alendor growled. "They're going to attack
Amenkor the first day of spring."

†

I gasped, lurched upward before realizing I was lying on the floor of
the throne room. The cold gray stone of the vaulted ceiling arched
above me, interrupted a moment later by Avrell's concerned face.

He knelt at my side. "Alendor is dead."

"I know."

He nodded, and along with Keven, helped me to stand. I staggered slightly, felt myself trembling, couldn't seem to make it stop.

"What did you find out?" Eryn asked. Behind her, I could see Alendor's body draped across the stone steps of the dais, face down.

The raw rage that enveloped me almost made me gasp. "That he and Baill have betrayed us."

"To who?"

I caught Eryn's eye, then Avrell's, and finally Keven's. "To the Chorl. They're going to attack Amenkor the first day of spring.

"In two days."

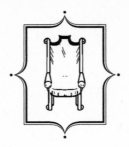

Chapter 12

I STARED at the ceiling of my chambers in the darkness. The faint sheen of moonlight illuminated the open doorway to the balcony, the curtains billowing inward from the breeze.

I breathed in deeply, smelled ocean and salt and smoke from the hundreds of sconces that had been kept lit on the palace walls the last two nights, since I'd learned that the Chorl intended to attack the first day of spring.

Today.

I let the breath out in a long, heavy sigh, then sat up and shifted to the edge of the bed.

I wouldn't be able to sleep. I doubted if many would.

I pulled on my breeches, a white shirt, my boots, and tucked my dagger into the belt, then drifted out onto the balcony and stared down at the city.

Amenkor. Torches lined the three walls surrounding the palace, as well as the lengths of wall on the juts of land leading out to the two watchtowers. Sentries occasionally passed in front of the flames, silhouetted briefly before passing on. In the city below, the streets should have been quiet for the most part, the only movements bakers getting ready for the morning rush a few hours off or guardsmen meandering the streets. Instead, there were groups of men at critical cross streets, their torches marking key defensive points throughout the city. The wharf was crowded with boats, carpenters even now working on the trading ships, frantically trying to install some additional defenses. Most of the palace's patrol ships were already out in the harbor, dark shadows sliding through the moonlit waters.

Drawing in a deep breath, I closed my eyes and slid beneath the river, focusing on the city below, concentrating until I could pick out the flickering white flames of the people I'd tagged with the White Fire over the last few days. Catrell and Westen had volunteered, as well as a few other guardsmen and Seekers, and they were now stationed at various locations throughout the city. Westen and his Seekers had been split between the city and the palace, their skills better suited to attacks from cover and in narrow, confined spaces. Catrell, now captain of the palace guardsmen in Baill's stead, as well as captain of the regular guard, had sent the majority of his men into the city. The palace guardsmen had been left on the palace walls and the watchtowers, a few more on the boats.

Baill had taken at least twenty guards with him when he vanished, cutting the palace guardsmen down to just over a hundred men. Catrell had had another hundred and fifty city guardsmen under his control before Baill left. With the thirty Seekers . . .

It wasn't much of an army. But with the militia we'd been training, with the citizens who had taken up arms and joined them, with Darryn and the denizens of the Dredge . . .

Divided among them all were the Servants, most able to provide some protection from the powers of the Ochean and her own Servants. As much as could be learned in such a short period of time anyway. Most of them, including Marielle, had volunteered to be tagged by the White Fire as well.

I could see those flames now, scattered throughout the city like stars.

I opened my eyes, let the river go.

Just before it slid away completely, I felt a surge, a ripple of power—

And one of the watchtowers exploded.

A fireball roared into the sky at the edge of the harbor, wood and stone and bodies arching up and out as a concussive crack of sound split the night. I jerked back from the edge of the balcony, gasped as debris began to rain down into the water of the harbor, boats silhouetted against the conflagration, and then the flames died back down.

A sudden, shocked silence fell. I could hear myself gasping, could feel my blood thudding in my veins.

Then a bell began to ring from the second watchtower, answered by others inside the city as the alarm began to spread. Activity along the walls doubled as men raced to positions. In the city, more torches were lit, bonfires raised along the lengths of barricades in the streets. The wharf erupted with frenzied activity, lines untied, trading ships casting off into the harbor. The patrol boats streaked toward the bay's entrance.

The door to my chambers crashed inward and I spun, Keven streaming into the room with twelve other guardsmen, a look of panic crossing his face as he saw the empty bed. But then he caught sight of me on the balcony.

"Mistress," he said, stepping quickly to my side.

"It's started," I said.

Keven stared out at the fiery ruins of the watchtower, his hand on the pommel of his sword. His eyes widened at the destruction, then his attention turned toward me. "We have to get you to the throne room."

I'd slid back beneath the river, could feel his tension, his fear.

But even as it registered on my senses, the fear was suppressed and the tension slipped into controlled channels, harnessed and used. This is what he'd been trained to do.

I felt the next surge of power a moment before the second watchtower exploded, a pulse that shivered across the harbor like a ripple on water, its source somewhere beyond the influence of the throne. Keven didn't flinch as the fireball that had been the tower rose into the sky, didn't even turn in that direction, his eyes never leaving my face, his jaw clenched.

I met his gaze, the urge to draw my dagger and rush down to the city below almost overwhelming. My hand already gripped the handle of my dagger, anger making me tremble. Anger at this attack, at what they'd done to *The Maiden* and the other trading ships.

Anger over what they'd done to Laurren and Erick.

But I'd be more effective here at the palace.

I blew my breath out in exasperation, then nodded. "The throne room."

†

The palace was strangely empty, the hallways echoing as we made our way down the corridor to the main entrance to the throne room. Most of the Servants were already out in the city, along with the guardsmen. But Avrell and Eryn were waiting for me. Neither looked like they'd gotten any sleep.

"What's happened?" Eryn asked immediately as the guardsmen opened the double doors and began lighting torches and candelabra. Avrell, Eryn, and I moved down the walkway to the dais.

"The watchtowers have fallen," I said. "They'll be entering the harbor soon."

She nodded grimly. "The patrol ships and trading ships should halt them for a while. Did you see how many of them there were?"

"I didn't see them at all." I stepped up the dais and sat down in the throne, felt it settling into its usual shape beneath me. An echo of the city's emotions flooded through me—terror, resistance, fear, anger; a seething turmoil—but I held it back, looked down at Avrell and Eryn. "I won't let them take Amenkor."

Both nodded, signed the Skewed Throne symbol over their chests, the gesture startling coming from them. It sent a shiver down my back.

"Remember," Eryn warned, "Reaching drains your strength, makes you weak. Don't overextend yourself trying to help those in the city. They can take care of themselves. Save your strength for later, in case you need it."

I frowned in irritation, saw the answering stiff-lipped admonition in Eryn's eyes, and grudgingly nodded.

Then they were moving, both marked with the White Fire now, both heading to the outer walls and the city below with looks of determination, Avrell to the middle wall, Eryn to the inner.

Keven took their place, gazed up at me expectantly. "Keep me informed of what's happening."

I inclined my head, drew in a deep breath, closed my eyes. . . .

And plunged myself into the river, the force of the throne behind me.

The rage of emotions that represented the city crashed into me like a wave, threatening to drag me under in the riptides. I struggled, cried out involuntarily, flailed against the currents of hatred and fear. I could feel the city's attention drawn toward the burning watchtowers, could feel the shuddering apprehension as they watched the entrance to the harbor in the darkness, all of the bells in the city ringing, the patrol ships and trading ships that had managed to cast off the only counter to the heightening anxiety. The men and women in the ships sped toward the entrance with grim determination, and I latched onto this emotion and stabilized myself in the torrent of the river.

Settling myself in the currents, I streaked out over the black water of the bay, the flames of the watchtowers getting closer. As I approached, I could feel the disruption the destruction of the towers had caused on the river, a disruption brought on by a tremendous release of power. Whirlpools had formed, one each at the centers of the watchtowers. I skirted around the first whirlpool's edge, felt its energy tugging at me, trying to draw me into its mouth.

One of the voices within the throne shifted forward, not Cerrin or Liviann, but Garus. He smelled of ale and roasted meat. *It took more than one person to do that much damage that quickly.*

They'll have to recoup, Seth broke in. *Regain their strength. We'll have a little time.*

A multitude of other voices agreed, but the tone of the agreement was grim.

What's wrong? I asked, and felt Cerrin shift forward to respond.

When the Chorl were pushed back from the coast the last time, they had not progressed to the point where they could combine their powers in such a way. This much focused energy means they're working together, augmenting each other, as we combined our powers to form the thrones. It seems the Chorl have learned a few things since they were here last.

Why didn't you warn me they could do this when they attacked The Maiden?

Because they didn't combine their strength then. They simply turned their separate attacks on one person.

Laurren.

My stomach clenched, and I thought about the Servants scattered about the city below, waiting to deal with the Chorl and their powers. If the Chorl Servants attacked them with their combined strength . . .

But there was nothing that could be done about that now, so I forced the sickening sensation aside and focused back down on the harbor, on the black waters.

I noticed a flare of White Fire on one of the ships close to the harbor entrance and dove for it.

I found myself staring out through the eyes of one of Catrell's high-ranking guardsmen, the patrol boat rocking on the waves beneath him, the motion sharper and more violent than what I'd experienced through Erick on *The Maiden*. Swallowing hard, suddenly feeling nauseous, I realized it was because the boat was smaller than the trading ship.

And then something skimmed out of the darkness beyond the burning watchtowers, its edges limned with reflected firelight. The bow and spit pierced the cloaking darkness like a dagger, the sleek ship gliding almost silently on the water, painted black so that it melded with the night—

Then it was past the juts of land, within the harbor itself, moving fast and deadly, streaking straight for the wharf and the docks at the mouth of Amenkor's River, just like the ships that had entered the harbor of Venitte in Cerrin's memory. And behind it came more ships, as sleek and silent, like lances from the night, twice the size of Amenkor's patrol boats, all painted black, no light visible on the decks, even the sails black, the rigging, the masts. They were like shards of night, splintered off and sent hurtling toward the city.

The guardsman I inhabited jerked out of his shock and pointed, bellowed, "Ready! The ships have entered the harbor! The ships have entered the harbor!"

Cries rang out on all sides and the patrol boat suddenly listed, turning sharply to the left, directly toward the smooth lines of the first ship. The lead guardsman I inhabited clutched the railing before him to keep balance, shifted his weight, cursing silently. Fear slid down his arms like cold water, but he tightened his grip as he watched the ships knife into the harbor. Four of them . . . no, seven . . . no, twelve at least! And even as the patrol boat came up alongside the first enemy ship, he saw two more spits pierce the darkness beyond the harbor's entrance into the firelight from the burning towers.

But he had no time to watch and count the enemy ships. His patrol boat had drawn abreast of the first ship. He barked orders. Grapnels were heaved up onto the enemy deck even as it sped past, the length of rope attached to each grapnel tied down to the front of the patrol boat. Rope hissed, trailing into the darkness, then snapped taut.

The patrol boat lurched, guardsmen on the deck grunting as they lost their footing and crashed to the deck, the smaller patrol boat swinging around and crashing into the side of the larger enemy ship as it sped on. The captain of the patrol boat screamed at his men to get up as they were dragged alongside the ship deeper into the harbor, cursing as men regained their feet slowly, grasping a few by the scruff of the neck and hauling them upright, shoving them toward the side of the Chorl ship. A rope ladder with grapnels on the end was flung up the side of the enemy ship grinding at their side and men began to climb.

I felt fraying rope scrape into my palms as the captain of the guardsman seized the rope ladder nearest to him and began the climb up to the deck. Halfway up the ladder, a scream rang out, and as he glanced down the length of the patrol boat, he caught his first sight of the Chorl.

He gasped and froze. Leaning over the railing above, three blue-skinned warriors with black hair glared down at the patrol boat, then caught sight of the ladders and the grapnels holding the two ships together. Abruptly, two of the faces vanished, returning a moment later.

There was a flash off the head of an ax, followed by a solid thump of metal digging into wood.

Adrenaline flooded the captain's numbing arms with heat, overtaking the sizzling terror of the strange and horrifying faces of the Chorl. "Climb!" he bellowed, his voice tearing at his throat. "Climb, you bloody bastards! Before they cut us free!"

He lurched farther up the ladder, grasping the next rung even before the feet of the man above him had cleared it, pulling himself up with all his strength. His breath hissed between his gritted teeth. A few paces away, men screamed as the ladder they were climbing suddenly went slack and they fell back, hitting the deck of the patrol boat with a thudding crash followed by moans, but the captain didn't turn, didn't hesitate.

The man above him kicked out, almost catching him in the face as he dove over the railing of the enemy ship. The captain reached up over the railing next, pushed off with his feet as he pulled with his arms—

And then he was up and over, rolling onto the deck of the enemy ship, his back thudding up against a yielding body, his hand landing in blood.

He gasped, saw the dead, vacant eyes of the man who'd been climbing the ladder above him—

And then he rolled away. A curved blade swished out of the darkness and bit into the deck where he'd been, then he was up and balanced, sword drawn with a hissing snick of metal.

The blue-skinned Chorl spat what could only be a curse, face twisted in a grimace as he jerked his blade free from the deck and turned to confront the captain. Beyond the Chorl, beyond the stunted mast of the sleek ship, I could see the watchtowers retreating. The patrol boats hadn't even slowed the ships down. They were still streaking toward the wharf, toward the docks and the city.

I spat my own curse.

Where were the trading ships?

Then the Chorl struck, the guardsman parrying on instinct, my attention drawn back to the fighting that was spreading quickly across the Chorl's deck. More and more guardsmen had breached the railing, had pushed the Chorl back so that others could join the fight from the patrol boat below. I watched the interplay, settled into the flow, ready to intercede if the captain needed it. I could feel the instincts Erick and Westen had trained into me screaming to be let free, but I held back. The captain was competent, and Eryn's warning still rang in my head. I'd exhaust myself faster if I seized control of the captain's body.

The Chorl overextended himself, and the captain took advantage, his blade snaking in, punching through the Chorl's silky clothing and armor at the midsection. The blue-skinned man gasped, red blood spurting from his mouth, his hand gripping the sword slid into his belly.

The captain withdrew the blade and the Chorl fell to the side with a low, gurgling growl.

As he turned, I caught sight of movement at the aft of the ship. A woman, dressed in filmy clothing, the glint of gold at her ear.

I also caught sight of another Amenkor guardsman from the patrol boat, fending off two Chorl not three paces away.

To hells with Eryn and her warning.

I claimed the captain, took two paces forward and with coldly calculated movements used his sword to kill the Chorl the other guardsman faced. I felt the captain's surprise as he lost control of his own body, but shrugged it aside.

Captain! I said. *Kill the woman! She's one of the Chorl Servants!*

"What?" he gasped. The guardsman he'd just saved clutched

at a wound along his side, bewildered. "What are you talking about?"

This is the Mistress! I shouted, letting anger bite through his confusion. *Kill the woman! She's vulnerable right now, but I don't know how long she'll stay that way!*

Then I spun, the captain's sword flicking out, slicing through the neck of the Chorl that had been coming up from behind, blood flying in a wide arc.

The guardsman stared in shock, eyes widening as I turned back, letting the captain take control of his own body again, retreating back into the White Fire. He shuddered as he regained control, but then stiffened with resolve, shaking his head.

"Kill the woman!" he growled, motioning toward the Chorl Servant with his bloody sword. "Pass the word that we're to focus on getting to the woman! We'll try to flank her on both sides!"

The guardsman I'd saved hesitated, then nodded and moved to the left. The captain watched him go, then turned, saw another group of guardsmen fighting heatedly to the right, and charged into the fray.

I surged up out of the captain's body, up above the ship, its sails, rigging, and mast rushing past beneath me as I scanned the battle in the harbor. There were twenty-five of the Chorl vessels, seven of them crawling with Amenkor guardsmen, patrol boats latched onto their sides like leeches. In their wake, four other patrol boats had been crushed, guardsmen flailing in the waters of the harbor among the debris. A few other patrol boats were cutting through the waves, picking up the survivors. There was nothing else they could do. There was no chance the patrol boats could catch up to the Chorl ships already past them.

The Chorl hadn't even been slowed.

Then, as I watched, one of the Chorl ships began to swerve, cutting sharply to the right, the men on deck toppling over as the ship tilted. Amenkor guardsmen were at the helm, steering the ship hard and fast toward a second Chorl ship, one not yet boarded. The Chorl on the deck of that ship began shouting, pointing at the spit of the other ship as it bore down on them. The ship began to veer away, the Chorl shrieking—

But it was too late.

The two ships collided with a reverberating crunch, wood splintering as the spit punched through the side of the second Chorl ship, chunks of wood planks flying. A shudder passed through the river, a shock wave of force that pushed me back, and everyone on both ships crashed to the deck and rolled, men from Amenkor as well as the Chorl tipping over the rails to the ocean below. The second ship listed, its sails falling limp as part of the mainmast snapped, rigging falling down onto the deck, into the water. The two ships slowed, began drifting off to the right, into the path of a third Chorl vessel, but it had time to swerve, the movements of the Chorl on its deck frantic, laced with sweat and terror. It cut left, its deck tilting harshly, skimmed past the aft section of the two stricken ships, then began to veer back onto course—

And suddenly Amenkor's trading ships slid into the fray.

Lines of flaming arrows pierced the night, cutting up and out from the decks of the trading ships, then turning and plummeting down onto the Chorl ships' decks and sails. As they struck, pouches of pitch tied to the arrows burst and caught fire.

Within moments, three of the Chorl ships' sails were aflame and fires were spreading across many of their decks. The trading ships and the Chorl attackers met, the harbor degenerating into a flurry of sails, rigging, ships, and screams. The Chorl ships were sleeker, faster, easier to maneuver than the trading ships, but the trading ships could sustain more damage, could take a more direct hit.

In the chaos, twelve of the Chorl ships broke free, two still fighting fires in the rigging or on the decks. They headed directly toward the wharf.

I spat a curse, felt the river roiling around me as the battle continued, then noticed three more of the White Fire beacons in the battle below.

I dove down quickly, stayed long enough with each person to seize control and pass the word about targeting the Chorl Servants.

Then I sped back to the palace, drew in a gasping breath and focused on the people in the throne room.

"What's happened?" Keven asked. He was surrounded by other guardsmen. They'd encircled the dais, were standing ready with swords drawn, facing outward. A page boy waited at Keven's side, eyes expectant, as if Keven had just been about to issue him an order.

"They're almost to the wharf," I said. "Twelve ships made it past the patrols and trading ships. The rest are battling it out in the harbor."

Keven nodded. "Based on the reports I've heard from the men watching on the walls, that's only half their fleet."

"I know," I said, frowning. "I expected more ships, expected more of a fight."

"Maybe this is all they have," Keven said, but I could tell he didn't believe that, even without the throne, without the voices of all of the previous Mistresses murmuring warily. I could hear it in his voice. "We'd only seen four of their ships before this, after all."

I shook my head. "No. They're planning something else." I stared down at the throne room floor a long moment, thinking, then glanced back up. "Keep watch on the harbor. I'm going to check out the wharf."

Keven nodded, then turned back to the page boy as I closed my eyes and sped up and out of the palace.

As I swooped over the walls surrounding the palace, I saw

guardsmen lining the battlements, packed in tight, arms pointing toward the fiery conflagration on the waters of the harbor. Situated on the top of a low hill, the walls like tiers, they could see the battle as it progressed, could see the mass of ships as they wove in and out among each other, flaming arrows arching up into the night in all directions, a few ships dead in the water, listing as they burned, their masts black skeletons in the reaching flames. And they could see the sleek Chorl ships that had escaped the patrol boats and the trading ships and were racing toward the docks, their shapes silhouetted by the fires of the battle behind.

I skimmed over the rooftops of the city, the streets below packed with people, men and boys fighting through the crowds of women and children heading toward the outermost wall of the palace, guardsmen hurrying the people along. Terror drifted up from the streets like smoke, the guardsmen at the gates funneling the people through as quickly as possible, shouting and bellowing orders. The crowds thinned as I passed down into the lower city, the streets now filled with men manning the barricades we'd spent the last few days erecting, others streaming toward the wharf, where the first Chorl ships would land.

As I neared the docks, the black Chorl ships rushing in fast, I spotted a flare of White Fire behind a hastily constructed barricade, recognized Borund in the torchlight a moment before I slid into the Fire at the core of his soul.

"Here they come," Borund said, and his voice was steady even though his hands shook. He held a short sword awkwardly in one hand, the other on the edge of the barricade of crab traps, netting, empty crates, and furniture that had been hastily thrown together. He glared out over the top of the barricade, down the length of a dock.

Out on the water, the twelve Chorl ships had separated, each angling for a different point on the wharf, spread out like a fan.

One of the ships was heading directly for Borund's position.

He glanced to either side. I felt a frisson of fear as I realized William stood to his right, his hair more tousled than usual, his eyes widened in fright. To either side, a mix of sailors, guardsmen, and tradesmen watched the approaching ships, crouched behind the barrier. Most had a look of disbelief on their faces, as if this couldn't possibly be happening, as if they expected any moment to be woken from the dream.

"Ready!" someone shouted, and Borund flinched, swallowed hard, and turned toward the man standing on top of the barricade. A captain of the guard I didn't know, his face tight with hatred, with confidence. "I said, ready!"

A shout went up all along the barricade, swords raised, or daggers, a few knives and spears, even a fishhook.

The captain turned toward the advancing ships, and in a deep voice that carried all along the barricade, bellowed, "Amenkor!" dragging out the last syllable into a battle cry.

All along the wharf, men raised their weapons to the night and took up the cry, a roar of pure defiance.

On the river, the frayed tension I'd felt earlier, the terror, settled into a sense of purpose as the broken battle cry formed into a chant.

Borund stared around at the men in fear, his hands shaking even more. He licked his lips, tightened his grip on the unfamiliar short sword. His palms were sweaty.

I frowned. I could hear his heart thudding in his chest, could feel the tremors running down his arms, could taste the sourness in his mouth.

Borund was close to panic.

"They haven't slowed," William said abruptly.

Borund jumped, startled, his head snapping around to William. "What?"

William nodded toward the ships. The fear had left his face, had faded from his eyes, a consequence of the chanting; it seemed to have bolstered him. "They haven't slowed," he repeated. Then he swore. "They don't intend to slow," he said, and pushed back from his position at the barricade, began shouting toward the captain still standing on the barricade. "Get down! Get down! They aren't going to slow down! They're going to ram the docks!"

The battle chant faltered.

And then the first Chorl ship slammed into the docks, its bow plowing through the planking, wood splintering, cracking with sharp retorts and flying up into the air. Tremors shuddered through the wharf, juddering up through Borund's legs and shivering in his teeth as he clenched them tight, ducking his head as shrapnel from the docks was flung up over the barricades. More ships plowed into the docks to either side, wood shrieking, the battle cry lost in the rending of wood against wood, in screams as flying debris cut into flesh, as terror overcame resolve and a few men began to flee. Borund gasped as something cut into his shoulder, the wound like fire, and then he slammed flat onto the wharf behind the barricade, reached up and grabbed the back of William's shirt and hauled him down to safety. The sound escalated, the Chorl ship grinding its way closer, and Borund squeezed his eyes shut, gasped as the sound intensified, as it crashed around him until it seemed to fill the world, reverberating in his chest, in his heart. He suddenly realized the Chorl ship wasn't going to stop, that it was going to crush him as it plowed through the dock and hit the wharf—

And then the roar of splintered wood retreated, dying down into the distance as the other Chorl ships ground to a halt.

Silence settled, broken only by moans and the clatter of the last of the debris as it fell from the sky. People began to pick themselves up, brushing splinters of wood from their hair, their shoulders, coughing at the dust. Someone close panted loudly and whimpered, the sound wet and painful.

Borund let out an explosive breath, his heart still racing at triple the speed. His shoulder burned.

"Holy shit!" William swore. Blood leaked from a small gash above his left eye.

Wood slapped onto wood, a sound Borund recognized instantly. "They've lowered planks!" he hissed, his voice no longer steady. "They're disembarking!"

And they both jerked as someone down the length of the barricade screamed, a bloodcurdling scream that sent cold shivers into Borund's blood.

"Amenkor!" the captain bellowed again, and Borund saw him standing up twenty paces away, dragging men up off of the wharf as he began making his way down the barricade. "Get up, you bloody bastards! For Amenkor! For the Mistress!"

At his side, William suddenly stilled. Borund saw something kindle deep inside William's eyes, something deep that burned through the last of his fear.

"For the Mistress," William said softly, almost to himself.

Then he leaped up, his own sword brandished high, and he screamed, "For the Mistress! For the Skewed Throne!"

And he began a charge over the barricade. Men on all sides who'd wavered, who'd acted as if they were stunned and shocked, suddenly gripped their swords tighter, roared with hatred and released terror and tension, and tore over the barricade after him.

Borund heaved in a deep breath in surprise, held it, then lurched to his feet with a shouted, "William!" He reached the barricade in time to see the rush of men led by William encounter the first of the blue-skinned Chorl. William's blade struck out, unwieldy and unfamiliar in his grip, but it sliced into the first startled Chorl's arm, cut through the cloth at the elbow, blood splattering—

And then the crowd of people overtook William and he was lost from Borund's sight.

Borund gasped as he saw the end of the dock—or what remained of the dock; the Chorl ship having smashed through its upper half—degenerating into a melee of swords and screams and blood.

"This can't be happening," Borund murmured. He took a step back from the barricade, scanned up and down the wharf, saw men fighting on the docks, on the wharf, on the barricade itself in the torchlight. He took another step back, shook his head. "This—"

Someone lurched up onto the barricade directly in front of him and Borund cried out, the sailor stumbling on the uneven footing. He was splattered with blood, his face strangely open with shock. In that frozen moment, Borund felt as if he could see into the young man's soul, as if the sailor's entire life had been exposed.

Then the sailor pitched forward. His foot caught in the barricade and he sprawled down over it, head hanging, arms limp, hands trailing on the ground.

A sword had cut open the man's back from shoulder to hip.

Borund gasped, jerked away, bile rising in the back of his throat. He stood there, trembling, his mouth working but no sound coming out. Sweat broke out over his entire body, and the pounding of his heart in his veins escalated, drowned out the sounds of battle, the screams and clash of swords. He felt suddenly cold.

He stood shaking for a long moment, the world reduced to nothing but the bloody gash on the sailor's back and the thunder of his heart.

Then he dropped his own sword as if it had caught fire . . . and he ran.

I felt a momentary flash of anger, almost reached out from the Fire and seized control of him, forced him to pick up the sword, to charge onto the dock as William had done.

But then the anger died.

I let Borund go, watched him flee into the streets behind the wharf in panic. I couldn't stay here and force him to fight; Amenkor needed me for other things. Fighting was Borund's choice.

I pulled back from the docks, scanned down the length of the wharf at the twelve Chorl ships and the pitched battles going on everywhere.

A horn sounded. A heavy, deep, sonorous note that held and held, then faded.

I glanced up and frowned at the horizon, where the sun was just beginning to rise.

None of our signals were horns.

Then I froze, my gut clenching. The stench of Borund's panic filled my nostrils as I sucked in a deep breath, but I fought the sensation back.

At the entrance to the harbor, where twin towers of smoke rose into the sky against the dawn from the smoldering watchtowers, more ships were gliding into the bay. A massive ship, half again as large as one of Borund's trading ships, led the group, other smaller ships fanning out behind it. These ships were not as sleek as the initial attack ships, but they were definitely Chorl. Hulls painted black, decks packed with blue-skinned warriors, the smaller ships began to edge out in front of the lead ship, sails billowing out in the breeze coming from the sea. The lead ship's sails were white, some type of spiny shell painted on the largest in yellows and golds.

A man dressed in yellow robes on the lead ship raised another shell to his mouth and the horn sounded again, echoing across the water, throbbing in my ears. A woman stood next to him, dressed in iridescent blues this time, her ears ringed with gold.

The Ochean.

Deep inside, I felt the Fire pulse, its warning flames licking upward. I shivered at their frigid touch.

On the dock below, the Chorl renewed their attack in a frenzy. Our lines were pushed back. Someone called for a retreat and the Amenkor men scrambled back behind the barricade and attempted to hold there.

I rose higher into the dawn, despair washing over me as I watched the Ochean's second wave of ships flooding into the harbor, spreading like oil on water. The battle between the trading ships and the first Chorl ships in the middle of the bay had thinned, at least half of the ships on both sides burning. Debris floated on the surface, bobbing in the waves. And bodies. Dozens of bodies. Some clinging to flotsam, others simply floating, empty faces turned to the lightening sky.

The Ochean's ship reached the remains of the ships and slowed, edging through the wreckage. The conch-shell horn continued to sound at steady intervals, like a death knell. Some of the survivors in the water shouted out to the passing ships, but they were ignored, Chorl and Amenkor alike. The fighting on the decks of the remaining ships paused as the fleet slid past, the faces of the men exhausted, hope dying in the Amenkor men's eyes as they were surrounded.

I sped back to the wharf, saw the men at the barricade falter as the new wave of ships came into view, hidden before by the smoke and fire and ships of the first wave and their battle. The Chorl pressed harder, broke through the barricade to the south, near the half completed warehouse district, blue-skinned men spilling through the gap and onto the wharf and the streets beyond like ink, Amenkor men racing toward the walls of the palace before them. And with that one break, the entire barricade began to crumble.

I watched as the new Chorl ships drew up to the remains of the docks and the wharf, watched as planks were lowered and more of the Chorl warriors disembarked, flooding the wharf with men. And with them came the Chorl Servants, dressed in pale greens, shell necklaces around their necks, gold earrings glinting in the early morning sunlight. The Ochean strode down onto the wharf surrounded by Servants and surveyed the barricade, still loosely held in a few locations.

She motioned to a few of the Servants, who broke off with warrior escorts of their own and spread out along the barricade and the pockets of resistance that remained.

Once in place, they raised their arms and I felt the river gathering, felt it being manipulated.

William, I thought with horror, my gut wrenching. I didn't know if he was still down there, or if he'd fled when the line began to break. I couldn't find him either. He hadn't been one of those tagged with the Fire.

I wanted to close my eyes as the pressure on the river built, wanted to lash out. But I knew it was useless. I couldn't stop all of the Servants, couldn't hope to hold them back. And there was no one close who'd been tagged with the White Fire in any case. I couldn't manipulate the river when Reaching unless I worked through the Fire.

Save your strength, the voices of the throne whispered.

I cried out when the Servants released the pressure—in despair, in frustration.

Amenkor was dying. I could see it. I could feel it.

Fire exploded from the hands of the Servants, rushing forward to slam into the barricades, enveloping Chorl warriors and Amenkor defenders alike. Fresh screams rose into the air with the scent of burned flesh and oily smoke.

"Fall back!" someone bellowed—the captain from the initial attack, still alive, blood covering one eye from a cut across his forehead. "Fall back to the second barricade!"

The Amenkor resistance held a moment more . . . and then

lurched back, the men retreating slowly at first, then breaking into a run as the Servants released more fire.

I shifted, glared down at the Ochean as she climbed over the remains of the barricade accompanied on the left by a man I didn't recognize dressed in yellow robes, holding some type of reed scepter, his face twisted into a scowl. They were surrounded completely by blue-skinned warriors.

I did recognize the warrior to the Ochean's right. Circular tattoos on his cheeks; a ragged half ear.

He was the one who'd led the attack on *The Maiden,* the one who'd met with Alendor in the cove and taken our food.

I spun, flashed past the Chorl as they entered the lower streets beyond the wharf, searched the lower city for flares of the White Fire, for a particular flame . . . and found it.

I dove down, seized control of Captain Westen's body where he watched the wharf from the rooftop of a building. A group of twelve Seekers, both young and old, surrounded him.

I turned to them, eyes flashing. "This is the Mistress. The Chorl have broken through the barricade on the wharf and entered the lower city. They have their Servants with them, dressed in green. They'll be heading this way. I want you to target the Servants. Take out as many as you can before they reach the marketplace."

The Seekers nodded, faces settling into the same dark, dangerous look I'd seen on Erick's face so often beyond the Dredge. These men and women didn't radiate fear. They were strangely empty of emotion, all of it crushed.

Erick had never felt as depthless to me as most of the Seekers did now. But perhaps I had simply known him better, longer. Perhaps the emotions were there, just hidden deeper than usual.

The Seekers scattered, descending from the rooftop and spreading out in the streets below. I followed their movements for a moment through Captain Westen's eyes, then released him, lingering behind in the Fire.

Westen shuddered, closed his eyes and bowed his head, breathing in deeply.

When he'd recovered, his mouth twisted in a tiny smile. "Well," he murmured. "That was certainly strange."

Then he shifted, all thought centering on the hunt. He reached down into the shadows of the roofline at his feet and drew forth a crossbow and a pouch containing steel bolts. Slinging the pouch over one shoulder, so that the opening rested on his hip, within easy reach, he sprinted in a low crouch along the edge of the roof to a corner, scanned in the direction of the wharf, where thick columns of smoke now rose into the lightening sky from the burning barricade. Hooking the crossbow to his belt, he slid over the edge of the roof, holding onto the stone abutment, then climbed down the brick wall like a spider.

He jumped the last few feet, crouched down in the alley's entrance, then darted across the street, heading toward the wharf.

A moment later, he heard running footsteps and ducked into the shadows of a doorway, absolutely still as a group of Amenkor guardsmen tore by, mingled with a few random citizens, all bloody, some wounded. The sounds of the battle were growing nearer.

Once they'd passed, Westen took a quick look out into the street, then to the door at his back. He eyed it carefully, then stepped back a pace and kicked the door in.

He moved into the interior rooms as the piercing cries of the Chorl rose on the street behind him. Without turning, he strode into the back rooms, found the stairs to an upper floor and sprinted up those, noticing that the stairs continued to the roof before moving again to the front of the building.

Sidling up to a window, he glared down onto the street, watched ranks of Chorl move past, wincing at their harsh, barked commands. None entered any of the buildings, continuing on down the street, in pursuit of the fleeing guardsmen.

Westen grunted, settled down next to the window so that he'd be hidden in the shadow of the room, then reached out and swung the window outward.

The breeze brought with it smoke and blood as well as the taint of sea salt.

Westen ignored it all, pulled out his crossbow, and proceeded to load a bolt.

He scanned the room—a bed, two dressers, a wardrobe, a table with a jewelry box and a chair. Reaching out, he dragged the chair closer to the window and sat, angling the crossbow down to cover the street.

He began to wait.

His mind flickered through numerous images as he listened to the sounds coming from the street. Foremost was a woman, her hair a light brown and her eyes green, smiling as she held out a sheathed dagger. A child clutched her leg and she ruffled the boy's hair. Concern bled through Westen's cold Seeker reserve as he thought about them, and I suddenly realized it was his wife and child. I hadn't known he had a family, found it surprising that any of the Seekers had families.

More images of the two flashed by, mixed with worry that they'd made it to the palace in time. Then he shoved those thoughts aside and concentrated on the sounds in the street. They were getting closer. He could hear explosions in the distance, wondered how the other Seekers were faring.

Smoke drifted down the street and he tensed, leaned forward, and shifted the crossbow.

Shouts, in the strange language of the Chorl, and then the street was flooded with Chorl warriors, this batch moving slowly, swords drawn, escorting—

Westen didn't smile, didn't react in any way, but all thoughts of his family, of the other Seekers, of everything but the street below faded away. His vision seemed to narrow as he concentrated, as my vision narrowed on the river, but without the strange textures of the river that told me so much. He edged the crossbow to the left, then down, sighted on the flash of green among the blues and browns of the Chorl warriors. The Servant's face came into focus, the skin smooth, tinted the palest of blues, the lips a much darker blue. Her eyes flashed left and right as the group moved, her jaw set in a stern line. Three gold earrings glittered in each ear, and there was a trace of a tattoo at the edge of her throat, hidden beneath the iridescent green dress.

For a moment, Westen hesitated.

But the image of his wife and child resurfaced, followed by a flood of hatred for these invaders.

He pulled the crossbow's trigger.

He was moving before the bolt struck the Servant in the chest, flinging her backward, her arms flailing outward, her face startled. A roar erupted from the Chorl in the street. He heard them entering the building below, furniture crashing to the floor as it was thrust aside, and then he was at the stairs leading to the roof, sprinting up them two at a time. He burst out through the trapdoor to the rooftop, hauled himself up into a roll, then slammed the trapdoor back down into place and dashed across to the roof's edge.

In the street below, he caught a brief image of Chorl surrounding the fallen Servant in a rough circle, their faces enraged as they searched for the culprit. The Servant's face was slack, her green dress stained a dark, grisly black-red, the bolt sticking out just above her left breast, directly over her heart.

Then Westen leaped from the roof, thudding down hard onto the roof next door, rolling back up into a sprint.

Just before I withdrew from Westen, I felt a surge of satisfaction from him at the Servant's death.

I lifted up, surveyed the scene in the lower city, saw buildings on fire in three different locations, saw two other Seekers streaking across rooftops or edging through the back streets, all of them retreating slowly to the marketplace and the second line of barricades as the Chorl advanced. But the Seekers were slowing the Chorl down. Their groups weren't running from street to street anymore, the Servants held back as the Chorl warriors sent out advance parties to flush out the Seekers before they struck. As I watched, one Seeker's bolt took a Servant in the shoulder, too high for a killing stroke, and the Servant lashed out, the flare of pain and fury as she unleashed the fireball like a slap in the face. The fireball exploded on the second floor of the house, heat searing upward, the blast so powerful the windows burst outward, glass shards flying down into the street. But the Seeker was already sprinting away through a back narrow, cursing himself under his breath.

Closer to Amenkor's River, the Chorl had almost made it to the second barricade.

I sped toward the marketplace, found Captain Catrell, slid into the Fire at his core.

They're almost here, I said.

He grunted in surprise at my voice, those men nearest him frowning. "Mistress?"

Westen and the Seekers have slowed them down, but they're going to reach the second barricade any moment. You won't be able to hold it long. The Ochean's Servants will break through it.

"Then we'd better prepare our own Servants for some defense," he said under his breath. He barked orders and three page boys took off at a run. One came back almost immediately, Marielle in tow, her white Servant robes discarded and replaced with ordinary breeches and a brown shirt. The white robes would have been too easy to target. I'd wanted my own Servants to meld into the fray.

To be gray.

The guardsmen surrounding Catrell parted as Marielle stepped forward. She was shaking, her face a mask of terror. I thought of Borund, my heart dropping.

"You'll be fine," Catrell said.

Marielle snorted, but I reached out on the river and touched her through the Fire, abandoning Catrell, saying, *Catrell is right, you'll be fine.*

Marielle relaxed instantly, keeping her voice low. "I didn't want to go on the ship."

I frowned. *What?*

"The ship. *The Maiden.* I thought, in your chambers when you were tagging Erick, I thought you were going to put me on the ship, too. I was terrified. But Laurren went instead, and I was so relieved." I felt her gut twist with pain and grief. "And look what happened to her! I should have gone instead! She should be here, defending the city, not me!"

But she isn't here, I said. *You are.*

"Here they come," Catrell said quietly, his voice grim, no sign that he thought Marielle conversing with herself was strange entering his voice. Then he bellowed out orders, men shifting up to the edge of the barricade on all sides.

Marielle's terror had returned, supplanting her grief.

You know what you have to do, I said.

She shuddered, then shook herself. Her shoulders straightened, and she glared out at the empty marketplace before the barricade.

Chorl began pouring from the streets into the square. Marielle closed her eyes, drew in a deep breath to steady herself—

And I felt the river shift, felt it gather in a wall before the bar-

ricade. An invisible shield centered at Catrell's position and extending in both directions for at least twenty feet.

I grunted.

"A Chorl Servant," Catrell said, motioning with his sword.

I glanced in that direction, frowned as the woman emerged
from the side street, thankful there was only one. The Chorl warriors around her halted, leaving a wide open space between her and
the barricade.

She raised her arms, the green of her sleeves flapping in the
breeze. I felt the river gather, heard Marielle whimper.

And then fire exploded toward the barricade.

The men cried out, lurched back, and ducked behind the
makeshift barrier, but Catrell held steady, his face grim, his jaw
clenching.

The fire struck Marielle's wall, and she gasped, wincing. I resisted the urge to help her, bit back a sharp sickening memory of Laurren, of feeling her burn to death. But Marielle held the wall tight,
shunting the fire upward as she'd been taught so that it shot harm-
lessly into the air over the heads of those behind the barricade, heat
radiating downward in palpable waves.

Then the fire cut off. Sweat lined Marielle's face, but she
straightened.

A cheer went up from the Amenkor guardsmen as they realized
the barrier had held, and Marielle smiled.

In the marketplace, the Chorl Servant stepped forward, shoving warriors aside, her eyes enraged. She raised her hands to try
again, and I felt Marielle brace for the impact, steadier this time,
more confident.

"Take the Chorl Servant out as quickly as you can," Catrell said
to the men at his side, issuing orders even as the second blast of fire
struck Marielle's wall and I lifted free from the Fire at Marielle's
center.

The second barricade seemed to be holding, the palace Servants holding off the Chorl's Servants all along its length. I slid from Fire to Fire inside Amenkor's Servants, helping some to tighten their shields or boost their confidence, others to push back and attack, but I never stayed long. The group of Chorl near the River had reached the barricade there, but had run into a different problem: Darryn and the denizens of the slums. The militia had come out in force, backed by hundreds of other residents who'd managed to survive the winter. They surged across the Dredge's bridge into the Chorl's flanks brandishing anything they could lay their hands on as weapons, Darryn at the forefront, screaming into the smoke and wind drifting inland from the ships burning in the harbor. What they lacked in organization, they made up for in numbers, the mob overwhelming the Chorl warriors, crushing them into the barricade where the Amenkor guardsmen were holding them off with little effort.

But the wharf and the lower city were both in shambles, entire streets on fire, smoke rising into the midmorning light in thick, black columns. The battle in the harbor was over, trading ships nothing but burning husks, a few of the sleek Chorl ships moving toward the wharf, battered but still whole.

Then I caught a flicker of Fire, nothing but a sputter, barely visible. It came from the Chorl ships already at the docks.

It came from the Ochean's ship.

I hesitated, ready to return to the throne room, ready to warn Avrell and Eryn and the others on the walls of the palace. I'd been out too long as it was, had been using the river, had been Reaching from person to person.

But the Fire flickered again, and so I dove for it, speeding through the columns of smoke, feeling the heat from the fires below as the city burned, intending to simply check out the Fire and then leave. No lingering as I'd done with the others.

I slid down into the Ochean's ship, slid into the Fire—

And almost screamed with the pain. An all-consuming pain, like white hot flame, seething in my arms, my legs, my back, my chest. It felt like a thousand needles being shoved into my skin simultaneously, digging deeper and deeper with each breath, piercing all the way down to the bone. Each breath, each pulse of blood, sent the pain shooting through my body again, and again, and again, until the pain began to grow numbing, until I felt my heart ready to burst.

Until I remembered that this wasn't my body.

With effort, I forced the excruciating pain to recede, to fade into the background. But I couldn't force it to stop. It throbbed with the beat of a heart, ever present, ceaseless and unending. But it receded enough that I could focus on the body I inhabited, enough that I could recognize the man writhing beneath the pain.

Erick.

I almost screamed again, almost unconsciously jerked Erick's body, a movement that might have killed him. Shock overcame me, utter and complete shock. Followed by a horrible, tortuous, unbelievable joy.

And then, instantly crushing the joy, a terrible, choking grief. That I'd thought he'd died, that unknowingly I'd left him, abandoned him . . . to *this*.

I wanted to sob, felt the pressure building up inside me, inside Erick, knew that if I let it out it could kill him. He was almost dead, his body tortured, bruised, and crushed. I tasted blood on his lips, felt hundreds of small cuts on his arms, on his legs, his back and shoulders and abdomen. Hundreds of pinprick burn marks. Something inside was broken, a rib, each breath sending sheets of pain into his right side, and the cut he'd received during the battle on the ship hadn't completely healed yet, seethed with its own fire. His throat was raw and torn, to the point that I knew he couldn't scream even if he wanted to. And the muscles in his neck . . .

He must have screamed, I realized. Even when he could no longer make a sound. He must have screamed and screamed, for the muscles in his neck were strained to the breaking point.

Shifting carefully, I tried to open his eyes. Only one of them complied, the other swollen shut and caked with blood. Even that small movement increased the pace of his breath, to the point where he was panting, his breath hissing in and out through a clenched jaw, blood, spit, and snot blowing in strands from his lips.

He lay on the floor in the corner of a lavishly decorated room, bolts of blue-and-green cloth draped from the ceiling, covering the outlines of a bed, hiding the rough wood of the ceiling and the walls. They drifted as the boat rocked, undulating in the waves. Pillows littered the floor, strewn in all directions, most blue and green as well, but a few a vibrant yellow or red.

The pillows closest to Erick were splattered with blood.

I heard a footfall, saw two sandaled feet move into view, the edge of a yellow robe.

One of the Chorl crouched down next to Erick, his tattooed face impassive. "Awake?" he said, the word awkward in his mouth, harsh, with a strange clicking sound at the end. He grinned, the expression sending a shudder through me. "Amenkor burning."

Erick didn't react. He had retreated deep inside himself. I could sense him huddling in a far, far corner, locked away from the pain.

But rage flooded through me. I couldn't suppress it, could feel Erick's breath quicken, his heart beating faster.

The Chorl must have seen my rage in Erick's eyes, for he shifted closer, eyebrows raised. He grunted, the twisted grin returning.

With careful, practiced ease, I felt him reach out on the river, felt it . . . churn. I couldn't see what he was doing, could only sense it.

But I felt the consequences instantly. Every prickling needle on Erick's skin erupted in white-hot fire.

Erick screamed, back arching, his heart shuddering, faltering, dying—

And then the sensation ended. It had only held for a moment, a single breath.

But it had brought Erick to the brink of death. His heart thudded once, hard, then relaxed back into a faint weakened beat. Erick's body relaxed as well, slumping to the floor, trembling.

The Chorl leaned back, considered Erick for a long moment, then snorted in contempt and stood, moving out of view.

I wanted to lash out, to seize the river and hurt the Chorl bastard. Hurt him as the Ochean had hurt Erick, torture him so that he screamed with pain without me even touching him. I wanted to kill him.

But I couldn't. Erick's body couldn't take it.

So with utmost care, I slid free, felt him exhale softly, his eye closing. I watched his huddled, battered form for a moment more, wanting to touch him so badly I ached.

There was nothing more I could do here.

And I couldn't abandon the throne room, couldn't abandon Amenkor.

But I couldn't leave him here. Not with the Ochean. Not now. Who else . . . ?

I pushed up and out of the Ochean's ship and scanned the lower city, found the Fire I was looking for and dove into Westen's body. He was close to the second barricade, hidden in an alley, attempting to get close enough to pick off a few more of the Chorl Servants from behind. But he was almost out of crossbow bolts.

Westen, I gasped, my voice sounding more frantic than I felt. *You have to get to the Ochean's ship at the docks!* I felt him frown in confusion. *Erick's alive! He's being held on the Ochean's ship, guarded by a*

Chorl dressed in yellow. Kill the guard if you have to, but get Erick out of there! You'll have to be careful. The guard can use the river. And Erick's hurt. You won't be able to move him far.

I left Westen's body, felt his shock as my words sank in. Then he hardened, as he'd done before, grabbed his crossbow and pouch, and sprinted down the alley, back toward the wharf, without a word.

I hovered in the alley, fretting, hesitating between following Westen and heading back to the palace, but an explosion near the barricade, followed by a billowing black cloud of smoke, forced my decision.

I lurched above the buildings, saw an entire section of the marketplace barricade enveloped in flame, spent a moment worrying about Marielle, then fled toward the palace and the throne room.

"Keven!" I barked as soon as I'd settled into my body. Weakness rippled through my arms and I gasped, but it hadn't sunk in deep yet, only made my hands tremble a little. I gripped the edges of the throne hard to stop them. Guardsmen and page boys were running in and out of the chamber, lining up to give reports. The guard surrounding me had doubled.

Keven broke away from a breathless guardsman in mid-report and vaulted up the three stone steps to the dais. "Yes, Mistress." His face was lined with worry, with anger and frustration.

"The Chorl have breached the second barricade. They'll be at the outer gates in moments. Close them. Now. Close them all."

"There are still people trying to get within the safety of the walls," he said calmly.

I grimaced. "It's too late. Everyone will have to fend for themselves."

He nodded, as if he'd expected the response but felt obligated to report. He turned and barked a command, one of the guardsmen surrounding the throne rushing off to the tower to sound the appropriate warning bells.

Then he turned back to me expectantly. "The harbor? The lower city?"

I sighed. "The battle in the harbor is over. And the Chorl brought in another wave of ships in addition to the first. I didn't count them. There were too many. The Ochean came with them. They overran the barricade on the wharf in moments, with the help of her Servants. Westen and the other Seekers managed to slow their advance, and our own Servants halted them at the second barricade for a while, but as soon as they broke through that, I came here."

Keven's eyes emptied of all emotion, became stoic. It was obvious he'd heard some of this news before now, but not all.

I watched him, considered not telling him the other news, but then decided he—of anyone in this room or on the palace walls—deserved to know.

I leaned forward. "Keven."

He glanced toward me, his expression still blank.

"Erick's alive."

For a moment, the words didn't seem to register. But then something deep inside stirred. His shoulders straightened and he drew in a long, slow, full breath . . . and held it. "Erick's alive?"

I nodded. "He's being held on the Ochean's ship."

His jaw clenched, unclenched, then clenched again. The spark in his eye hardened, began to seethe with fury. His brow creased and in a rough voice, his eyes meeting mine with raw intensity, he said, "We have to save him."

I held his gaze, let him see my own rage. "I've already sent Westen to get him."

Keven drew in another breath, as if to protest, as if to say that wasn't enough.

But then he nodded.

Satisfied, I leaned back, broke eye contact. I gazed down into the throne room, surveyed the long walkway between the four stone pillars on each side, the scattering of statues and tapestries and candelabra in the recessed areas behind the pillars. I scanned the guardsmen surrounding the throne, the page boys, some servants from the palace ready with paper and ink, or a few trays of food or drink.

I frowned.

"Keven."

He turned back.

"Keep everyone off the promenade," I said. "And keep everyone away from the central corridor in the palace to the throne room as well. Remove the guardsmen at the doors to the inner sanctum and leave those doors open. I want a clear passage from the inner gates, up the promenade, to the throne room."

When his eyes flared, I shook my head and smiled. "If the Ochean and the Chorl breach the inner gate, I want no resistance."

His brow creased with disagreement. "What about you? What about here, in the throne room?"

My smile faded, and I glared out at the open doors of the throne room, out into the corridor beyond, thought about Erick on the Ochean's ship, thought about the intensity in the Ochean's eyes when she'd recognized the Fire at Erick's core on *The Maiden*. There was no reason for her to have kept Erick alive. Unless . . .

"I don't think she's come for Amenkor," I said. "I think she's come for the Skewed Throne. Let her try to take it."

Keven hesitated, uncertain, ready to argue, but in the end he complied. Stepping down from the dais, he motioned a group of guardsmen near, began issuing orders, more forcefully, more vehemently, than necessary. But he issued the orders.

I drew myself away from the throne room, pushed myself up to the tower, concentrated on the three walls below me, on the gates. Fire flared at the inner gate and the middle gate—Eryn and Avrell, respectively.

I dove down to Avrell, and said, *They're coming*, then settled back to wait.

Like the others, he shuddered as I spoke, then regrouped and moved up to the edge of the wall above the gates, motioning to a captain of the guard beside him. "Get ready. The Mistress says they're coming."

The captain turned and passed the word down the wall. Avrell glanced toward the gate in the outer wall—closed, so that he couldn't see what was happening beyond. As he watched, the guardsmen on that wall suddenly broke into activity, archers leaning out through the crenellations, firing at the Chorl on the far side. Men began tipping boiling oil over the wall, or chucked stones onto the attackers below.

And then suddenly the gate exploded.

Chunks of wood and stone blasted into the air, arching up and over the outer ward, shattering into buildings, caving in rooftops.

"Mistress' tits!" the guardsman to Avrell's left whispered in shock.

Avrell shot him a disapproving glare, then turned back to the dust cloud caused by the explosion. The men on the wall were scrambling away from the gate entrance, fleeing along the parapet. Another explosion followed, more debris raining up and out through the air, landing with distance-muffled thuds. A building near the gate collapsed with a slow grinding crunch.

Then, through the dust and debris, Chorl poured into the streets.

Avrell straightened as everyone on the walls tensed.

"What in hells was that?" The captain of the guard had reappeared, his eyes wide.

"I don't know," Avrell said. "Are the gates sealed?"

"For all the good it's going to do us."

Avrell grunted.

The Chorl headed straight for the second gate, a massive wave of blues and reds and purples and browns, the greens of a few Servants scattered among them. Tension along the wall mounted as they approached, men shifting from foot to foot, armor scraping against stone.

"Ready!" the captain called when they were two blocks away, but still out of sight. Their piercing war cries could be heard, growing louder and louder, echoing off the buildings into the afternoon sky.

Shouts of "Ready!" echoed down the wall, men stepping forward, craning to see.

Then the Chorl appeared on the street below, a mob of blue skin and raised swords, the blades curved strangely, their war cries suddenly roaring. It crashed into the gates and wall like an ocean wave, increasing as more and more of the Chorl appeared, surging forward like a tide.

They struck the gates, then split and piled outward. The captain roared, "Now!" but his voice was drowned out in the cacophony of noise. His sword arm slashed downward and all along the wall Amenkor guardsmen responded, arrows flying, stone arching outward, falling indiscriminately among the screaming mass of blue-skinned men. To Avrell's left, two burly men hoisted a vat of bubbling oil up into the crenellation and tilted it over the edge. Fresh screams arose, the Chorl below retreating from the scalding oil. Someone else chucked a flaming brand down after the oil and fire seared the wall. Black smoke, reeking of charred flesh, billowed up into Avrell's face.

He pulled back from the wall coughing, face twisted in distaste.

Before he could recover completely, the roar of the Chorl died down abruptly.

Avrell staggered back to the wall, forearm lifted to cover his mouth and nose, still coughing. Through tear-blurred eyes, he glared down at the space below the gate.

Then his eyes widened.

The Chorl were falling back, leaving the square and street open. Guardsmen still heaved things over the walls to either side, but all fighting in the immediate area had halted, men crowding back to the edge of the wall, perplexed.

In the square below, the edge of the Chorl force parted and the Ochean stepped forward.

Tense mutters passed among the guardsmen as she moved forward, halting just out of reach of the archers. Her black hair shifted in the gusting breeze from the harbor, and the folds of her iridescent blue dress trailed on the ground behind her. Shell necklaces hung down from her neck, and strings of shells had been plaited through her hair.

She surveyed her forces, the gates, the walls, her face unreadable, her pale blue skin flawless.

Then her gaze fell on the top of the gates, on Avrell's position.

Her expression hardened, grew taut, and she raised her arms, blue cloth arching from her wrists to her waist as she held her hands outward, palms facing the wall.

I felt the force gathering on the river, reached out to Avrell to warn him, but he'd already seen the danger.

Eyes widening in fear, he lurched back and to one side and bellowed, "Run!"

He'd taken two steps, the guardsmen to either side turning to frown at him in confusion, when the pressure on the river released.

The gates exploded, the force shuddering through the stone wall beneath Avrell's feet. Then a concussive blast hit him from behind, flung him forward to the parapet, the skin of his hands scraped raw on the stone. He gasped, rolled to one side, and struck the stone of the crenellation with his back, grinding to a halt. Something soft landed on the parapet before him—a body, the guardsman already dead, eyes wide in shock—and then the body slid off the wall and Avrell could see wood and stone flying outward, away from the wall.

Avrell gasped again, realized he could barely hear his own breath, sounds muted, felt a trickle near his ear and reached up to his jaw. His shoulder screamed at the movement and his hand came away bloody.

Boots pounded past, their thuds like muffled cloth. Through the fog of dust from the gates, he could pick out shouts and screams, too soft and chaotic to make out words.

The stone beneath him rumbled, shuddered again, and he felt the wall shift, suddenly leaning inward.

He jerked himself up onto his elbow, ignored the sharp pain in his chest, and scrambled to his feet. His dark blue robes were covered with grit, his hands throbbing where they'd been skinned raw. He huddled against the canted wall, coughed as he tried to make out what was happening.

The gates had fallen. The stone above where the gates had stood had collapsed, and the walls to either side were threatening to give way as well.

He stood on the parapet, guardsmen running past, retreating from the walls, and stared. Chorl filled the street below, surging in all directions, their main force angling straight for the inner gates.

The wall trembled again, the motion piercing Avrell's numbness and shock, and he suddenly said, "Eryn."

He shook himself, pain shooting up from his elbow and shoulder where he'd hit the stone parapet. Clutching that arm to his chest with the other hand, he began to stagger back along the parapet, looking for a way down to the street.

I left him, pushed up through the middle ward, past the huge three-horse stone fountain in front of the merchant's guild, the plaza already swarming with Chorl, up through the streets to the inner wall, the inner gate, and settled inside Eryn.

She'd seen the middle gate fall, had seen the dust, debris, and smoke from the outer gate. Her jaw was set, her hands flat on the stone wall before her as she stared out into the street. "Avrell," she said to herself.

Then the Chorl flooded the street below, came screaming up to the wall, and the arrows began to fly.

Eryn didn't pay any attention, guardsmen bellowing orders all around her. Instead, she closed her eyes, concentrated inward.

I felt her heart slow, felt the faint tremors of concern and fear leave her, her arms steadying.

The river around her calmed, the turbulence caused by the guardsmen, by their raw terror, by the death, faded away, evened out.

Until, when the roars of the Chorl died down as they had at the middle gates, when the Chorl retreated and the guardsmen on the wall fell silent and Eryn opened her eyes, she stood in a pool of total serenity.

On the street below, the Chorl parted and the Ochean stepped forward. She surveyed the wall as she had before, and her arms lifted.

Eryn drew in a deep breath, her hands on the stone before her, and summoned the river.

It solidified fluidly, the wall of force she constructed flawless as far as I could see, stretching from the ground to the top of the parapet, completely covering the gate, and curved like a shield.

She finished it a moment before the Ochean released.

I saw the Ochean's power flash across the square, raw and blunt, channeled like a battering ram and aimed at the center of the gates.

When it hit Eryn's wall, it struck like a solid punch to the gut. Eryn gasped, her eyes flying wide, one arm leaving the wall and clutching her stomach. The shield she'd created flexed, wavered, the force of the Ochean's blow being shunted to the side as swiftly as possible. For a single moment, it seemed that Eryn would be overwhelmed. The wall stuttered, frayed at the edges—

But it held.

In the square below, the Ochean stepped forward, her eyes flashing with hatred. The Chorl began to mutter, shocked. Then she spun, clapped her hands and shouted an order.

Instantly, three of the Ochean's Servants stepped forward.

The Ochean swung back to the gates, arms outstretched, face livid. The three Servants fell into position around her, one each to either side and a step behind, the third directly behind her and two steps back, so that they formed a rough diamond.

The three Servants clasped their hands before them and bowed their heads. Lines of force wavered into being on the river, connecting them to the Ochean, solidifying into thick conduits.

The voices of the throne drew in a sharp breath.

Except that wasn't true. Most of the voices seemed merely confused, murmuring with worry, some stunned into silence by the previous explosions. Only the Seven had drawn breath.

They're Linking. They've advanced farther than I suspected, Cerrin said.

Then I have to help her.

I reached, even as Eryn steadied her shield, a thin pain shooting up from her stomach. Even though her shield had held, she'd still felt the force behind the Ochean's blow. I began to weave the river into a second shield behind Eryn's.

No, Liviann said, and I felt her step forward, felt Cerrin recede. *We can't teach you how to supplement Eryn's power as the Servants below are supplementing the Ochean's—there's no time—but we can show you how to effectively reinforce Eryn's shield.*

She reached through the Fire with Cerrin's help, the rest of the Seven stepping forward as well, all of them guiding the shield's lines that I'd already put in place, shifting them slightly so that my own shield wove into Eryn's, slipped along its edges, forming buttresses between Eryn's shield and the physical stone walls themselves.

As the last currents slid into place, Eryn straightening and murmuring a soft, grim, "Thank you, Varis," under her breath, the Ochean unleashed another hammer blow of power.

On the river, the hammer descended with horrifying strength, not just the power of the Ochean and three Servants, but more than ten times the power.

It struck, and a solid core of heat and pain exploded in Eryn's gut, like a sizzling ball of fire. Both Eryn and I gasped, Eryn's arms wrapping around her stomach as she staggered. The shield held, power dissipating outward, shuddering along its length, the buttresses bleeding the power down into the walls themselves until the stone began to shudder. More power slammed into the shield, pressure building, the tremors of the wall increasing, until a few of the guardsmen cried out. Eryn's shield began to collapse, crumbling in from the sides—

And then the Ochean's power halted.

At the same time, a horrendous crack reverberated through the inner ward as the stone of the wall split. Guardsmen leaped back from the sundered stone, shouts rang out, but the wall held.

Eryn gasped and collapsed forward, holding herself up on the edge of the parapet with one arm, knees weak. The captain of the guard shifted forward in concern, to where Eryn hunched forward, arm still clutching her stomach.

Eryn waved him off, forced herself to straighten and stand, her breath coming harsh and fast now, gasping. The white hot fire radiated up from her abdomen, seething, shooting flares of pain down her arms, into her heart. But she closed her eyes, reached out and steadied the wall of force before the gate yet again, sucked in another deep breath and held it as the Ochean gathered her power, and that of the Servants, for a third strike.

Eryn's shield never had a chance, even with my help, even with the guidance of the Seven. It held for one short breath, two—

Then it collapsed.

And the gates exploded.

Eryn sagged to the stone wall in front of her as it shuddered, groped blindly for the stone as debris flew outward behind her, dust enveloping her in a shroud. She coughed as she tried to breathe through the grit, raised an arm weakly to her mouth, covering it with the sleeve of her white dress. Grit settled into her eyes, too fast for her to blink it away, and she felt herself slipping down the stone of the crenellation, felt it shuddering beneath her hands, ready to crumble, to collapse.

Then someone gripped her beneath the arms, a guardsman, heaved her up as she coughed and hacked, and dragged her away, the fire in her gut exploding with the movement, tasting of acid and blood in the back of her throat.

She held on to consciousness a moment more, enough to see the captain whose name she did not know hauling her to safety.

And then everything went black.

I pulled away, stared down at the wreckage of the inner gates, watched as the parapet Eryn had just been pulled off of caved in, stone raining down onto the base of the promenade. I lifted up, shifted to the tower, and turned, staring down over the city, the taste of acid and blood moving with me, tainting the river. The harbor was filled with burning ships, the water crammed with bodies and debris, rising and falling with the waves stained red with blood. Smoke billowed through the afternoon skies, rising in thick columns from the city, from the harbor, from the watchtowers. Even as I watched, a building in the middle ward collapsed, dust rising in a thick cloud. And everywhere there was fire—on the wharf, in the warehouse district, in the inner city. Even in the slums.

It was the vision. Amenkor lay in ruins, the stench of smoke and blood and death clogging the air.

I turned from the image, sank down through the tower, down through the stone to the throne room, and settled into my body, breathing in with a hard, shuddering, painful gasp, tears at the corners of my eyes, weakness coursing through my arms, through my chest. And still the taste of acid and blood lingered.

Keven stood at the throne's side, guardsmen lining the walkway, stationed behind the pillars. I frowned in irritation, thought about ordering them all out of the room, but halted when I saw the set expression on Keven's face.

"They've broken through the gates," I said instead, my voice ragged, hoarse, my throat raw. "The Ochean is inside the palace."

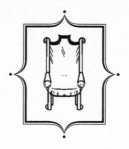

The Throne Room

KEVEN SHIFTED NERVOUSLY, the throne room utterly silent. Outside in the corridor, through the open double doors, the palace felt deserted. No servants tread the halls, no guardsmen guarded the entrance to the inner sanctum, nor the entrance to the throne room. The only sign of life came from Keven and the score of guardsmen lined up in the spaces between the columns along the central aisle.

She'll come straight to the throne room, Cerrin said.

I tensed at his voice, then relaxed. The voices had remained quiet since helping Eryn at the gates, so quiet I'd barely noticed they were there. Now, I felt them all—all of the previous Mistresses, the Seven who had created the Skewed Throne, the men and women who had touched the throne at some point and died because of it, like Alendor. They were all quiet, even the madmen, the silence in my head, behind the protective wall of Fire that still encircled them, eerie.

I could feel Cerrin and Liviann at the forefront, hovering at the edge of the white flame, Liviann slightly behind Cerrin. I could feel Atreus and Alleryn, Seth and Garus and Silicia, could smell their individual scents, all mingling.

She'll try to seize control of the throne, Cerrin added, his melancholy voice intense. *You can't let her take it, no matter the cost. The Chorl are ruthless. They'll destroy everything.* I could hear the echoes of the pain over his wife's death in his voice. Of his daughters' deaths.

"I don't intend to let her take it," I said, and a few of the guardsmen jumped at the sound of my voice.

Then, out in the corridor, came the tramp of boots on stone.

Everyone tensed, Keven taking a step forward, his hand falling to the pommel of his sword.

"Leave them to me," I said sharply.

He frowned without turning, but he didn't draw his sword.

The sound of footsteps grew louder, closer.

Then a group of five Chorl warriors stepped into the doorway to the throne room and halted, curved swords drawn and at the ready, gazes darting around the room, taking in me, Keven, the guardsmen along the sides.

They hesitated, unsettled, obviously expecting more resistance.

Someone barked a command in the corridor, then stepped to the center of the group of warriors.

The Chorl captain. The man with the circular tattoos on his cheeks, his ear half cut off.

He surveyed the throne room, his face set in a dark frown as the men to either side of him relaxed, his eyes finally settling on me.

I could see his hatred, could sense his malevolence, could almost taste it, like smoke.

Inside my head, I felt the voices in the throne stir.

See, Cerrin whispered.

The other voices murmured agreement.

Still watching me, he motioned to the side, and more Chorl warriors flooded the corridor outside. But they left a narrow space between them.

When her escort was in position, the Ochean moved into view, followed by the Chorl man in yellow robes carrying the reed scepter,

both stepping up to the Chorl captain as the others closed in behind them.

The Ochean hesitated at the edge of the throne room, then
stepped inside, alone, walking down the aisle between the pillars
imperiously, as if she'd already seized control, as if the throne—the
entire city of Amenkor—was already hers. Her captain followed her,
a pace behind, a few of the warriors behind him, fanning out to the
sides, their stances wary, gazes locked solidly on the guardsmen at
their flanks.

The Chorl in yellow robes remained behind, frowning.

My eyes narrowed with anger. When she'd made it halfway
down the aisle, I stood abruptly, felt the weakness from Reaching
shiver through my legs to the point I almost collapsed. But I steadied myself, shoved the weakness back.

The Ochean halted, lowered her head slightly as she considered
me, jaw clenched.

Behind me, I felt the throne begin to twist, reshaping itself into
another form. I felt its power reaching out, the voices stalking the
room like a predator hunting its prey. I could feel their hatred, as
harsh and malevolent as the expression on the Chorl captain's
face . . . or on the Ochean's.

Her eyes widened in surprise as the throne twisted, as the
power of the throne filled the room, but she crushed the reaction
swiftly, her glare settling back on me. Behind her, the man in yellow didn't bother hiding his surprise.

I smiled. "Welcome to Amenkor."

I didn't know if she understood the words, but she heard the
sarcasm, condescension, and hatred in my voice.

Her frown deepened, almost into a scowl.

Then she lashed out using the river, a whip crack of force that
snapped across the shield I raised at the last moment. I felt the tip
of the lash skid across the invisible barrier, sending ripples of force

out into the river, but before they could dissipate, I flung a barrage
of daggerlike shards across the throne room.

They hit her own shield like ice pellets, shattering into a thousand scintillate fragments of visible light. The guardsmen gasped.
Keven lurched forward, suddenly aware that I'd already been attacked, but—my voice cracking through the room—I barked,
"Stand back!" The Ochean spat something herself, her captain and
warriors edging back toward the doorway.

Keven growled, and I flashed him an angry glare.

"Don't interfere," I snapped. "No matter what happens."

Sword half drawn, he stepped back behind the throne grudgingly, sheathing his blade.

I turned back to the Ochean. Her eyes flashed, her shield pulsing. A solid wall of force, like Eryn's, the weave tight, controlled.

She had more practice at using the river than I did, more experience. Perhaps even more experience than Eryn.

A shiver of doubt coursed through me.

But you have us, Cerrin said, and his voice was no longer sad, no
longer weak. It was angry. All of the Seven radiated anger, had
shifted forward, ready to help.

Drawing a steadying breath, my heart thundering in my ears, I
stepped down the three steps of the dais to the main floor.

The Ochean watched me coldly.

I thought about the dagger at my waist, about the drills Eryn
had put me through in the courtyard, about Erick and Westen and
the hours of training with the Seekers.

And then I struck.

The blow fell on the Ochean's shield with blunt force, like a
mace, and I heard her grunt. I smiled in satisfaction, but the emotion was fleeting. Her wrist flicked and a blade, curved like the
Chorl warriors' blades, slashed into my own shield. I shunted the
stroke aside, let the power bleed out into the river, struck back with

the mace again, raining blows down left and right, dodging her sword slashes, shoving them aside when they struck, grunting with the effort. Sweat broke out on my forehead, began to trickle down my face, but I concentrated on her blade, watched the fluctuations in her shield as each of my blows landed, searching for a weak point.

We began circling each other, the Ochean edging left, me right. Her hands, fingers long and supple, flicked as she directed her sword. The shells in her necklace and laced through her hair clacked together, a strange counterpoint to the soundless and mostly invisible battle waged between us. Shards of light, in all colors, sparked from the shields occasionally, flaring and dying in a heartbeat, the guardsmen and Chorl warriors gasping at the more intense displays.

I could feel myself beginning to tire, to flag, drained by the Reachings I'd done to keep track of the battle in the city below, so I increased the intensity of the mace's blows, shifted them subtly so that they struck at odd angles, and still her shield held, shuddering under each blow, but steadying in a heartbeat, not weakening in the slightest.

My own shield began to fray at the edges. I pulled back some of the power from the mace, used it to fortify the shield, and just when I felt I'd have to break off my attack entirely, the Ochean withdrew, her sword rippling away on the river.

I gasped, noticed we were both heaving, sweat dripping down our faces, staining our clothes.

We'd circled enough that our backs were facing the pillars, the throne to my left, its shifting form at the edge of my vision. The guardsmen and Chorl warriors were utterly silent, waiting, no one daring to enter the walkway between us. Not when they couldn't see the weapons being wielded.

The Ochean said something, the words sharp, but edged with respect.

Then she sneered, emitted a short, piercing shriek, and her arm lashed out.

She'd changed tactics. Instead of a curved blade, she hit me with a barrage of fistlike punches, aimed at my midsection at first, then shifting the blows outward.

I hissed through my teeth, felt some of the force seeping through the shield, striking my body with light taps. But if the shield failed . . .

I cried out, poured all of my strength into the shield, not even attempting to counterstrike, and even that wasn't enough.

I needed more strength, more power.

The voices in the throne responded.

I felt the surge of their support, felt the shield around me sharpen as Alleryn and Atreus reached forward with subtle flows, felt additional strength pouring into my arms from Seth and Garus, Cerrin allowing the previous Mistresses to help through the Fire. The Ochean's eyes widened slightly, only for a moment, and then the pummeling redoubled, her eyes narrowing, the fists striking at random now, left, right, midsection, thigh, chest, one sharp jab to the head, to the throat, but the shield held.

I began to fight back, Liviann and Silicia taking over part of the shield. Using daggerlike thrusts, I slashed across the Ochean's shield, cut across her eyes, saw her flinch back, then recover. I used every technique Erick had taught me beyond the Dredge, everything Westen and the Seekers had taught me in the rooms deeper within the palace, everything to maim, to kill, to distract—

And then I realized that even with the throne behind me, even with the Seven and their knowledge, my strength was fading.

But how . . . ?

I suddenly recalled Eryn in the garden, beating at my shield, no longer attempting to pierce it, simply hitting me over and over with force, battering me heedlessly.

Because she was attacking me somewhere else, subtly, the blunt force merely a diversion.

I continued slashing with my dagger, but began searching the river, searching my shield—

And there, I saw the pinhole, saw the threadlike conduit snaking back toward the Ochean, saw my strength being leeched away and used to supplement the Ochean's, just as Eryn had done during training.

I felt a seething flash of rage envelop me, caught the Ochean's eye across the aisle between us, then withdrew the power I'd focused on the dagger slashes and with a speed Eryn had drilled into me in the gardens formed a needlelike dart of raw force—a second, a third—and fed them into the Ochean's conduit one after the other.

The Ochean screamed when the first dart struck, her attack faltering. The second slammed into her a heartbeat later, followed by the third, spinning her around, her hands clutching her side, the conduit between my shield and her snapping as she withdrew it with a jerk.

The pummeling fists dissipated. Her shield wavered, flickered, and began to fail as well, but even as I stepped forward, even as I seized part of the river to retaliate, it shuddered and held.

But her conduit had given me an idea.

Breath coming in hoarse gasps, the Ochean spun back, eyes flashing, straightened as much as she could, pain clear on her face, one hand still clamped to her side. She spat something vicious, her face twisted into a cruel scowl, contorting the subtle beauty of her features. With her free hand, still half-turned, she lashed out again with the sword, the stroke heavier, weighted with more force, more thrust, shuddering into my shield, forcing me down into a low crouch. I cried out as it struck again, and again, then retaliated with my own strokes, using the lash as she'd done earlier. But my cries were exaggerated, the cracks of the lash meant to distract, as she'd tried to distract me.

I began to form my own conduit. Not to siphon off strength, as the Ochean had done. No. This conduit was meant to work in reverse, to send something to the Ochean.

What are you doing? Liviann snapped. *She'll send something back, as you did! Something more lethal than darts!*

Let her work! Cerrin spat, cutting off any further remarks from the Seven.

I ignored them, formed the river into a small funnel on my side of the shield, let the tail of the funnel snake outward, toward the Ochean. It stretched, shuddered beneath the flows of the battle on the river above it, stretched and thinned—

Until its tail touched the Ochean's shield.

I felt her gasp, saw her begin searching the river for the conduit, her eyes flicking left and right. The sword strokes lessened, their strength reduced as she concentrated elsewhere.

What's she doing! Liviann snapped, screaming at the other voices in the throne, trying to gain the support of the other Seven. *Garus! Seth! She's going to get us all killed!*

Wait, Cerrin said. He'd seen. He understood. I could hear it in his voice.

Give her a chance, Liviann, Garus growled, although there was doubt in his voice.

I brought the mouth of the funnel close to the Fire at my core. White tendrils of flame began streaming down the tail, snaking as the conduit twisted and roiled in the currents, but moving steadily toward the Ochean.

The Ochean's sword strokes halted, her attention completely on the river, her head snapping to the side, frantic.

The Fire had covered half the distance between us . . . two thirds.

If I could tag her—as I'd tagged Erick, as I'd tagged Eryn and Avrell—if I could tag her . . .

I could use the Fire to seize control of her.

The Fire had almost reached her when the Ochean saw the conduit.

She lashed out instantly, a short, decisive gesture, like a cleaver being brought down on a block of wood.

The funnel I'd created snapped, its tail severed where it had been attached to the Ochean's shield, severed at the tip, so that none of the Fire reached her.

The funnel snapped back, the Fire, the river, lashing out, striking me hard, shattering my shield and throwing me back. I screamed, crashed into the pillar behind me, head cracking into stone, and crumpled to the granite floor, stunned.

I'd barely taken a breath when half the voices of the throne shouted *Varis!* in warning, the sound mingling with the Ochean's shriek of triumph.

I flung a shield up, half dazed, felt the Seven pouring their own strength into it, felt the river roil as the Ochean manipulated it, her sword falling fast and swift. Twisting where I lay, blows raining down on the shield, filtering through with bruising force, I gasped, tried to strengthen my defenses, felt the Ochean's sword change to fists, to thrown daggers, a lash. I heard the Ochean stalking across the floor, felt her presence as she stood above me, her hands stretched out, fingers spread, her face a hideous mask of scorn and hatred and cruelty. Her eyes blazed with determination, any pain I'd caused earlier with the darts masked, buried beneath her contempt.

And I saw my death. I felt drained, barely able to sustain the shield, even with the strength of the Seven, of the other voices of the throne, infusing me. I'd expended too much energy following the battle in the city below, used up my reserves. My muscles trembled with every blow, the seepage through the shield increasing, each stroke sinking deeper and deeper into my flesh.

I felt a shudder of regret pass through me, heard it break free in a sob of pain, of heartrending defeat. I thought of everything I'd worked for over the last winter: the reconstruction of the warehouses, the desperate search for food, the setup of the work force and the communal kitchens. I thought of everything that Amenkor had accomplished, all lost now, burning beneath the

Ochean's fires, nothing but charred, smoking husks on the harbor and in the streets. I thought of Avrell and Borund, of Catrell and Westen, struggling to hold together the city as Eryn went insane, then struggling to recoup when I'd supplanted her as Mistress and the food supply ran short, unknowingly fighting against Alendor and his alliance with the Chorl.

And I thought of Erick, of his beaten, tortured body lying in the room of pillows, in the Ochean's personal chambers.

Tortured by the woman glaring down at me now, eyes flashing with malice.

Erick.

She'd kept him alive, even when she knew she'd taken everything from him, when she'd learned everything she could about Amenkor and the throne.

Beneath the Ochean's assault, beneath the despair, I hesitated.

Why? Why had she kept him alive? There was no reason, no need. Not any longer, not once she'd decided to attack Amenkor first. But she'd kept him alive anyway, had brought him here to Amenkor to witness the attack. . . .

I felt the hesitation shift into certainty.

She'd kept him alive because she wanted him to see what she'd done to Amenkor when it was over.

I felt myself weakening, felt the shield I held faltering, edging closer and closer to my body, more and more of the force of her blows passing through to strike my body. My hands were raised now, as if to ward off the attack.

In another few heartbeats, my shield would fail.

But perhaps . . .

I cried out, harshly, and as if my strength had given out completely, I let the shield fall.

The voices of the throne gasped. Liviann leaped forward, tried to take over as she had once before and reestablish the shield, but

I used the Fire to hold her back, heard her scream with frustration, flail against the restraint, felt the other Seven reach forward and haul her back, subduing her.

The Ochean hesitated as the shield failed, as if she thought it were some kind of ruse, but then a slow smile touched her dark blue lips, her almost black eyes. A malicious smile. A triumphant smile.

She drew in a deep breath . . .

Then struck me again, fists punching hard and sharp, once to my face and once to my stomach. My lip split, the pain like fire, and I gagged, curled up into a ball as I'd learned to do on the Dredge, knees tight to my chest, arms close, hands covering my face. But the fists didn't stop. They continued, struck my back, my butt, my forearms, my shoulders, the back of my head. The voices of the throne cried out in protest, tried to seize control, raise the shield again, more of them this time, not just Liviann, but I forced them all back, held them all in check, felt Cerrin block their access through the White Fire. I suffered through the Ochean's beating, felt my strength flagging, thought of Erick lying among the bloody pillows, thought of the denizens of the slums pouring out across the Dredge's bridge to attack the Chorl, thought of all the death and destruction in the city below. . . .

And finally the punches slowed . . . and stopped.

I lay on the throne room floor, trembling, barely able to breathe, my back, my shoulders, my arms and lower legs bruised by the force of the Ochean's hatred. My muscles screamed with pain. I shuddered, tasted blood from my split lip, but dared not move. I wasn't certain I could move.

Above me, I heard the Ochean gasping, her breaths thick with phlegm. I listened as she slowly calmed, heard her dress rustle as she lowered her arms.

When her breathing had almost returned to normal, she spat

on me. I flinched, but didn't move, let the spittle trickle down my neck, beneath my chin, mixing with my blood. I kept my hands tight over my face, and waited—for ten heartbeats, for an eternity—

Then I heard her move away.

I drew in a shallow breath and held it, listening intently as her footsteps retreated. Carefully, I lowered one hand, peeked out through my spread fingers.

The Ochean had moved to the center of the aisle again, had turned to face the Skewed Throne, twisting and morphing on its dais. Keven had shifted forward, his face grim, hand on his sword.

I silently cursed him, willed him to stand aside.

The Ochean stepped forward, moving toward the throne.

Keven tensed, made to draw his blade—

With a careless motion, the Ochean used the river to fling him out of the way.

He struck the stone pillar to one side, grunted as he collapsed to the dais, and didn't move again. But I could still see him breathing.

I felt a renewed surge of hatred.

The Ochean stepped up to the dais, movements poised, casual, even though her blue dress was stained with sweat. She turned at the top, surveyed the throne room, expression triumphant, locking meaningfully on the Chorl captain's face, on the man in the yellow robes with the reed scepter. Something passed between them, something I didn't understand, but the Chorl captain's eyes blazed with hatred a moment before he gave her a grudging nod. The man in yellow merely frowned.

The Ochean's gaze fell on me. I saw a flicker of satisfaction when she saw me watching.

She wanted me to see, as she'd wanted Erick to see Amenkor's destruction.

Then she sank onto the throne.

I lifted my head, all pretension set aside. It hurt, more than I expected, and required almost all of my strength. But I wasn't as beaten and drained as I'd led her to believe.

On the dais, the throne shuddered and twisted. The Ochean sucked in a sharp breath of surprise. Her eyes widened and she suddenly stilled, muscles rigid, back stiff.

The voices of the throne paused. The predatory presence of the throne in the room hesitated.

Then the voices rose into a shriek . . . and pounced. As they'd pounced on me when I'd sat on the throne almost five months before. A maelstrom of screams, roaring for attention, howling their hatred, their fear, their disgust. A hurricane that leaped toward the blue-skinned woman who sat on the throne.

And they dragged me along with them.

†

I found myself back in the marketplace, trapped in a crowd, jostled and crushed as everyone tried to shove their way to the center of the plaza, everyone screaming, yelling to be heard over everyone else, the voices all melding into an indistinguishable roar. Fear lanced through me as I stumbled and almost fell, shorter than most of those around me. With sudden horror, I realized that here, if I fell, I'd be trampled to death.

But someone reached out and grabbed me by the arm, hauled me upright and pulled me close to them.

"Careful now!" Cerrin bellowed, smiling tentatively down at me.

"What's happening?" I asked, trying to be heard over the noise.

Cerrin's face grew stern. "The Ochean touched the throne. She's trying to seize control."

"We can't let her!"

"I know." He glanced around at the faces in the crowd, gripped me tighter as the mob suddenly surged left. Someone's elbow jabbed into my side, made me gasp. "They're fighting her," he said, nodding to indicate the people—all of the previous Mistresses, all of those that had touched the throne before this. "But she's strong."

I glanced around, noted the pure hatred of those in the crowd, saw the panic beneath the anger, the fear. I could smell it, a rank stench of sweat and blood. But the faces of all of the old Mistresses, of all of those that had touched the throne over the last fifteen hundred years, were determined.

I turned back to Cerrin. "Take me to her."

He stared down into my eyes, frowning, his own eyes filled with doubt.

But then he nodded.

We began working our way through the crowd, Cerrin shoving the terrified and frantic people aside, forcing a passage wide enough for me to squeeze through, then roughly following behind. A few people backed off when they saw it was me, a few spat in my face for betraying them.

I ignored them all, anger building as the crowd grew thicker, more desperate. I started using my elbows, my fingers, jabbing into tender muscles, punching soft flesh. I came up against a man—face unshaven, several teeth missing, hair patchy, thin, and wild—who leered down at me, reached forward to grab my breast. I kneed him in the groin and stepped on his back as I passed.

Then suddenly, I broke through an edge, stepped out into a small space barely three paces across, the Ochean before me, her back turned. She slashed at the crowd around her with a sword, curved like the Chorl warriors', the strokes smooth but with a hint of desperation. Bodies lay at her feet, most moaning, blood flowing from cuts to their faces, to their chests.

She seemed to sense someone behind her, spun.

Her eyes widened in shock and she jerked back.

I smiled, then reached out and touched her.

✝

I stood on a porch built of thousands upon thousands of wooden poles, like reeds but thicker and segmented. Huge green leaves covered a latticework of more wooden poles overhead for shade, and lay in thick layers on the floor. I could feel more of the poles beneath the leaves through the soles of my bare feet.

I moved to the edge of the porch, out into the sunlight.

Below, the land sloped down to a pristine beach, the sand a blinding white, the cove beyond a myriad range of greens and blues. The porch was surrounded by more huge, flat leaves, by dense foliage and tall trees, the trunks bare until they branched out at the top into dozens of huge, serrated palms. Closer to the beach, I could see small houses made of the same poles as the porch, thatched in the palm fronds, sandy paths leading from house to house, down to the beach, where strange boats had been drawn up onto the sand. Long and narrow, they could fit barely two men side-by-side, and had no sails.

I stared down at the scene, hands crossed arrogantly over my chest, and watched the people moving among the huts, or down on the shore. Blue-skinned people.

My people.

Then, the ground shuddered.

I frowned, reached out to steady myself against the edge of the porch. But the trembling had already subsided.

Down on the beach, the people near the boats and in the shallows had halted their activities, were now staring inland, their hands raised to shade their eyes as they looked up.

I turned, shaded my own eyes against the glare of the sun, and stared up beyond my summer palace.

The land rose in a gentle slope beyond the palace, to the base of a huge peaked mountain, the sides of the mountain covered in dense jungle, the peak itself conical.

The mountain had been silent for almost fifty years, but now . . .

Now, a thin column of smoke rose from its crater.

†

Back in the marketplace, I frowned, then concentrated, shifted the focus of the throne, filtered through the Ochean's memories.

†

And found myself back in the summer palace, in one of the interior rooms, seated on a throne built of the thick reeds, draped with cloth in greens and golds and purples and skeins of shells. Chorl warriors stood to either side of the throne, wearing breeches of dark blue filmy cloth, their chests bare and covered with tattoos in circular patterns. A figure knelt before me, bowed down, head pressed into the floor. He was dressed in yellow breeches, the tattoos on his chest curved crescents, like sickles, and black instead of dark blue.

The kneeling man raised his head.

"Ochean, the prophecy says—"

I hissed, cut him off. "I don't care what the prophecy says, Haqtl!"

The Chorl warriors around me shifted uncomfortably, and I sensed their anger. This man was a priest, communed with the gods.

And the warriors were pledged to the gods, not to me.

I clenched my jaw, forced my irritation and impatience down.

In a grudging voice, laced with undertones of scorn, I said, "Continue."

Haqtl, his expression darkening, began again. "The prophecy says the mountain will destroy us. It was sung ages ago, and now the time has come."

I shoved myself up out of the throne, began pacing before it. "You know this for certain? The gods have spoken?"

"The gods have spoken. They forewarned us ages ago, and there have been signs. The land rumbles. Poison gases boil from the ocean, killing the fish. And then came the Fire of Heaven from the west."

I spat a curse, heard the warriors shift again. I stifled a growl, suppressed the urge to slap Haqtl, to beat him. I knew the gods had not spoken, that there were no gods, that the priests were opposing me to gain more power, as usual. They were seizing upon the now constant rumbling from the mountain and using it against me. And the sea always boiled before the mountain erupted. It had done so before.

But the Fire of Heaven . . .

I shuddered as I recalled it sweeping in from the ocean, falling on the islands of the Chorl. It had covered the evening harvest in a pall of fear, the weak-souled villagers in their ships screaming as it approached, trying to make it back to shore.

For all the good it did them. There had been no escape. The Fire had touched everyone.

And the power! The raw energy! I didn't know where the Fire had come from, but I wanted it, needed it if I was to continue to rule the Chorl.

I could not deny the priest the Fire of Heaven, no matter how much it galled me.

The anger seethed beneath my skin, forced my hands into balled fists. This should not be happening. Not during my reign, not now. I'd crushed the priests, had regained the power of my family, power that had been stolen from my father.

This should not be happening!

I spun toward the warriors, saw them frowning at me darkly, their expressions troubled, rebellious.

My gaze fell on the captain of the warriors, on Atlatik, on his half-missing ear and the tattoos that riddled his face.

The warriors would side with Haqtl, with the priests, with the gods. I could see it in Atlatik's eyes, in his stance. He would do anything to thwart me, no matter what he felt about the gods, about the priests and their manipulations.

I emitted a strangled sound of frustration, the urge to lash out, to wipe the doubting looks from his and the warriors' faces, almost overwhelming.

But I needed them. I couldn't control the islands without them.

I moved to stand before the priest, glared down at him imperiously, almost reached out to strangle him when he glanced up, his eyes victorious.

"What," I spat, then tempered my voice, gritting my teeth. "What is it that the *gods* expect us to do?"

Shifting position, Haqtl's expression became serious. "We must abandon the islands. We must take to the ocean and attack the lands to the east, as we did once before."

I recoiled from Haqtl in shock, fell back into the throne, the shells of my necklace and those on the throne clattering together.

Even the warriors seemed stunned.

"What do you mean?" I said, voice weak.

Haqtl stood slowly, gathered himself together, and said calmly, "I mean that the mountain will destroy the entire island when it erupts. If we stay, we will all die.

"We must find another place to live. And the only other place to live is the coastlands to the east."

✝

I shuddered, drew back from the Ochean's memory, my stomach sick with anger, with hatred.

Then I shifted the focus again.

✝

The ground jolted, seemed to fall away beneath my feet. I screamed in the darkness, warriors reaching out to catch me before I fell, and then we continued running, fleeing, following a line of torches through the trees to the port, men and women and children shrieking into the night as they picked themselves up off the ground where they had fallen.

Behind, hidden by the jungle, something hideous, something horrendous, roared. A bellowing sound, like a thousand claps of thunder, that slammed into the air around me, that drowned out the screams of all of the people running to the port. My heart pounded in my chest, thudded in my ears, and I gasped, felt my escort tearing down the path around me, heard them shouting commands, shoving stragglers aside.

The ground lurched again as we crested the rise and stumbled down the slope to the beachhead, following the torches to the docks on the bay where the ships waited. Men, women, and children crowded onto decks, others scrambling up the planks.

My ship was docked at the end of the pier.

The mountain roared again, the wood of the dock shuddering, then we reached the plank and sprinted up onto the deck. As soon as I was aboard, the ship cast off, edging out into the water.

I turned, chest heaving, arms trembling with terror that was slowly beginning to calm.

Behind, on the dock, people were screaming as they tried to find room on the ships. Some had already cast off, as we had, were pulling away from the island as quickly as possible, their decks packed with panicked men and women. As I watched, some tumbled overboard.

Then the air seemed to shudder, another booming thunderclap resounded, and I jerked my attention upward.

The mountain had exploded. Thick jets of magma leaped into the sky from the crater, throwing up spumes of ash and steam and gas in a thick roiling column as black as the night. Lava flows were already streaming down the mountain's sides, rushing to the ocean.

Another thunderclap. A shuddering of the air. And what seemed like the entire western side of the mountain trembled, then slid slowly, horrifyingly, into the water.

I stared at the destruction in shock, the tremors of panic fading as the ship drew farther away from the island. But they were replaced with tremors of fear, with a hollow feeling of hopelessness, of disbelief.

The priests had been right. The mountain was tearing the island apart. There were other islands in the chain, other places to flee to, but none large enough to support the Chorl for long. If the mountain continued to erupt, the Chorl would die.

The only option was the coastland to the east. We'd attacked them once before, been repelled after five vicious years of fighting. But we'd grown since then, learned much.

A cold sensation filled the hollowness. My brow creased in thought, with purpose. I could use this. I could use this against the priests, against Haqtl. I could turn his own gods against him.

A smile touched my lips.

Perhaps the gods were correct.

Perhaps it *was* time to cross the ocean.

✝

I shivered at the cold calculation of the Ochean's mind, skimmed farther ahead in her memories, saw the Chorl fleet gather and head east under the Ochean's and the priests' direction, watched them attack a group of islands—the Boreaite Isles—and overrun the ports. They began raiding the trading lanes, seizing entire ships and taking them back to the isles, converting them into fighting ships to expand their fleet. I watched, sickened, as they slaughtered entire crews.

And then they'd attacked *The Maiden*.

✝

"What do we do with him?" Atlatik asked, voice rough with contempt.

I glared down at the crumpled form of the guardsman on the deck of the ship we'd just conquered. All of the other crew had been killed, and Atlatik's warriors were tethering the ship to our own so it could be towed back to the isles, the fires being put out by the Chosen.

Before I could answer, my mind spinning—he had part of the Fire of Heaven inside him! I could taste it!—someone approached from behind, Atlatik stepping to one side.

Only one other person could force Atlatik to move.

"Haqtl," I said, trying to swallow the bitterness that flooded my mouth at his name.

"Another victory," he said. "We must thank the gods."

I almost snorted, but pursed my lips instead. "The gods have favored us today."

"In what way?" Suspicious, wary. As he should be.

I smiled.

"This man has the Fire of Heaven inside him. I can feel it."

Atlatik gasped, glanced down at the man who lay unconscious on the deck, his hand moving unconsciously to the tattoos on his neck, stroking them as he uttered an inaudible prayer. He'd almost killed the man, before I'd even gotten to the ship.

Haqtl knelt down next to the bloody body, spread one hand over the man's head and closed his eyes. I felt the Elements shudder as he probed, searching.

Then even Haqtl gasped, standing quickly, as if he'd been jerked upright. He turned to me, eyes blazing with fervor. "We have to heal him, find out where he came from, find out everything we can about him."

Interesting. I could see how I'd gain control of Atlatik and the warriors, could see how I could get even the priests to follow me. This man was the key. This man, and the piece of the Fire of Heaven he carried inside him. He could lead me to the Fire itself, Haqtl would drag the Chorl there even against my wishes. I could see the intent in his eyes, could feel his body trembling with it.

But of course I wanted the Fire as much as Haqtl, wanted it even more.

I broke Haqtl's gaze, glanced down at the warrior's body. Such strange pale brown skin. And no tattoos. It made me shudder.

"Oh, I intend to find out where he came from," I said. And when we finally begin attacking the coastline in ernest, we'll attack there first.

Haqtl breathed a sigh of relief.

Neither Haqtl nor Atlatik saw the underlying twist in my smile.

†

I withdrew from the Ochean's memories, stared hard into her face as my hand dropped to my side. I'd relived her memories in a matter of heartbeats, her expression still locked in shock as she recognized me.

Then it twisted into bitter hatred.

She lashed out with her sword, but the blade passed through air as Cerrin yanked me back into the crowd. The mob closed in around us instantly.

"What did you find out?" Cerrin asked.

"Why they're here, why they attacked us. Why they returned." I caught his gaze. "They had to come. The island they were living on has been destroyed. They didn't have any other place to go to."

Cerrin grunted, then swore, glancing around at the turmoil of the throne.

"What?" I asked. I could sense a change in the mob, a subtle shift.

The voices were beginning to panic.

"She's beginning to win," Cerrin answered. Overhead, the sun-lit sky above the marketplace began to darken, clouds roiling in. Cerrin glanced toward them, then back down at me. "I don't think we can defeat her."

His voice had changed. The melancholy air had returned. The hatred that had enlivened it had bled away, replaced with resignation.

Around us, the jostling had eased. There didn't seem to be as many people anymore.

"We can't let her have the throne," I said, and desperation tinged my voice.

"She's too powerful," Cerrin said, and now his voice seemed dead.

The clouds had completely blanketed the sky now. The crowd had thinned to half its original number, the people that remained milling about in uncertainty, most with expressions of defeat on their faces.

Liviann suddenly appeared at my side, trailing Atreus and Garus and the rest of the Seven. "Do something! You can't let her win! She'll destroy everything!"

"I tried!" I spat. "I thought the throne would destroy her, as it did Alendor, as it almost did me!"

Liviann scowled. She turned to Cerrin. "What else can we do?"

He shook his head. "Nothing."

"We can't let her take the throne," Liviann hissed. "We can't. Not the Chorl. We defeated them once already. We can't have them back. Remember what they did. Remember the death. Remember your wife, your children, for the gods' sakes!"

"I know!" Cerrin spat, his face strangely enraged and vulnerable at the same time. "I know! They killed them, slaughtered the people of Venitte, decimated the entire southern coastline! Do you think I don't remember?"

"Then do something!" Liviann screamed.

"What?" he spat. "What can we do?"

Liviann fell into bitter silence, glanced toward me.

"Can we destroy the throne?" I asked quietly. I was thinking of their attack on Venitte, of the fires, of Cerrin's daughters. Of Erick and Laurren's sacrifice. It would all have been for nothing if the Chorl claimed the throne.

Liviann harrumphed.

But Cerrin stilled.

"What?" Liviann asked.

He stared at her in silence for a long moment, then said quietly, "We can."

Liviann frowned.

Around us, the crowd had been reduced to no more than a hundred people.

Garus shoved himself forward. "You know we can, Liviann. And it might be the only way."

"Would you rather have the Chorl take control of the throne?" Alleryn spat. "I don't like it any better than you do, but considering the consequences. . . ."

The rest of the Seven nodded in agreement.

"We'll die," Liviann said, but her voice was quiet.

"We're already dead," Cerrin said. "We've been dead for far too long."

Liviann shot him a glare, then focused on me.

There were only fifty people left in the square now.

"Here," she said, taking Cerrin's hand, "we'll show you how."

When she touched my hand, I gasped.

†

The clouds over the marketplace had darkened, rushed past so close to the ground I thought I could reach up and touch them. The buildings at the edge of the marketplace were gone, had blackened and vanished. There was no one left on the plaza anymore, no more voices, no more bodies, except for me.

And the Ochean.

She stood ten paces away, her blue dress sweaty, torn in a few places. Her chest heaved as she breathed in deeply, almost panting, but her expression was hard, determined. She still held the curved sword in one hand.

Reaching down, I drew the dagger from my belt, the blade dull in the half-light of the plaza.

"I can't let you have the throne," I said.

The Ochean hesitated, then grinned.

She settled into an open stance, her sword steady.

I slid into a crouch, dagger held before me.

We held each other's gazes a long moment.

And then the Ochean lurched forward, brought the sword down in a diagonal strike.

I dodged, not even attempting to parry, knowing that my dagger wouldn't last long. This was a distraction, nothing more. A ruse. But I'd try to hurt her as much as I could nonetheless, using everything Westen and Erick had taught me. As I moved, I hissed, cut upward under her guard, but she was too quick, spinning back and out of reach as she brought the sword around, slashing across my midsection. I leaped back, felt the blade slice through my shirt, felt a stinging line of fire across my stomach, felt blood. But it was only a scratch.

I settled instantly into another crouch, the Ochean doing the same. I tried to ignore the cut, but I felt my shirt sticking to the wound.

In my peripheral vision, I noticed that the marketplace had shrunk. The clouds were lower still, the darkness on the sides pulling inward as the Ochean solidified her control of the throne.

The Ochean smirked as she saw the blood staining my shirt. Anger rose, but before I could use it or suppress it, she attacked.

Her blade flashed as she cut and I dodged, stroke, counter-stroke. I ducked under her guard, nicked her on the arm, and she cursed, thrust out hard. Sidestepping, I tried for another mark, but she twisted, turned her own blade inward, the edge slicing down along my thigh. I screamed, backpedaling fast to get out of reach.

I glanced down at my leg, the scent of blood sharp. This cut was deeper and burned with a white-hot intensity. I sucked in a breath through clenched teeth, blew it out through my nose. Sweat dripped from my forehead, from my hair, from my chin.

I settled into a guarded position. The Ochean did the same.

She closed in again. But this time, I couldn't dodge as quickly, the slice along my thigh burning, seething in pain. I cried out, cut in hard, and twisted as she lunged, missed, brought my dagger back up and out, but her elbow crunched into my wrist. My hand went numb, and I dropped the dagger, even as she grabbed me hard about the waist and drew me in tight against her, my head against her shoulder.

Before I could react, she brought the sword up, placed its edge against my throat.

I gasped, tried to arch away, but she tightened her grip, pressed the blade even closer, enough that I felt it cut into flesh.

I grew still.

She chuckled, the sound reverberating through my skin, her breath against my cheek.

Then the muscles in her arm tensed as she readied to slit my throat.

I closed my eyes and dove, down and down, deep inside myself, deep below the plaza, deeper and deeper into the throne, into its essence, into its heart. I felt the others in the throne brushing past me, like spider's silk, their threads subdued and tangled in the Ochean's power. I felt their wrath at being overtaken, and it drove me onward.

Until suddenly the spider's silk of the others thinned, until only seven threads remained, converging and twining together the deeper I sank, throbbing with life, with power. I followed the threads, dove faster as I felt the Ochean's blade far above begin to cut deeper, felt skin parting, felt blood beginning to flow—

And then suddenly the threads ended, all seven coming together at the throne's heart: a blinding, pulsing, pure-white light.

I hesitated a moment, transfixed. The ends of the seven threads at the center of the light touched, were held together by the Seven who had created the throne, by the strength of the magic that had bound them, by the strength of the throne itself. The raw energy, the pureness of it, made me shudder in awe.

Then I reached out, and with a twist, broke the seven threads apart.

†

I gasped, breath entering my lungs with a shudder, and reached up for my throat. My arm screamed with pain, my hand touching blood, and my heart stopped, fear slashing through my heart—that I'd been too late, that the Ochean had cut my throat.

But then I heard someone else gasp, heard voices cry out in shock.

I opened my eyes and stared across the stone floor of the throne room. The blood came from my split lip, not a cut throat. The pain came from the bruises of the Ochean's rage.

The Ochean.

I lurched upright, almost passed out as every muscle in my body shrieked, but steadied myself with my hands.

The Ochean still sat on the Skewed Throne. Her face was intent, focused inward, but it was the throne that caught my attention.

It had settled into a shape: a granite seat, wide, with arms that flared slightly to the side; short, fat legs; a back rounded and scalloped like a seashell.

But something wasn't quite right. One of the arms of the throne hadn't changed to fit the new form. Its top was curled, the side shaped like an S.

Like the arm of my throne.

Something pulsed, as if a wave had swept over the room, a wave felt only in your skin. The air thickened, grew suddenly heavy, and began to tingle. The guardsmen to either side shifted back; the Chorl at the door backed out into the corridor. All except the Chorl captain Atlatik and the Chorl priest Haqtl.

The Ochean stiffened, cried out sharply, then arched back, the muscles in her neck standing out in a silent scream.

Beneath her, the throne began to twist, slowly at first, then the pace accelerated, faster and faster, shifting from throne to throne, passing through all of the previous forms, from ruler to ruler starting with my own and working backward. A grating sound filled the room, began to shudder through the stone of the floor, through the pillars, escalating to a piercing shriek.

And then suddenly the throne stopped. On a form I'd seen once before, when Eryn had first thrust me onto its seat: a rough granite block with a straight rectangular back.

Its original form, before it had become the Skewed Throne, before the Seven had lost their lives in its forging.

The grating sound peaked, steadied, began to tremble—

And then it snapped.

There was no sound, no light, no smell. There was nothing to feel, nothing to touch.

Except on the river.

On the river, something exploded.

I felt the force blow over me, a gale that thrust me back, that shoved me hard into the pillar behind me, that deafened me with its intensity. It washed over me for a heartbeat, two, three . . .

And then it faded.

The density on the air sank down to nothing.

I sat on the floor and breathed in deeply, blood coating my neck, my entire body throbbing, my lip pulsing with the beat of my heart . . .

And then realized something was missing.

I could no longer feel the city, could no longer feel its pulse, the throb of its life, of its people.

I felt strangely empty. Hollow.

On the throne, the Ochean's body suddenly slumped forward, then tilted and fell to the dais, her dress rustling. Behind her, the throne split, a jagged crack appearing in the granite down its back.

No one in the throne room moved.

I shifted, winced as I pulled my legs underneath me and forced myself to a crouch, then up, using the pillar for support, until I faced the Chorl captain, until I faced Atlatik.

Trying not to tremble, gathering what little strength I had left, I growled, "It's over."

I don't know if he understood me, but he glared at me. Behind him, his warriors suddenly stepped forward, surrounding him and Haqtl in a wall of men.

Instantly, the palace guardsmen under Keven's control leaped forward, swords snicking from sheaths. I had my own escort in no more than a breath.

Pushing myself away from the pillar at my back, I stepped forward, raised my hands as if I were going to use the river, as the Ochean would have done.

Haqtl barked a sharp order, and I felt the river ripple as he erected a defense around them both.

I hesitated. I couldn't sustain another pitched battle using the river.

Haqtl spat something else, his voice leaden with scorn. He motioned toward the Ochean's dead body, to the cracked throne on the dais, and spat on the ground. He would have felt the power of the throne being released, could sense that there was no power there now.

And he could sense that the throne had nothing to do with the White Fire, what the Chorl called the Fire of Heaven.

Behind me, I heard Keven stir where he'd collapsed, regaining consciousness.

Atlatik frowned as Haqtl spoke, seemed shocked when he spat in the direction of the Ochean. But he was listening, his eyes never leaving my face.

Keven stood and came to my side, one hand on the pommel of his sword.

"Go!" I shouted at the Chorl. And then I gathered as much of the river as I could, saw Haqtl's eyes go wide, saw him reach out and catch Atlatik's arm.

Atlatik broke. With a barked order, the Chorl on edge, they began a careful backward retreat to the door of the throne room.

The palace guardsmen shifted forward, following them.

As soon as they left the room, vanishing in a sudden dash down the outside corridor, I let the river go, sweat pouring down my face.

"Mistress?" Keven said, and I heard the request in his voice.

"Kill them," I said, voice wavering with exhaustion, thinking of Erick, of Laurren, of everyone who'd died in the city today. "Kill them all."

And then I collapsed.

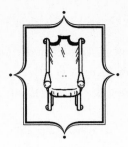

Epilogue

I AWOKE IN MY CHAMBERS, the breeze from the ocean billowing in the curtains over the balcony. Keven was speaking quietly to Avrell and Eryn near the open doorway, half hidden by the curtains.

I tried to sit up, but moaned instead.

The conversation broke off, and all three rushed over to the bed, smiling. Eryn seemed on the verge of tears, and even Avrell's smile was strained, the skin around his eyes tight. His arm was in a sling and tied across his chest.

"Don't get up," Keven commanded. "The healer said you weren't to move."

I didn't tell him I couldn't move. Every part of my body protested when I breathed.

I caught Avrell's eyes, held them. "The Chorl."

He straightened. "They retreated to their ships and left."

"Once the Ochean died," Keven added, "all of the fight seemed to leave them. We harried them to the wharf, slaughtered them as they boarded their ships."

I sighed in relief. Amenkor had been the Ochean's target,

Haqtl's target, not Atlatik's. And they'd wanted the Fire of Heaven. Once Haqtl realized the Fire wasn't here, there was no reason to stay and fight. Not when they'd lost the Ochean.

"And the city?"

Avrell smiled thinly. "It will survive."

I snorted, but nodded, settling back into the pillows.

"Varis?" Eryn stepped forward, her face lined with concern. There were shadows under her eyes, and it looked as if she'd aged ten years. One arm lay over her stomach and I remembered the pain she'd felt as she'd resisted the Ochean's advance at the gates. "Varis, the throne—"

"I know," I said, cutting her off.

She didn't know what to say, her expression lost.

Then Keven cleared his throat and Eryn stepped back awkwardly. "There is one other thing," he said, then hesitated, as if uncertain he should tell me.

"What?"

He glanced toward Avrell and Eryn, then said, "Westen brought Erick back."

I sat up instantly, sucked in a sharp breath, and through gritted teeth said, "Take me to him."

All three seemed about to protest.

I let my expression darken.

"Take me to him *now*."

†

Westen had hidden Erick in a back room of a tavern near the wharf, afraid to move him any farther from the ships in the condition he was in.

The captain of the Seekers opened the door warily, the room beyond dark, so that I couldn't even see him through the crack. But a moment later, he opened the door completely and stepped aside, going to light a lantern.

I moved to the edge of the bed that had been shoved into the far corner and stared down at Erick. Avrell hovered at my side, ready to catch me if I fell. Keven stood on the other side.

Erick's eyes were closed, his face twisted up in pain. Sweat glistened on his forehead, and his skin was pale, the bones of his cheeks clear. His torso was covered in cuts and burns, the skin around most of the wounds red and swollen. Where the Ochean had not touched him, you could see the older scars, covering his chest, his arms; the scars of a Seeker.

"The healer said he should recover," Westen said from deeper in the room. His voice was muted.

I nodded. I couldn't speak. Something had forced itself up from my chest and lodged itself in my throat, something hot and solid. I swallowed, but it didn't seem to help.

I reached out a tentative hand and touched Erick lightly on the forehead.

For a moment, his pain seemed to ease, as if he sensed the touch, but as soon as I withdrew, his face contorted again.

I fought for control, and when I felt composed, turned to Westen.

The Seeker had seated himself in a chair against the wall, his arm resting on the table beside the lantern. Like Eryn, he also looked older, and I thought suddenly of his wife, of his son, wondered if they'd survived the battle.

But instead, I asked, "The priest? The man who guarded him on the ship?"

He shook his head. "He wasn't there." He sounded disappointed.

For some reason, I wasn't surprised.

I nodded, glanced back to Erick.

Avrell shifted awkwardly. "Do you think they'll be back?"

I thought about the Ochean, about Haqtl and the priests and the volcanic islands that had been their home, about the Chorl captain, Atlatik, then sighed.

"They'll be back," I said. "They have nowhere else to go."